"Shayla Black and Lexi Blake never fail to heat up the page, and the Perfect Gentlemen series is no exception. Hot and edgy and laced with danger, the stories in the Perfect Gentlemen are just that—perfect."

—J. Kenner, *New York Times* and international bestselling author of the Stark series

THE NOVELS OF SHAYLA BLACK ARE . . .

"Sizzling, romantic, and edgy!"

—Sylvia Day, #1 *New York Times* bestselling author

"Scorching, wrenching, suspenseful . . . A must-read."

—Lora Leigh, #1 *New York Times* bestselling author

"Wickedly seductive from start to finish."

—Jaci Burton, *New York Times* bestselling author

"The perfect combination of excitement, adventure, romance, and really hot sex."

—Smexy Books

"Full of steam, erotic love, and nonstop, page-turning action."

—Night Owl Reviews

THE NOVELS OF LEXI BLAKE ARE . . .

"A book to enjoy again and again . . . Captivating."

—Guilty Pleasures Book Reviews

"Utterly delightful."

—Night Owl Reviews

"A satisfying snack of love, romance, and hot, steamy sex."

—Sizzling Hot Books

"Hot and emotional."

—Two Lips Reviews

Scandal
NEVER SLEEPS

SHAYLA BLACK
AND LEXI BLAKE

BERKLEY BOOKS, NEW YORK

BERKLEY

An imprint of Penguin Random House LLC
375 Hudson Street, New York, New York 10014

Library of Congress Cataloging-in-Publication Data

Black, Shayla.
Scandal never sleeps / Shayla Black, Lexi Blake.—Berkley trade paperback edition.
p. cm. (The perfect gentlemen ; 1)
ISBN 978-0-425-27532-0 (softcover)
1. Murder—Investigation—Fiction. 2. Man-woman relationships—Fiction.
I. Blake, Lexi. II. Title.
PS3602.L325245S33 2015
813'.6—dc23
2015015654

PUBLISHING HISTORY
Berkley trade paperback edition / August 2015

PRINTED IN THE UNITED STATES OF AMERICA

10 9 8 7 6 5 4 3 2

Cover design by Judith Lagerman.
Cover photograph © Lynn James / Getty Images.
Interior text design by Laura K. Corless.

Penguin
Random
House

To the one who truly helped us form and shape this story.
We truly feel this couldn't have happened without you,
our lovely friend from New Zealand.
So this novel is dedicated to the amazing Kim Crawford. . . .

PROLOGUE

Gabriel Bond really wanted to murder his best friend. He even knew how he'd do it—by beating Maddox to death with that damn camcorder.

"Do you understand the trouble you've caused, Mr. Bond?" The very fussy school counselor Mr. Ogilvie sat back, his bushy gray brows rising over his eyes like judgmental twin caterpillars.

Gabe had always loathed his last name since no one at the exalted Creighton Academy would call him anything but "Mr. Bond." It made him sound like some kind of stupid secret agent. Currently, they'd come to the point in the James Bond film when the floor opened and dropped him into a vat of man-eating sharks while the bad guy monologued. Gabe was fairly certain he would rather swim into the Great White's mouth and allow himself to be eaten alive so he didn't have to hear the horror about to transpire.

He should have known nothing good would come from screwing

a member of the rival debate team. Especially when it hadn't been a student of the all-girls Murray Heights Academy for Young Women, but their faculty sponsor. Damn, she'd looked maybe twenty, and in exceptional shape. She'd had the most gorgeous pair of breasts he'd ever seen in his young life.

Roman Calder stepped up beside him. "I don't think my client should answer any questions."

Sometimes Roman took his position as the president of the Creighton chapter of the Future Lawyers of America way too seriously.

"Mr. Calder, you're in trouble, too. All of you boys are. This is a serious offense. While Mr. Bond has shamed our academy, the rest of you broke the rules as well. What did you think you were doing, sneaking off to a bar? What will your parents think?"

His father would likely high five him and breathe a sigh of relief because he now had confirmation that his only son was neither asexual nor gay. His mother would roll her eyes and take another drink from her ever present "coffee" mug that smelled suspiciously like vodka. Only his younger sister would worry.

This entire incident was Mad's fault. Mad the instigator. Mad, the dude who'd taped his best friend's one-night stand without bothering to ask first. Fucker. Gabe felt his face flush slightly, but he'd learned enough about the world to know when to bluster his way through.

Yeah, Mad had taught him that, too.

"Mr. Ogilvie, I don't understand why my friends are here. Maybe they were out after curfew, but it's no secret that nearly every student is from time to time." Another thing Gabe had learned was when to throw himself on his sword. God, he was going to miss his friends. If his stupid dick got him expelled, he had no illusions about what would happen. His parents would ship him to another prep school, and he would have to start all over. "Please, if you'll let them off the hook, I'll admit to everything."

"Martyr," Mad coughed like the idiotic douche he could be.

Gabe very slowly lifted his hand behind his back and shot his bestie the middle finger.

Connor Sparks stepped up. "No, Gabe. We went into this together. We go down together." He frowned. "I wish I could have played against Exeter. It's going to be hard to miss out on the league championship."

Daxton Spencer shook his head, following Connor's lead. "Yeah, I think the whole school will be deeply disappointed. Without our captain, we're sure to lose."

Smart bastards. Gabe repressed a smile and couldn't help but feel a spark of hope. Creighton took lacrosse and the league championship very seriously. It brought money and prestige to a school that valued both greatly.

The counselor, who in Gabe's opinion had always had it out for them, leaned forward. "If you think for one second that sports will save you from the punishment you've earned, you're wrong. This establishment has rules, and I follow them. I've seen the video evidence. It's disgusting. Perverse. What is wrong with you boys?"

Dax and Connor looked around, then at one another, and shrugged.

Mad grinned as if silently admitting their list of faults was long and distinguished.

"You think this is funny? Expulsion is the only acceptable outcome for this mess. We raise *gentlemen* at this school, and you six have proven you're anything but. And you, Mr. Hayes . . ." Ogilvie turned to Zachary Hayes, the quietest of the six.

Their contemplative buddy never made a move without thinking through the outcomes and consequences first. Zack frowned.

Gabe felt his stomach drop. God, he was getting Zack kicked out. Zack, the freaking class president and valedictorian. The one with the brightest future.

"I'm surprised at you," the counselor continued. "I knew you would find nothing but trouble when you fell in with this crowd. I believe I warned you."

All eyes turned back to Zack. With dark hair and winter blue eyes, Zack often seemed ready to permanently retreat inward. He'd been at Creighton for two months before Gabe had really talked to him. Mad had been the one to bring the quiet kid into their group. Gabe had soon realized that Zack was smart and funny . . . and could sometimes figure a way out of a bind. For five years, it had been the six of them against the world. They shouldn't have fit. Connor and Dax had naturally become pals because they were both athletes. Roman and Zack were the obviously ambitious types. And somehow he'd been the nerd taken under the wing of the most obnoxious, devious-minded rich boy at school, Maddox Crawford.

They felt like brothers, and he couldn't be the one who fucked up everything. In a year, they would graduate and they had plans to attend Yale together. They'd coached Connor through trig and made sure he'd gotten an A so they wouldn't be separated in the future. One for all and all for one, and all that shit.

Maybe his dream was about to be dashed, but he wasn't going to screw over his friends. They had a pact.

"It's my fault. I blackmailed them into sneaking out with me." He was willing to tell any lie that might work.

"Dude, that was weak." Dax rolled his eyes. "Like anyone would believe that. Look, Mr. Ogilvie, you know how the press is, willing to say anything salacious about us rich boys to make a buck. Do you really want *People* magazine running an article that exaggerates about Creighton's super entitled boys running wild and taking women who have barely given their dubious consent to bed?"

Gabe gaped at his friend. *What the hell?* "Her consent wasn't dubious, asshole."

"The press won't care," Roman pointed out, then turned to the counselor. "That scandal won't look good for the school, either."

"I don't make my decisions based on the press, only the rules of this school. And I fully intend to talk to my counterpart at Murray Heights this afternoon. Miss Jones will be dismissed by the end of the day. I have no doubt they will call the proper authorities as well. No school worth a whit wants a sex offender working on campus."

Shit. He'd landed a nice, remarkably limber young lady in a heap of trouble. Hell, *he'd* come on to *her.* She'd simply been trying to help a guy have fun. Why should her good deed be punished?

Gabe raked a hand through his hair. His day sucked. He needed to hang it up and become the loner he'd been before Mad had taken him in and shown him how to stand up for himself. "Please don't do that."

"He can't for two reasons: First, the age of consent in the state of New York is seventeen, so engaging in sexual relations with Miss Jones wasn't illegal, and she is, therefore, not a sex offender. Second, I don't recall that sexual intercourse with another consenting adult is an offense one can be expelled for. If that's the case, Ogilvie would have to expel most of the senior class, especially if they've met Augustine Spencer."

"Hey! That's my sister you're talking about," Dax objected.

"What? She's a giver. I mean that in the nicest possible way," Roman assured. "But back to the point. Ogilvie could probably have Ms. Jones fired . . . but he has no proof the incident ever occurred."

"Of course I have proof. I saw the tape."

Roman turned with the smooth expertise of a kid who'd spent his share of time in mock trials and won them all. "Mr. Bond, did you sign a release or in any way give Mr. Crawford permission to tape you in coitus with the lovely Miss Jones?"

He shot a nasty look Mad's way. "No. Hell no, and don't be stupid. If I had known, I would have clocked the fucker." Ogilvie's bushy brows slashed down in a judgmental scowl, and Gabe remembered where he was. "I mean, I was entirely unaware and would have protested vociferously had I realized the encounter was being taped."

Gabe *had* decked him afterward. He'd broken Mad's nose, but Mad just seemed to view it as one more story he could tell over beers someday. He'd shrugged it away, like he did everything else—with the negligent grace of a man who knew there was a billion dollar trust fund waiting for him at the end of the yellow brick road of prep school.

"I might have forgotten to ask." Mad smiled benignly. "You know art doesn't apologize."

And neither did Mad.

Roman slapped his hands together in jubilation. "I believe we'll discover that Miss Jones was unaware as well. In this state, no recordings, video or audio, may be made or used as evidence in a civil trial without the informed consent of one of the participants. They can fire her for moral turpitude, but they need that tape to hold up in a court of law. Since there was no consent to tape the encounter and it happened out of the public eye, that tape won't hold up and Murray Heights lawyers will likely advise the administrators not to open the school to a lawsuit they can't win. I'm afraid you don't have a tape."

Ogilvie's face had turned a florid shade. "Listen here, you little shit, this isn't some court case. I don't need permission. You're all being expelled and there's not a damn thing you can do about it. This school turns out not simply gentlemen, but *perfect* gentlemen. Do you know how long I've wanted to get rid of you, Maddox Crawford? I've anticipated this day, longed for it, since the moment you walked through those doors, you overindulged bastard. I'm taking you down—and sending your friends with you just to make you miserable."

"Is this because I pulled that prank on your car your first year here? You need to get over that." Mad rolled his eyes.

Of course this was happening because Mad had done something stupid.

What the hell was Gabe going to do without them? He couldn't fathom it. He even hated summer breaks. He would go to his parents' place in the Hamptons and sit like a piece of furniture because he didn't fit in there. The only part of going home he enjoyed was seeing his little sister, Sara. Besides her, he'd only ever fit with these five guys. One way or another, they'd all been on the outside. Gabe studied too much. Zack was an introvert. Roman spent much of his time with his head in a law text. Dax's father was some bigwig in the navy and his mother was a New Orleans socialite. Connor was a scholarship kid with nothing in his pockets. And to most, Mad was an asswipe . . . though a strangely likeable one. Gabe had never been more attached to other people in his life and he had zero idea how he would survive without them.

They all stopped, looking at each other as though trying to process the fact that their prep school cocoon was over.

Ogilvie took a long breath. "Good. Now you understand how the world works, boys. When you fall in with a bad crowd, you get taken down with them. You may all go and pack. I'll be speaking to your parents this afternoon. And good riddance to you, Crawford."

For once, Mad didn't have a pithy comeback. He'd gone stony, his eyes blank.

How was this happening? They weren't bad guys. They looked after each other. They'd only wanted a drink, and Emily Jones had been so damn pretty, Gabe hadn't thought twice.

Gabe was about to turn around and walk out when Zack finally spoke, his voice low and filled with an authority none of them had ever heard before.

"I know how the world works, Mr. Ogilvie." Zack stood and straightened his tie. "Do you know about the Brighton Endowment?"

The counselor snorted. "Of course. It's an annual three-million-dollar grant. It means a great deal to this school."

"It does. Did you know my father is very good friends with the donors responsible for that endowment? They listen to him. William Markovic considers me a second son, in fact. If you go through with this, I will have a long conversation with Mr. Markovic, and this school will find itself three million dollars short next year—and every year thereafter. I'll ensure the rest of the staff and faculty know exactly why. I think you might find yourself out of a job as well."

"You don't have that kind of power," Ogilvie blustered.

"You think I don't? My father was the ambassador to Russia for years. He's been close friends with the last three presidents, including the current commander-in-chief. My father wants one thing and one thing only from me. Everyone who's met him knows that he gets what he wants. My future is mapped out. If I do the right things—get the grades, remain class president, go to the appropriate college—then I accomplish everything I should. If you derail me from this path, I'll get my ass kicked in ways that would make your head spin. But it will end even worse for you. I recently got my SATs back. I had a perfect score. I'm getting into Yale, and Skull and Bones will be waiting for me senior year because they know what my father's friends have already figured out: I will be the president of the United States one day. Now, you can be my friend or my enemy. You decide."

Ogilvie said nothing for a long moment, then he cursed under his breath, not quite meeting Zack's gaze.

"I'm glad you understand me. You're a low-level counselor, so I'm going to stop wasting my time here and make an appointment with the dean. He takes my calls, you see. You can't get rid of us. I'll also make sure the lovely Miss Jones suffers no ill effects. Since my friend here was smart enough to use a condom, I don't expect any other complications. I'm also going to assume that Dax and Connor did the right thing and destroyed that tape."

Connor gave him a thumbs-up. "We burned it early this morning, but we'd planned to mention that later." Because they'd had to break into Ogilvie's office to finish the deed.

"Damn it," Mad cursed. "That was a good piece of film."

Zack sighed. "Someday you're going to go too far, Mad, and I only hope we can save you then. As for this time, we didn't do anything but be young and stupid. Miss Jones is single, and because Gabe has a five-o'clock shadow by noon and a surprisingly large dick, I understand how she might have believed he was older. The only one who did anything criminal was dumbass over here." He pointed to Mad.

"It was?" Mad tossed his head to flip his hair out of his eyes. "I just thought it was a beautiful act that should be recorded for posterity."

With a shake of his head, Zack went on. "We're finished now, gentlemen. I believe it's lunchtime and the cafeteria has likely done something amazing with gelatin. Let's go."

Zack started for the door, and Gabe watched him openmouthed. Where the hell had that confident, convincing speech come from?

"This isn't over," the counselor swore.

Zack sent him a pitying look. "It is. I have a surprisingly shitty life, but this is one case where I have power and I'm going to wield it."

They followed Zack out, Mad nearly pulling Gabe along. Ogilvie didn't challenge them. Lightning from the heavens didn't strike them.

"Guys, it can't be that easy," Gabe said as they emerged into the sunlight. They were suddenly surrounded by classmates pointing at them and chattering about the scandal.

"Dude, did you really screw that blonde?" one asked.

"I can't believe you got into a bar," another stated.

Zack put a hand on Gabe's arm as the rest started receiving high fives for sticking it to the man—and the chick—though Gabe was sure they meant two different things. "It is that easy. Let it go. You bent a few rules but didn't do any real harm, man. It's going to be okay. Ogilvie needs to understand there are no gentlemen here."

"That's not true. Bond was a gentleman and allowed the lady to come first." Maddox snorted. "I think I should get T-shirts made, plaster 'Perfect Gentlemen of Creighton' across our chests. The old curmudgeon would love that . . ."

Gabe prayed the stupid moniker didn't stick. "I'm still going to kill you, Mad."

Mad put an arm around him. "Promises, promises."

ONE

New York City
Present day

Gabe stared at the urn and wondered what had gone so wrong. One minute, life had been something resembling normal. Well, normally fucked up. The next minute, he was standing in a church full of somber shock and lilies with at least seven hundred people at his back, waiting for the proper reaction to hit him. "You son of a bitch. How could you leave like this, Mad?"

He kept his voice low, given the fact that most tabloids would love to run a story about Maddox Crawford's best friend cursing his very name before he was laid to eternal rest.

Damn, but Mad would have hated the idea of eternal rest, of peace. The fucking bastard had never rested. He'd always been scheming up a new plan and forever instigating chaos.

He'd also left behind problems Gabe didn't even want to think about. But he would have to in about six months, when his sister had her baby.

He stared at that ridiculously expensive urn and thought about smashing it in rage. It would serve Mad right to be vacuumed up by a handheld sweeper.

He turned away and caught a glimpse of his sister. Sara sat in the well-polished pews of the Church of St. Ignatius Loyola. She was discreetly in the middle, not wanting to call attention to herself. Wearing a black Prada sheath, with her tawny hair in a neat bun, she looked like she belonged amid the marble finery of the Upper East Side church because she did. Sara was Manhattan born and bred. Unlike her older brother, she'd never been shipped off to boarding school. Even in the face of grief, she comported herself like a lady.

Her eyes might be red, but she stared straight ahead, her shoulders back and her head held high. And she was carrying Maddox Crawford's baby. That fucking asswipe hadn't kept his promises—any of them.

I'll watch after her, Gabe. You don't have to worry. I love her. It's stupid but for the first time in my life, I'm in love. You're my best friend in the world. I know I've been a jerk in the past, but I've always taken care of you. Now I'll take care of her, too.

He'd been a dumbass to let Sara date Mad. It should have been a no-brainer that the asshole would seduce and dump her. Mad hadn't been as faithful to Sara as he had been to his MO. Christ, everything about their relationship had been utterly predictable—except Mad's die-in-a-plane-crash routine, but the rest of it . . . Fuck, he could have written that book.

"Hey, I think they're ready to start the service," a quiet voice said from behind him.

Gabe turned. There stood Roman Calder in his customary three-piece suit, which Gabe knew he purchased from a London tailor twice a year. He made the voyage from DC to the UK under the auspices of diplomacy, but it was really about those suits. And now that Roman was here, Gabe wanted to know one thing. "Is he coming?"

Roman sighed, his face falling slightly. "You know how busy he is.

He sent me. And you'll have me for a few more days. I'm staying over for a fundraiser."

Gabe shouldn't have expected a different answer. Mad had been a terrifically controversial figure. In a world where the one-percenters were vilified, Mad had been the poster child for rich, bad-boy behavior. If he wasn't screwing some small company out of its profits, he'd been humping a supermodel.

Gabe wished he'd stuck to those women and left his sister alone. "Let him know we missed him."

He turned and started back down the aisle. There wasn't a family pew. Mad had been the last of his line, his father having died of a heart attack two years before. That had struck Gabe as odd, since he'd been sure Benedict Crawford hadn't possessed a heart.

"You have to forgive him. You know he's torn up. He got the news during a press conference," Roman said under his breath. "A fucking reporter brought it up after his speech on the immigration reform bill. He was completely caught off guard."

Gabe had seen the news clips. Hell, everyone in the country had seen the president of the United States stop in the middle of a Q and A with the press, turn, and walk away. "Tell Zack not to sweat it. We all get it. He's got huge responsibilities."

Roman followed him down the second pew, where Dax had reserved their seats. "You have to understand how the press would interpret his attendance. After the way Mad lived the last couple months of his life, I couldn't advise it. He hates that he can't be here."

Gabe knew exactly how the last two months had gone. After Mad had dumped Sara, he'd gone a little crazy, drinking by the gallon and painting the town red with models and actresses. But Gabe suspected what others couldn't: Mad had been protecting someone. No idea who. His best guess was that, after dumping Sara, he'd found a new mistress and used all the other women to divert the tabloids' attention from the new object of his desire. That had been Mad's MO, and he'd heavily relied on bait-and-switch tactics when he had been hounded by the press. Gabe should probably let it lie, but he wanted to know the identity of that woman. He wanted to know if Mad's new mistress had any inkling of the pain she'd caused by luring Mad away from Sara.

"I hate that I have to be here in the first place." Dax stood and stuck out a hand. Like everyone else in the church, he looked grim.

Gabe shook it, studying his old friend and wondering where the hell the years had gone. It was hard to believe they'd all been kids together, their worst problems being math tests and how to sneak over to the girls' school so they could make out. So many of his childhood memories were shared with the other men in this pew. And the one in that damn urn. "Brother, it's good to see you. I thought you were somewhere in the Pacific."

"I came home the minute I heard. I had some leave." Dax's gaze shifted as he stared at the place where Mad's coffin lay. "Why the coffin? He's not in there. From what I understand, there was barely enough left to cremate."

Gabe's stomach threatened to turn. He didn't want to think about how Mad had died. Sure, in his darkest moments he'd thought about killing the fucker himself, but damn, he'd loved the guy, too.

Never let 'em see you sweat, Gabe. That's the key to bullies. You walk by. You flip 'em off. If they give you real trouble, you take them down in a way that ensures they stay down. You go for the kill because that's the way of the wild, my man.

Gabe had learned that lesson from him. At the time, Mad had been talking about the bully upperclassmen at their school, but Gabe had taken that lesson into business. If he was going to take down someone, he made damn sure they couldn't get back up. Ever.

"The coffin is there for show. Apparently, people want something substantial to stare at during the service. That's what the coordinator said." Gabe sighed. "The picture doesn't count, and the urn is too small."

There was a large poster of Maddox in front of the empty coffin. He was dressed in a custom-made Brooks Brothers suit, smirking at the camera like a douchebag. But then, he'd always looked like that.

Would his baby inherit that smirk? That never-ending thrill for life Mad had possessed?

Damn you for leaving us behind. And damn you for what you did to my sister, but I fucking wish you were here.

He sat on the pew, his brain buzzing. He'd gotten the news five days ago and it still hadn't quite penetrated. He kept expecting to turn around and see Mad walking toward him with that damn smirk, drink in hand. It was wrong to consider someone as alive as Maddox Crawford dead.

"Hey," a familiar voice said. Gabe turned to find Connor, dressed in a button-down shirt and pressed slacks. Just another normal guy— except for the fact that Gabe knew he was Agency. The CIA had claimed Connor long ago, and any illusion of normalcy he donned was really a mask. "Sorry I'm late."

Gabe stood and put his hand out. Connor took it. "It's good to see you."

It had been at least a year since they'd been in the same room. They kept up via e-mail and the occasional phone call where Connor never mentioned what country he was in. "You, too."

"Do you know anything about his death?" Gabe murmured. "Have you looked into the incident?"

They all leaned in. Connor dealt in secrets. Oh, he might say he was simply an analyst, but there was no way Connor wasn't an asset, as they would call him in the Agency. Even though they'd been friends for years, Connor had changed, become more distant, colder. Deadlier. No, Gabe didn't buy that Connor sat in front of a computer. Connor got his hands dirty.

"I don't know anything, guys," he said with an apologetic frown. "I'm sorry."

Roman shook his head. "It's not a CIA matter. The FAA is handling it. Trust me, I've been up their ass about it. So has Zack."

"I called in my contacts," Connor said. "They told me the investigation is in its early stages. They have the black box and they're carefully probing the wreckage. There were reports of high winds in the area where he went down. The working theory is the plane hit a storm system and the pilot lost control."

Gabe had heard that theory. It was difficult to think that a storm had taken down Maddox Crawford. He'd been a force of nature himself. Mad should have been shot by a furious husband—or brother.

"I promise, I'll make sure you all get the final report," Roman murmured. He nodded toward the aisle. "Is that who I think it is? What's her name? Tavia?"

Gabe looked up. A gorgeous blonde with killer cheekbones strode quickly toward the coffin. Mad had hired Tavia Gordon—and paid her well—to be his public relations guru. And he'd kept her hopping. From what Gabe could tell, Tavia had spent all her waking hours putting out the fires Mad had been prone to start. Though a bit tall and fashionably thin for his taste, she had a delicate, aristocratic face. No denying she was an icy beauty.

He'd wondered more than once if Mad had thrown Sara over for Tavia. Because there must have been a woman. With Mad, there always had been. Had his buddy worked his playboy angle to throw the paparazzi off his PR Girl Friday/mistress so she wouldn't be inundated? He'd wondered if Mad had been trying to protect Sara, but given the cruel way he'd cut her out of his life . . . Gabe gnashed his teeth. He couldn't focus on that now or he'd think very ill of the dead.

As Tavia dashed to her seat, she pulled a tissue out of her Gucci bag. He'd never seen her look less than perfect, but today her eyes were a bit puffy, her nose red.

The pastor stepped out, and the great organ began a mournful dirge. The Mander Organ, one of the most famous organs in North America, now played for Maddox Crawford. He would have enjoyed that.

"Hey, should we bring Sara up here?" Roman asked, his eyes straying back. "It looks like she's alone."

Oh, she wasn't alone. Not in the strictest sense, but he wasn't going to mention her pregnancy to anyone yet. "No, we chose to sit apart. The tabloids tend to ignore her. I'd like to keep it that way."

They wouldn't ignore him. He tried to keep a low profile, but Mad's death would likely send the damn tabloids into a feeding frenzy. The last of the Crawfords gone to his just reward, marking the end of an era.

God, when had he gotten so fucking old?

Dax settled in. "Why here? I never imagined Mad having a church funeral. I always thought when he went, we'd give him a Viking funeral in the swimming pool at some swanky hotel in Vegas. Seriously, I looked up how to loop those pool noodles together to make a proper raft for his corpse. I was thinking of killing him at the time. It was right after he hired those hookers, then stiffed me with the bill for both of them."

Connor's lips turned up briefly. "That send-off sounds fitting. Mad never wanted to be predictable. Or we could have an Irish wake. But I can't believe he wanted all this pomp and circumstance in a house of God."

Only because the others hadn't known that deep down Mad actually adored all the attention from reporters and TMZ. He'd laughed when the paparazzi chased him down Park Avenue. The man had never met a scandal that hadn't flipped his switch. He'd also had a deep devotion to history. Sort of.

Gabe snorted. "Jackie O's funeral was held here. You know he always thought he should have been born a Kennedy. Since he hadn't been, he decided to one-up her with more spectacle."

Roman groaned. "Dumbass."

Connor took a deep breath, obviously stifling a laugh. "He always did think he was American royalty, the bastard. So are you giving a big speech?"

"No. Since Mad planned this whole shindig before his death, he farmed that out. His lawyer hired a Broadway star to read the letter he left behind to the world. Can you believe that? The fucker wrote his own eulogy and hired a Tony winner to read it."

Roman looked down at the pew, repressing a laugh. "I thought I recognized that guy. God, Mad was such a douchebag. I miss him already."

"The priest is going to say a couple of things, after which I was supposed to persuade Christina Aguilera to sing a moving hymn. Yeah, that didn't happen. Apparently she's got a life and a career. So Mad will have to settle for the Met's new diva. She was available—but not cheap. I ignored his request for a burlesque dancer and an open bar in the sanctuary." Gabe rolled his eyes, not even asking what Mad had been thinking. Anything to raise a brow . . . "The good news is, there's no reception line and none of us have to speak. We can keep a low profile."

"Maybe he knew what we'd say if given a mic and the chance," Connor muttered.

Someone shushed them, and that had them all grinning. It was good to know that twenty plus years later, they could still get into trouble.

Gabe sighed as he caught sight of the urn again. They'd always been good at getting into trouble. Now Gabe would have one last opportunity to clean up Mad's mess.

An hour later, Gabe settled his sister into a limo. The crowd was finally starting to thin out. So many people, and they were all a blur to Gabe. He'd kept his head down, hoping he didn't have to talk too much. Funerals, he'd discovered, annoyed him mightily. Just when he needed to be alone to mourn and think, he found himself surrounded by others. He didn't need to comfort a bunch of people who hadn't really been close to Mad. He needed to comfort the one who had been the closest.

Or at least she'd thought so. But his sister was overwrought and battling morning sickness that lasted long into the afternoon, so he was letting her go.

"Are you sure you're going to be okay out at the beach? I'm sorry I can't leave the city for a couple of weeks. There's too much to do. I'm meeting with Mad's lawyer Monday, and I need to spend the weekend prepping. At the very least, I'm going to have to deal with the foundation or whatever group he left the company to."

Sara nodded. Her demeanor appeared perfectly calm, but he didn't miss the way her hands fisted around the handkerchief on her lap. "We'll be okay. The Hamptons are quiet this time of year. I'll stay for a while and think things through. After the news has died down, I can come back and have the baby. If anyone asks, I'll say I had a fling when I traveled to Paris on business in June." Her eyes took on a faraway look. "I really believed that if he had time to think, to miss what we had, he'd come back. That will never happen now."

"Sara, I know you loved him, but he was only a man. And not always a good one."

Tavia Gordon, racing from the building, snagged his gaze. He wondered vaguely how she ran in those towering shoes. Shaking his head, he stepped between Sara and Tavia to block his sister's view. He didn't want her to be hurt any more by coming face-to-face with Mad's possible mistress.

Sara frowned, the cool breeze tugging at the few loose tendrils of her golden hair. "Are you all right?"

"Fine. You go on. Take care. I'll call you after I meet with the lawyer." He needed to figure out how big the clusterfuck was. Crawford Industries should go to Mad's heir. Gabe intended to fight the will to ensure his niece's or nephew's future.

She nodded. As Gabe closed the door, she turned to the driver. Then the limo pulled onto Eighty-fourth Street. As he watched the car roll out of sight, another woman caught his eye.

She stood out in the crowd. Short and curvy, with a massive amount of wavy strawberry-blond hair, she was like a sprite among the elven supermodels. Every other woman walking down the street looked emaciated and fashionably plastic to him, but Little Red was obviously not a devotee of surgical beauty. No, those breasts were real.

Gabe couldn't take his damn eyes off them. They weren't huge, but a nice handful, he estimated. They would be soft. He could tell from the way they moved. She wore a black dress with tiny white dots and a Tiffany blue belt that cinched her waist, showing off her hourglass figure. He pinned her age somewhere close to twenty-five, maybe a year or two older, but something about her—maybe her fair skin and curls—drew him in.

"Hey, I thought I lost you." A young man in a stylish suit caught up to her and slid his hand into hers.

Had she been in the church? No. Surely he would have noticed her. Besides, he knew high-quality clothes when he saw them and hers, while pretty, were mass-produced and inexpensive. Her shoes were well made but not designer, and her purse looked a little like a burlap sack. Doubtful that she was one of the label whores exiting Mad's funeral.

As they walked by, she smiled up at the man, her unabashed affection hitting Gabe straight in the gut. How long had it been since a woman looked at him while her obvious joy lit up his world? Maybe never. The women he dated always had their eyes on a prize: moving up in the world. No matter how nice they seemed, they were ambitious females on the prowl, always looking for more money, more power, a better social position. They didn't want him; they wanted the life he could provide. Which meant that the women he dated didn't hold hands as they walked down the street. Nor did they smile up at him brilliantly with undisguised sensuality. They sure as hell didn't have soft, real breasts that bounced gently with every step.

Gabe watched as the couple made their way down the sidewalk and disappeared around the corner. He hissed. She had a spectacular ass, too. Simply watching her curves made his whole body heat up. He couldn't remember the last time that had happened.

Sex had become a rote activity, something he did because he needed it. But watching the girl with the strawberry-colored hair, he realized how long it had been since he'd simply wanted a woman because she flipped his switch. He hadn't seen her at the funeral, so he had to think she was just another pretty girl taking in an autumn afternoon in Manhattan.

He stared at the space where she'd been standing. If she hadn't been holding hands with another man, he probably would have been a schmuck and followed her. It was just as well she wasn't available since he had a job to do.

Gabe sighed and started back up the steps. The others were waiting for him at a bar down the street. A good deal of Mad's friends and coworkers were meeting for a few hours of drinking and storytelling and trying to forget that Mad was gone forever. He stepped back into the church and was assaulted by the silence. So quiet now. He could hear his footsteps as he crossed the floor.

The cathedral was beautiful with its marbled arches and bronze doors, but it seemed cold to him. Pretty and empty without people to animate it. A little like his life had become. Materially, he had everything a man could ask for, and he was starting to wonder if any of it was worth the work. He'd gone numb. That girl on the street was the first time in months that he'd felt something beyond anger, anxiety, and sorrow.

No matter what had happened between Mad and Sara, the grief over his friend's passing lodged in his gut—for the man he'd known more than half his life and for everything that should have been.

Damn, he wished the last words they would ever exchange hadn't been said in anger. He couldn't help but think that during his final encounter with Mad, he'd told his best friend that he wanted him dead.

That night, he had been.

Gabe stepped into the chapel, searching for the priest who had performed the service. Tradition required the family of the deceased to make a "donation" to the church. Mad hadn't had any remaining family, and he'd written Gabe a letter with the directions for his funeral, should anything happen to him. As pissed as Gabe had been at the man, there had been a time when they'd been closer than brothers. Executing this duty was up to him, so Gabe had a check for ten thousand in his pocket for the priest. If only he could find the man.

As he trekked inside and looked up the aisle, he stopped because he wasn't as alone as he'd thought. A man in a dark suit stood in front of Maddox's urn, his head down. His shoulders moved, and he turned slightly so Gabe could see his square jaw and the set of his brow.

An odd sense of relief swept through Gabe. He'd come. Somehow, even though he'd been told otherwise, he'd expected all his friends to be here to mourn the loss of one of their own.

"Mr. President, your detail sucks. I could have snuck up on you."

The president of the United States straightened but didn't turn. "I think you would find that task difficult, to say the least. My detail is surprisingly attentive."

That was when he noticed three red dots of light on his chest. He scanned the sanctuary and found the snipers. Yes, he could be dead in about two point three seconds. "Damn, Zack. Could you tell them who I am and not to shoot?"

Zack turned and flashed one of his rare grins. The quiet man had been cold and shut down since his wife's murder two years ago. Gabe couldn't think of the event in any other way. Joy Hayes had been cut down during a campaign rally. He'd been standing in the crowd with Dax and Mad. Sometimes, he could still hear that shot and the resulting screams. He could still see Zack's face as he realized Joy was gone. Sometimes, when he closed his eyes, he saw Zack holding his dead wife to his chest while the Secret Service did their damnedest to haul him away. He'd won the election in a landslide three days later.

It was good to see his old friend smile again.

"Gentlemen, this is Gabriel Bond. I doubt he's here to hurt me. Please don't take out one of my oldest friends." Zack strode down the aisle and his grin faded. He put out his hand. "We've already lost enough today."

"We certainly have." Gabe took Zack's hand but hauled him in for a manly hug. "Damn, it's good to see you."

Zack stepped away, his eyes tired as he put a hand on Gabe's shoulder. "You, too. You have no idea. How are you holding up? I know you two weren't on great terms when he died, but this has to be hard on you. You were the closest to Mad."

Gabe thought about lying, but he couldn't. "It's fucking hard. I'm struggling to believe that he's really gone. I looked at myself in the mirror after I got the news. Do you know what I saw? A man who learned how to properly knot a tie because Maddox Crawford taught him. I kissed my first girl because Mad engineered the situation."

Zack nodded. "And I found my first real friends because Mad sat next to me in class one day and cheated off my pre-algebra exam. That was the first time I sat at your lunch table. He told me he could use me so we might as well be friends. At least that's what he said. I found out later the asshole was a mathematical genius and he hadn't cheated at all."

"I figured his scheme out when we were in college. He came up with a reason for us to hang out together until the group was tight. Mad gathered us together. He wanted a family since his didn't give a shit about him, so he made one for himself. It's interesting that he chose outsiders. I guess he always considered himself one of us, even after we became the popular kids. Maybe because he knew he could count on us."

Gabe needed a freaking drink. Or twelve. God, he needed to sit and bond with his pack, to remind himself that he belonged somewhere.

"Is there any way you can ditch the snipers and come down to the pub with us?" he asked. "We're meeting at this place down the street. All of us. Me, Roman, Connor, and Dax. The guys would love to see you."

Gabe didn't mention that he needed Zack, needed the gang together even though they would never be whole again. What had happened?

He'd thought they would go to each other's weddings. Dax had eloped in Vegas, and none of them had been there, though they had thrown him one hell of a divorce party two years later. Zack had been the only one of them who had gotten married with proper pomp and circumstance, before it had ended in horror.

Now Mad had suddenly met his maker after a tragic, unexpected death. They needed something good.

Zack's grin was back. "Roman won't be happy to see me. In fact, he'll be perfectly dismayed, but I think if we sneak in the back, we can manage an hour or so. Maybe two. I'm not due back in DC for a bit. What do you say, Thomas?" He looked to his left.

Gabe followed his line of sight and saw a tall African-American man in a black suit. He stood at least six foot five and was built like a linebacker. Even indoors, he wore mirrored aviators and looked like the badass he certainly was. "I think you've gone insane, Mr. President." He smiled, showing even, white teeth. "You also know I love a challenge. Give me five to scope the logistics, then we'll move. I smuggled you in here without the press noticing. I'll get you in there, too." He took a cell phone out of his pocket and hit a button. "The Professor is thirsty, boys. We're going to get the boss a drink."

Zack sighed. "The Secret Service loves me. I hope this bar has a back room."

"If they don't, we'll make one, Mr. President." It was still surreal to think his boyhood friend was the most powerful man in the free world.

Zack shook his head. "Please don't call me that, Gabe. Let me pretend to be Zack for an hour or so."

Gabe knew exactly what Zack needed. "Oh, if you want to feel like one of the guys, we can do that for you. In fact, we'll be happy to remind you of the days you were a dumbass kid, Scooter."

Zack groaned, but at least something besides desolation lit his eyes. "Don't call me that, either. It's bad enough that my Secret Service call sign is The Professor. I don't need to be reminded about that damn scooter incident."

But the scooter incident had been so much fun. "I promise nothing."

E verly Parker looked around the swanky bar and felt out of place. This wasn't her crowd, even though she worked with some of these people. She wasn't a big bar hopper. She didn't watch the clock and wait for five p.m. so she could hit her favorite watering hole. No, she was a work-long-hours-and-go-home-to-a-good-book-and-hot-bath kind of girl. But tonight she wanted to be someone else—anyone who hadn't buried her mentor and friend an hour ago and wasn't now staring down the possibility of losing both her job and the roof over her head.

"Hey, are you going to nurse that drink all night long?" Scott Wilcox leaned over and winked. He was on his third margarita. "Because I think you should down a few glasses of wine and be my wingwoman. Harry from accounting is here and I swear I'm going to die if I don't go out with that hunk of man soon. He's the only truly beautiful boy at work. He should be mine."

Everly smiled. After she'd started at Crawford last year, she'd met Scott during her orientation. Initially, she'd mistaken his playful nature for a come-on. But he'd finagled her into having coffee with him shortly thereafter and apologized for giving her the wrong impression. He'd admitted that he hadn't been himself because he'd recently been through a rough breakup with his boyfriend. Scott sometimes used his happy-go-lucky face to mask his somber moods. To finally see him let go of his lost love and dip his toe in the dating pool with a hot guy thrilled her.

Honestly, Everly wasn't sure she believed in true love. Attraction and affection, yes, but love? Her father had been burned by the concept. He'd taken the shock and sorrow of his wife's abandonment to his grave. Her mother had always seemed so distant, as though she'd spent her life up until the moment she'd walked out on them longing for something else.

She shook her head. "Scott, I don't even know what a wingwoman would do."

He sat back and thought about it for a moment. "Well, first you should go over there and talk me up. Tell him how perfect I am, what a great guy I can be. If that doesn't work, then slip him a roofie so I can have my wicked way with him."

She rolled her eyes. Sometimes Scott had a vivid imagination. "Sure. I'll get right on that."

"I tried," he said with a long sigh, his gaze trailing to the back of the room.

Everly followed his stare. A waitress in a female version of a tuxedo carried what looked to be a cheese plate past a large black man wearing a nondescript suit and aviators. He guarded a door that led to what she could only imagine was a VIP section.

"See that? I heard a rumor," Scott whispered in her ear. "While you were in the bathroom, Marty from processing stopped by and told me the craziest story."

"You shouldn't listen to him. He's a horrible gossip."

"Do you want the scoop or not?"

She was kind of afraid that the next big scoop after Scott's would be "Wonder Girl Gets Fired After Kindly Employer Dies." She'd shot through the ranks like a comet, and now she was going to hit the ground with a great big thud. She wasn't sure what she was going to do when the new boss came in and found out his or her head of information security was a too-young-for-her-position hacker who everyone except Maddox Crawford thought couldn't handle the job. Maddox had been her champion, her mentor in this crazy corporate world. He'd also been a surprising friend.

At first, she'd been so shocked by his death. The devastation still hadn't worn off. But now, almost a week later, her brain had begun working overtime, and she had questions—the sort no one seemed to want to answer.

Maddox Crawford had been an experienced pilot. Had his death really been an accident?

Not according to that mysterious, inexplicable e-mail she'd received last night.

"All right. What's the big scoop?" Everly decided to disregard her own advice. She would listen to any gossip that took her mind off her troubles. She needed one good weekend before she faced whatever crap Monday morning would bring.

She took a healthy gulp of the sauvignon blanc she'd ordered. Scott was right. She needed to live a little before the hammer came down on her head. If things went the way she suspected, she would be lucky to afford box wine next month.

"You know how the Great Crawford had some seriously powerful friends, right?"

She didn't follow the gossip rags the way everyone else did. In fact, she purposefully avoided that tripe. Why fixate on the problems of celebrities when she had so many of her own? Besides, when it came to people like Maddox, more fiction than truth filled the tabloids. They wanted a good story, and real life tended to be too boring. The Maddox she knew had worked hard—twelve hour days, often six days a week. He'd cared about his employees. She bet no one reported that. "He knew a lot of people. Men in his position often do."

"But he knew one very *powerful* person," Scott whispered.

She wasn't sure what he was insinuating. "I don't doubt that. He was in a lofty position, Scott. It's not so surprising he knew key players."

Scott huffed, his frustration evident. "Damn it, don't you know who I'm talking about? Zachary Hayes, the president of these United States, the hottest man to ever hit the White House. They were friends as teenagers, according to rumors. I've heard the president is a senti-mental man. I think he secretly attended Crawford's funeral and is even now somewhere in this bar."

Maddox had told her once that he'd attended the same prep school as the current president and that they'd been close back in the day. The two of them had been part of a small group of friends who had dubbed themselves the Perfect Gentlemen. Everly wasn't sure if they'd meant the name to be ironic, but she suspected so, given Maddox's less-than-polite reputation. The rumors of their high jinks had been the stuff of legend . . . and they'd come up in some really low-blow campaign ads against Hayes.

She let out an exasperated sigh. "Yes, the president of the United States is here. I'm so sure."

Scott looked pointedly back toward the VIP room. "Have you seen the surprising number of men in black suits hanging around here?"

"Scott, the majority of people in this bar came straight from the funeral. Are you really shocked they're wearing dark suits?"

"And the sunglasses?" Scott shot back. "How many people besides crazy, scary feds do you know who wear sunglasses inside a crowded bar at dusk?"

She turned and caught a glimpse of two overly large men standing by the entry to the back room. When a woman stumbled toward them, they gently but firmly turned her away. Everly caught a glimpse of metal. Maybe Scott was onto something. "Holy shit. I saw a SIG Sauer."

Scott's brow rose. "A what?"

Clearly, Scott hadn't been raised around firearms. "It's the weapon the Secret Service uses. I know because my father was a cop and a complete gun nut. I knew how to shoot practically before I could walk. I don't know if that guy is actual Secret Service, but he's carrying a similar piece."

Scott stared at the doorway being guarded by the aforementioned black-suited, aviator-wearing bodyguards. "Think about it. The hottest of all the commanders-in-chief might right now be sitting in that room, downing shitty tequila."

"Somehow, I think they'd give him the good stuff. And it's probably not him. More than likely, it's some pretentious CEO or trust-fund playboy Mad knew. Surely, the president would go someplace more secure. Besides, if he were here, the press would be crawling everywhere."

Scott shrugged as if he saw Everly's wisdom but still liked his own theory better.

Grinning, she canvassed the room to see who else from Crawford Industries had come to pay their liquid respects to Mad and noticed Tavia walking her way. The stunning, polished executive dashed toward them, her standard professional smile in place.

"Good to see you here, dear. I thought you'd go back to Brooklyn after the service." Like many raised on the Upper East Side, she said the word *Brooklyn* as if it was a virus she didn't want to catch. Those poor deluded people thought the city only existed between Midtown and Harlem, and wouldn't dirty their designer shoes by walking on the rest of the island. But in every other way, Tavia had proven personable, if a bit high-strung. The woman could barely sit still.

"Scott convinced me to stay for a while." It hadn't taken much. Her loft had been so quiet for the last five days. The silence had become intolerable. She hadn't realized how much she'd come to depend on her boss's friendship.

For the last couple of months, he'd shown up on her doorstep out of the blue and uninvited with some project to talk about. They'd spent hours gabbing and eating. At first, she'd worried that she would have to fend off a lecherous boss, but he'd actually been surprisingly sweet. Kind, even. He'd taken a profound interest in her, but not as a lover. Somehow they'd fallen into a comfortable companionship, as if she'd known him all her life. There had not been a single spark between them.

She was going to miss him so much. The ache she felt at not seeing him again definitely hurt. Everly took a sip of wine, wishing again that she was someone else and somewhere else. Escape sounded great about now.

Tavia tapped a Prada wedge against the floor. The shoes might have been a few years old, but they still looked sleek and classy. "Hey, I wanted to pass on a little insider info. Crawford's lawyer is meeting with the executor of his will Monday, so it looks like we'll have some news about the company's future soon."

Scott went a little green. "So the pink slips could go out in quick order. God, I don't want to look for another job. It took forever to find this one."

Tavia shook her head, her pale hair jerking over her shoulders. "There's always a shake-up after someone new takes the reins, but you should be fine in the executive development program. They usually take out the players at the top. The new guy tends to like to bring in his own leadership team. If anyone's going to get the boot, it will be me and Everly."

Scott rolled his eyes. "It could be any of us. I'm not exactly a peon, thank you very much. I'm rotating through all the departments until the program ends."

Three margaritas and a funeral had left Scott prickly and morose.

"Which means you'll be valuable, Scott," Everly assured her friend. "You know something about every part of Crawford, having spent six months in most of the major departments. You'll be fine."

"Exactly," Tavia agreed. "But before I'm kicked to the curb, I need to make sure the new boss understands the importance of the foundation's work. It's excellent PR, and we all know Crawford Industries needs that now. With all the turmoil lately, our stock is down substantially. I'm hoping the new head honcho will think it looks bad to fire me two weeks before the annual fundraiser. If he keeps me until then, I'll have a little time to convince whoever takes over that I'm worth what Maddox paid me."

The fundraiser was the most important social event of the year at Crawford. Two weeks didn't seem like a long time to sway a new boss, but the woman was right. Crawford Industries' support of the International Women and Girls Education Foundation Tavia's family had founded was vital. It was a true public relations gem. For a playboy like

Maddox to give generously to fund education for females in third-world countries had bought him a lot of good press and goodwill.

So why had Maddox told her privately that he wasn't going to the gala this year? Everly frowned. He'd said it casually over dinner one night when they'd been going over her plans to strengthen their cyber-security systems. He hadn't exactly explained other than to say it was complicated. Then again, everything was complicated with Maddox Crawford.

He'd spent time with her, but he hadn't trusted her with his secrets. And she'd understood that—right up until his plane had gone down and she'd received that mysterious e-mail.

Before his death, Everly had suspected he was hiding something. Now, she was almost certain of it. She wished she'd asked more questions and pressed harder.

But she wouldn't be able to unravel all his mysteries tonight. Starting Monday, she'd probably have lots of time to figure out what Maddox had been up to because she'd be looking for a new job. Tonight, she wanted to get blitzed enough to sleep through the night.

One white wine wasn't going to accomplish that.

"I'll be right back." She gulped the rest of the vino in her glass, then stood and scanned the place. The bar was packed and seemed hopelessly understaffed. It wasn't likely the waitress would make it back any time soon.

Everly couldn't help but notice a couple of well-dressed waitstaff coming in and out of the back room, but they didn't stop to help anyone else. If she wanted another drink, she would have to fend for herself.

Everly moved past the tables of coworkers. She stopped and said hello to some, but could barely handle the speculative stares of the rest. She knew exactly what they thought. Despite the company being a large, multinational conglomerate, the corporate office of Crawford Industries still functioned like a small town. Gossip abounded, and there was no one they liked to gossip about more than the boss.

She'd been linked to Crawford from the moment she was hired. Her first day on the job, he'd shown her around personally, sparking rumors that she was his mistress. When he'd bumped her up to head of cyber-security after only six months on the job, the chin-wagging had become unrelenting. Though that made her job difficult, Everly had put her head down and worked. She'd stopped a corporate spy and helped the FBI track down a ring that had used Crawford subsidiaries for phishing expeditions. Still, no matter how effective she'd proven herself, the employees still speculated that she'd slept her way to the top.

Everly sighed. What a joke. She hadn't slept with anyone in well over a year, and her long dry spell didn't look like it would end any-time soon. At least the tabloids hadn't printed the rumors of her non-existent, torrid affair with Maddox. She had to be thankful for that small miracle.

She elbowed and nudged her way up to the crowded bar and tried to get the bartender's attention. Unfortunately, she only counted two people working.

She held out a hand as one headed her way. "Can I get a drink?"

He walked right past her, but he did stop for the two blondes at the end of the bar. They were thin and gorgeous. Story of her life. She'd always been short and slightly more plump than fashion dictated. Damn it, that didn't mean she didn't need a drink as much as the skinny chicks.

The bartender turned and headed her way again.

"I'd like a glass of wine, please."

Nothing. Not even a "Hey, I'll be with you in a minute" that she wouldn't believe anyway. He walked to the opposite end of the bar and started prepping what looked like cosmopolitans. The female bar-tender walked by, even more dismissive than the first guy.

The male walked by again and delivered the drinks to the two supermodels at the end of the bar. This time she was ready. She leaned over, hoping that maybe he hadn't heard her the first two times.

"Hello, could I get a glass of . . ."

He started to stride past her again, but a large hand zipped out beside her and over the bar, stopping him in his tracks. "I believe the lady needs a drink. I'd appreciate it if you would help her now."

That was the deepest, sexiest voice she'd ever heard in her life. It was attached to a really masculine-looking hand.

The bartender's eyes widened. "Of course, sir." He finally turned his attention to her. "What can I get you, ma'am?"

At the moment, Everly wasn't interested in wine.

She glanced over her shoulder at her rescuer. The sexiness didn't end with his voice. Vaguely, she noted that while she'd had to shove her way through the crowd, the mass of humanity had seemingly parted for him. He stood alone, though closer to her than strictly necessary. Tall and broad, with close-cropped golden brown hair and the bluest eyes she'd ever seen, her Good Samaritan stared down at her with a bit of a smile. Her tummy knotted.

"He needs to know what kind of wine you'd like. Let me guess." He gave her a considering stare. "A sweet red?"

She shook her head. "No. Um, a sauvignon blanc. I prefer white wine. Red tends to upset my reflux."

Way to go, Everly. That was a super sexy comeback to the hottest man she'd ever met. Of course he wanted to know about her digestive issues.

"Well, we wouldn't want that." A hint of amusement lurked in his voice. "The lady will take a sauvignon blanc, and I'll have a Scotch. The Glenlivet twenty-five."

The bartender immediately went to work.

"Thanks." She felt herself blushing. She probably looked like an idiot schoolgirl to him and could only hope she hadn't drooled. She'd never seen him before, but she would bet he belonged in the VIP room. Maybe he was an actor. He certainly looked good enough to be on the screen. "I couldn't seem to get him to hear me."

Mr. Gorgeous's lips curved up as he leaned against the bar. "I don't think his ears are the problem. The man seems a bit blind to me."

Everly wasn't sure what he meant, but she found it impossible to look away from him. "I guess he's really busy tonight. The place is packed. I even heard the strangest rumor that the president is here."

The man laughed and sidled closer. "I'm sure the leader of the free world can get better booze at the White House." He held out that big hand of his. "Name's Gabriel."

Like the archangel except in a really well-cut suit. His name was fitting. She put her hand in his, and he immediately covered it with his other. His palms swallowed her hand, the heat from his skin warming her own.

"I'm, um . . . Eve. I-it's nice to meet you."

She didn't like the idea of this man calling her the same thing as all her business associates. Only her family had ever called her Eve. Tonight, she didn't want to be the woman worrying about her job and how she was going to afford her loft. She'd rather be someone whose only pressing concern was to flirt with a hot guy. This conversation was likely to go nowhere, but she could fantasize about the handsome stranger.

Everly knew she was something of a wunderkind computer geek, but maybe Eve could be a flirty seductress. Eve could drink her wine and pretend that the gorgeous man beside her saw her as an irresistible woman.

Yes, she would like to be Eve tonight.

"It's nice to meet you, Eve. You live around here?"

She shook her head. "No, I have a place in Brooklyn. How about you?"

"I was born on the Upper East Side, but I get out as often as possible."

The bartender put the drinks in front of them. "Here you go, sir."

Gabriel passed him what looked like two hundred-dollar bills. "Keep the change."

So he was wealthy. It wasn't surprising since he'd admitted he'd been born in this part of town. She sipped her fifteen-dollar glass of wine. "You're a generous man."

He took a healthy swig of Scotch. "Not really. This is expensive booze. I can't help it; I'm a Scotch snob. I like it to be a single malt and at least able to vote. I'm more flexible on my other tastes." He cast a sidelong glance back toward the table she'd been sitting at. "Is that your husband over there?"

Everly looked back. Scott was sitting by himself again, Tavia now engrossed in another conversation at a nearby table with others on Crawford's management team, gesticulating as quickly as her lips moved. "No. He's just a friend. I'm not exactly his type."

"Then most men here tonight are blind it seems."

She could almost feel his gaze like a physical caress, moving from her eyes to her chest. His stare lingered there for a moment before he shook his head as though he was correcting himself. At his inspection, she stifled the urge to shiver. "Are you with the VIP party that's occupying all the waitstaff?"

He grimaced, though it did nothing to mar his beauty. "I'm afraid I am, but I needed to get out for a minute. I thought I'd stretch my legs and fend for myself. Now I'm happy I did. I saw you on the street earlier."

"Really?" He'd noticed her?

Gabriel nodded. "You were walking down Eighty-fourth. I suppose you were coming here. Were you with the crowd at the church?"

Nope, she'd hovered near the back, not wanting to see the casket that represented the death of a friend she would long mourn. She didn't want to talk about the funeral now. Since Gabriel lived in the area, he'd probably been doing something happier today. Why bring down his mood, too? Besides, tonight she was Eve—a woman without problems. "I was in the mood for a drink."

"Well, I was, too. Maybe we can share a couple. This place is crowded though."

Was he merely making an observation or actually suggesting she leave with him? Her heart rate tripled. Yes, she knew she shouldn't run off with a stranger. Serial killers could be beautiful, too. And yet, the idea of getting to know this man intrigued her.

"Gabe? Come on, man. We're waiting on you. They found the cigars, but Zack won't light up until you come back." A tall, muscular man with chocolate eyes and black hair in a buzz cut joined them, glancing at her with a smile. "Hello. My name's Dax. What's yours?"

Gabriel narrowed his eyes and put a hand on his friend's shoulder. "Her name is I Saw Her First."

Dax put his hands up as if to concede the point. He looked terribly amused. "Well, that's a lovely name, but Gabe needs to go see our old friend, who won't be here much longer because he has important things to do. He's leaving in twenty minutes. Something about a crisis in the Middle East. Like that won't be there tomorrow."

"All right." Gabriel sent her what seemed to be a regretful smile. "It was nice to meet you, Eve. I don't suppose you're hanging out here all night?"

She didn't want to let him walk away, but apparently her little fantasy was going to end sooner than expected. And it was probably for the best. Running off with a stranger for a hot fling while her life was in turmoil wasn't smart . . . though the escape would have been nice. "No. But it was nice to meet you. Thanks for the drink."

Before she was tempted to blurt out her phone number, Everly turned away and rejoined Scott.

"Who's the hottie?" He watched Gabriel and Dax disappear into the back of the bar. "Or should I say *hotties*, plural? I didn't get a good look at them, but you can tell a lot from a man's backside. Tell me one of them is gay and we're about to get lucky."

She sighed and took another sip of what would likely be her last glass of wine for the night. "Nope. We're definitely not getting lucky."

The kind of luck it took to snag gorgeous Gabriel only seemed to happen to other girls. She took another drink and wished she'd been able to play Eve a little longer.

TWO

Gabe couldn't stop thinking about Eve. He tried to focus on the conversation around him, but all he could see were those wide hazel eyes and the way her reddish hair tumbled around her shoulders, curling down to those lush breasts.

It had been a very long time since he'd gotten hard simply by looking at a woman.

"I'm just saying, Liz is going to be pissed." Roman had ditched his jacket and tie and looked every inch the Beltway player he was. He sat back and puffed on his cigar. "Did you tell her?"

Zack shook his head. "I'm not stupid. I'm going to tell her I came up here to meet with the UN delegation from . . . I don't know. Pick some war-torn country. I'll tell her I was trying to make peace or something."

Elizabeth Matthews was Zack's press secretary but she'd also served as his work wife since Joy's death. Gabriel was grateful Zack had her to lean on. His old friend had been so hollow for the longest time. Even as he'd accepted the highest office in the nation, Gabe had known his friend felt dead inside. Two years into his first term, and he was finally joking again. Gabe suspected lovely blonde Liz had a lot to do with that.

"Zack, come on, man. You're the leader of the free world and you're scared of your press secretary?" Connor shook his head.

Roman patted his boss on the back. "We're all scared of Liz. She might look cute, but that woman has three rows of teeth and they're all razor sharp. Trust me. When she finds out—and she will find out because she's also got eyes in the back of her head—she'll kick his ass."

"I'm sure kicking isn't what Zack would like to do to her ass." Dax winked. "Shit. Did I say that out loud?"

They all looked to Zack, but he laughed. "You've spent way too much time on that boat of yours, man. You've forgotten the fine art of diplomacy."

"I don't think he ever had it," Gabe replied. "Don't you remember Dax was the one who got us all detention because he told the math teacher where to stick his calculator?"

Dax shook his head. "Yeah, that was not a fun day. Mad snuck out the back window because he had a date, and we had to cover for him. Asshole."

Connor laughed. "Damn, but I'm going to miss him." He shook his head as though clearing his thoughts. "So, are you ever going to give in to temptation and ask Liz out?"

Zack scoffed. "I don't know if you've noticed, but my job is kind of demanding. I don't have a ton of time for dating."

Gabe leaned forward, warming to the topic. "Excuses, man. We've all got demanding jobs. You know you like her."

"Yes, you all have demanding jobs. And how many of you are married?" Zack pointed out. "None. Zero. Zilch. Besides me, Dax is the only one of you to give matrimony a whirl, and that didn't work out so well."

"Hey, I am looking for the next Mrs. Spencer," Dax said. "Who will surely be an ex after a year or two on the job."

"Well, naturally, since you admit being your wife is work," Roman shot back. "Besides, I think it's traditionally called *marriage*."

"Hey, military wives call it a job. They don't have it easy. There's a reason Courtney left me," Dax admitted. "But that shouldn't stop Zack from sneaking around the White House and getting a little something-something. Tell me you haven't thought about doing it in the Lincoln Bedroom. Or in that room with all the china. Why the fuck do you need all that china? How many plates does one man need?"

Zack took the ribbing with a good-natured wave of his hand. "Stop. You're killing me. And no, I am not pursuing Liz. I can't take a crap without the press trying to snap a picture. Have you seen that blog? What's the name?"

"Capitol Scandals," Roman supplied with a hearty groan. "It's the hottest thing in DC right now. I've tried to get it shut down five times. It keeps popping back up like a rat that won't eat the poison. I would love to get hold of whoever runs that sucker."

"They ran a report on the size of my dick. I'm not kidding you. It was called 'A Well Hung Commander-In-Chief.' Apparently they talked to some of the women I dated before I got married." Zack sighed. "I can't date now. Even if I wanted to, I couldn't manage it. The press would be all over the poor woman. I wouldn't put any female through the daily grind of being the president's girlfriend. It's better this way. I can focus on the job."

"You can focus when you haven't had sex in . . . what, a couple of years? I think I'd go a little crazy," Connor admitted.

"I can't have the woman I want, so what's the point?" Zack sat back.

Gabe was fairly certain he wasn't talking about his wife. He'd seen Zack and Joy together. They'd been more like friends and partners than ardent lovers. He certainly hadn't sensed any passion in their political marriage. She'd come from a wealthy family and possessed a graciousness that won Zack as many votes as his policies. But when Zack and Liz occupied the same room, electricity arced between them, strong and palpable.

Kind of like the electricity Gabe felt between him and Eve. Lovely, sexy Eve.

"Well, I think we should talk about who's taking home Little Miss 'I Saw Her First,'" Dax said with a shit-eating grin.

"Someone called dibs?" Connor asked, proving that even a super spy could sound like a goofy teenager under the right circumstances.

Back when they'd been kids, the girls were few and far between, since they'd attended an all-boys school. When they'd found themselves in the presence of a female, they'd taken to calling dibs. It was silly and juvenile, but he freaking had dibs on Eve.

"I was just talking to a woman at the bar," Gabe explained. "She was having trouble getting a drink, so I helped her out."

"Did she lose the drink in her breasts?" Dax asked. "Because you seemed to be trying to find it there with your stare."

"Asshat. She was just a nice woman." *With a great rack.* "She's definitely not the next ex–Mrs. Spencer."

Gabe wondered what she was doing now. It was getting late. He'd been back here with the guys longer than twenty minutes, so she'd probably already left, likely on her way home to Brooklyn. He hadn't even gotten her last name. A tragic oversight on his part.

Roman was frowning down at his phone. "Motherfucker. Okay, Connor, I need you to figure out who's running Capitol Scandals and assassinate him."

"I'm an analyst," Connor began. "I don't do assassinations. What did the loudmouth write now?"

Roman squared his jaw, his lips thinning in a sure sign of anger. "He's claiming Maddox was murdered."

The knot that had been sitting in Gabe's gut for days tightened. "What proof does that prick have?"

Roman scrolled down the screen of his phone, scanning the text. "He claims he has an inside source. I don't know if that's the FAA, NTSB, or someone else. Damn it, I hate this. I fucking hate this." His phone hit the wall with a violent thud.

Grief. It sat there, a tightrope connecting them all. They could laugh and joke and pretend everything was normal, but Maddox was dead, and a piece of them had been ripped away forever. It was another reminder that their childhood was gone.

"I'll look into it." Connor put a hand on Roman's shoulder. "I haven't taken a vacation in years, so I've accrued tons of time off. I'm taking it now. Since I'm off the clock, I'll figure out who the source is and shut them down."

"Shut down the whole fucking site. They're vultures." Roman's head fell back, and he took a long breath. When he brought it back up, his eyes were infinitely tired. "Sorry. It's been a long week."

Since Gabe had gotten the news, it seemed as though time had slowed to an unbearable crawl. The idea that now they would have to hear conspiracy theories about Mad's death played out in the media for months weighed him down. "His plane crashed. Are they saying someone caused it?"

Zack stood and reached for the bottle of vodka he'd ordered. "They're flashing salacious headlines to grow their readership. You have to ignore it. I promise I'll get in touch when the FAA report comes in." He poured a shot. "Come on, guys. I've only got a few minutes before I have to go. Let's not waste it on things we can't control."

Zack was right. There was nothing they could do about any of it tonight, just like Gabe couldn't fix the mess his sister was in. And he couldn't change the fact that Mad was gone and he felt hollow inside. He could, however, honor his friend.

Gabe held up his glass. "To Mad."

They all raised their drinks.

"*Za ná-shoo dróo-zhboo,*" Zack said in a perfect Russian accent, his vodka held high.

To our friendship. Zack had spent seven years with his parents in Moscow. His father had been the U.S. ambassador, so Zack had learned the language fluently as a kid.

Gabe remembered the first time they'd snuck out of the dorms and gathered in the groundskeeper's shed. Mad had filched a bottle of bourbon from the headmaster, and they'd all taken shots. And Zack had said those same words in Russian. *To our friendship.*

A bittersweet moment passed as they drank, that memory fresh in Gabe's mind because one of them was missing—and would be forever.

"No more of that," Dax said, putting his glass down. "Mad would be horrified to know we're getting emotional. Now let's talk about how we're going to get Gabe laid tonight because I, for one, think he needs it."

The last thing he needed was his friends thinking he needed help getting sex. "Not happening, guys. Do you think I've forgotten the incident a few years back?"

"I know you forgot it." Roman stood and stretched. "You couldn't possibly remember after everything you had to drink that night."

"I woke up in Jersey with three women who swear I asked them to marry me. I snuck out when they started pulling each other's hair. That catfight saved me. No, thanks. I'll find my own dates."

His twenties really had been interesting. His thirties . . . not so much. Since his father had passed, he'd lost himself in responsibility, and now he'd give just about anything for a few hours without thinking of all the people relying on him. Was asking for an evening of guilty pleasure really too much?

"You found a date, then left her? You're off your game, man," Dax ribbed.

"Do you mean the chick with the strawberry-blond hair I saw you talking to earlier? Because if not, then I totally call dibs." Roman was standing at the door, peeking around the corner. "Damn. That girl is hot. She's got some curves on her, unlike most of the other ladies here. Does no woman in this town eat cheeseburgers?"

Eve was still here? Gabe got to his feet and strode across the small room. He'd been sure she would be gone. He followed Roman's line of sight.

She was sitting alone now, pulling out her wallet. She looked around the bar as though searching for someone. When her pretty hazel eyes found his, they flared briefly, but then she suddenly seemed to find the table deeply interesting.

"Oh, you need to hit that." Roman elbowed him. "I'd sure like to."

Gabe stepped back, returning to his seat. He was in a bad place and he'd be using her to forget his troubles. It wasn't fair. "I can't use my best friend's funeral to get laid."

Zack stared at him as if he'd lost his damn mind. "We're talking about Mad. I'm surprised he didn't ask for an orgy to be held over his casket."

Gabe couldn't help but laugh. "Well, he left a hooker fund—twenty grand—for any of us who happened to be single at the time of his death and in need of temporary solace."

Gabe didn't want a hooker. He wanted Eve, and she was about to walk out the door. Maybe if he was honest about what he wanted, she wouldn't be hurt. Maybe she'd come here for a drink because she needed something, too.

All he knew was he would regret it forever if he let her walk out.

He grabbed his jacket. "I'll talk to you guys later."

"Treat the lady right, Gabriel," Dax said with a grin.

He intended to. He hoped he could convince her to give him a chance because suddenly nothing seemed more important than spending the rest of the night with her.

I t really was time to head home. Everly wasn't sure why she hadn't left when Scott had. That wasn't exactly true. She knew what she was waiting for, or more specifically, whom. She simply wasn't sure why.

She dragged out the necessary cash to pay her bill. Scott had found the courage to talk to his crush. He'd left with Harry from accounting thirty minutes earlier. It was already dark, and she needed to get home. Instead, she'd sat around, nursing her drink and hoping for another glimpse of Gabriel.

Now she wished she'd left sooner. He'd caught her staring. Of course, he'd been with a friend. The minute his gaze had found hers, she'd put her head down. When she looked back up, he'd been gone.

Was he waiting for her to leave? He might think she was some kind of creepy female stalker. If he was an actor or someone famous, he might have to deal with adoration from strangers constantly. It was definitely past time to exit. She just lacked the check. And damn it, there was never a waitress around when she needed one.

She glanced at her cell while she waited and found a text. The number came up as unknown.

I have the info about Crawford's death I promised in my e-mail. I'll contact you with a date and time to meet. Don't tell anyone. Come alone.

A chill zipped through her. She wanted to believe the person contacting her was some whacked-out loon, but she'd received that mysterious, very lucid e-mail yesterday suggesting that she check into Maddox Crawford's activities in the days before his murder. Not his unfortunate accident or his death. His *murder*. When she'd tried to trace the source, she'd come up with an e-mail sent from an anonymous account, the type anyone could grab off free mail sites. She needed more information to be able to track the person down.

If he wasn't a deranged creep then . . . what? A sick jerk playing a prank on her? A vindictive coworker trying to trip her up to prove she couldn't do her job? A creepy reporter fishing for a story? Or someone really trying to give her vital information about Maddox? Everly thought through the angles. The latter seemed far-fetched . . . but not impossible. She couldn't brush it off. Since getting tipsy apparently wasn't on her agenda tonight, as soon as she made it back to her loft, she'd start digging. Everly owed Maddox at least that much.

Part of her wanted to text the mysterious bastard back and ask what he was up to. But she needed to be smarter. If inquiries with her cell provider didn't net her any information . . . well, she knew a few tricks to hack her way into obtaining phone numbers. This jerk could try to hide, but she had ways to peel back the layers and find the truth.

She shoved her phone into her purse and stood. Pay the bill. Get home. Start investigating. Maybe try to sleep. Her stomach growled. She should probably eat first, but she definitely wasn't going to hang around and look like she waited desperately for Gabriel.

Everly marched to the bar. "I need my bill, please."

Shockingly, the bartender stopped. "It's already been taken care of. Thank the gentleman in the suit there."

She turned in the direction of the bartender's gesture, and there stood Gabriel. His tie was slightly undone and his hair was mussed as though he'd run a hand through it. He was just as stunning to her senses as he'd been before.

As he approached, Everly had no doubt this man could make her tingle from head to toe. "Um, thanks."

"You're welcome. It's much quieter out here than before." He glanced around the now half-empty bar. "What happened to your friend?"

"He left with someone else."

His grin nearly took her breath away. "Did he find someone to spend the night with?"

"I'm sure he's hoping so, though I'm not convinced that guy plays for his team."

Was this stranger flirting? Why was she flirting back? She should stop. He was too good-looking and obviously rich. All she could boast was a decent loft in Brooklyn, one she would no longer be able to afford if she lost her job. She could be out on the streets in weeks.

Ugh, wasn't she a bright ray of sunshine?

"So, where did your friend go?" she asked.

He glanced back toward the VIP room. "That party broke up. Everyone had to get home. But I was thinking about staying up for a while. What are your plans tonight, Eve?"

That was a loaded question. Her current plan included going to a lonely apartment where she could worry about her future and try to figure out if someone had murdered her friend. She could be alone with her fear and doubt . . . but she didn't really want to. "I was getting ready to leave. What about you?"

"So was I. I thought I'd get some dinner before I called it a night. I don't think the food here is going to be any good. Giovanni's is one block over. Italian might be nice. I can promise you won't have any trouble getting a glass of wine there."

"You're asking me out?" It was a little surreal. She saw much more attractive women still in the bar. Why had he chosen her? Maybe he liked a curvier girl. Some guys did.

His face settled into a polite mask. "I don't know that I would call it a date."

"What would you call it, then?"

He stepped closer, into her personal space. "Eve, I want to be honest with you."

Eve. She wasn't Everly to Gabriel. Which meant that he didn't expect her to be a good, polite girl. She didn't have to be shy about what she wanted.

She stood a bit taller and met his beautiful blue eyes. She could see the five-o'clock shadow darkening his jaw and wondered what it would feel like to brush her fingertips over his face, to run her thumb across that full bottom lip of his. "Honesty is good."

She wasn't being entirely honest with him, but it didn't matter. They were sharing a moment out of time. She wouldn't see him again. She didn't even know his last name.

"I'm looking for an escape tonight. I can find it in the bottom of a bottle or I can take you out of here and try to make us both feel good. Why don't you let me buy you dinner and plead my case?"

He was asking her to sleep with him. A one-night stand. She'd never had one. She'd slept with two men in her whole life, and they'd both been her boyfriends. Sex had been all right, but something about the look in Gabriel's eyes told her this would be far better.

He wanted to escape. She wasn't sure from what, but she glimpsed a world of worries and sorrow in his expression that drew her. She understood loss and longing. She knew what it meant to need a few hours of escape. Hadn't she been wanting that herself?

A single memory pierced her in that moment. Two days before he died, Maddox had shaken his head over her nonexistent dating life. He'd tried to persuade her to let him set her up on a blind date, but she'd said she didn't have time. She'd needed to get some reports done and go through the purchase orders on the new hard drives and security systems. He'd rolled those piercing eyes of his.

You need to live a little. Your whole life can't be spent behind a computer screen. Life is often about taking risks. Sometimes you have to leave yourself to figure out who you really are.

She didn't have to be herself. Not tonight.

"Kiss me." The words were out of her mouth before she could stop them. She was never bold or brazen when it came to men. She'd never demanded anything sexually of a lover, but she wanted Gabriel to kiss her. She wanted to see if that spark she felt translated to something truly physical.

She expected some discussion, and when he hesitated, she was more than willing to admit that she'd been hasty. Everly was about to shake her head and try to laugh the incident off when he cupped her face and his body brushed hers. He tilted her head up and his mouth descended.

Soft. His lips were soft on hers. Gentle. He moved with predatory grace. His fingers sank into her hair, and her hands seemed to naturally find the lean muscles at his waist. Even through his crisp dress shirt, she could feel the heat of his body. It practically poured off him and into her, warming her skin and making her come to life.

He was gentle, but Everly knew precisely who was in charge. His lips locked onto hers, leading her. A little tug on her hair told her which way he wanted her to move.

Everything about him—scent, taste, feel—made her melt. She forgot where she was, forgot that they were in public. The noise of the bar receded until all she could hear was her own heart beating furiously in her ears. Nothing mattered at all but the feel of his body under her hands, the masterful way he moved her.

"Is that what you wanted, Eve?" He breathed the words against her mouth. "You wanted to see if I can kiss? I can give you more. I don't simply want to kiss your lips. I want to strip you down and find out if you're as sweet and soft everywhere as you look. I want to run my tongue over your skin until I memorize how you taste. I want to kiss you so long and hard that you'll forget you were ever kissed before." He lifted his head up and dragged in a breath. "So what do you say? Will you have dinner with me?"

She swallowed. His words made everything but her need fall away. "It's not dinner I'm interested in anymore."

THREE

"hat's one suite for the night, Mr. Bond. Do you need any help with your luggage?" The woman behind the counter at The Plaza arched a brow as she glanced at Eve, who stood in a corner, staring up at the coffered ceilings and the huge chandeliers of the elegant, marbled lobby. In fact, since they'd arrived, she'd looked everywhere but at him. Doubt was creeping in. Her darting gaze and tense body language told him that. She didn't do this kind of thing often, he'd bet. If he let her think for too long, he could lose her.

Gabe tapped his fingers impatiently at the desk clerk as Eve adjusted her purse, her hands skimming along the strap with nervous energy. She definitely wasn't cool and calm about the one-night stand she'd agreed to.

A gentleman would put her in a cab and send her home, but he wasn't a gentleman tonight. Maybe he never had been and old Ogilvie had been right. Yes, he knew it wasn't fair to mask his grief with the lust he planned to slake on her. But he needed her too much now to play fair.

"I don't need help with luggage, but I do need something else." He fished out a couple of hundreds. "Keep my stay here quiet. I don't need reporters showing up."

"Sir, at The Plaza we believe in the strictest confidentiality," she said, but she took the cash anyway.

When he was done in a few hours, he would leave out the back entrance, or better yet have Roman pick him up so they could start prepping for this meeting on Monday with Mad's lawyer. If there was a person on earth who knew how to avoid the press, it was the White House chief of staff.

Gabe knew that a smart man would not spend this evening with Eve, but would go home and prepare all weekend for Monday's legal skirmish. He intended to fight for his niece's or nephew's rightful inheritance. He didn't care what the will said or what charity Mad had left his money and worldly goods to. The safety and security of his fortune belonged to Sara, damn it. But Gabe didn't want to think about that now, not when he had a warm, intriguing redhead to help him temporarily forget.

He stared at her. She made his blood pump, made him feel alive. No way he would let her off his hook tonight. He needed some of her softness, a few hours where he didn't have to think about anything but pleasure. Monday would be soon enough to battle Mad's final wishes and his own demons.

After taking the keycard and shoving it in his pocket, he strode to Eve and slipped his hand in hers, tangling their fingers together. He didn't usually engage in public displays of affection, but the skin-on-skin contact made him feel connected to her. Knowing what they'd do next gave him something to look forward to. Even better, the gesture seemed to reassure her. He needed that because they were about to be alone. Gabe planned to have her aroused and naked in the next five minutes.

As they strolled to the bank of elevators, her heels clacked against the sleek floors. He was grateful as hell that most of the tourists seemed to be out for the night, likely heading to Midtown for a show.

With a ding, one of the elevator doors opened to reveal a uniformed attendant. "What floor, sir?"

The young man's earnest question made Gabe grit his teeth. There was already too much space between him and Eve, too much time between now and the moment he sank deep inside her. He fished out another bill. "I'll give you fifty if you sit this ride out."

The attendant was more than happy to comply.

Once they were alone, he hit the button for the nineteenth floor. The doors closed.

Eve sent him a puzzled stare. "Why did you—"

Gabe didn't let her finish the question, merely backed her against the wall and fastened his mouth over hers. Demonstrating his hunger was way better than explaining it.

The second his body pressed flush against hers, his senses rioted. He noticed a million things about Eve at once. She smelled decidedly feminine. Her curves were lush. Even in heels, she was petite, barely reaching past his shoulder. She fit naturally in his arms. And damn, she radiated warmth like the sun after a bitter winter.

Eve gasped slightly before she yielded to his lips, but she kissed with a passion that stemmed from her whole being. The woman ignited him.

Since the first kiss had already addicted him, Gabe went in for another.

As he molded his lips to hers again, he buried his hands in the silk of her hair and tugged with enough force to tilt her face and grant him easier access to her mouth. She responded perfectly, following his lead, answering with abandon. When he let his tongue run along her bottom lip, her mouth flowered open for him.

Fuck, he wanted to eat her up.

His heart pounded as Eve kissed him with artless enthusiasm and anchored her hands on his waist—as if she needed to steady herself while he devoured her mouth. Her fingers explored the muscles of his back, clutching him as if she'd never let go.

As the elevator ascended to their floor, she slid her leg against his in blatant invitation. Gabe wasn't about to refuse her. He took total possession of her mouth, plunging his tongue deep to stroke hers.

Normally, he preferred to play the smooth lover. He usually dated women who wanted to prove they were as good in the bedroom as they were in the boardroom. Most of his lovers had been cool and practiced—and not one of them had made him as crazy as Eve.

She hesitated at first, her tongue tentative. But he persisted until she met him with an endearing hesitance that rapidly turned bold, then demanding. Gabe gladly accepted the challenge.

He glided a hand down to cup one cheek of her incredible ass. The flesh in his grip was round and juicy, and he was sure she probably bemoaned her curves but they were perfect. His free hand joined his other, and he filled his palms with her lush derriere and used the leverage to drag her hard against his body, rubbing himself against her belly. She gasped.

"Are you all right?"

She blinked up at him, her eyes heavy with arousal. "Yes. I just . . . I don't . . ."

He shook his head. "No *don't*s tonight. Tell me what you want. Tell me what you like."

Her lips curled up in the sexiest little grin. "I love it when you kiss me."

No problem. He was going to kiss her. Everywhere.

The elevator stopped. The doors slid open. He felt like he was freaking sixteen again and he couldn't wait. He needed her on a physical level and he wasn't going to be satisfied with anything less than total possession.

She headed out of the little car but walked too slow for him. Maybe she wasn't comfortable in the heels she wore. Maybe her mind was hazy with arousal. Maybe she was rethinking everything. Gabe couldn't allow that. Their suite was at the end of the hall, and he had to get her inside before she changed her mind.

He bent and shoved an arm under her knees, his other around her back, and hauled her against his chest.

"You picked me up." She was very observant.

"I'm a full-service lover," he offered wryly as he strode down the elegant hallway, focused on getting inside that room and getting her naked.

Her grin became a smile. "That's good to know, Gabriel."

He liked how she said his name. Somehow she made it lyrical, as though she was savoring the syllables. She drew them out like his name was the most sensual word she'd ever spoken. He didn't correct her. All of his friends called him Gabe, but he liked Gabriel with her. "You are incredibly beautiful. Did I mention that?"

She wrapped her arm around his neck. "And you're both gorgeous and strong. I don't think a man has ever picked me up."

So strength was a turn-on for her? He could show her a thing or two because he definitely wanted to impress the lady.

But mostly, he was desperate to get inside her. The need rode him hard.

He had to set her down when he reached the suite and scrambled to find the key. He was never nervous and fumbling. Damn it, he was usually smooth, always in control. He blamed Mad. He blamed her.

Gabe stopped caring whose fault it was the second he managed to slot the keycard in the lock and slide the door open. Finally, they would be alone.

As he gestured her inside, Eve entered on shaky legs. He appreciated knowing he wasn't the only one bowled over by the chemistry between them.

He closed the door and scanned the room. The curtains gaped open, the lights from the street giving the room a glow that silhouetted her figure. He watched as she walked in, her hips moving in a sultry sway as she set her purse on the couch.

"This is a really nice room," she murmured.

He didn't give a shit about their surroundings. "I want to see you."

Even in the low light, he noticed her breath hitch. "You want me to turn on the lamp?"

"That's not what I meant." He never took his burning gaze from her. "I want to see you naked. Take off your dress. Show me your breasts."

"I'll close the curtains." She started to turn to the windows.

He caught her elbow, gently restraining her. "Don't. We're up high. No one can see in. Take off your dress. Let me see you in the moonlight."

Her gaze tangled with his, and he could see a hint of her trepidation. A gentleman might have backed down. But he knew what he wanted. She must want him, too, or she wouldn't have agreed to spend the night with him. He wasn't giving Eve the easy way out.

Finally, she turned her back to him and lifted her arms, struggling to reach the metal tab. "There's a zipper down the back."

He moved closer. "Let me."

Gabe ran his hands up her spine before finding the zipper. She lifted her curls out of his way, exposing the graceful column of her neck. Her skin looked pale, almost incandescent in the low light. He couldn't help himself. He leaned over and kissed her nape, feeling her shiver under his touch.

Slowly, he eased the zipper down, his fingertips brushing her spine. Once he passed her neck, she let her hair fall free, the strawberry-blond mass tumbling well past her shoulders, gliding over her fair skin. Her tresses were soft, too. Not severely flat-ironed. Different, like the woman herself. Fuck, he could lose himself in Eve.

She shrugged, allowing the straps of her dress to fall past her shoulders and drop to her waist.

Her bra looked plain and white. He was used to lacy garments meant to entice a man, so he had no idea why the sight of her utilitarian bra made his cock jerk. She hadn't been seeking a man this evening, much less intending to seduce a lover. When she'd dressed, it had been for comfort. But now, she was here with him, slowly peeling away her clothes.

With practiced ease, he unhooked her bra with a twist of his hand and slid his fingers under the straps to strip them off. He closed his eyes and allowed his hands to roam across the wealth of smooth skin he'd exposed. He drew her back against his chest and grazed his way up her abdomen until he found her breasts. Full and real, he loved the weight of them in his palms. He drew his thumbs over the nubs of her nipples and Eve rewarded him with a long intake of breath.

"That feels so good." As she leaned back against him for support, she shuddered and thrust her breasts up like twin offerings.

He would absolutely take everything she had to give.

Gabe filled his hands with her flesh, cupping and rubbing and discovering every inch of her breasts before he grew impatient to have her totally bare and pushed the dress over the curve of her hips. It pooled on the floor at her feet.

Her underwear matched her bra. If she were his, he would buy her La Perla. He would dress her like a goddess in silk and lace and know that she wore the most come-hither lingerie for his eyes only. She could wear her ladylike dresses and cover herself with all appropriate modesty if she wanted—but only until they were alone.

As he stripped off her panties, a wild possessiveness blazed through his system. Gabe turned her to face him, well aware that he needed to slow down but utterly incapable of doing so. He took in the sight of her breasts. They looked every bit as perfect as they'd felt.

"You're beautiful."

"I don't feel that way." She tilted her face up to his, drinking him in with her stare. There was nothing coy about her expression. She looked at him with naked yearning. "Not most of the time. But you make me feel sexy."

"You are. I want to be very clear about how beautiful I think you are." He kissed her again, lifting her up and out of her dress, heading back to the bedroom while his mouth ate hungrily at hers.

She didn't fight him, didn't fidget to make him set her back on the ground. She simply wrapped her arms around his neck and let him carry her. Her fingers sank into his hair and she held tight while her tongue danced against his.

Luckily, he knew Plaza suites like the back of his hand. He maneuvered her toward the bed, his cock throbbing insistently.

He wouldn't last long. God, he couldn't believe he was even thinking that. Usually, he could go for hours, but Gabe knew the minute he got inside Eve, he was going to lose control. He needed to make it good for her now because he'd barely touched her and already he wanted to throw her against the wall and shove his way inside her.

As he approached the mattress, he stopped and eased her onto the luxurious bedding. She lay back on the elegant duvet, her hair fanned out and her legs spread. Wanton and yet so innocent. He pulled at his shirt, hearing a button or two pop off, but at the moment he didn't give a shit. The need to be skin to skin with her drove him to haste. He unbuckled his belt and shoved his pants down.

"Foreplay." Freaking hell. He was so ready to go, he'd forgotten about that. Women liked foreplay. It tended to be necessary for them.

She shook her head. "The kissing was foreplay. We're totally good."

I wish. He had to slow down. He wasn't exactly a small guy. She needed to be ready to take all of him.

Gabe drew in a deep breath. "Need you aroused. It's okay. Give me a minute."

"Gabriel, I am more aroused than I have ever been in my life. I'm a little worried about what kind of stain I'm going to leave for the staff on their pretty white linens. So really, can we get this train moving?"

He gripped her ankles and slid her down the bed, spreading her legs wider in the process. His cock twitched when he saw that she was right. Her pussy was wet. Juicy. He could see its slick gloss from above, even in the shadows. A little kissing, some groping, and she was ready to go. He'd never had a woman respond to him so readily. "Tell me again."

"I'm ready," she vowed. "I am *really* ready."

"No, tell me this isn't normal for you," he corrected. It was stupid.

She was right there, able and willing to give him the pleasure he sought—but he craved more. He needed to know that tonight was special for her. "Tell me you want me and not just sex."

She gave him a sheepish smile. "This isn't at all normal. I guess I've gone a little crazy tonight, but I don't do one-night stands. I can count the men I've had sex with on one hand and I wouldn't need all my fingers. And I've never, never wanted anyone as much as I want you right now. Gabriel, I don't need foreplay, just you."

Hallelujah. He needed her, too.

Gabe fumbled for his wallet, looking for the one condom he kept in case of emergency sex. He hadn't needed it lately. The sucker had sat there for months while he dealt with everything that had gone wrong in his world. Now something was finally going right.

He tore the little foil wrapper open and managed to roll it over his dick with shaking hands. He didn't need to stroke himself to get hard. He was a fucking rock, as though every available ounce of blood in his body had rushed south and stayed.

Once the condom was secure, Gabe was all over her. He gave Eve his weight, climbing on top of her while parting her legs wider. He pinned her wrists above her head, leaving her open and vulnerable, spread beneath him, a feast for his every sense.

As he buried his face in her neck and inhaled her scent, he crushed her breasts against his chest. "Wrap your legs around me."

His command sounded gruff and thick, but Eve complied, her legs winding around his waist, opening herself fully to him. Gabe groaned. *Hell, yes.* He didn't need to work to align their bodies. He rubbed his cock against her soft opening. It knew right where it wanted to be, locking in on her pussy like she had a homing beacon.

He plunged his hands into her hair again, nipping at her lobe, inhaling her skin, savoring that moment before he sank to the hilt and fucked her breathless.

"Please, Gabriel. Oh, please," she whimpered against his skin. "Don't make me wait. I've never felt like this."

He was fairly certain he never had, either. He'd had so much sex since his first tangle between the sheets at fourteen. The last few years, most of it had been become dull, nothing more than another bodily function. But this felt like something more—something electric, inexplicable. Really damn perfect. He wanted to make the sharp, agonizing moment before he plunged into her last. He needed to enjoy the sizzle burning his skin and feel her slowly set him ablaze. But Eve pressed kisses up his neck and jaw, arching underneath him, silently begging.

Fuck waiting.

Gabe pressed in, forcing her to take his full length in one thrust. She cried out, her nails digging into his back. The pain mixed with the pleasure of her snug heat and shot down his spine. He hissed out and tried to shove in even deeper, but her pussy was so tight. He withdrew slightly. She was so wet and ready, the friction felt perfect. Mind blowing. Damn, he couldn't remember any woman who had ever responded so quickly and completely to his touch. He knew he'd never had one give herself so honestly.

Their bodies were like one. Eve enveloped him in a grip so tight and hot. And he loved every second of their closeness.

He crushed her to the mattress while he thrust back in, so deep, every inch a pure, toe-curling pleasure. So good. No, fucking amazing. Every time he pushed into her, he swore it couldn't get better . . . and then it did. His heart raced. His blood sang. Tingles erupted. Hell, his head swam with euphoria. He couldn't last. She was too hot, too perfect. The sensory overload was too damn much.

He settled into a hard rhythm, pushing them both to the brink. The bed squeaked. The duvet abraded his knees. Gabe didn't care.

Instead, he focused on Eve, angling up until he found that spot that made her gasp and call out his name. Her pussy clenched, nearly strangling his dick with exquisite pressure, and he couldn't hold back a second more. As she moaned out an incoherent cry, he felt her flutter and grip him as she came in his arms. That was it. He was done for. With a primal shout, he let go.

The orgasm shook him, seemingly endless. With a long groan, he thrust in relentlessly, soaring with a dizzying pleasure. Sweating, he pulled back as sensation raked him to new heights.

Gabe repeated the motion until the ecstasy seized his muscles. Pleasure exploded again. He let out a shocked, hoarse cry, until he couldn't even gasp for another breath. Until he felt dizzy and replete. Until he had nothing left to give.

Finally, he fell on top of her, spent—for the moment.

A peace settled over him, and he rested his head on her breast. He listened to her heart beat in a rapid, measured rhythm.

In that moment, Gabe didn't think he'd ever get tired of this . . . of her.

They were only supposed to have this night. He'd picked a hotel instead of his penthouse because he'd wanted to have her, then leave as soon as he'd finished. But he knew in that instant he wouldn't. Couldn't. He needed more. Even as he lay on top of her, still tucked inside her and panting, the thought of having her again made his cock begin to swell once again.

"Stay the night with me." He lifted his head to look down at her.

A languid smile spread across her face. "All right, but I think you said something about food."

"Well, I always try to take care of a lady." He leaned down and kissed her.

He'd bought a few more hours with her, maybe even the whole night.

Gabe intended to make it count.

FOUR

Everly came awake slowly, not wanting to leave the sweet dream she'd found herself in. She was safe and perfectly happy. With Gabriel's arms wrapped around her middle, the heat of his body warmed her. She smiled in contentment.

And then she felt a hand on her breast. Her grin became a moan. "Tell me it's not morning yet."

He moved in closer, his lips caressing her neck. "It's still early. The sun's not quite up. I don't have to be anywhere for hours. How about you?"

"Not for a while." She still needed time to process Mad's death, the turn of her life, her future . . . But she didn't have to do it today.

Gabe rolled her over and his mouth caught hers. "Good. Then we have time. I already called for coffee. It should be here in twenty minutes or so. We can take a shower. Then I'll call in for some breakfast. I find myself very hungry."

He'd been hungry all night. Gabriel had taken her over and over the night before. After the first time he'd made love to her, he'd called down to the concierge and ordered a bottle of champagne, dinner for two, and a box of extra large condoms. She'd blushed at the idea that some random bellboy was bringing up birth control, but Gabriel hadn't blinked an eye. He'd tipped the young man, sent him on his way, and then he'd done his damnedest to go through the entire box.

She'd finally fallen into an exhausted sleep sometime after three in the morning. He'd wrung so much satisfaction from her body, Everly hadn't been able to imagine wanting more.

A few hours of sleep had cured her of that. He'd barely started kissing her and her whole body was hot, alive, buzzing. Sex with Gabriel was like nothing she'd had before. Despite the fact that she didn't know much about him, she felt a connection she couldn't deny. Everly loved the way it felt to be underneath him. When he was on top of her, she felt oddly safe and protected, as though he was sheltering her with his big body.

It sounded silly and naive, but when they were together, she felt as if she belonged with him.

He sucked her bottom lip between his as he made a place for himself between her legs. She could already feel his hard cock against her and couldn't help but wince. It had been a long time since she'd had sex—until last night when she'd had a whole lot of it. Everly also couldn't deny that Gabriel was a bit better endowed than her previous lovers. Make that a whole lot better.

His head snapped up. He frowned. "You okay?"

She didn't want to say anything that would make him stop. She only wanted to be close to him, and that was worth a little discomfort. "I'm fine."

In the early morning light, she could see the way his five-o'clock shadow had filled in. The hair on his face matched his head, all golds and shimmering browns. She liked the way the stubble felt as it gently scraped her skin.

"You're sore," he said with a self-satisfied grin. "We had so much sex last night that you're tender."

She blushed again. "That's not something to be proud of."

"Oh, I totally disagree," he shot back with a chuckle. "It means I did the job well. But I think I can make this right."

"Gabriel, I'm fine." He'd made it right about six times the night before. She was willing to give him whatever he wanted.

He started shimmying down her body, sliding against her in a slow grind. Every inch he eased down, he suckled and laved her skin. He laid sweet kisses against her neck and chest and nipped playfully at her breasts. After the initial hot passion of their first lovemaking, Gabriel had turned out to be a chameleon. Sometimes he liked to play and take his time, touching and kissing every part of her. Other times, he would roll her over and she would find herself penetrated and calling his name within seconds. He kept her off balance and always made sure she had a screaming good time.

His tongue delved into her belly button. "I can make you forget that you're sore."

She had no doubt. Still, she liked to play his game. "How are you going to do that?"

His eyes flashed. "I'll kiss it and make it better."

Gabriel looked down at her sex, leaving no doubt as to his intention. She squirmed. They hadn't done that yet. He'd kissed her everywhere but there, and it probably wasn't a good idea. She hadn't showered. "I don't really like that."

He held her down with his big body, hovering right above her mound. "Don't like what?"

She tried to close her legs, but two hundred pounds of muscle lay between them. "Oral sex. It's . . . awkward. I'm really okay without it."

He reared back. One brow rose in obvious disbelief. "Seriously?"

She couldn't imagine what she tasted like. The couple of times she'd allowed a lover to try had been embarrassing and she hadn't gotten a lot out of it. "Yes."

"Well, I'm not. Trust me, I was planning on getting your mouth on my cock this morning. I guess I'll have to persuade you. See, the way

I figure it, you're very likely a fair woman and you'll repay me once I take care of you."

"I'm really not . . . It's not my thing." She shook her head.

But his mouth was already descending.

"How about you stop thinking for a few minutes? I don't know what your other lovers did, but I intend to make sure you like this." He rubbed his nose right over her pussy and took a deep breath. "You smell incredible. Like sweetness and sex. So fucking good."

His tongue lashed out, and she couldn't stop him. She couldn't stop herself from looking down her body, watching as he licked at her. Then his mouth covered her pussy. Heat slammed through her system. No hesitation. No uncertainty. Gabriel knew exactly what to do, how and when to do it to make her back arch and a cry escape her lips. He was slow and sure and incredibly thorough. His fingers parted her, opening her to the rasp of his teeth and tongue as he very gently and deliberately devoured her.

She gripped the sheets to stop herself from clutching his hair. Not to pull him away, but to make sure he didn't stop. He licked and sucked, leaving not an inch of her unloved. When his tongue circled her clitoris, she was certain she was going to die happy.

"You taste so good, Eve."

The sound of her nickname startled her. She was only Eve to those she loved. In her head, the name was almost an endearment. Usually, she preferred Everly. Last night had been make-believe. Her name hadn't mattered then. This morning, she wanted more. She wanted Gabriel to call her by her real name because she wanted him to know the real her.

Dangerous thoughts. She had too much on her plate for more than here and now. Besides, for all she knew, Gabriel was actually married with three kids. Damn, but that thought was disconcerting. She didn't even know his last name.

"Hey, don't tense on me." His fingers played in her pussy, thrusting up and curling against her G-spot. "Don't think, baby. Just feel. Give me a couple of hours more. Stay with me."

He didn't want to leave any more than she did, it seemed. The thought made her sigh as he lowered his head once more.

His tongue found her clit as he pressed his fingers up again. Suddenly she didn't give a damn about being sore. All that mattered was the heat and thrill sparking between them. When he sucked her clit between his teeth one more time and moaned, she went screaming over the edge.

She bucked against him, but he held her hard, hips pinned to the mattress, forcing her to take every sensation he had to give. Her entire body jolted. Lightning pleasure crackled down her veins. Anyone staying on this floor had to have heard her wails of ecstasy.

Once the peak passed, Gabriel eased away. Her whole body softened as she came down from the high—until she saw him on his knees, over her, reaching for a condom.

He was a magnificent man. She could look at him all day. From his piercing blue eyes to that square jaw to a truly amazing chest, his body provided one gorgeous sight after another. She let her stare drift down to abs she'd only seen in magazines and those notches at his hips bespoke long hours in the gym. He rolled the condom on with a deft hand, covering what had to be the most voracious cock she'd ever encountered. Not that she'd experienced many, but it was hard to believe anyone else could compare with his stamina.

"I thought I was going to repay the favor." She didn't mind. Now that he'd shown her what the big deal was about oral sex, she wanted to know how he tasted.

He shook his head impatiently as he pressed the broad head of his erection against her. "No time. Need it now."

He lowered his body over hers and thrust in deep, his lips plundering hers even as his cock did the same below. She tasted her own arousal on his lips.

"I don't want the morning to end," he groaned, rumbling the words against her lips.

Everly didn't want this to end, either. They could stay right here in this hotel. They could live here and do nothing but make love, eat, and drink. What a lovely fantasy.

She wrapped her arms around him, knowing she would miss him after this and would forever rank other men by the night she'd spent with Gabriel.

He sank in, his hips surging forward then easing back until he found the perfect rhythm. It didn't take him long to send her up, up, until she hung on to the edge by a thread again. This morning, she would never have believed she was capable of multiple orgasms. Now she knew that not only could Gabriel give them to her, but with him they were inevitable.

His body stiffened. "Oh god, Eve. Fuck, that feels so good."

Then he pushed in again, his swelling cock providing exquisite friction against the most sensitive spot high and deep. She screamed as he called out to her again, then they collapsed in a tangle of arms and legs and sighs.

Panting, he rolled to the side of the bed and slung his arm over his head. "You know, we could go on a date sometime."

She turned to face him. "I thought this was one night only."

He reached for her hand and brought it to his chest. "It doesn't have to be. There's obviously a spark between us. No reason we can't explore it. Give me a second."

"I thought we agreed to just a night." She might dream about him, but she knew what reality was. They came from two different worlds. Everything about the man screamed money and privilege. She was a girl from the wrong side of the tracks who was about to find her way right back there.

He stared at her for a moment as though he was trying to figure her out. "And if I changed my mind?"

She needed him to be realistic. "Are you looking for a girlfriend, Gabriel?"

"No," he said, his gorgeous lips turning down. "I'm not in a place where that's a good idea. The next few months are going to be . . . difficult to say the least. I won't have much time to spare and I need to spend it on my family."

Against her better judgment, her heart sank. Well, at least he was honest. He'd been kind. He'd given her more pleasure than she'd ever hoped for and now he was giving her the truth. She couldn't be angry at him for that.

She pressed a chaste kiss to his lips. In the morning light, his hair looked more golden than brown. "Good-bye, Gabriel."

Everly turned away from him and started to rise from the bed. Somehow, she managed to keep herself together. She didn't want to make a fool of herself, and the last thing he probably wanted was a weepy female. Gabriel was too perfect, too good to be true. It was far better if they parted now.

He curled a hand around her arm, stopping her. "I don't want you to go."

She didn't turn, but let herself be drawn against his warmth again until his chest seared her back. "Believe me, if there was any way we never had to leave this hotel again, I just might take it right now. But you know as well as I do that we've both got lives."

"Do we? Today's Saturday. Do you have to work? I don't. I don't have anywhere to be until Monday morning."

She caught her breath. It was a bad idea. She was already in over her head and she'd barely spent twelve hours with the man. "Gabriel, you said you don't want a girlfriend."

His lips brushed her ear, his warmth caressing her. His big arms surrounded her. "I said I can't have one right now, not that I didn't want one. What I can have is a weekend. Forty-eight more hours of pleasure. Forty-eight hours where we don't leave this suite, where you don't wear clothes or worry about tomorrow or think past your next orgasm."

When he cupped her breasts, she sighed. "I don't know if I can handle another orgasm."

Gabriel chuckled behind her. "I think you can. We fit together as if you were made for this moment with me. Look how these pretty things fill my hands. Come on, Eve. Stay. I'll play by your rules."

"I think it's a bad idea." But her body was already behaving like a traitor, softening, priming itself for surrender. "I understand how one night is about sex. I don't know if a weekend will feel as casual to me. I'm a girl who usually thinks with her heart."

He turned her to face him, his blue eyes gentle. "Baby, I can get sex from a lot of women. I don't mean that to be crass, but last night was more than sex for me. I felt more connected to you than I've felt to anyone in a long time. I wasn't lying. I can't have a romantic entanglement right now so I'm going to be selfish and ask you to stay with me. The next few months of my life are going to be a challenge professionally and personally. Maybe it's not fair for me to ask, but I want to spend a few days with you so I'll have something to remember."

Connected. Yes, she'd felt that, too. Somehow despite their lack of words, she'd felt connected to this man by a force more than the physical. Their chemistry was something she'd never felt before. Was she really ready to let it go? Last night, he'd given her a reprieve from all the difficulty in her life, so she could relate to his troubles. He'd offered her the opportunity to forget again. She could be Eve for a little while longer.

"First, I'm going to need a shower."

His smile lit up the room. Then he loomed over her. She drank in the sight of his muscled body before he plucked her off the mattress. God, she would never get used to that. When he picked her up, she felt light and delicate. Not words that she usually used to describe herself. "I have a better idea."

Ten minutes later she lay back in the tub, warm water caressing her body. From behind her, Gabriel folded her into his arms. His erection poked against the small of her back, but he seemed more than content to simply sit with her now.

"So if we're going to spend the weekend together, are we exchanging last names?" he asked.

Everly shook her head. Though she probably shouldn't, she found herself negotiating the weekend with him, setting rules together. Their verbal volley somehow made the moment seem like a very sexy game. "No last names. And no work talk. I don't want to even think about that."

He hummed with a long, satisfied sigh. "I'm all for not talking about work. I think politics and religion should be off the table, too. Boring subjects. We can find more interesting topics to talk about. You liked the movie we were 'watching' last night?"

While their bodies had been tangled together. "I did. *Key Largo* is one of my favorites. My dad and I used to watch movies all the time. He never liked TV. I think it was too violent for him."

"My parents were very strict about TV and movies," Gabe said. "I didn't actually realize movies had colors until I went to a friend's house during a break. We had TV at the academy in the game room, but it was set to one of those stations that played documentaries and 'classic' shows. I think the headmaster believed that if we didn't have cool shows to watch or video games to play we would study more. That did not happen."

"You went to boarding school?" She shouldn't be surprised. She'd known he was wealthy.

His legs slid along hers. "From the time I was seven. I spent nine months out of the year at various boys' schools in Connecticut. How about you? All girls' school? Maybe a Catholic school with a little skirt and pigtails."

"Squash the Britney fantasy. Definitely no private schools for me. I grew up in a small town upstate. There was a combined elementary and middle school. It was a little rural. It's safe to say I didn't fit in. I was the only kid in my class not in 4H."

He caressed his way over her skin again, brushing her breasts as he kissed her ear. "You didn't want to raise prize pigs? I'm trying to see you on a farm."

Everly laughed, feeling oddly content with him. No, what she felt went beyond that. She felt as if she belonged with him.

She'd come to the city almost a year before and she'd found a few friendships, but things felt so weirdly right with Gabriel. It was as if they'd created their own cocoon and nothing could touch them. "No farm for me. My father was a police officer."

"Seriously?"

That was the reason he'd hated modern TV. He dealt with police procedure all day. He hadn't wanted to come home at night and watch actors do it—often badly—on TV. "Yes. I was not the best daughter in the world for him. While everyone else was busy showing off farm animals, I got into computers."

His chest moved with his chuckle. "Tell me you're a sweet little black hat hacker."

He might love old movies, but it was obvious he'd seen some new ones, too. She sat up and swiveled, settling against the side opposite him and took in the gorgeous sight of Gabriel relaxing, his big, muscular chest half out of the water. He still hadn't shaved and that burgeoning beard made him look gloriously masculine. "First, there's no such thing as a sweet black hat. They're called that for a reason. They're mostly anarchists or criminals. I was more into civil disobedience. Oh, and I really was into *Lord of the Rings*. I might have hacked into Peter Jackson's company trying to find the early trailer. I was fifteen. You could say I was a little bit of a late bloomer."

His eyes lit with mirth. "Now that is fascinating, Eve. You're a nerd goddess. Computers and hobbits. Is there a sci-fi fan somewhere in there?"

She felt herself blush. Maybe she should have been a little less honest. She was supposed to stay away from Everly. Why couldn't Eve have been into fashion and art?

"Hey." He leaned toward her. "Baby, I wasn't really making fun of you. I was teasing you a little. I find you completely fascinating. I would never have guessed that you were into computers."

"What would you say I am into?"

He studied her for a moment. "If I had to guess, I would say you work in counseling of some kind. You're the person everyone talks to and relies on. You're responsible. Thoughtful. I would also bet that you're lonely because you don't shift your burdens to other people. They can talk to you, but you don't want to drag your friends down with your problems."

She sucked in a shocked breath. He was surprisingly insightful.

"I'll be honest with you, Gabriel. Right now I don't have many friends. I'm fairly new to the city and all I do is work." The closest friend she'd had in the Big Apple was now gone. "This weekend is absolutely the most exciting thing that's happened to me since . . . maybe ever, and I might have wrecked it because I told the hot guy what a nerd I am."

He reached for her hand, and the water sloshed around her as he dragged her into his lap. The tip of his cock probed her pussy. How did this man manage to take her from feeling insecure to aroused in an instant?

"You are the sexiest nerd I've ever seen," he murmured. "I want to hear all about your life as a hacker. Tell me every story."

"I thought we were staying away from personal details."

"Screw that. I only agreed to no last names. I want to know you. I want to know everything about you." He dragged her down for a hungry kiss. "Later."

Everly gave in and let him take her where only he could.

Gabe couldn't help but watch her. Sure there was a movie on the big screen, but Eve was naked and splayed across the bed. She lay on her stomach, her chin propped on her hands and her ankles crossed. Her ass looked plump and round and so sweet he couldn't help but reach out and caress it.

She looked back at him, wearing a mysterious smile. Her skin appeared luminous in the evening light. "You are an insatiable man."

He was completely crazy about her. He tried to remember when he'd ever spent this much uninterrupted time with a woman, and he couldn't.

Eve. She made him feel a little like Adam. They'd shared two days in their own private paradise, and with the singular exception of ordering room service, they hadn't seen or talked to anyone. His phone was filled with messages, but he didn't care. Sara hadn't called and she was the only one he might allow to interrupt this time with Eve. Maybe.

"Come here. I promise I'm utterly sated. I don't think I could get an erection if I wanted one." He was lying. His dick was as crazy about her as the rest of him, but right now he really wanted to hold her. It was getting late and he would have to leave in the morning. He'd shirked all his meetings this weekend, but that's why he paid his lawyers. They'd be prepared for tomorrow. Right now, he could only focus on how much he'd hate saying good-bye to Eve.

Last night after she'd fallen asleep, he'd lain awake while his brain whirled, trying to craft a new way to persuade Eve to stay. For the first time, he understood why Mad had strung the press along in the last months of his life. His old friend had been trying to protect the woman he'd truly cared for—whoever she was—but Gabe had seen how those games had hurt Sara. He couldn't put Eve up in some swanky building, then pretend to date other women to keep the press off her. But if he didn't, those vultures would be on her the instant they discovered the two of them were involved, especially given all the interest in Mad's death and the uncertainty with Crawford Industries.

She got to her knees, his nerdy goddess. He wondered briefly if he had a position open at Bond Aeronautics, his company. He hired programmers all the time. He could wait a few weeks, then see if this euphoric craving for her wore off. If it didn't, he could find her and hire her and persuade her that, oh baby, the boss needed a little attention. They could keep the whole thing under wraps until the press died down.

Hmm. If he wanted her to say yes, he'd probably have to work on his presentation.

She settled against him, cuddling his right side. She was a perfect armful. "I've always loved this movie."

Casablanca was playing on the television, but he'd mostly been watching Eve. She fit perfectly against his side. In the last two days, he'd had her often and well, but he'd found the one thing he liked even more than making love was talking to her. He'd avoided talking about his sister, his friends, or the parts of his past that would enable her to identify him. She didn't seem to have any idea who he was, and he liked it that way. She seemed to think he was just another guy, not a man who had reporters hounding his every move, who regularly showed up in gossip rags. He kind of liked being a regular Joe and not Manhattan's most eligible bachelor. Eve had agreed to stay with him with no strings, no promises of presents or favors or hopes of being seen with him.

Eve liked him. Just him as he was.

"Did you used to watch this with your dad?"

She nodded against his chest. "Oh, yes. He would play it at least once a year. We would eat Chinese food and watch this along with *North by Northwest*. He said it was the perfect double feature. Romance and adventure. The Chinese food was made by refugees from Jersey. The Pollizzi family. It was awful. They liked to say it was fusion. Chinese and bad Italian should never go together. Although the Kung Pao lasagna was legendary."

She made him laugh. Being with Eve showed Gabe how grim he'd become.

The offer to fly her to Beijing so she could experience true Chinese food sat right on the tip of his tongue. He could show her the city's most impressive restaurant. He could fly her there himself or take the private jet with a pilot so he could make love to her for the whole fourteen-hour flight.

Instead, he simply squeezed her tight. "I hope you've found some good spots here."

Her face lit up. "I love the city. So much good food. I think I've gained twenty pounds from trying everything."

Most of his previous female companions didn't eat a lot, much less show such enthusiasm. Eve was unabashed in her joy. She'd eaten every bite of her Belgian waffle that morning and relished in the fries served with their steaks this evening.

All he had to do was feed the girl and she was putty in his hands.

"Does your father miss you?"

She went still, and he knew he'd stepped into something.

"I'm sorry, Eve. He's gone, isn't he?"

The question seemed to rattle her, and she sighed. "I lost him not too long ago. I don't know. Sometimes it feels like yesterday. Sometimes it feels like forever ago."

"How about your mom?" He asked the question cautiously. He was so curious about her background, but she'd been serious about the no-last-names thing. He didn't want to scare her off.

She remained quiet for a moment, then turned her face his way. "She left when I was young. It was just me and my dad. How about you?"

He was more than willing to discuss his background if it kept her talking. "Well, you know I grew up wealthy."

Her nose wrinkled in that cute way that let him know she wasn't impressed. "Yes, I think being able to afford this super expensive suite for three nights is proof that you've got some bank, Gabriel."

He went still. "Wait. Um, I thought you were paying for this. I told them it was all you."

Her mouth fell open, her eyes widening in shock.

Gabe let her off the hook with a laugh. "I was joking, baby."

"Jerk," she huffed, but settled back in.

He loved teasing her, too. "So like I was saying, grew up rich, but that is not a guarantee of happiness."

"Why did they send you to boarding school?" she asked.

He was sure the concept was foreign to her. Eve's father probably had been very protective. He couldn't see her dad letting her reside in a different state nine months out of the year. "Because every male in my family for the last hundred years has attended Creighton Academy, and I wasn't going to be any different, according to my father. My family came over on the Mayflower. My many-times-great grandfather was one of the first official US prisoners of war. Him dying in a Redcoat jail was a serious point of pride to my father."

She frowned, her brow creasing sweetly. It made her look like a grumpy kitten, though a sexy one. "I'm pretty sure I'm related to John Wilkes Booth."

"That is unfortunate. My mother would surely have forbidden me to see you." He kissed her forehead. "Again, I'm joking. I'm merely pointing out that I had a reputation to live up to."

"That must have been rough. You weren't allowed to be a kid, were you?"

"No. I had to represent my family. My father was raised a certain way and he passed that on to me. He was distant, though I believe he loved me deep down. It's funny how our perspectives can change as we age. Now I see he tried to connect the only way he knew how." He hadn't discussed this in years, and never with the honest insight he was sharing now. He and Sara spoke about their parents, but he never wanted to criticize them to her, so he hadn't been completely open about his feelings. Maybe because he'd spent so much time naked with Eve, it felt so natural to open himself up. It seemed right to talk to her.

"And how was that?"

He smiled with the memory. "We flew. He started taking me up in puddle jumpers when I was six. Scared the hell out of my mother, but I loved it. I got my pilot's license at seventeen but I was flying long before that. I was lucky I never got caught."

Eve caressed his chest, her touch soothing. "Wow, the biggest concession I got from my dad was when he let me ride in the back of his patrol car and I let everyone think I'd been arrested. I was eight. I thought it made me look tough. Then I actually got arrested because of the Peter Jackson incident and it really ruined me forever."

"I can imagine." He wished he'd been there for that lecture. He was sure it had been a doozy. He wondered what she would say if he told her he'd recently been at a party with the famous director.

"So your dad taught you how to fly," she said with a little bit of wonder in her voice.

He would love to take her up. Climb about twenty thousand feet where the world receded and a man could see forever. "Yeah. He was a cold man, but he gave me that. I think of him when I fly. He died a few years back. Heart attack. I think it started earlier though. The FAA took away his license because he failed the medical exam. Once he was grounded, he wasn't the same. My mother went a year later from cancer. I miss them. I wouldn't have thought I would, but I do."

She sat up and looked down at him, her eyes solemn. "That's something we have in common. We're orphans. I know it sounds silly since we're adults, but after Dad died, I couldn't get that word out of my head. I guess it doesn't matter how old we are. We still need our parents. I only had one, but he was enough."

"He did a good job." Tenderness welled inside him.

"Yours did, too, Gabriel."

He couldn't help but chuckle at that. "Oh, I wish I could agree. You don't know me outside of this room. You don't know the things I'm capable of. I am everything my father wanted me to be. Ruthless. Successful. Unrelenting. Stubborn. Arrogant."

He was the man whose hands had twitched at the thought of Mad screwing around on Sara. He was the man who was still going to find the woman who'd fucked his sister over and ensure she did not benefit in any way from Mad's death.

Eve straddled him, cupping his face in her hands. "I don't believe you. I think you're more yourself in here than you are out there. I know I feel that way. I haven't felt as safe in months as I have the last two days. I really don't want it to end."

Gabe curled his hands around her hips, reveling in her curves. His cock was at full staff again. "I don't, either. Come here, baby. Let's make tonight count and we'll talk in the morning. Maybe things will look different to you then."

He drew her down and prayed he could persuade her to give him more.

The next morning, Everly stared down at her phone and sucked in a shaking, shocked breath. Now she knew exactly how Pandora felt. She'd opened that box she wasn't supposed to open and unleashed chaos on her world.

"Hey, baby. Are you sure you don't want anything more than coffee?"

She darkened the display on her phone the minute she heard his voice. "No, I'm good. It's too early for breakfast. I'll get something on my way to work."

"All right. I'm going to take a quick shower. Then we're going to talk, all right?" He appeared in the doorway, obviously comfortable with his nudity. "You sure you don't want to join me?"

"Sorry. I've got some really important e-mails from work. I should go." After what she'd discovered moments before, she needed to run, not walk, back to Brooklyn.

He was Gabriel Bond. She'd spent the weekend with aeronautics tycoon Gabriel Bond. He was a multi-billionaire playboy. She hadn't needed to dig very deep. All she'd had to do was Google *pilot, Creighton Academy,* and *blond man.* The search engine had spit out more details than she'd been prepared for. Entire websites were devoted to his love life. He dated models, actresses, and gorgeous socialites. He absolutely did not have a fling—much less a lasting relationship—with a cop's daughter. She didn't even comprehend the world he moved in. Worse, she'd read another piece of horrifying news: Maddox Crawford had been his best friend. That explained why he'd been in the bar on Friday night. He'd attended the funeral, too. Everly wondered how she'd ever explain her connection with Maddox to Gabe?

It was easy; she wouldn't. He'd said himself that he wasn't the same man outside this room. She wasn't the same woman. And obviously she'd lost her mind, spending an entire weekend naked with a man who only shared his sheets with the most beautiful women in the world.

He strolled back in carrying his cell phone. "This is ridiculous. I'm not going to let you simply walk away. Here, give me your number and I'll call you. I've got a ton of stuff to do today, but maybe we could have dinner later this week."

She took the phone from him and looked down. Eve. He'd already started the contact with that name. He had no idea Everly was her given name. Would he feel betrayed now by her white lie? Did it matter since he wasn't the sort of man who would stay with her forever?

He stared, waited. His anticipation dissipated. He scowled. "You don't want me to call, do you?"

Everly paused. It would be smarter if she didn't but . . . could she really stay away?

She was about to respond—she wasn't really sure what she planned to say—when she heard a firm knock on the door.

"Put your number in. Please." Gabriel leaned over and kissed her, as if adding a little sugar to sweeten the pot. "That's probably the coffee service I ordered. Look through the menu again. I know you said you had to leave but I would feel better if you ate something. I'll be right back."

She watched him walk toward the living area, unable to take her eyes off how fine and taut that bare backside looked.

He turned at the door, snagging a robe from the closet and tossing the second one her way. "Slip this on. I fully intend to tip the delivery guy, but he doesn't get to see you naked. That's for me."

He winked at her, then headed for the door. As Everly belted the robe, she heard the snick of the lock and the squeak of the door opening.

She was such a coward, she thought, staring at that phone. She should input her number. When Gabriel came back, she would confess her connection to Maddox, admit that she'd violated their anonymity rule. He knew she wasn't from his world and he hadn't seemed to mind. Maybe she was making too much out of this worry. Maybe they would be all right.

Or they would be a complete disaster. She needed to focus on keeping her job. Dating Gabriel Bond would likely be a roller coaster ride without a seatbelt. Everly wasn't sure how long she could hold on. His glittering realm wasn't something she could comprehend. Now that she'd seen picture after picture of the beauties he'd dated and probably taken to bed, insecurity rushed over her. Besides, he'd told her from the beginning he didn't have time for a girlfriend. Sure, he wanted more sex, but that wasn't love. In fact, that wasn't anything beyond an erection and an orgasm. Okay, so he seemed to like her as a person, but that didn't change the fact that he hadn't wanted a relationship when he'd walked through this door. He probably didn't really want one now. And how did she know this wasn't an "I'll call you" thing, an empty promise that would never come to pass?

She didn't . . . but Everly still took a deep breath and punched her number into the phone anyway. The ball was in his court. What was life without a little risk?

"Gabe, my man, we need to talk," a masculine voice said from the front of the room.

She peeked through the doorway to find two tall men, both radiating power and impatience, striding into the room. One had dark, thick waves of hair he'd clearly tried to tame and wore a stylish charcoal suit. The other, a rugged guy with dark blond hair and a nick of a scar slashing down his chin, was dressed in dark slacks, a black T-shirt, and a windbreaker.

"We've got trouble," the impeccably dressed man warned.

Everly's stomach took a nosedive. It looked like her time in paradise with Gabriel was over.

FIVE

Gabe strode out the service entrance and climbed the ramp that led to the street, scanning his surroundings for photographers.

"Dax is with the car," Roman explained. "We'll talk when we're sure no one can hear us. You know, if you had answered your phone, we wouldn't have had to track you down."

Connor shifted in front, hyperalert for any threat. He wore a light jacket, though it already seemed too humid for anything with long sleeves. On the other hand, Gabe supposed his CIA pal had more than one firearm to conceal. Sure enough, when Connor turned, Gabe caught a glint of metal under Connor's arm. He was carrying. That wasn't unusual, but his tense demeanor meant trouble.

Gabe frowned. What had the two of them so keyed up? Foreboding gripped his gut.

"We're good." Connor nodded. "Let's go."

The secret agent emerged into the sunlight, jogging to the waiting limo before opening the door and gesturing them inside.

Gabe nearly growled his frustration as he followed Roman. "You better have a damn good excuse for pulling me out of bed."

Roman hadn't cracked a smile. He hadn't made a joke or leered at Eve once. He was behaving completely out of character. "Oh, I have the best excuse of all. I'm trying to save your ass, man. And don't blame me. Connor is the one who found it."

It? Gabe scowled. He needed to get his head in whatever the hell game they were already playing. Unfortunately, his brain was still replaying his time with the woman he'd left upstairs, and wondering how soon he could see her again. "What is this amazing thing Connor found?"

"When we get in the car. Go," Roman snapped.

At this time on a Monday morning, plenty of people walked the street. Any one of them could be a photographer. Gabe knew the drill: duck into the car as quickly as possible. Instead, he turned and looked up at the hotel he'd left Eve in, wishing like hell he was still there with her.

She'd barely been able to look at him after he'd told her he needed to go. She'd immediately nodded and agreed, and he didn't need to be a genius to know she thought he intended to ditch her. There wasn't a hell of a lot he could do about that now. He could say all the right words, but she wasn't going to believe him until he called her.

If, in fact, she'd given him the right number. After her hesitation, he wasn't sure.

Holding in a curse, Gabe bent and folded himself into the limo. His friends followed into the air-conditioned interior, closing the door behind them. Roman settled beside him on the black leather with a sigh. Immediately, the limo took off.

"You said Dax was here." Gabe sat across from Connor and speared him with a questioning stare, assuming they'd now have to wait for their friend.

"I've got the wheel, brother." The window between the front and the back of the limo buzzed down, and Dax nodded at him in the rearview mirror.

"What the hell?" Had he left the navy for a career as a limo driver?

"In all honesty, I've had more than enough crappy surprises this week. So if the three of you cooked up some elaborate practical joke that ruined my morning with Eve, I'm going to kick every one of your asses."

"In your shoes, I'd be pissed off, too. She was hot." Dax expertly guided the car into the early morning traffic. "And you guys are safe to talk. I rechecked the car. No one's listening. Unless the NSA has some new toys."

Connor shook his head as he reached into his briefcase. "No. We're good in the limo when we're moving. I seriously doubt the tabloids are chasing us with sophisticated listening devices."

"Don't underestimate them," Roman shot back. "And I'm not only worried about reporters. I'm worried about the police, too."

Gabe sat up a little straighter. They had his attention now. "Police?"

Roman sat back, looking utterly exhausted. Now that he studied his old friend, Gabe could clearly tell that Roman hadn't slept the night before, and nothing as pleasant as a woman like Eve had kept him awake. "Connor has a lid on our problem for now."

"But there's no way this doesn't get out—and soon. I got to this particular reporter, but she thinks her source had already sold copies." Connor held the tablet he'd extracted from his briefcase. "She said she tried for an exclusive, but the seller wouldn't give her one. I've got an associate doing his best to hunt down any other copies."

Gabe was starting to get angry again. "Copies of what, damn it?"

"Of this." Connor turned the screen of the tablet in his direction. "Recognize it?"

Of course he recognized the dining room of Cipriani. He had lunch there all the time. The maître d' was an old family friend. He knew there were hotter spots, but it had been a favorite of his father's and had become a sentimental pick for him. Every time he sat there, Gabe remembered all the times his father had taken him and tried to teach him about the business. "Of course I recognize my table at Cipriani. Has eating scampi thermidor become a crime?"

As the video started rolling, he realized exactly what event had been recorded, and his stomach took a deep dive. He could see himself, though only part of his face occupied the top left of the screen. The right side was filled with the back of a man in a gray suit, drinking a Scotch, his hands tapping on the glass with a nervous energy.

"Oh, shit. This is my last meeting with Mad."

Roman nodded. "Someone must have recognized you. Or more likely, they recognized Mad. He was all over the tabloids the last few weeks of his life. I believe this was taken with a cell phone by someone sitting at the table next to you."

Connor shot him a disgusted stare. "You should have noticed."

"Turn that thing off." He didn't need a reminder of what had happened that afternoon. It played through his head all the damn time, like a never-ending nightmare. Well, except the last few nights. With Eve, he'd slept like a baby . . . when he hadn't been inside her. This weekend he'd been able to forget that he was mourning Mad and the terrible way they'd ended a lifelong friendship.

Despite what he'd told her about not having time for a girlfriend, he knew it wouldn't be long before he gave in and dialed her number. If she'd given him a false one, well, he would find her anyway. He needed her. It was selfish to even think of bringing her into his crap right now, but somehow during the weekend they'd spent together, she'd become necessary to him. That was the truth.

Roman took the tablet and flipped it off. "Obviously, Gabe was far too busy arguing with Mad to notice anything at all."

"Oh, it isn't the argument that's the problem. It's the threats." Connor stared at him like he was a suspect. "You threatened to kill Mad. You want to explain why?"

He'd threatened Mad in numerous ways at that lunch. "Guys, I was angry about the lousy way he treated my sister. You know they dated a couple of months back. It ended ugly."

"I told you that was a mistake," Dax supplied helpfully as he turned the limo.

The green of Central Park was to his left, the site of his crime coming up on his right. The restaurant where he'd promised Mad that he would have revenge had a marbled front with a few small windows covered in crisp white drapes. He preferred the table that overlooked Grand Army Plaza. As a child, he would stare at the gold statue of Sherman while his father droned on about the importance of business. He stared at the façade of the building as they drove past.

Gabe remembered that last fight with Mad vividly. Gabe had left him with the check and walked in the park for about an hour. He'd sat on a bench and known that all around him tourists and locals were enjoying the day, but he hadn't seen it. He'd only seen his friendship with Mad crumbling. He'd been so brutally, violently angry, and if he'd had the chance in that moment, he might have choked the life out of his best friend.

But he hadn't had the chance. Later that evening, after Gabe had cooled off a bit, he'd driven out to the airport to talk to Mad again. Unfortunately, he'd missed the plane taking off by seconds. He'd thought he would have more time for everything to work out.

Instead, Mad's plane had gone down.

"We all know he broke up with Sara in a nasty way." Roman used the same soothing tone he took on the Sunday morning news shows when butting heads with the opposition. Roman Calder was known as the pundit whisperer. He could calm the most ferocious mouthpiece for any lobby or special interest with the sound of his voice—and very tight logic.

Gabe had no interest in being calmed. His friends didn't know half of what had transpired. "He dumped her via text, and two hours later he was strutting down the red carpet with a blond actress, bragging about their fabulous sex life. Do you have any idea how that made Sara feel?"

"I can imagine." Connor crossed one leg over the other and sat back. "But you knew what Mad was like when you let him date her."

"He wasn't like that with her." That fact baffled Gabe most. "He was . . . perfect with Sara. He'd seemingly matured and stopped drinking so much. Hell, he even seemed to have given up other women and stayed home with Sara every chance he could. We went out to the Hamptons and didn't leave the house for a week. They seemed so happy."

"Sara is beautiful and kind," Dax said, his voice low. "She'll be fine, Gabe. Hell, she'll probably find a good man and get married in the next couple of years and forget all about Mad."

"She can never forget about Mad, damn it. He made sure of it. That's the fucking problem."

"Sara's pregnant, isn't she?" Connor said, his eyes narrowing. "That's why you were so blazingly pissed in that video. Mad got Sara pregnant and dumped her."

Damn. He hadn't intended to tell anyone, but Connor had always seen too much. "Less than a week after she told him, yes. Sara finally admitted it to me the morning of that lunch. Keep that information quiet."

Roman slapped at the door, his calm demeanor fleeing in an instant. "There will be no fucking way to keep this quiet, Gabe. Not once that tape gets out. And if there's any question about who you're threatening, I'm sure the police can drum up a witness or two to come forward."

Confusion was starting to make his head pound. "The police? Why the hell would they care who saw me threaten Mad that day? Mad's plane crashed. Capitol Scandals's claims aside, it was an accident."

Connor held up a copy of the morning's paper. "Not according to the *Times*. We've gone past the tabloids, brother. Real papers have picked this story up."

The headline jumped out at him in black and white, sending him reeling.

BILLIONAIRE'S CRASH DEEMED SUSPICIOUS

"Oh, shit," Gabe muttered as the implications fell into place.

"You don't even want to know what the other papers are saying,"

Roman explained with a sigh. "Apparently the FAA has found some trace chemicals that shouldn't have been there and say it's evidence of an incendiary device on the plane. The working theory is that someone left a timed explosive on his aircraft."

Gabe's whole body went cold. Mad had been murdered. "They're going to think I killed him."

"Well, you did mention ending him on that tape. More than once," Dax threw in. "We're two minutes out, boys."

"Now I'm glad I'm staying in the city for a few days because of that damn fundraiser." Roman straightened his tie. "Zack had to go back to DC, but while I'm here, I'll do everything I can to help keep this tape out of the press and the hands of police."

"We'll try. But some things are impossible, even for us," Connor admitted.

"Roman, I didn't kill him. I wouldn't have." Maimed him. Beat the shit out of him. Maybe forced him to the altar with a shotgun.

Connor held up a hand. "We know. But someone did off him. The problem is, the list of suspects is practically as big as Manhattan's phone book, and the NYPD is going to pounce on the easy suspect. That's you. I'm already trying to whittle the list down and figure out who really had the motive and means to bomb his plane. Dax and I are going to start talking to his employees quietly, and Roman is going to look into Mad's more intimate connections. We'll try to keep Sara out of this, but questions are bound to arise. You didn't directly mention her pregnancy in the video, but now that I know about it, I see both you and Mad allude to it."

Roman sat up, buttoning the jacket to his three-piece suit. "We have bigger problems right now, and knowing that Sara's pregnant makes the timing more critical. We need to get in and sign the papers concerning Mad's estate. It's urgent that we move to consolidate as quickly as possible. I've already talked to the probate judge and explained that the health of the company is at risk and the jobs Crawford Industries provides are vital to the economy. The will is well written and there shouldn't be any complaints against it. Mad didn't have relatives, so this should be a smooth transition. I think we can avoid a freeze of your assets if we're careful. I hope."

"I'm trying to buy us a few days to figure out what the hell's actually going on," Connor explained.

Gabe sat back in utter shock at the turn of events. An hour ago, he'd been warm and happy in bed with Eve. Now Roman was talking about freezing his assets? The world had tilted and he definitely didn't like where he'd landed. "Why would anyone freeze my assets?"

"Not all of them, just Crawford Industries." Roman winced. "Because you, Gabe, are the new CEO. Maddox left everything he owned to you and you alone—money, houses, cars, and his business. If that video isn't motive enough, then the billion dollar company you inherited as of this morning almost surely is."

For the second time in ten minutes, Gabe felt the world shift. He had to hope he was still standing when it stopped.

Everly walked out of the elevator, her mind still on Gabriel. What had she done? Why had she given him her number after she'd figured out who he was? It had been impulsive. She didn't have his phone number. He hadn't offered it. He'd kissed her, told her he had to go, and walked out. No more promises about calling. He'd looked grim as he'd dressed quickly, and he'd left as if fleeing the scene of a crime.

The only bright side? Maddox Crawford would have gotten a kick out of her having a one-night stand with his best friend after his funeral.

As she'd left the hotel, she'd had the oddest feeling that someone was watching her. There had been the usual crowd out on the streets. She'd run past a couple of photographers who had likely been waiting for celebrities. The Plaza had its share. They couldn't possibly care about her or know that she'd spent the weekend holed up with Gabriel. She'd wondered if they'd taken pictures of him as he'd left.

The paparazzi was his life. He wouldn't call and if he did, she would have to think about not answering. They were far too different to make anything lasting work. He likely wouldn't call at all. She was almost certain getting her number was a way to smooth over an awkward parting. His friends also had impeccable timing. They'd whisked Gabriel away at the perfect moment to avoid a long good-bye.

Hell of an exit strategy.

If she had to bet, she would put her money on the fact they were through. No matter how good a time he'd had, no matter how close they'd felt, Gabriel Bond wouldn't have an actual relationship with a woman like her. She'd been a good lay and a good time. Now it was over.

She'd been forced to "walk of shame" it until she'd managed to hail a cab to Brooklyn so she could shower, change, and pull herself together for what was likely to be a difficult day.

Everly walked into the elegant lobby of Crawford's corporate offices. Sometimes the fact that she was an executive still felt a bit surreal. The first time she'd been invited to the top floor, she'd felt like she'd finally made it. Now she worried how long she would last at Crawford and if she could even find another job.

"Good morning, Ms. Parker. It's good to see you here so bright-eyed after an undoubtedly long weekend." Jennifer, the corporate office's general receptionist, sat at the desk, a discreet Bluetooth device in her ear. She answered calls and sent them to whomever they needed to reach. But she also served as the hub for gossip in the office. Information both true and false flowed through her like a river before she sent it into the tiny world via her tributary of secretaries.

Jennifer had a light in her eyes that Everly didn't understand. She knew one thing, though. When Jennifer looked that happy, she had a truly juicy scoop on someone. "Yes, I hope everyone had a chance to relax. The funeral on Friday took a lot out of everyone, I suppose."

"Sure did," she replied with a wink. "Some of us more than others. Ms. Gordon was looking for you. I told her you were running a little late because you had to pick up a new external hard drive you ordered last week." She pulled out a small blue bag from an electronics store. "Here it is. It was delivered Friday, but she doesn't know that."

Everly took the drive, grateful for the excuse. She needed this to back up the contents of her hard drive before she tried to fix the problems with her frustratingly slow computer. "Thanks for covering for me."

She didn't want to have to explain why she was so late. Her staff wouldn't question her. She was easy on them. As long as they completed projects and did their jobs, she was flexible on the hours they worked. Most of them had earned their office moniker of "Geek Squad" by staying insular and holding weekly Magic: The Gathering tournaments. And for productivity's sake, she didn't dare get them started on *Game of Thrones*. All in all, though, she preferred her team to the cattiness of the rest of the groups.

She started toward her office, thinking about the day ahead. She needed to check over the reports for the last week. She'd had concerns on the retail side that there might have been a breach. If so, she would have a headache on her hands. But at least it would keep her from thinking about being unemployed.

"Everly, I'm so glad you're here. Are you all right?" Tavia poked her head out of her office, sounding concerned but looking so chic in a simple black sheath and sky-high heels with a distinctive red sole. Everly had seen the outfit a few times; it never failed to look striking.

"Fine." Everly frowned in confusion. "You?"

Tavia gestured with a manicured hand. "Thank goodness. I've worried about you all morning. Come in. Quick. I don't want to talk where everyone can hear us."

Everly glanced around and was really surprised to find way too many eyes peering above cubicle walls at her. They quickly looked away, the gawkers going back to the screens or reports awkwardly, as though trying not to look obvious.

Why was everyone staring?

She took Tavia's hand and let the woman rush her into the office with its four floor-to-ceiling windows and stunning view of Central Park. The back wall was covered with pictures of the blond beauty posed beside dozens of young women from all over the world. Tavia looked so different in those pictures. She was dressed casually in most. In some, from when she went to Muslim countries, she wore a hijab to cover her hair.

Tavia saw her staring at the pictures. "I'm hoping to open a new school with the money we raise this year." She pointed to the most recent photo. "I found this village in India in desperate need of a girls' school. They have a boys' school, but the girls' building burned down and no one has raised the money for a new one."

"How is the search for that missing girl going?"

Two months earlier, Everly had gone to lunch with Tavia after one of the girls from her school in Liberia had vanished without a trace. Tearfully, Tavia had clutched the girl's picture and vowed to find her.

"We're still looking. It's difficult in that part of the world. Epidemics go hand-in-hand with insufficient medical care, but once we established that Janjay hadn't fallen ill . . . the other options for her disappearance aren't so palatable. I have to hope she ran away." She shook her head sadly. "Girls get taken for many reasons. It's a reality I simply can't accept. Boko Haram is starting to work in that part of the world. Now we have to worry about ISIS as well. They'll try to tear down everything I've built."

Boko Haram was a terrorist group that believed all things western were evil, and that included educating females. They had kidnapped an entire school of girls, forcing them to convert to their extreme form of Islam. ISIS, another terror group, was moving into Africa. Everly could understand why Tavia was scared for the young women she tried to help.

"Do you want me to see what else I can do?" It felt wrong not to offer. "I'm sure the security guys at Crawford's international offices are working as hard as they can, but I'll ask them for an update."

Tavia smiled with regret. "Oh, you're so sweet, but please don't take their attention from the field. Their work in finding the girl is too important to tear them away. I'm sure they'll tell us what they've found as soon as they're able, but we can't risk leads going cold."

Which must be why Everly hadn't received any expense reports or requests for reimbursements. Sometimes their field agents were too busy for paperwork. The rest of the time, operatives hated what they called desk jockey stuff. "You're right. I wish I could do more."

"Your specialty is computer security, and the corporation needs that desperately, too. But Crawford's boots on the ground in war-torn parts of the globe have the experience in this arena. I hope luck is on our side. Now, how are you holding up?"

"I'm okay. I'll be better after the new boss comes in and we know one way or another whether we're keeping our jobs."

Tavia's brow rose. "Sweetie, I was talking about what happened this morning."

So she was going to have to explain why she was late. She wasn't sure why Tavia needed to know. The woman wasn't her boss. "I needed some time. I'm fine now. I should get to work."

Tavia circled back around to her desk. "You weren't scared of those reporters?"

Everly blinked. How had Tavia known about the small group of tabloid bloodhounds outside the hotel? She'd hustled to a cab and left them behind to wait for their real target. Since she'd likely shown up in the background of some shot, Everly supposed she had to make explanations. Maybe a white lie would get her through this. "I got a little drunk last night and decided to stay here in Manhattan. You know how it is, trying to navigate the subway when you're toasted."

Tavia turned the screen of her computer around. "I don't know that anyone's going to buy that story. Not when your name gets attached to someone like Gabriel Bond. Sweetie, you need to be prepared. They didn't have your name this morning, but they'll find it—quick."

Everly stared in horror at the byline on the Internet news story.

NEW MISTRESS?
WALL STREET'S BAD BOY BOND RETURNS TO FORM

Underneath the headline there was a photo of her running to the cab in her wrinkled dress, her hair whipping in the wind and one hand out to stave off the press. "Oh, my god. That's me. They're talking about me."

Tavia sank into her chair, crossing her long legs. "You can't be too surprised. You had to know they would, if they caught you."

"Why would they care?" Why the hell did it matter to anyone that she'd had a wild weekend?

"Of course they're going to care." Tavia stood again, as if too restless to sit. "They report about anyone remotely connected to that group. Did you really let Gabriel Bond pick you up at Maddox's funeral?"

"I met him at the bar after the service. I honestly didn't know who he was until I put it together this morning." And on the way back to work she'd thought about some other things, too. One particular memory had surfaced.

I need to let you meet Bond sometime. You'd like him, Everly. He's a good guy. Not too thrilled with me right now, but I have hopes we'll work things out eventually. He's my best friend in the world. We have to work it out.

Maddox had been eating her stew and talking about the group of men he'd grown up with, but he'd only referred to them by their last names, with the exception of Zack Hayes, whom he'd referred to as Mr. President . . . though he snickered every time he did. But Maddox had often talked about Bond.

Tavia's expression softened with sympathy. "If you didn't know who he was, then you must not have known his reputation. I'm afraid he's a real player." She winced. "He's torn through most every beauty in Manhattan, but he never stays with one for long. Pig."

She held out her free hand to stop that line of conversation. "I wasn't trying to be his girlfriend. He was alone. I was alone. It seemed like a good idea at the time."

He said he'd call her. He'd taken her number. Wall Street's Bad Boy ring her? Ha!

Tavia sighed. "If you lie low, it will blow over soon. He'll move on to the next woman, and the press will forget you. I wanted to make sure you were ready for the gossip. No one in the office can seem to talk about anything else this morning."

Everly felt her skin heat. In some ways, this was her worst night-mare. She couldn't stand the thought of everyone gossiping behind her back about her liaison with yet another man. At least this rumor was actually true. But up until last night, she hadn't had a sex life—nothing anyone would find interesting anyway. Suddenly, she preferred her coworkers chin-wagging about how young she was for her job.

It wasn't fair. If she'd been a man, no one would have questioned her or cared at all.

"Everly, don't worry about it." Tavia shook her head. "It really will blow over in a couple of days. I understand why you left with him. He's a stunning man. I've only met him once, but I was impressed by how charismatic he was. He could have talked me into bed, too."

"I can't believe those reporters were waiting for me outside of the hotel. Why did they hang around? Gabriel left before me." Though not very long before her. Once he'd gone, she had wanted to get out as quickly as possible. The room seemed too empty without him.

"Most likely, he left via the back door."

"Why wouldn't he tell me to do the same?"

"I'm sure you were good camouflage for him," Tavia explained with a sympathetic wince. "It's the way these men work. They're excellent in bed, but they don't care much about women like us out of it. How do you think they recognized that you spent the night with him and weren't a guest in some other room? I'm sure one of Bond's employees tipped off the paparazzi. That would keep them at the front of the hotel so he could slip out the back."

Humiliation washed over her. He'd told her he would call. He had called, all right—just not her. He'd dialed the reporters down on her head so he wouldn't be bothered.

Tavia stood up again and strode over, giving her a big hug. "Oh, sweetie, I'm so sorry. I hate that this happened to you."

The door opened. Valerie Richards, the head of the accounting department and Tavia's most frequent lunch partner, stood there. She was petite but reminded Everly of a fairy—one slightly evil and bullying.

"I thought for sure you would take the day off because we all know you must have had a few sleepless nights." Valerie smirked her way.

"Put the claws back in, please." Tavia shook her head. "She's been through enough."

"Well, apparently she's been through Gabriel Bond, too." Valerie looked Everly up and down, obviously finding her wanting.

The woman had been trouble since the minute they'd been introduced on Everly's first day at the job. Since then, the woman had done everything possible to undermine her, even though they didn't work in the same department.

There was only one way to handle a bitch. Well, besides punching her. Unfortunately, breaking Valerie's surgically perfected nose would only get her in trouble.

Everly stepped away from Tavia. "You don't go through a man like Gabriel Bond. You hold on and ride him like the stud he is. Now, if you're through sulking because I had a better weekend than you, I think we should all get back to work."

With a bully like Valerie, Everly refused to let the woman see her sweat. What Tavia's sympathy couldn't do, Val's mean-girl play had. Everly squared her shoulders and exited into the hallway with her head held high.

Scott was on her in an instant. "Hey, how did your weekend go?"

"As if you don't know. You could have called me." Now that she thought about it, she was a little mad at him. She would have given him a heads-up if the tabloid world had turned on him.

"I tried. Your phone's been off since Friday night or you would have gotten the whole story of my swinging and missing with Harry. Apparently, you had better luck."

Damn it. She'd muted the ringer and hadn't checked her voice mail this morning. Gabriel Bond had rewired her body for sex and fried her brain. Of course, he'd likely forgotten all about her the minute he'd made his getaway, while she'd been obsessing over him. "Sorry. I forgot I turned it to vibrate. Are you sure you want to be seen with me right now?"

"Of course," he replied as they trekked the hall. "You're, like, the new celebrity. You bagged another PG. I can't believe it. That's legendary, you know. Are you going for the full set? *That* would be a coup."

Thank goodness they'd made it to her office. She slipped inside, Scott right behind her, and thought seriously about never coming out again. "What are you talking about? Full set of what?"

Scott gave her a sad shake of his head as he shut the door behind them. "Perfect Gentlemen. You really need to read more. Gabriel Bond and his five best friends were called the Perfect Gentlemen at Creighton Academy."

She didn't need a history lesson. "I remember some negative campaign ads about Zack Hayes. They called him an imperfect gentleman, I guess in reference to his prep school gang."

"I'm sure." Scott rubbed his hands together, obviously warming to his subject. "Six of the most powerful men in America, and they're childhood friends. They stick together. They all backed Hayes when he was running for president. Roman Calder even left his prestigious and very lucrative law firm to become Hayes's campaign manager."

"Well, I think Hayes repaid him by making him the White House chief of staff. None of this explains why you think I would pursue a 'full set.'" Her desk was covered in mail. Where had it all come from?

He shrugged as he sat in the chair facing her desk. "Two very prominent actresses challenged one another last year. The first one who slept with all six got bragging rights and dibs on a major movie role that had Oscar written all over it. Rumor has it they both got Bond and Crawford. One of them screwed Roman Calder, while the other found her way into Captain Daxton Spencer's bed at a USO show she gave for the troops. But neither one could get Sparks or Hayes. Sparks is only a rumor. He doesn't really fit with the rest of them and he's never seen with them, so I wonder if there are really only five."

Sparks wasn't a rumor. Maddox had mentioned him fondly, but she tried to stay on subject. "That's horrible. Why would any woman think it's a good idea to 'collect' them all?"

"Because they're hot and to show you can," Scott said suggestively. "You've already had two of them."

"No, I haven't." The idea that people believed she was collecting bed partners made her ill.

He winced a little. "So the rumors about you and Crawford are untrue?"

She was so sick of that. Scott had never asked, but Everly wished they'd already crossed that bridge so she didn't have to discuss it now. "I never slept with that man. We were friends. Is that so hard to believe?"

"No one imagined that Crawford had female friends."

"He did. Look, I had no idea the man I left with on Friday night was some bad boy from Wall Street. If I had, I would have stayed away from him."

Would she really? Would she have had the strength to refuse Gabriel?

It didn't matter at this point because it was over. Tavia was right. In a few days, the rumors would die off and they would find someone else to talk about.

"I'm sorry," Scott murmured, giving her shoulder a little squeeze. "I shouldn't have assumed you were sleeping with the boss. You're not that kind of person. I'm trying to take my mind off the fact that I struck out Friday night." He sighed. "Rumor is that the new boss will be here tomorrow. I know everyone thinks the nonexecutive employees are safe, but I don't buy it."

"Tomorrow?" Wow, whoever the new CEO was, he wasn't wasting time.

Scott nodded. "Yeah, though no one knows his name. The rumor is Crawford always intended to leave everything to some animal charity. Or his favorite hookers. So we'll either be taken over by elderly cats or a woman covered in body glitter calling herself Crystal Clit. I'm hoping for the hooker. A couple of strategically placed stripper poles would liven up the place. But I'm betting on the charity because they've already sent in a man who's interviewing some of the employees. Hot guy. He didn't set my gaydar off, though. I think he plays for your team." He hesitated. "Sorry if I upset you."

Weariness dropped over her like a blanket. So much rumor and innuendo . . . And tomorrow she got to deal with the person or cat who would likely kill her career. "It's all right, but I think I should get to work. If the executioner is coming, I need to be ready."

Scott sighed and nodded, then headed for the door.

"Hey." She couldn't let him leave without knowing one thing.

"Yes?"

"So Gabriel Bond isn't a nice man, is he?" He'd seemed nice. He'd seemed real.

Scott shrugged, his face softening with sympathy. "I don't know that he's mean. But he's rich and I doubt he's ever been refused anything in his life. He's pretty much American royalty, and they don't tend to give a crap about the little people, you know? You're better off without him."

His words detonated like a bomb inside her, destroying what small hope she'd had that Gabriel wouldn't leave a dent in her heart. Scott departed, leaving her alone again. She had things to do anyway.

She pulled out the new external hard drive and plugged it in. She didn't trust the Cloud services of the world. They were far too easy to hack into. And she should know; she'd done it. So she only backed up to external hard drives she could control.

With a few keystrokes, Everly started a complete system backup.

Once she was sure her files were secure, she could run diagnostics and figure out why her system was running as if it was powered by a tired hamster.

As the task ran, she sat back. Tears pricked her eyes, but she took a deep breath to banish them. She'd made a mistake and she was going to forgive herself. After all, they'd just shared a fling—even if it had felt like more. Now it was over, and she'd learned the hard way to never look back. Always keep moving.

And she had to deal with mail. Somehow even knowing she was very likely to be let go, she couldn't just leave this stack here. There were tons of invoices and interoffice memos. Despite the fact that Crawford was a high-tech company, they still used an awful lot of paper. She'd been trying to fix that.

She picked up a small padded envelope. No return address, though it was postmarked from DC. The package was addressed to her, the mailing label typed and taped securely on. She turned it over and opened it. Two things fell out, a camera and a handwritten note.

To Alice,

Drink me. Let's go down the rabbit hole together.

Crap. She'd received a package from a weirdo.

Everly stared at the digital camera for a moment. It wasn't an expensive model, more like the kind a mom might buy to put in her purse and take pictures of her kids at the park. These days, though, everyone used their phones. This was at least five years old.

Curious.

She turned it over to flip on the screen and see the pictures this new crazy had sent her. Damn. The screen was cracked, a perfect starburst of destruction right from the center, almost as if someone had destroyed the viewer on purpose. If she wanted to see whatever images the camera might have captured, she had only one option.

Everly opened the camera and located the micro SD card, flicking the lever that held it in. The little square that likely contained something super gross popped right out.

Drink me, the note had said.

Why the *Alice in Wonderland* reference? Alice had imbibed a potion that enabled her to go down the rabbit hole and enter Wonderland. If Everly viewed the contents of this card, where would it lead her?

She couldn't help but think about the texts she'd received.

"If I get a virus from this, someone dies." Everly shoved the card into the slot on the side of her laptop. The backup was running in the background, but she could still pull this information up.

A few hums later, the machine identified the card. Someone had named the little disc "red pill."

Awesome. So the loon had mixed Alice metaphors with references from *The Matrix*. She frowned. In that movie, taking the red pill meant facing reality while the blue pill allowed a person to go back to their happy, completely false life. She clicked on the red pill, and her screen blinked, bringing up the menu. It appeared to be a series of pictures. All had been labeled with one date, nine days earlier.

The day before Maddox Crawford died.

A chill zipped through her. She clicked on the first photo, and the room turned even colder.

Everly recognized the apartment building immediately because it was hers. A man stood outside, pressing his finger against the intercom door. Maddox. He'd come to see her that night.

Evidence. Instinct told her she was looking at evidence, but she wasn't sure of what.

She moved down to the second photo. The photographer must have been in the building across the street because he'd captured a shot of her through her open living room window. She'd opened it that night because the evening had been cool and she'd wanted the breeze.

A knock sounded on her office door, startling her out of her memories.

Everly looked up in time to see Scott poke his head in. "Hey, you're needed in a meeting. Something about a breach in our retail sector."

She nodded stiffly. Because backing up to the external drive was taking up CPU cycles, she couldn't save the pictures on the SD card anywhere else. Damn it. She'd have to come back to this later.

"Of course." She released the SD card and shut her laptop. "I'll be there in a minute."

Scott gave her a little salute, then ducked out again.

Before she could make a clean exit, her phone chimed with a text. She glanced at the screen. Naturally, it was from an unknown number again.

> Meet me on Thursday to discuss your trip down the rabbit
> hole. Tell no one, sweet Alice, or I'll disappear and you'll
> never know the truth about what happened to our poor Mad
> Hatter.

Shit. This was all about Maddox, and she couldn't tell anyone.

Everly thought briefly about taking everything she'd received to the police, but whoever had found this evidence wanted her to have it, not the cops. If she did give it to the authorities, would the source disappear, along with the truth about what happened to Maddox?

She locked up the SD card and the camera in her safe. She would have to think about the best course to take later. For now, she had a job to do.

SIX

"So Mad dumped Sara to nail a woman who worked for him? Fucking bastard. I knew he'd found someone else." The following morning, Gabe sat in Mad's chair at Mad's desk. In Mad's corner office. In Mad's building. He took a deep breath, trying to quell his anger. Mad had bequeathed him everything—including his problems.

"It's only a rumor." Connor sank into the chair across from him. "I heard it from several of the employees I talked to, but there's no solid proof."

His friend was dressed for business in a tailored suit and tie, his Italian loafers finishing off the ensemble. With dark blond hair that had just started to gray at the temples, Connor looked like any of the thousands of wealthy, successful executives who walked the streets of Manhattan every day. Gabe knew that was a mask. Connor possessed a ruthlessness under his facade. He'd always been far too serious, but that focus had turned darker in the last few years. Sometimes Gabe wondered if the boy who had taught him to play lacrosse had been wiped out completely by the spy.

Gabe snorted. "Rumors usually have some kernel of truth to them."

The kernel of truth would be that Mad had spent time with this woman. Gabe only knew one way Mad had ever spent time with any woman, and that was between her legs. While Sara had been pining and dealing with morning sickness, Mad had moved on to the next bed.

Connor nodded, conceding the point.

"Who is she?" Gabe wanted to know so he could put her severance package together. The one good thing that could come from knowing was the pleasure of firing the woman Maddox had left his sister for.

Connor's eyes narrowed. "Why do you want to know?"

"Because I'm letting her go. I can't have her here." Surely Connor would understand that. "And while we're at it, I want to hire an investigator to pull up any and all dirt on this woman."

"Then I won't tell you her name. Even if it's more than a rumor, you have no idea what this woman's situation is. She might not have even been aware of Mad's relationship with Sara. You know how persuasive Mad could be when he wanted something . . ." Connor shot him a cynical glance. "Give the bastard points for one thing: he kept Sara out of the press, unlike that pretty redhead you took to bed over the weekend."

Gabe had seen the pictures. Eve's hair had been blowing in her face, obscuring most everything except her big hazel-green eyes and the intriguing tilt of her chin. Guilt sat in his gut. He should have told her to leave out the back. Hell, he should have escorted her home. He should have protected her. Eve didn't understand his world.

He hadn't called her yet for two reasons: he wasn't sure what to say and he wasn't sure if he had anything to offer her right now except a whole lot of trouble. So he'd forced himself to stop dialing her number about a hundred times. She'd already been punished for spending the night with him. He couldn't imagine what the press would write about her for actually dating him.

"They'll leave her alone if I walk away now. I'll go to dinner with some vapid model tonight and the press will forget."

He maintained acquaintances with a few women who made their living in front of a camera. They were casual, mutually beneficial dates. The women were guaranteed to be photographed for stepping out with one of Manhattan's most eligible bachelors. And he was guaranteed casual sex.

But he wouldn't sleep with his date tonight, not when he wanted Eve so much.

"Agreed. I'll have your assistant give Ashton a call and find a date for Roman, too. If the two of you are seen with a couple of models, the press will likely forget about Eve." Connor sat back casually. "Do you want me to dig for her last name? As far as I know the press is still scrambling to find it, but I'm sure I could figure it out."

Gabe didn't doubt Connor could find out everything from her last name to what she ate for breakfast, but it wouldn't change the problems in his life. "Not now. Maybe if things die down in a couple of weeks . . ." He winced with regret. "Even then, she's probably better off without me." He had to focus on the clusterfuck he'd inherited, not his love life. "Now tell me the name of Mad's mistress."

"Mistress sounds nice, considering I expected you to call her a whore."

He'd thought it. "Tell me. I'll find out anyway. I'm serious about the PI. I have to find out every bit of dirt I can use against her. We don't know who she is or what she's capable of. I'd rather be prepared if she tries to come after Mad's fortune or decides to use the press to make a name for herself. I don't want Sara to have to read whatever interviews this woman gives."

"Fine. I've mostly talked to entry-level employees and various worker bees, since they're the most likely to answer honestly. I didn't bother with the executives. They're too worried about their jobs to talk about anything else. You should know that we've managed to keep the news about Mad's will out of the press. If you work fast, the employees' first word about their new CEO will come from you."

"I snuck in this morning at five. I didn't want any questions." Gabe was already tired. He didn't admit to Connor that he'd come in so early because he couldn't sleep, couldn't think. He wanted Eve and he couldn't have her.

"Good thinking."

"I'll meet with the four VPs before lunch. The minute we're through, I'll release a company-wide announcement so they don't have time to gossip." He sent Connor an impatient glare. "Now stop stalling. Who was Mad's last mistress?"

"Come on, Gabe. You can't fire this woman. The last thing you need is a lawsuit, and if you let her go based on gossip, that's what you'll get. If we believe all the watercooler fodder, Mad slept with at least one of his VPs, several department directors, and a good portion of the secretarial pool. You know how Mad was. His dick did not discriminate. He had a very egalitarian sex drive."

"I don't give a crap who he slept with before Sara," Gabe admitted. "I want to know who he dumped her for. I won't do anything stupid."

With a frustrated groan, Connor shook his head. "Yes, you will. No matter what I do, you'll probably hear her name anyway. According to the rumors, he was spending a lot of time with his VP of information security. Her name is Everly Parker. I haven't had time to meet with her, but I looked through her records. She was hired just shy of a year ago and promoted to head of the department six months later. In the last three months, she's been seen with Mad after-hours and out of the building. One person even said Mad spent time at her place. Quite a bit of time."

He'd been fucking his head of cybersecurity? Nice.

"How old is she?"

Connor pointed to a folder on the desk. "Twenty-seven."

"So she's more qualified to be a centerfold than a VP of security." Gabe gripped his temper by a bare thread.

"That's ridiculously young, I'll grant you. But look through her records. I found the photo from her employee ID. She's wearing glasses and her hair is in some sort of bun—not Mad's usual. I think you should go easy on her until you find out what's up. She's brilliant, in fact. Her IQ hovers somewhere around genius level, and she's implemented some really innovative ideas. I suspect she's actually capable of her job."

Gabe snatched up the file and tossed it in the trash. No data or schoolmarmy photo was going to change his mind. "I don't care. The new management team will be changing direction, and I'm sure I can find someone better qualified for Ms. Parker's job. I'll give her a decent severance and hope the door doesn't smack her ass on the way out. But I won't have her here. Eventually, I'll give this whole company to Sara. The last thing she needs to deal with is Mad's ex-lovers."

"If that's how you feel, you'll have to can a lot of women. Are you going to fire Tavia Gordon, the PR guru, too? She and Mad had a fling a few years back. You'll get a shitload of bad press for letting go of the head of a charity that educates poor girls and women in underdeveloped countries because you've decided she's a whore."

Gabe winced. "Stop using that fucking word. I never said it."

"You imply it with every action you're taking." Connor rolled his shoulders, and some of the tension sloughed away. "Be reasonable. You know it's not fair to judge Everly Parker before you've met her. I understand you're pissed as hell, and Mad isn't here to take it out on. But don't punish her."

"Why do you give a shit about this woman?"

Connor stood. "I don't. I'm doing this for you."

"So I can avoid the bad press and a lawsuit? Newsflash: I've handled both before. I'm still standing."

"What will you do when your conscience starts eating at you, Gabe? If you fire her unfairly, given the current job climate, she may be hard-pressed to find this kind of job—or even another decent one—in this town. Two years down the road, you won't be blaming her anymore for Mad leaving Sara. You'll realize that Mad made his choices. Then you'll look up Ms. Parker. If she's doing poorly, you'll blame yourself. And you'll shoulder guilt I don't want you to feel."

"Because you'll feel it, too?"

Connor turned back, his face carefully blank. "I don't feel anymore, Gabe. And I can't tell you what a relief that is. Being back here in the States with you guys . . . it's the only emotion I've felt in years. Frankly, it makes me uncomfortable, but I owe you, Dax, Roman, and Zack. You four are the only real connections I still have."

"If you were in my shoes, what would you do about her?"

"Nothing. I wouldn't care enough to do anything, but then I don't have a sister."

"What if someone hurt one of us?"

Connor's eyes went dark. "You don't want to know. But if you want my advice about Everly Parker, get some perspective before you make a move, then proceed with caution. Maybe you're right about the PI. It could give us leverage if she does decide Mad owes her something. I'll get a team working on digging up any and all dirt we can on her. But you stay calm."

That wasn't happening. Connor might be right, but Gabe didn't think he could let it go. So he didn't say anything.

"I'm going to grab Dax and find some coffee." Connor nodded toward the door. "Then we'll continue our interviews. Roman is still at the hotel."

The White House chief of staff had insisted on staying somewhere more anonymous than one of their places to cut down on the possibility of reporters camping out in front of their buildings.

"Thanks. I'll see you in a bit."

"I'm also going to continue looking for our favorite asshole blogger. He's been leaking wild speculation about Mad's crash and calling it 'details.' I could easily ignore him when he commented on the size of Zack's dick. But if he doesn't shut up about Mad's death, I'll be forced to take him down." Connor sighed. "Think about what I said."

"Sure."

Gabe did. For roughly twenty minutes after Connor left, he pondered his friend's advice . . . then tossed it all out. He wasn't exposing

Sara to the woman who had taken her place. His sister was simply too fragile now. When the time came, he would have a long talk with Tavia Gordon and any other woman who had come before Sara. He would make it clear that they weren't to talk about their relationship with Mad around his sister, but Everly Parker had to go. She would likely be bitter that she'd been summarily relieved of her job. Not his problem. He wouldn't give her the chance to undermine Sara again.

He punched the button on the speaker that linked him to the smartly dressed assistant outside, Hilary. She was in her midfifties and had been Mad's father's right hand for years. The woman knew where the corporate skeletons were buried and would likely be a key asset during this transition. Best of all, Mad hadn't been sleeping with her. "Hilary, did you set up the meetings I asked you to?"

"Of course, sir."

"I need to move Everly Parker's meeting, please."

"All right." He could hear her shuffling through papers. "What time should I pencil her in?"

"Now." It was five minutes past nine. If she wasn't in, that would be one more strike against her.

"I'll see if I can reach her." The line went dead.

Gabe began to pace, not really paying attention to the stunning city skyline. He wanted this nasty business out of the way. After Everly Parker was gone, he could focus on assuming the reins of Crawford Industries and making sure everything was running with smooth efficiency until Sara took over. When his sister wasn't sick and grieving, she would be able to assume the reins of the company. She had an MBA and had been an executive at Bond since she'd graduated. All she needed was a bit of time to recover from the shock. And if he got rid of the woman who'd taken her place in Mad's life, she would find the transition easier. Sara could use a challenge, and this company would be her child's inheritance.

But the shift must be quick. Bond Aeronautics wouldn't run on autopilot for long.

Then, when everything had finally settled down, maybe he could dial Eve's number. His fingers twitched every time he thought about it. He wanted to call her now, to explain everything and ask for her patience. He wanted to apologize for the reporters. He'd paid for privacy, but he should have known better and ensured that she left the hotel without being hounded.

The thought that she was out there—scared, alone, and confused—made his gut twist.

A muffled female voice broke into his thoughts. "Hi, Hilary. Am I late? I didn't know I had a meeting this morning."

"Don't be shy. He asked for you, dear." Hilary opened the door and pushed it wide. "Mr. Bond, this is Everly Parker. Everly, this is the new CEO, Gabriel Bond."

He looked up, past Hilary, and caught sight of a riot of strawberry-blond hair and familiar curves. She gasped. His jaw dropped. Well, he didn't have to apologize to Eve now, and he wouldn't need her number after all. No. Because she stood in the doorway, staring at him with those wide eyes he hadn't forgotten. Her expression looked so innocent. But then she had that act down, he supposed. It was nothing but a lie. Anger started to thrum through his system.

Eve, the woman he'd thought he'd randomly picked up the night of Mad's funeral, was also Everly Parker. What were the odds that their meeting had been a mere coincidence? Definitely not in her favor. More likely, as Mad's mistress, she'd known the man had no family and intended to leave everything to his best friend. She'd obviously taken the death of her sugar daddy so hard that she'd gone looking for another. Gabe gritted his teeth. From there, it had been a simple matter to spread her legs and get under his skin. Hell, he'd practically invited her to.

It had worked, and he resented the fuck out of her for it.

"Gabriel?" She asked the question as if she was completely stunned.

Did she really expect him to believe that she'd had no idea who Mad's friends were?

Gabe crossed his arms over his chest and cursed himself. He'd been taken in by a pretty hustler who thought she could protect her cushy job by sleeping with the new boss. Perhaps she'd intended to get the same deal with him that she'd conned Mad into. At least he wouldn't feel that guilt Connor had warned would hit him later. No. He was going to enjoy every moment of this.

"Miss Parker, please come in. Sit. I think we have a few things to talk about. Don't you?"

How was it possible that her weekend fling was her new boss? Everly closed her eyes and shuffled inside.

She was fairly certain this was how Little Red Riding Hood felt when she'd been invited into her grandmother's cottage that fateful day in the woods. My, what big teeth her personal big bad wolf had. Gabriel Bond wasn't looking at her the way he had during the days they'd spent together. In fact, his cold, predatory stare now made her want to walk back out the door.

Luckily, she had too much pride to do that.

She forced herself to enter the office as if her heart wasn't pounding in her chest and settle in the leather chair opposite the big, masculine desk. Why was he looking at her with such contempt, like she was a piece of trash? Everly hoped she was hallucinating that . . . but she didn't think so.

Was he really that angry to discover his fling had come back to haunt him?

"Yes, we have a few matters we probably should have discussed before now."

Everly prayed she looked calmer than she felt. She'd been hoping that she would see Gabriel again, but not as Maddox's replacement and her new boss. This was definitely awkward. But he didn't seem uncomfortable so much as angry.

Dread tightened her stomach.

"Thank you, Hilary. That will be all." He nodded to the administrative assistant, who shut the door behind her. She would likely be on the phone to Jennifer in seconds. Despite being older than most of the assistants, she had been Maddox's go-to girl for the gossip grapevine.

"Eve?" A single brow rose above his blue eyes, holding a wealth of accusation.

She didn't pretend to misunderstand. Now that she was here, she'd deal with the situation and be as professional as possible. "It's something my father and close friends call me. It was probably dumb to give you that name since most everyone else calls me Everly. But I noticed that your friends call you Gabe instead of Gabriel, yet that's the name you gave me."

"I use my names interchangeably and would have happily told you that my friends call me Gabe. Hell, you could have guessed that yourself. But how was I to get Everly out of Eve?"

He had a point, and she wasn't being totally honest. "Sorry. The truth is I wanted to be someone else that night. Meeting you felt more like a fantasy than the terrible reality I found myself in. After that first night, it seemed easier to stick with Eve."

"Interesting," he said in a droll tone that belied his words. "I suppose the cause of your 'terrible reality' was the funeral?"

Maybe he understood a little. "Yes. It had been a hard week, losing a boss, a mentor . . . a friend. At the time, I had no idea that you were his friend, too. You didn't mention him all weekend."

One broad shoulder shrugged negligently. "That's true. But I didn't lie to you about my first name."

She tried not to grimace. Gabe had to be under an enormous amount of strain, losing his best friend and having to assume control of Maddox's company. Maybe under different circumstances he'd be more even-tempered. Then again, she didn't know him well, so maybe not.

Everly smoothed down her skirt, needing something to do with her hands as she collected her thoughts. "I didn't lie. Some people do call me Eve. My real name is somewhat unique, and that night I wanted to be anonymous. I was a little unsettled."

"Ah, so obviously you didn't give me your real number, then. Because if you were unsettled, I would understand you giving me a fake number to go with the fake name." His fingers tapped the screen of his phone.

Her cell started to trill. She felt heat creep up her cheeks.

He switched his cell off. "You couldn't have been too scared. You wanted me to call."

"I was anxious when we first left the bar Friday night. By Monday morning, I thought I knew a little about you. I didn't, though. Not really. In fact, I didn't know a damn thing about you." Tension forced her to sit tall in her seat, her shoulders back.

"You had no idea who I was?" He sounded unconvinced. His face looked even more skeptical.

"None. You were an attractive man in a bar who procured me a glass of wine and flirted. I was interested. We had sex." Everly had explained her rationale and didn't feel like defending herself anymore. "Did you really have any plans to call me again?"

He considered her a moment before sitting back in his chair. "No. I was being polite. Ninety-nine percent of weekend flings won't call. You should know that by now."

Even though she felt the lash of his anger, Everly refused to cry. She would stay calm and not show him how much his words had hurt. "Then it doesn't matter if you knew my real name or not, does it, *Gabe*?"

"I've been going over Friday night in my head and I've come to a couple of conclusions." His monotone voice held none of the sensual affection of their weekend together. "Perhaps you wanted anonymous sex with a stranger and that's why you withheld the truth. Or maybe you thought I would recognize your name and not sleep with an employee."

That was unfair. "Employee? So you're our new CEO. That hasn't been publicly announced yet, so how could I have known last Friday that you would soon be my boss? I didn't even have a clue until I stepped in this room two minutes ago."

"I'm not going to play this game with you, Eve. I mean, Everly. You'll have to forgive me. I associate you with your hookup name."

"Are you serious?" Pure indignation kept her from leaving the room. How dare he start this with her. "You don't know me yet you're accusing me of some premeditated seduction."

He looked at her blandly, but his lack of denial might as well have been a silent agreement.

Everly's fury frothed. "I read up on you yesterday, Mr. Bond. Trust me, I have nowhere near your experience. But then, men like you can get away with any kind of sexcapade. Women like me . . . I've had one single fling in my whole life, and I get called a whore."

"Everyone wants to put that word in my mouth today. I didn't call you a whore, but I find it interesting that you go right there. A whore is a woman who accepts money for her services. I didn't pay you. Were you expecting something from me today, like the deal you had worked out with your last lover?" He shook his head. "If so, it wasn't much of a negotiation since you already gave yourself away."

Everly had no idea what he was talking about and she didn't give a damn. That weekend, she'd wanted him and believed that he cared a little. And right now, she'd rather bite off her own tongue than admit that. "Why did you want to see me this morning? Clearly, you had no idea who I was until I came here."

"But you knew exactly who I was. By your own admission, you looked me up."

He was twisting her words. She decided it would be a bad idea to admit she'd been curious about him. He would use that information against her somehow, she had no doubt. "After we spent the weekend together. After I was mobbed by reporters on my way out of the hotel and everyone in this office saw the news."

"I felt a bit bad about that. Now I wonder if you didn't call them yourself."

"Why the hell would I call the press to print my own humiliation? Do you think that, as an employee of Crawford Industries, I want to be known for sleeping with the 'bad boy of Wall Street' and the new boss? I thought those days we spent together were special, but I guess I fell for your usual scam." She leaned back, trying not to be angry at herself for being gullible. "I'm probably one of thousands."

He stood suddenly, pushing off the chair, radiating a powerful vibe that seemed to take up all the space in the room. "I certainly wouldn't call it thousands. The tabloids exaggerate. I'm certain I haven't fucked my way out of the low hundreds yet but I can't be sure. One loses count after a while. So let's get to the heart of the matter. What exactly were you expecting to come from this plot of yours?"

He paced the office like an animal stalking its prey. Everly felt surrounded, watched.

She raised her chin, refusing to fall victim. "What plot? All I expected out of this meeting was to learn what the new CEO needs from me."

He stepped right in front of her, so close she had to stand. If she'd remained sitting, he would have loomed over her, giving him the psychological advantage of forcing her to look up at him. She wasn't about to allow that.

Even though she barely reached the middle of his chest, she stood her ground. Tension sizzled around them, making it hard for her to breathe.

He seemed amused as he stared down at her. "You want to know what your new duties are, Miss Parker?"

"I want to know if you're planning to fire me or not. If so, you should know I fully intend to sue you."

Resentment boiled right under her surface, a volcanic rage that he'd twisted something meaningful and beautiful into a mercenary, ugly act. Anger threatened to erupt. They could have handled this like grown-ups. It shouldn't have been difficult. They were two consenting adults, but he acted as if she'd done him some great wrong.

His mouth tugged up in a little smirk. "Oh, you're going to sue me? That should be an interesting hearing. Well, I haven't fired you yet. You know how it goes with new management. We need to come in and figure out where everyone's talents lie. What are yours, Everly?"

Her blood burned even more. Yes, it was anger. Being close enough to feel the heat of his body couldn't possibly be revving her up, not after the way he'd treated her. "I'm one of the best computer security experts in the business. It's why Maddox hired me."

"Yes, I believe you played up your nerd roots. It was clever. Unusual. I have to admit I found that aspect of you deeply intriguing. But I know a thing or two about business, and you don't fit anyone's idea of an executive. I was wondering why my dear friend Mad had hired someone so young."

"Because I'm very good at what I do."

"Computer security." Definite doubt resounded in his tone.

She wasn't going down without a fight, no matter who he was. She'd almost resigned herself to the idea that she would be laid off, but now she was going to fight like hell. No way would she be dismissed and escorted out of the building with her tail between her legs. "Yes. I've been instrumental in bringing this corporation into the twenty-first century. The last head of security's firewalls were crap even a second grader could hack through. I know what you're implying, Mr. Bond, but I was hired because I know my business. So you can handle me one of two ways. You can sit back in that chair you inherited—like everything else in your life—and we can go over my role with the company or you can stand over me like a misogynist who's enjoying his intimidation shtick. You pick."

His eyes flared with heat. He stepped closer. "There's another option."

"What's that?" No matter how much he crowded her personal space, she would not back down. She couldn't show him how much his presence disrupted her concentration or that she'd done nothing but think about him since leaving The Plaza.

"I can do this." He gripped her face in his hands and slanted his mouth over hers before she could stop him.

With a sweep of his tongue, Gabriel reminded her of the pleasure he had to offer a woman. A shock of hot desire jolted through her. Everly knew she should push him away, and she raised her hands between them. But instead of shoving him, she gripped the lapels of his suit coat and pulled him closer.

There was no hint of smooth lover in this kiss. He took control as his lips forced hers open wider and he surged deep. He slid his fingers into her hair, dictating the angle and depth of his penetration. His body crowded hers, dominated. He pressed close, letting her know that his urbane suit merely masked his primal nature.

"Eve, I know I shouldn't do this. I can't stop." His hands slid down her back to cup the globes of her ass. "It's wrong and I can't fucking walk away."

She couldn't seem to make him. Gabriel knew intuitively how to make her body ache for his touch.

He grabbed her skirt in his fist and yanked it up as he dropped his head into the crook of her neck, his lips at her throat. The heat of his palm slid up her leg. Somewhere in the back of her head, a faint voice warned Everly this was getting out of hand. But with Gabriel so near, touching her again, everything felt right.

"Tell me to stop," he breathed against her lips before he captured them again.

Resisting him would be smart, sensible. But her body was having none of that. He'd primed her to expect nothing but pleasure from him and she'd ached the night before, wishing she could have his flesh pressed to hers. She'd longed for the connection she'd felt when he thrust deep inside her.

She drowned in his scent for an endless moment. "I know I should."

Allowing him to touch her now was wrong. The nights they'd spent together, neither of them had known they would soon be boss and employee. Now they did. Crawford Industries didn't have an anti-fraternization policy. She couldn't think of a single reason they shouldn't see each other, except that he'd made his contempt for her plain. He'd made it obvious that he'd used her while blaming her somehow.

Those thoughts gave her the willpower to push him away. "Stop, Gabriel. I'm not going to be your convenient lay."

He stared down at her, his face savage, but he didn't allow her out of the cage of his arms. "Convenient? There is nothing convenient about this, Eve . . . Everly. Fuck. I lied. I was going to call you. I was going to call you right up until the minute I realized you'd lied to me. I almost dialed your number a hundred times in the last twenty-four hours. Yesterday morning, I wanted to ask you to come home with me because I felt good with you. I wanted to forget about every awful fucking thing happening in my world and lose myself in you again."

She knew they shouldn't, but his words struck a chord of sympathy in her. Losing and burying his best friend of over two decades had surely wrought grief. And seeing her walk through the door this morning had, no doubt, been a shock.

Her heart softened. "I wasn't trying to deceive you."

"Don't talk. I don't want to fucking talk." He crushed her mouth under his again.

He kissed her as if his life depended on it, and Everly couldn't help but wrap her arms around him. This was the Gabriel she knew. Passionate. Giving. Seductive. She opened to him and gave back.

With a moan, he pulled her leg up and curled it above his muscled thigh. Everly fitted herself against his body. Her head fell back as tendrils of pleasure started to course through her. Normally, she was safe and cautious, but being anywhere close to this man blew away every ounce of self-preservation and logic she possessed until she craved his touch again.

Gabriel maneuvered them back to the desk, turning so he could set her on the surface. "You're so responsive. Do you have any idea what that does for me?"

With her skirt bunched around her hips, he easily fitted his hand over her silky underwear, cupping her pussy. She braced her hands on the desk and spread her legs a bit wider as she fell further under his spell.

"It feels so good when you touch me." No other man affected her the way Gabriel did. All he had to do was look at her and her body softened, preparing for him. Breathless for him.

He growled as he worked his fingers over her panties, right where she ached for him. "You're already wet. Hot and soft for me. Is this why Mad was so crazy about you? I wish like hell I didn't, but I understand why he dumped everything to have you."

His words hit her like a bucket of ice water, jolting her from his spell. She gasped and shoved him away, jumping to her feet and tugging her skirt back in place with shaky hands.

He looked dazed for a moment, as though trying to process what had happened. "Eve, I didn't . . . Damn it, I didn't mean to say that."

No, he'd meant to keep that sentiment to himself. *Bastard.* "My name is Everly. I would prefer Ms. Parker, especially if you think I slept with Maddox." She tossed her head back, righteous anger fueling her. "If you want me gone, you'll still have to fire me. I'm not going to let you intimidate or shame me into quitting a job I'm good at."

She felt so stupid for giving him the opportunity to use her response against her. While she'd been feeling sorry for him, she'd almost overlooked his low opinion of her and allowed him to maneuver her flat on her back. He'd probably kissed her to see how much of herself she would let him take. To prove she was the office whore? In his book, her responsiveness would undoubtedly be one more strike against her.

He turned away, showing her his back as he took several long breaths. "I'm not going to fire you. Yet. Instead, I'll apologize, Ms. Parker, for my primitive actions."

God, he sounded so cold. His control infuriated her. "You mean for nearly raping me on the desk?"

He zipped back around to her, his eyes narrowing. "Are you serious?"

Damn it. Just because he'd been an ass, that didn't mean she had to sound like a shrew.

Everly dragged in a breath. It would be easy to blame him but unfair. "No. I'm sorry. I was there with you. It was a mistake. It's obvious neither one of us is the person the other thought. It would be best if we pretended last weekend never happened."

A bitter laugh huffed from his throat. "Don't you think I'd love to forget? I've been telling myself to do exactly that since the minute Hilary escorted you through my door. It's not working. Do you know what I'm thinking about right this second, Everly?"

He drew out her name as though tasting it and savoring its flavor.

Her heart raced. Her body burned for more of him. But she shook her head. "No."

Gabriel saw through her denial. "That if I'd kept my mouth shut, I could be inside you right now. I could have laid you out on that desk and spread you wide and thrust my cock deep. I wouldn't have taken off my damn pants. I want you too much to wait for that. I could have just dropped my zipper and worked my way to that snug, wet place I've craved since the moment we met. I would have fucked you until you screamed out my name. Only then would I have let go. Every single time I look at you, I remember how beautiful you are when you come for me. So you tell me how I'm supposed to forget."

His words shook her to her core because the feel of him, of their shared pleasure, haunted her, too. She didn't know what to say or how to turn it off. Everly only knew it couldn't continue.

"Gabriel . . ." Regret filled her voice. "We can't."

He scrubbed a hand across his tired face. "You're right. Professional. Fine." He steadied himself with a long breath. "Sit down, then. We have a few things to talk about."

Finally, they were going to discuss the situation in a civilized manner. At least she hoped so. Everly was just about to sit when the door opened.

"Mr. Bond, I'm sorry." Hilary gave the gentlemen who walked in, dressed in serviceable suits, a stern glare. "They insisted."

The taller of the two flashed a badge. "Gabriel Bond?"

Gabriel's jaw tightened, and he straightened his jacket. "Yes. Can we do this here?"

The police had come to see him, and he didn't seem at all surprised. In fact, the resignation in his manner said that he'd been expecting this. She frowned.

Then the shorter detective pulled out a pair of handcuffs. Everly tried not to gasp as the detective slapped them against his thigh. "You can come down to the station willingly or we can formally arrest and charge you. The press would eat that up. But it's your choice. Either way, I suggest you take this seriously. You're our primary suspect in Maddox Crawford's murder."

"Murder?" Had she heard that right?

Maybe . . . the text and e-mail she'd received weren't from some crackpot stirring up trouble. All the implications stole her breath. Unfortunately, she could think of a lot of people who'd wanted Maddox dead, but why would anyone think his best friend had murdered him?

Would the evidence she'd received damn or free Gabriel Bond? And how could she even know what she had or how accurate it was if she didn't follow instructions and meet the man on Thursday?

Gabriel sent her a grin that held not an ounce of humor. "You say you're good at your job. I hope you're competent at all forms of security."

Everly nodded. Her dad had been a cop. She'd grown up with a lot of his knowledge; she wasn't merely a computer nerd. "You need protection."

"It couldn't hurt. Find Daxton Spencer. He's somewhere in the building interviewing employees. Then track down Roman Calder and get them both to the precinct." Gabe turned back to the detectives. "Gentlemen, can I take my car and meet you?"

"We have a car waiting. We wouldn't want to inconvenience you or have you get lost along the way. We know how you rich boys sometimes mistake your private jet for the station house."

"At least take him out the back." Everly's head was spinning. Above it all stood one fact: He was now the head of Crawford Industries, and since Mulford, the head of building security, was on vacation in Australia for two weeks, Everly was his stand-in. That meant she had to protect Gabriel. The company didn't need more press right now. She didn't know whether he had actually killed Maddox, but he was innocent until proven guilty. "Let me get an escort. I can call to the desk."

The taller detective smirked her way. "No worries. We've got that handled."

Gabriel looked back at her as they led him out. "Find Dax and call Roman ASAP."

She nodded, staring as the detectives escorted him out of the office and headed for the elevator. The moment they'd gone, her head exploded with questions. What the hell was going on? And had she actually been sleeping with a killer?

SEVEN

"Where is Gabriel Bond and is he under arrest?" Everly asked the female officer who ran the front desk at the 19th precinct for what seemed like the five hundredth time.

After Gabriel had been marched out of the office, Everly went into crisis-management mode. Despite shaking hands, she'd picked up the phone and asked Scott to find Dax Spencer while she'd used a number Hilary had for Roman Calder. She hadn't been sure it would work. Most normal people didn't have the White House chief of staff's number in their contact list. She'd expected to be routed through rounds of assistants, but the man had answered on the first ring and promised to be down at the precinct as soon as possible. His no-nonsense voice said he hadn't been shocked by her call—or the reason for it—at all.

Why hadn't he or Gabriel seemed surprised that Gabe had practically been arrested for the murder of Maddox Crawford?

Everly braced herself against the nearby wall. What the hell did she really know about Gabriel Bond except that he was rich and very good in bed? After the nights they'd spent together, she would have sworn he wasn't a violent soul. She also hadn't expected him to accuse her of being Mad's mistress or seducing him for her own gain, so clearly, she didn't know anything about him.

She blew out a breath. Later. Her job had to come first. Gabriel needed her to come through. So did Crawford Industries.

"Ma'am, as I explained to you before, I'm not allowed to give out information to anyone but his lawyer. Are you his lawyer?" The very matter-of-fact woman stared a hole through her. She definitely wasn't going out of her way to be helpful. And since she controlled the door between the entrance and the rest of the building, Everly had been sidelined here. But she wasn't giving up without a fight.

"Yes. Yes, I am his lawyer." If lying got her through, she would give it a try.

The guard rolled her eyes. "No, you're not. When you first arrived, you told me you were his employee. Go back to the office and send his lawyer."

"I'm—" *Both*, she started to say.

"She's good," a man said, approaching a wall of glass dividing the reception area from the inside of the station. He stared, and Everly wondered who he was and how he'd gotten admitted to the station's inner sanctum. "And it looks like Mr. Bond's lawyer is here. I would love it if you could let him in."

With a loud *whoosh*, the door behind her opened and a familiar man strode in, dressed in what had to be several thousand dollars' worth of designer suit. He carried a leather briefcase, and as he stepped in from the street, flashbulbs burst everywhere and the rumble of shouts from outside filled the place.

"Damn." The woman at the front desk shook her head and picked up the phone. "We're going to need some crowd control at the front of the building, and tell Johnson and Klein that I'm going to kick their asses. Their stupidity for bringing Bond in so publicly is now my problem. They're going to pay."

The man in the suit stepped forward with confidence. "My name is—"

"I know your name, Mr. Calder."

Roman smiled tightly. "Very good. I'm Gabriel Bond's lawyer."

The woman sent Everly a pointed glance. "That, I'll believe. As soon as I'm sure the press won't invade, I'll sign you in." She sighed. "I wish you rich boys would stop murdering each other."

"Allegedly murdering," Roman Calder pointed out.

"Yeah. Whatever. This is supposed to be a cushy precinct." She stepped to the doors and flung one open. The sound of the crowd outside became a dull roar again. "You leeches step back. I mean it. Everyone get your asses off the steps. Do you think I won't use tear gas on you? Because I did not like the way you talked about my man, Tom Cruise. Yeah, I'm talking to you."

The policewoman let the door swing shut but continued to make faces at them through the glass.

"Hello, I Saw Her First." The man who'd appeared through the glass now walked up behind Everly and smiled down at her—way down since he had to be at least six feet four. Besides looking absolutely stunning, he seemed familiar. He was dressed very differently from his elegant counterpart, in a black T-shirt that showed off his hard chest, a light windbreaker, and a pair of jeans that hugged his obviously toned body. His dark hair was cut in a military buzz that accentuated the angles of his masculine face.

"I'm sorry?"

He held out a hand. "How quickly they forget. Dax Spencer. We met at the bar last Friday night."

Gabriel's friend. Of course. She'd met him, but her brain had been on Gabriel. "I'm glad Scott found you."

"Dax, did you secure the transportation I asked for?" Roman queried.

Dax nodded. "She's a fine vehicle. It's been a while since I got to take one of those beauties out for a stroll. She'll be ready when the interview is over."

Roman's eyes narrowed as he looked at Everly. "I thought the VP of security for Crawford had someone contact Dax." He froze before his very serious face turned mischievous. "Oh, please tell me you're the head of security."

Dax frowned. "No. This is Eve, Gabe's girl from the other night. You know, the one he can't stop talking about."

That was an interesting piece of information she had absolutely no idea what to do with. Two hours ago it would have thrilled her. Now it just confused her more than ever.

The two men stared at her, and Everly felt a little awkward discussing her professional and personal life with two strangers. "I'm, um . . . both, sort of. My name is Everly Parker. I run Crawford's cybersecurity department. I'm filling in for the head of building security since he's out on vacation."

"Thank god. For a minute, I thought the day would be boring." Roman Calder pulled out his phone and punched in a few numbers. "Yes, I need to speak with Captain Charles. You tell him that Gabriel Bond's lawyers are in the lobby and we're ready to talk to the press about the fact that we've been refused access to our client. If we're not allowed to see him in the next thirty seconds, the top story on the evening news will shine a bright light on this precinct's abuse of a man's constitutional rights."

Despite the unmanned desk, a buzzing sound alerted them to the fact that someone had opened the precinct door.

"Thank you. Let's go." As he ended the call, it became glaringly obvious that Roman Calder was a man used to getting what he wanted, when he wanted it.

"I'd like to come back there, too." Everly wondered what role she could play here, but she wasn't going to leave her post because it seemed as if Gabriel had his own backup. She represented security for Crawford Industries right now. She had a responsibility to its new CEO.

And okay, a little piece of her wouldn't rest until she knew he was all right. Even though he'd been an ass, and now had this cloud of suspicion hanging over his head, she still felt a pull between them.

Besides, she'd been accused of being Maddox's mistress and sleeping her way to the top, so she knew how it felt to be accused of something that wasn't true. If Gabriel was innocent, this must feel wretched.

If.

Roman opened the door for her, gesturing her inside. "Oh, I insist. I have to hear this story. Well, first I have to make sure Gabe doesn't do anything stupider than he's already done, so please tell Dax the story. He can fill me in later."

Everly frowned as she walked through, then waited for the men. Roman sounded amused. She wouldn't have pictured the male-model gorgeous, ever-so-serious Roman Calder doing something as trivial as gossiping.

The men stepped in behind her, and Everly realized she didn't know her way around. Roman obviously did, and he took the lead, striding toward the back of the building. How many of his previous clients had found themselves being questioned here? She and Dax followed, and Everly nearly had to jog to keep up.

"While you work on getting Mr. Bond out of here, I'll find a way to slip him past the press as quietly as possible," Everly said. Because clearly they couldn't just walk past.

"Don't worry about it," Dax insisted.

Maybe he didn't understand how overwhelming being shouted at by a couple of dozen people with the power of the press behind them felt. She was thankful they hadn't been assembled there when she'd arrived. "Of course I'm going to worry. That crowd outside was awfully aggressive."

"Them? They're a bunch of babies. Give it half an hour and the nationals will show up," Dax explained. "They're pains in the ass. But don't you worry. I've got an exit strategy already, so we can leave in peace."

"Care to share?" If Dax had already done her job, why had they wanted her to stay?

"Need-to-know basis." He winked. "Let's talk about something important. Mr. Bond? Really?" He grinned. "Don't you think that's a little formal, given the circumstances?"

She ignored that question as Roman led them through another door. She kept her voice low, both to cut down on potential gossip and ensure she didn't disrupt the detectives working around her. "He's my boss. So I need to know."

"I'll bet he was surprised to find out he was your boss." Dax stopped as they entered a narrow hallway.

A man in a captain's uniform called out to Roman. "Mr. Bond is in here. You can talk to him. He hasn't said a word, and I stopped the questioning when he lawyered up."

"If I know Gabe, he lawyered up before you got him here, Captain," Roman shot back. "These two are with me. They'll be watching from the observation room. If you have a problem with that, I can get the chief on the phone. I promise you if he won't take my call, I can find someone higher up the chain of command who will."

"They can stay." The captain scowled as he pointed to a window in front of the little room. "You won't be able to hear anything until Calder says it's all right, and we'll be recording the session."

He stepped aside and let Roman enter the interrogation room.

Everly slid into the adjacent space and looked through the two-way mirror. Gabriel sat in the utilitarian space, his face a polite blank. He didn't smile or show any sign of relief as Roman walked in. He merely stood and shook hands with the man.

"Wait, Everly Parker?" Dax frowned. "You said your name was Eve the other night."

Was this day never going to end? "My name is Everly. Eve is a nickname."

Dax crossed his big arms over his chest with a shake of his head. "Shit. I can imagine how Gabe took that. Tell me he behaved himself when he found out."

"I could, but why lie?" She shot him a perplexed glance. "I don't really understand why he would be angry. Not that our personal affairs are any of your business." She turned back to the scene in front of her. "I'm just here to do my job. Forget I said anything."

"But he didn't fire you yet, right? I'm going to count that as a win."

She remained silent for a long moment before giving in to the urge. The scene back in the office kept playing through her head. "Shouldn't I at least be given a chance to prove I'm good at my job? Does he have someone else he wants in my position? I understand that there's a lot of turnover when a new boss comes in, but I think his objection was way more personal. I don't understand why he was so angry."

"No doubt. You have to give him a little time. I was helping him out by conducting preliminary interviews with the employees to get a feel for the company and individual roles. One of the things I heard more than once was that you and Maddox had a . . . very close relationship. Gabe couldn't have taken that information well. He and Maddox had a falling out over Maddox's romantic entanglements, if you know what I mean."

She didn't except in the vaguest sense. Everly only knew she was so tired of that gossip. "I wasn't sleeping with Maddox, if that's what you're implying. I did *not* get my job by screwing the boss."

He held his hands up in surrender. "I had to ask because I doubt Gabe was feeling levelheaded enough to do the same. He likely heard that rumor and accepted it as fact because the only way Mad spent time with a female was when he took her to bed."

Everly knew his reputation. She'd heard of his many affairs with women at the office, but the possibility—even a hint of it—had never come up between them. He hadn't treated her strictly like an employee, but he'd never come on to her. Instead, he'd behaved more like they were pals. "He never touched me. He didn't even try. I think he was lonely and needed a friend."

Dax's eyes narrowed. "I find that very interesting and out of character. We've been Mad's friends for years and he never went looking for more companionship. In fact, he was the one who taught me to be wary of getting close to anyone else."

Everly didn't know why the truth seemed to upset Dax, but she really wanted someone to believe that she hadn't been one of many in Maddox's bed. "I can't explain why, but he was close to me. I cared about him." In fact, she felt his loss more deeply than she'd expected. "He talked about all of you. He called you his brothers, but he only mentioned you by last names. It was odd."

"In school, all of the teachers referred to us that way. Mr. Spencer, Mr. Bond, and so on. I'm sure they thought it would civilize us. Mad kept it up even after we left the academy. I'm sure if he was here right now, he would slap me on the back and say 'Spencer, have you smartened up and left the navy yet?'" Dax laughed, but it was a bittersweet sound.

"I didn't pay that much attention to who Maddox talked about. You were merely his friends to me. So I didn't know that Gabriel was Bond or . . ." It probably sounded silly, and now she wished she'd paid more attention to the tabloids. But she couldn't change the past. "I listened because Maddox seemed to want to talk."

"If he was talking, it was because he trusted you." Dax shot her a speculative look. "I'm going to guess that you're still here because you care for Gabe at least a little."

She flushed guiltily and cursed having such fair skin. Sometimes, it revealed her every emotion. Still, she wasn't going to incriminate herself. It would be stupid to forget that Dax was Gabriel's friend. His loyalties lay there, no matter how nice he seemed.

"Good. Look, Everly, I'm going to ask you to do something that's not fair to you. Gabe needs some time to process everything that's happened. Don't judge him until he's had a chance to really think about everything."

"I'm not going to judge him at all," she lied.

She'd already judged him. Yes, he'd lost a good friend, so he wasn't at his best now. But even on a good day, he was a playboy who couldn't possibly take a relationship seriously. He could offer a woman orgasms—and not much else. She'd already gotten everything good out of Gabriel Bond.

Now that she thought about it, his attitude reminded her of her mother's. From what Everly could tell, her mother always believed she'd married beneath her. No matter how much her dad had loved her mother, he hadn't been enough for her. She'd needed more and eventually she'd left her family behind to find it. Everly had no desire to replay her dad's life. Though she'd loved her father dearly, he'd spent years pining for a woman who couldn't love him. Gabriel might desire her, but he wouldn't build a life with a woman who brought nothing but herself to the relationship. Certainly not a woman he thought slept her way into a career.

"I'm going to be professional with him," she assured Dax. "I have a job to do. As long as that's the extent of our relationship going forward, we'll be fine."

Dax shrugged. "That will work for now. If you stay close to him, he'll come to the proper conclusions."

"And what are those, Mr. Spencer?"

A smile tugged at his lips. "That you're not the type of woman who would hop from one man's bed to another so quickly, especially not for monetary gain."

Everly bristled. "Of course not."

"That you're the kind of woman who will only sleep with a man to gain comfort, because he makes you feel safe. You would do it because you want love."

The whole conversation was making her uncomfortable. Daxton Spencer didn't know her. She certainly hadn't slept with Gabriel Bond because she wanted his love.

God, she hoped she wasn't fooling herself.

"That makes me sound like a helpless twit. I think I preferred it when everyone believed I was a whore."

"No, you're too smart for that. But you're also innocent." He studied her with knowing dark eyes. "You don't come from the same world we do, and that might be a good reason for you to run as fast as you can. I'm asking you not to because I think you're good for Gabe. I think he needs you. And this situation is going to get worse before it gets better."

A shiver went down her spine, and she told herself the cause was nothing more than a blast from the air conditioning. Did Dax know something she didn't? Should she tell the cops she was getting messages and pictures from someone who said they knew the truth about Maddox's death? What if they gave her more proof that Gabriel was a killer? She couldn't say anything or turn over whatever she had to the police until she figured out if this mystery person was legit. Then she'd find out what he knew—and wanted.

In order to do that, she had to start connecting the dots between Gabriel and whatever else was going on.

"Why do the police suspect Gabriel of murdering Maddox?"

The smile slid off Dax's face and he went carefully blank. "Because he was the last person Mad met with, I suppose."

Everly's bullshit meter started ringing. Dax was lying. Or at the very least, he wasn't telling her the whole truth. He'd been full of expression until she'd asked that question. Her father would have called that his tell.

She sent him a plastic smile. Sometimes being female and curvy meant people underestimated her. Everly found it annoying most of the time, but she'd also learned to turn it to her advantage. "He should be released soon, then."

Being the last one to see Maddox alive shouldn't make Gabriel a suspect. But he was. And there had to be a better reason.

Dax gave her a noncommittal shrug and nod. "Why don't I find a more comfortable place for you to wait?"

So the big guy wanted her away from the interrogation? "I'm fine, but I am really thirsty. Do you think they have a vending machine or something around here?"

His face tightened but he took the bait. "I'll find one. Coke, Pepsi, or something else?"

"Anything diet is fine. Thank you."

Dax nodded her way, then went off in search of her drink. Halfway down the hall, he asked the officer stationed there, who gave him directions.

As Dax walked away, her cell buzzed in her pocket. She found a text from Scott asking if everything was all right. And another from Tavia asking the same. So the rumor that she'd followed Gabriel to the station after he'd been hauled in had made the rounds through the office grapevine.

She quickly wrote them both back to say that she was fine and waiting for more information. Once she'd finished, she pocketed her phone, then peered into the room where Gabriel was talking to Roman.

How had all those reporters figured out so quickly that Gabriel had been brought in for questioning? If the police simply wanted questions answered in their investigation, they could have interrogated him far more easily at the office. Instead, they'd threatened to arrest him. Which meant they must have some motive or proof that he was a suspect.

Obviously, Dax wasn't being honest with her.

Maybe the Internet would be. Well, not honest, but it might give her a clue as to why this interrogation seemed way more serious than routine.

She strode down the same hall through which Dax had disappeared and gave the cop standing there her most innocent smile. "I'll be right back. I have to call the office and let them know Mr. Bond likely won't be in again this afternoon."

The officer nodded. "Yes, I wouldn't expect him back today. He's going to have his hands full."

So everyone knew more than her. The officer made Gabriel sound like the primary—and perhaps only—suspect.

Digesting that supposition, she slipped away and found a bathroom, entering quietly. She was in luck. No one seemed to be here and, according to her little screen, the signal was strong. She pulled up the

search engine on her phone and typed in the words *Gabriel Bond,*
Maddox Crawford, and *murder investigation.*

Capitol Scandals popped up in seconds.

She clicked through and the site assaulted her with the tawdriest
headlines.

SENATOR CAUGHT WITH PANTS DOWN

FEDERAL JUDGE SELLS DISMISSALS FOR COCAINE

IS PRESIDENT HAYES THE HOTTEST
COMMANDER-IN-CHIEF OF ALL TIME?

But the biggest headline, with the huge red print, caught her eye.

BREAKING NEWS:
GABRIEL BOND KILLS
BEST FRIEND MADDOX CRAWFORD

SEE THE VIDEO THAT WILL ROCK WALL STREET

Tabloid journalism alone wouldn't motivate the police to suspect
Gabriel, but if they had a video . . . She clicked the link and enlarged
the shot on the screen. It was still small, but she could see Gabriel in
what looked to be a fancy restaurant. Someone sat across from him,
but only part of that man's back was visible. Gabe leaned forward, and
while only a portion of his handsome face entered the view, she could
tell he was very angry.

"Do you have any idea what you've done?" Gabe growled in a low
voice. "I told you to be very sure because you would wreck her life and
she would be hurt. You said you'd changed."

"Relax, Bond. Everything is going to be fine. It's really for the best,
you know."

She would know that voice anywhere. Deep but with that hint of world-weariness Maddox Crawford had always possessed.

As she watched, Everly felt a little shiver slide through her. Was this video of their final conversation?

"For the best? You talked to her. You know what's happening. You just don't care, you son of a bitch. Of course you don't give a shit. You know what I should have done?"

Maddox's hand fisted on the table, but his voice remained calm. "Don't say something you can't take back. Calm down. Everything is going to work out in the end. I need you to give me a little time."

"So you can go through another fifty women? I'm supposed to believe you'll change if you get a little more pussy? Fuck you, Mad. I'm going to kill you for what you've done. I'm not going to do it today. I'm not going to do it tomorrow. I'm going to wait until you think you're safe. Then I'll be there. Do you understand?" He stood, throwing his napkin down in obvious disgust.

"I understand you are one overly dramatic motherfucker, Gabe. Please sit down. I can't tell you everything. It wouldn't be good for you. But something's happening, and I need time to sort it out. I need to ask you if you've ever heard the name Sergei?"

"I don't give a flying fuck what you need. Don't ever call me again, Mad." Gabriel walked out of view.

And she watched as Mad's head fell forward. He cursed audibly, then tossed some cash on the table.

The video ended abruptly.

She watched it through again. Okay, so that explained why the police considered Gabriel a suspect. He'd clearly had motive and intent, but her head still rang with questions. Obviously, he'd been angry, but who was the female they'd fought about? And who was Sergei? Even if he knew, Dax wasn't going to tell her anything more than he had. She might get something from watching the interrogation. She wasn't sure why Roman Calder had allowed her here, but she wasn't about to miss the chance.

Everly straightened her clothes and tucked her phone away.

It was past time to put her heart on the back burner and start thinking with her head.

She had her mentor's murder to solve. She hoped that when she was done, her investigation didn't prove that the man she'd fallen for hard and fast during their weekend together had killed in revenge.

Gabe glanced at the clock. They'd been asking him the same questions for hours. "I'm sorry. I didn't catch that last one."

Roman sighed. "Probably because you're hungry. We were supposed to have lunch two hours ago. Is this really how you want to roll, detective? It's so cliché to hope that my client will give more if you starve him. Are you planning on denying him bathroom breaks as well?"

The detective shrugged, obviously willing to play the bad cop. Gabe wished the good cop would show up. "You can eat once you've sufficiently answered our questions."

"He's answered every single one," Roman shot back. "Several times."

The detective ignored him completely, choosing to focus on Gabe. "Were you aware someone was filming you when you threatened Crawford's life?"

Ah, finally a new one. "No. I wouldn't have done it if I had known."

"So you admit you didn't want anyone to know you planned to kill Mr. Crawford."

Maybe the detective wasn't smart after all. "I admit I didn't want to be recorded without my knowledge. Is this a good time to point out that, according to that video, I wasn't planning on killing Mad for a few years?"

"He's being sarcastic." Roman shot him a dirty look and leaned in, his voice dropping low. "Is this a good time to remind you that we're being recorded here, too?"

Gabe was getting really sick of the whole conversation. "I'm pointing out the flaw in their theory. They seem to think that snippet lays out my nefarious plans to murder my best friend. If it does, then it should clear me because I threatened to kill him a few years down the road, not a few hours."

Roman gaped at him. "Do I need to staple your mouth shut?"

"Please don't. He has a point." Detective Johnson sat back, his look turning thoughtful. "I assume you had good reason to be angry with him. I've read about Crawford. He wasn't the nicest guy in the world. You seemed to be fighting over a woman. I understand he had a very busy love life."

"As I've stated several times, Mr. Bond was angry with Mr. Crawford over a personal issue. The actual point of contention isn't relevant." Roman had been doing his best to deflect questions from Sara. The news that Gabe's sister had been involved with Mad and was pregnant with his illegitimate child would be like pouring gasoline on a blazing clue for the police. The press would follow. They would race to his house in the Hamptons before he could reach Sara, and once he cut through the swarm of reporters, he'd have to try to move his sister somewhere else with them following.

They'd dig until they found out about Everly, too. It was just a matter of time. Would he leave her hanging in the wind or try to protect her as well?

"I disagree," said the thirtysomething detective. "I think the woman those two fought over is incredibly important to this investigation, but we'll figure it out with or without Mr. Bond's help. How about we talk about what you did the rest of that day?"

He tapped his left hand against the desk. This was one line of questioning he would rather avoid. "I went to the park after I left Cipriani. I decided to take off from work that afternoon and I wandered around the park to think for a bit."

"And I suppose there's no convenient video of you doing that currently posted on the Internet." Johnson slanted him a dubious stare.

"Likely not." It would be easier if there were. "Can't you have the city pull the security feeds from the park?"

The detective didn't answer him directly. "And the rest of your day?"

Shit. How much did he tell the police? How much did they already know? "I spent it alone, thinking about that conversation with Mad. I had dinner at home. My housekeeper can verify that. I went to bed around midnight."

He hadn't exactly made it to the bed. When he'd reached his penthouse, he'd barely touched his food, but he'd torn through a bottle of twenty-five-year-old Scotch. He'd awakened the next morning on the couch with a dry mouth and a throbbing head. He'd gotten the terrible news about Mad an hour later.

His whole world had been upside down since.

Was Eve . . . Everly gone already? Had she done the smart thing by packing up her desk and walking out on this mess? Gabe wasn't sure he could accept that outcome right now. He still didn't know what she'd meant to Mad. But at this point, he wasn't sure he cared.

Anger rolled in his gut. Yes, he'd been planning on firing Everly. That had been an easy decision before he'd known who she was. Letting her go now . . . As much as he hated to admit it, he wanted her close. He couldn't explain why except that he needed to see her again, touch her. He needed to fuck her out of his system. Maybe he should agree to whatever deal Mad had given her. She could keep her job and sleep with him until he purged himself of this horrible longing.

"Gabe?"

At the snap of his friend's voice, he looked up. "Yeah?"

Roman stood and frowned down at him. "We're leaving. I've explained to the detective that unless they want to formally charge you, they need to let us go now."

"I would love to throw you in a holding cell and see if you soften up, but my captain doesn't like the growing swarm of press. You're free to go for now, but don't leave town. I'll have more questions." The detective sat back with a sigh. "I find it very interesting that Crawford went down in one of your planes."

Mad's private jet had been built by Bond Aeronautics. Gabe had overseen the build himself. He'd made sure it was the most tricked-out mile high club in the air. He and Mad had gotten their pilot licenses at the same time. They used to love flying together. Usually one flew while the other fucked in the back on their way to Vegas or Paris or some other suitably decadent party town.

God, he couldn't believe Mad was dead.

"I assure you the last thing my client wants is negative press. The stock of his company has already taken a hit." Roman flipped the lid of his briefcase closed. "He won't leave the city. If you have any more questions for him, please contact my office. Perhaps we can do this in a more private setting next time."

The detective stood and left the room, his disappointment obvious.

"Let's go. Dax is waiting to get you out of here." Roman straightened his tie. "I'll face the mob outside and try to defuse the situation. You and I are going to have a long talk later."

Because Roman must know he was hiding something. Clever bastard. Gabe would have to confess he'd been at the airport that day. He'd been standing there when Mad had taken off.

Yeah, Roman was going to love that.

"All right. Give me the night to figure a few things out."

He especially needed to figure out how to handle Everly. He'd done everything wrong this morning. He wasn't even sure what would have been right. He should have found out about her relationship with Mad and been utterly disgusted. He'd wanted to be. He'd definitely been angry, felt betrayed. But he wanted her way too much to hold that grudge. Her fling with Mad infuriated him on Sara's behalf, but for himself? It didn't matter.

Everly was too damn dangerous for his peace of mind. To complicate matters even more, he now wondered if she had critical information.

During the long, tedious interrogation, his brain had been working the angles of this case. Though grief was still strong, the shock of Mad's death was wearing off. Logic had begun to set in again. He'd started to wonder about a few things. Mad had hated DC. What had compelled him to fly there to see Zack, rather than just picking up the phone? Why had he updated his will three weeks before his death? Why had he been so explicit about the funeral arrangements? Gabe had been forced to watch the tape of his last conversation with Mad again, and without the filter of rage to blind him, he could see the bastard had been trying to tell him something.

Everly had been the woman in Mad's bed at the end of his life. She must know something.

"That's all the time you get," Roman replied. "We'll talk in the morning. Go to Connor's place and we'll all meet for breakfast. For tonight, lay low."

He couldn't do that. He had to find Everly. "I need to go back to the office."

Roman paused at the door. "Absolutely not. You're going into hiding. The less chance we give the press to photograph you, the better off we are. The NYPD is all over you. The FAA isn't done with their investigation, but they're definitely treating the crash as if it was foul play. These cops are fishing for a suspect at this point, and that dipshit tape of you and Mad makes you look easy. For now, they'll leave you be—unless you give them a reason otherwise. But we have to figure this shit out. So you will behave. Is that understood?"

"Sure." It was best to agree with Roman, then do what he needed to. Roman wasn't going to understand his need to see Everly. Or his reason. He had to track her down and get her where he wanted her.

Underneath him, with her hair spread out, begging him to end the sensual torture.

Damn it, he had to stop thinking about having sex with her until he talked to her again. He wouldn't touch her until he figured out what part she'd played in this chaotic mess. And what she knew that could get him out of it.

Of course, he might not have to worry about ever getting physical with her again. She might have decided he was a bad bet as her new lover since he'd insulted her, then practically been arrested for murdering her last one.

Roman stared at him, and Gabe worried the shrewd lawyer had figured him out, but Roman finally opened the door and stepped into the hall.

Gabe followed. As soon as he had a free moment, he needed to pull up her address. Now that he knew Eve was Everly, he realized he had access to all her employment records, including her address in Brooklyn. They could continue their discussion at her place. He had his own interrogation to perform.

He turned the corner, then stopped. She stood right there, in the hallway, her face turned up, mouth moving as she said something to Dax.

"Why is she here?" He kept his voice low.

Roman sighed. "She'd already arrived when I walked into the precinct. Once I found out she's on Crawford's security team, I thought she should know what's going on. Actually, I'm surprised you didn't fire her on the spot. Dax told me there was a rumor about her and Mad."

"And I'll find out if it's true or not." He intended to discover every secret that woman had. "I'm also going to find out what was going on in Mad's head the last few months of his life. I'm betting she knows something."

"It's possible," Roman admitted. "I don't know if he would have really divulged anything of value to her, rather than his lifelong friends. But toward the end, Mad hadn't seemed like himself, so maybe she does know something." Roman frowned. "Any idea what he was asking about that last day you two went to lunch? He sounded as if he was looking for someone."

He'd mentioned a Sergei. "No. Hell, for all I know, it was his new drug dealer."

"Stop being an ass. This is exactly why you should stay away from her. You're on the edge and you'll only dig yourself in deeper. Neither of you needs another pile of shit right now. Take a step back, and we'll talk in the morning. I'll interview her and let you know what I find."

Not happening. He needed her. Even if he pried nothing more than the truth about her relationship with Mad from her, he wasn't going to leave Everly alone.

She turned, and he caught sight of her smile. Even in the little hallway, he couldn't fail to notice how bright she shined. His breath caught. No wonder Mad had left Sara for her. Eve was utterly different than any woman Gabe had ever been involved with. His whole body responded to her.

The minute she caught sight of him, she wiped all expression from her face. "Mr. Bond."

She wanted to play it that way? Of course she did now that she'd witnessed his interrogation. He wanted to punch Roman for letting her stay. Her opinion of him had obviously tumbled after their fight this morning, and seeing homicide detectives grill him had likely dropped him a notch lower. Damn it. He needed to do whatever possible to make sure she didn't get away from him.

"Everly, thank you for tracking down Dax and Roman. There was no need for you to wait. I planned on finding you soon. We still have a few things to iron out."

Roman shook his head. "You're not going to listen to a damn word I say, are you? Don't cause a fucking scene. I'll talk to you in the morning. Dax, have you got this?"

"It's handled. I don't think anyone can follow us."

Roman nodded and strode toward the front of the building, cursing to himself.

Dax stepped up and shook his hand. "I'll meet you up top, brother. Go easy on her. Everly isn't what you think she is. And the press knows her name now, so I don't recommend that you send her home by herself. Bring her up with you in ten."

He strode toward the stairs.

So she'd made another conquest. That wasn't surprising. Apparently, it was what Everly Parker did best.

"I'm sorry you had to witness that mess." He was going to be polite if it was the last thing he did because attacking her wouldn't induce her to talk. He refused to give in to the need to fight with her. Or to fuck her.

Her expression was bland, professional even. Damn it, he wanted to see her smile again. "I had to be here. I'm able to do my job better if I understand what's going on. So what are you not telling the police?"

"What do you mean?"

She dropped her voice to a whisper. "It's obvious you're hiding something. You avoided certain questions when you were more than willing to answer others in painstaking detail. You tap your left hand when you get nervous. You did it several times. On the desk. Against your leg. And you were definitely nervous about any questions concerning your whereabouts after your lunch with Maddox on the day in question. So where were you?"

She'd seen way more than he'd expected. Hell, she'd seen more than the detective. "I explained that several times."

"No. You didn't explain the stretch of time between your stroll in the park and dinner at all. That detective is an idiot."

"Could we not do this here? And I should probably remind you that you're my employee. It's your job to protect me, not question me."

"How can I protect you if I don't know the truth? That's the problem with clients. They tend to give you half the information, then expect a hundred and fifty percent effort. Besides, from what you said earlier, you might very well fire me."

Maybe he wouldn't avoid a fight after all. She seemed to be itching for one. "Why did you come here?"

She brushed back her hair. "Because until you fire me, I have a job to do."

"Exactly what job is that, Everly? Did you come here to keep the press off my back? If that's the case, from what I've heard, you failed."

"I came to make sure you got out of here in one piece, especially since they wouldn't let you take your car. How else did you plan on getting home?"

"That's why I had you call Dax. He'll take us back to the office. Let's go."

"If you don't need me, I can find my own way back to work." She turned to go.

He grabbed her elbow, staying her. "No. You'll come with me. I'm still your boss."

Her eyes flared. "You don't have to be."

"Don't even try to quit. I can make sure you don't work in this city again."

"Maybe I don't want to work in this city." Her voice had gone low and stubborn.

"I've got long arms, baby. You'll find it hard to work anywhere."

Her eyes narrowed and her lips pursed. She jerked free from his grip. Her body tensed, ready for flight.

Things were quickly heating up. It didn't serve his purpose to fight with her. It would serve him even less for her to walk away.

"Damn it. Let me try this again, Everly. I'm sincerely sorry about the meeting this morning. You threw me for a loop, and I handled it poorly. My only excuse is that I've had a rough couple of days."

She hesitated, obviously mulling over his words. Then she softened just a bit. Oh, fight still lurked somewhere in there, but Gabe saw clearly that anger wasn't the way to deal with her. He needed to be sneakier.

Everly nodded at him, a silent acceptance of his apology. But she still looked wary. "Why don't you head home, and I'll handle things at the office? I promise not to quit while you still need me."

Gabe planned to use that impromptu vow to his advantage. He had to blast past the guard she'd put up against him and hope she would respond to being needed. If he made her think they were partners, maybe he could slip under her defenses. If he could find out what she knew and purge her from his system at the same time, so much the better.

He shook his head. "I need you with me, Everly. I need to talk to you. You spent time with Mad. I have to figure out what was going through his head during his last few weeks."

He took her hand in his because he'd always found it was easier to take charge than wait to be followed. And he liked the feel of her skin against his.

Thankfully, she didn't pull away, merely allowed him to lead her up the stairs toward the top of the building. "I realize you don't believe me, but Maddox and I weren't lovers, so I don't know anything. He asked me questions about myself. Sometimes, he'd talk about work, his friends, his day . . . but nothing deep."

"You may not realize what you know that might be important to this case."

She sighed as they rounded the next flight of stairs. "This morning has been such a whirlwind, I probably wouldn't know what was important if it hit me in the face."

"But I might." He liked how small her hand was, how her fingers tangled with his almost of their own accord, as if they knew they belonged there.

She kept up with him, proving beyond a shadow of a doubt that she was in shape. She jogged up the stairs without sounding winded at all. "Why are we going up? I thought we were leaving."

He finally made it to the top of the building. He stopped in front of the door and could hear the whooshing sound of chopper blades as Dax turned the engine over. "We are leaving. I'd like to see the paparazzi follow us now."

Her eyes widened as if she'd identified the sound, too. "We're going in a helicopter? I've never been in one."

"This isn't simply any helicopter. This is my baby. I designed it myself. I could go into all the brilliant engine innovations and give you specs on how far and fast it can go, but you'll probably be more interested in the fact that I convinced the House of Versace to design the interior. This is a flying luxury suite." And the interior was definitely tricked out so they could get busy. Not that he was going to seduce her now. But it crossed his mind.

She stared at him with wide eyes. "Gabriel, whatever you're thinking . . . that's a mistake."

"No, it's not. I need you, Everly. Help me figure out who killed my best friend because I didn't do it." It was time to play on those heartstrings of hers and seal the deal. To do that, he would have to open up and give her a little honesty. It might even make her feel guilty enough to give him what he needed. If she'd been sleeping with Mad, she might be shocked at what he was about to say. "I owe it to my future nephew or niece to figure out who killed him."

She paused, obviously putting the pieces of the puzzle together. Then she gasped. "Your sister. She's pregnant. She dated Maddox. He mentioned it once. That's what you two were fighting about."

"I'll tell you everything if you'll come with me. I'll put all my cards on the table, and you can show me yours. Then we'll see what kind of hand we're left with."

She nodded slowly, but withdrew her hand from his. "All right, but this is a professional relationship from here out. Our weekend was a mistake, an aberration. I'll help you, but you have to promise to forget about what happened between us."

Not in a million years. But she was right that it had been an aberration. Usually when he slept with a woman, he moved on right away. Usually, he didn't feel a thing beyond physical satisfaction. Everly made him feel more. She made him feel too damn much.

"Of course." It seemed to be his day for telling lies.

She nodded and started for the door.

Damn it. How was he going to keep his hands off her? He followed her, completely unable to pry his stare away from that curvy backside.

He tried to tell himself that Mad had her first, and she was the reason they were in this mess. He tried to tell himself that if Mad had been murdered, she might even be a suspect. He had a million and one reasons to not trust her, to stay as far from her as he could.

But a certain ruthless part of him found every reason possible to keep her close. She'd belonged to Mad, who had given him everything. His business. His homes. His money.

Why not his mistress?

As Everly opened the door, the bright light of day flooded the stairs. She stopped at the top and stared at the chopper. It was a gorgeous black and white body with a matching elegant cabin. Dax had thoughtfully left the cabin door open, but she made no move toward it.

"Are you scared?" Gabe asked.

"I've never loved heights, to tell you the truth." She retreated as though ready to scamper back down the stairs to safety.

He wasn't about to let her do that. He had no idea why Mad hadn't taken her up, but flight had been a big portion of Gabe's life for a very long time. His family business was all about getting up in the sky. Besides, if she was afraid, she might cling to him. She might be grateful to him for keeping her safe.

"I won't let you fall." He held out his arm.

"Gabriel . . ." she began.

"I am very professionally offering to escort you to your vehicle, Ms. Parker. And trust me, you haven't seen Manhattan until you've seen it from my vantage point. Let me show you." He could muster up some charm. It had all gone down the toilet when he'd let his anger rule. Charisma worked better. He would know her secrets and figure her out. And once he had, he would be ready to let her go.

She squared her shoulders and slipped her arm through his. "All right. I guess it is the best way to avoid the press. Are we going back to the office?"

Right before he answered, a thought struck him. He should gauge how she reacted to being surrounded by Maddox Crawford, see if she pined like a lover or clammed up guiltily like someone keeping secrets. "Let's go to Mad's and see if he left anything that might help us figure out what he was up to before he was killed. We might be able to piece together some clues. Would you help me do that?"

The light came back into her eyes, and he felt her inch closer. Yes, he would definitely catch more Everlys with honey than vinegar.

She hesitated, as if she knew better, but then nodded.

"Keep your head down." The rotors were really moving now. He had to yell over the sound.

When he started walking to the chopper, she did as he asked and stayed by his side. He settled her in and grabbed the headphones that linked him to Dax, passing another set to her.

"Are you two ready?" Dax asked, his voice coming in strong over the headphones.

"Everly's never been in a helicopter before, Dax," he replied. "Why don't we give her a tour? You know the drill."

There was a slight pause, followed by a little chuckle. "Well, now, brother, you know I never like to disappoint a lady."

The helicopter lifted off the pad, and Dax turned it up just enough to send her right into his arms. Yes, Dax remembered the drill.

He eased Everly back into her seat and helped her secure her seatbelt. He was satisfied to let her be. For now. Once they were alone . . .

Gabe smiled.

EIGHT

Everly glanced around the library. It was surprisingly classic, even staid, given the fact that it was in Maddox Crawford's bachelor pad.

Earlier, Gabriel had kept his promise to show her Manhattan from above. It had glittered like a jewel in the early evening. From those heights there had been no trash, rude people, or violence, only beauty. She'd felt safe with him. Which probably made her an idiot since he was a suspect in a high-profile murder. But her gut told her that he wouldn't harm her.

After the exhilarating ride, they'd landed on the helipad atop Maddox's building. The four-story brownstone was otherwise luxurious but unassuming. Since entering the place, Everly had been walking around a bit wide-eyed.

She'd expected everything flashy and modern, with all the latest gadgets and a flat screen as big as the one in Times Square. Instead, the place reeked of old-school elegance. Sure, he had contemporary leather sofas upstairs and Euro-modern cabinets in the kitchen—which should have looked out of place. But he'd also chosen fixtures and fabrics that bridged the gap between the Gilded Age and today, while keeping the character of the building. The plaster ceilings, medallions, moldings, and door casings blew her mind. Everything looked like it belonged in a magazine.

As they'd stepped down into the library, the sights hadn't stopped. The cove ceilings towered above them. On either side of the room, built-in shelves painted a pristine white arched across the length and width of the wall. Each was lined with hundreds of leather books, and the smell was divine. At one end, a huge picture window opened up to the "garden level" and provided light to the sturdy antique desk beneath. A massive marble fireplace with ceiling-scraping mirror-and-wood detail dominated the other end. Dark hardwood floors added a cozy richness to the place. A cushy reading chair in a velvet bottle green occupied one corner, along with a globe in a floor stand. A pale beige sofa with softly colored pillows sat right in the middle of the room.

Everything shouted class. For all of Maddox's faults, the man had possessed great style.

"Have you found anything?" Everly asked a couple of hours later as she caught sight of Gabriel at the big desk.

He looked up from what appeared to be a mountain of paper, a single sheet clutched in his hand. "Mad didn't like to deal with trivial details. No idea why he's keeping a receipt for booze he had at a party he threw two years ago. Did he want to be reminded of how much he overpaid the caterers? Seriously, he got scammed and hard. He paid a hundred thousand for champagne that wasn't worth twenty."

She sighed as she peeked at the receipt. "Given the date and quantity, looks like it's a receipt for the champagne served at the foundation's annual gala. The event is Tavia's baby, though Valerie started handling most of the ordering and catering two years ago. I'm not surprised she would spend so much. She likes expensive things."

He shook his head. "That's what I'm saying. This brand isn't expensive."

"Well, this was for charity. Maybe Maddox needed an additional write-off. Or the hotel likes to up charge."

"He liked to give money to a good cause, but overpaying for booze wasn't one of them. Did he fire this Valerie person?"

"No." Everly's world would be a better place if he had.

Gabriel seemed deeply interested in receipts. She was, too, but not from Crawford Industries. Everly had spent the last two hours hacking into a coffee shop system. She'd traced one of her mystery e-mails to a coffee shop computer in Midtown and now she was going through credit cards. The shop offered free wi-fi and had four computers available for use by patrons.

With a little luck, one of thirty-seven people who purchased a latte within an hour before or after the e-mail was sent would turn out to be her mystery texter. She had to hope he'd also sent her the photos. Too bad the SD card was locked up in her office.

She'd been trying like hell to get back to her computer and look at more than the first two images. But the meeting Scott had pulled her into that morning had lasted until quitting time. Then the other VPs had insisted she come with them to a strategy session over dinner to prepare for the new boss's arrival. When she'd finally left after ten that night, SD cards had been the last thing on her exhausted mind. Tuesday morning, looking at that card had been first on her agenda . . . until Hilary had called her into Gabe's office and the damn world had blown up. Everly had every intention of getting back to the office and viewing more of the photos.

"I'm surprised he didn't let her go." Gabriel huffed. "Mad could seem like a happy-go-lucky screwup, but he didn't suffer incompetence at all. Remind me to look at her file when all this blows over."

Would she even be with Crawford Industries—or Gabriel—by then? "Let's just do it now."

Darting across the room to the plush chair, she grabbed Maddox's sleek laptop, hit a few keys, and browsed.

"You have the permissions to view HR files?" he asked from across the room.

Everly didn't answer right away, but it didn't take longer than that to find what she needed. "I know how to get into the confidential HR files Maddox had access to. According to those, there hasn't been a single firing at Crawford in over two months, and the last person wasn't even in accounting. In fact, I couldn't find anything that would suggest he or HR intended to make a case to dismiss Valerie."

"He never failed to let go of someone who deserved it. Did you find anything else when you scanned his computer earlier?"

Before he'd settled down with boxes of receipts, Gabriel had asked her to check the two computers in the house, a laptop and a desktop. Both top-of-the-line and neither yielding much. From what she could tell, he'd done a purge of both systems fairly recently. "Other than a surprising amount of pornography? I didn't know the human body could do some of those things."

Gabriel chuckled. "I bet you got an eyeful. Mad always did enjoy the exotic. Sorry, I should have thought about that."

He stared at her with eyes full of warm regard. When he looked at her like that, Everly remembered how well she knew this man physically. She knew how it felt to have his arms wrapped around her, her body beneath his. She tried to shake the memories off.

"Somehow I'll survive, though I wouldn't mind bleaching my eyeballs." She gave him a wry glance. "But I also managed to check his datebook. He had a bunch of meetings but I didn't see one with Valerie or anyone else who handled accounting for the foundation galas, so it doesn't look as if he even questioned her about that receipt."

"The fact that it was front and center on his desk tells me he was keeping it close for some reason."

Silently, Everly agreed. "But he hadn't acted. Any thoughts why?"

Gabriel shook his head. "He was obviously interested in this particular transaction." He filtered through a few more scraps of paper and scanned them. "And two others a lot like it. This one was attached to the receipts for the foundation parties for the previous three years. Unless Mad was suspicious, I can't think of a single reason why he kept them in his personal space, rather than with the corporate files. Maybe he questioned Valerie off the record?"

"That doesn't seem like him. The Maddox I knew might not always share his agenda but he tended to meet things head on."

"Exactly." Gabriel sighed. "I'll have Connor peek into this woman's financials to see if he can find any hint of her skimming money. I'll also have him find out if she has an alibi for the night of Mad's death."

"Will that really help? She could have planted that bomb days or weeks ago."

"No, the plane had been used by another Crawford executive the day before. One of the services the private airport we use offers is a nose-to-tail check between every flight. Dax looked at the records. He texted me to say that Kingston, the owner of the airport, and his head mechanic inspected the plane three hours before Mad took off. Jerry Kingston has been a family friend forever. He's a nice old guy and had no cause to want Mad dead. If there had been a bomb on that plane then, they would have found it. So it was planted some time between ground check and takeoff. Mad was flying solo."

"Why was he going to DC?" That had been the destination listed on his flight plan.

Gabriel sat back and massaged his forehead as though he had a headache coming on. "Right after the crash, Roman told me Mad had called the day before and asked for a meeting with Zack. Mad refused to say why."

"Zack. You mean the president?"

Gabriel chuckled a little. "To me, he's Zack. Or Scooter, when I want to needle him."

She had to shake her head in disbelief since Zachary Hayes was known for his serious demeanor. "You call the president of the United States *Scooter*?"

When Gabriel smiled like that it was difficult to remember why she should stay away from him. "Absolutely, but I'm sworn to secrecy about how he acquired that nickname. I think he'd sic the Secret Service on me if I told."

It was so weird to think that the gorgeous guy in front of her not only knew the most powerful man in the world, but they'd grown up together. Gabriel Bond was the type of man who rode around in private helicopters and had dinner with the commander-in-chief. He was the type of man who was perfectly comfortable in limos and mansions.

He was the type of man who would enjoy a woman like her for a few nights, then cozy up again with women of his own class.

Everly had been raised in the middle of nowhere. She'd never actually owned a car of her own, just borrowed her dad's because he'd mostly driven his squad car. Gabriel's mother had been a debutante, while hers had left when Everly was six and took virtually every cent they had. She hadn't even bothered to say good-bye. In fact, she hadn't talked to her mother in years. She'd been forced to bury her father alone.

She and Gabe were from completely different worlds. She'd do well to remember that.

He sat back in his chair, stretching his big body like a lazy predator. "Do you want to order some dinner? I met with the housekeeper yesterday and gave her the week off while I sort everything out. But I can call Dax. He'll bring us something."

That sounded awfully cozy. "I should probably head home."

Because she was fairly certain that, even though this place had six palatial bedrooms and over eight thousand square feet, it was still too small and intimate to hold both her and Gabriel if she wanted to keep her skirt on and her bed solitary.

"That's not a good idea." He stared at her like he knew something she didn't.

"I can't stay here. I don't have a change of clothes. I don't have anything." Well, except her purse. But she hadn't stuffed it with a spare set of undies or her toiletries.

He shrugged. "The good news is, Mad has a whole closet of crap women have left here. I'm sure we'll find something that fits. The bad news is, your building is very likely surrounded by reporters now. Apparently, they learned your identity this morning, and someone tipped them off that you came to the police station with me. So unless you're desperate for your fifteen minutes of fame, I'm afraid you're stuck here with me."

"Why would they have any interest in me?" Sure they'd caught her leaving a hotel a couple of days before, but . . . "I spent one weekend with you."

"Everly, you have to understand how gossip works. They figured out the name of my mystery date earlier this morning and started asking questions. You coming to the police station with me only added a spark to that blaze. I assure you, the minute I was taken in for questioning, the story got even juicier for them. I guarantee those reporters called every employee at Crawford and buttered up anyone willing to talk. Can you guess what they said?"

She already knew, and it made her want to scream. "That I was Maddox Crawford's mistress."

"Bingo. So, since they saw you leaving the hotel after our night together, I assure you they're claiming you're now *my* mistress. There may even be wild speculation about a possible ménage à trois or some conjecture that I killed Mad in a jealous fit. I have no doubt they're also publicly wondering if you came to the police station today to provide me an alibi or the final nail in my coffin."

"Oh dear god." Never mind this day being terrible. She wanted to scratch the whole week and start over. "What a mess."

"Yep. Don't be surprised if you get called in for questioning, too. If that happens, Roman will go with you or he'll have one of his former partners represent you. I won't leave you alone in this."

Her jaw dropped. She stood staring at him, trying to process all he'd said. There was no way it could be true. No one could possibly think she was the mistress of one powerful man, much less two. "Who would ever believe that you would kill your best friend over me? It's ridiculous."

"Maybe but it makes for a great story. Tabloids aren't looking for the truth. They want whatever sells papers or gets page views. And they're definitely staking out your place." He snatched the computer from her grasp, hit a few keys, then turned the computer screen toward her.

She read the headline in horror.

AND A WOMAN CAME BETWEEN THEM . . .

The article included pictures of Maddox and Gabriel through the years. They'd also posted the shot of her running out of the hotel again.

Holy hell. It was really there. She turned to look at the gray shantung silk covering the window. The office was just below street level. With the curtains drawn, she couldn't see out but wished now that more than cloth and glass separated her from the outside world. "Do you think they followed us here?"

He gave her a short shake of his head. "No. Dax and I made sure of it. A decoy of me was seen going into my building, and Connor found an actress who looks enough like you to head into yours. She's going to walk by your window every couple of hours to keep them there."

"There's a strange woman in my loft? How did she even get in there? I've got my keys."

"Do you?"

She walked back to check her purse. Sure enough, her keys were missing. "You stole my keys?"

"No. Dax did that. He's got fast hands, but if he hadn't been able to lift your keys, I assure you Connor could have found a way in. If you're going to be angry with someone, be angry with me. It was the best way I could think of to keep the press off our trail. Neither of us can go home now, so I thought this was a good compromise since I had keys to Mad's place. He inherited a much larger mansion when his father died. He lists that as his address, but he preferred to stay here. It could take a couple of days for the reporters to figure out where we're hiding."

But they wouldn't be able to leave. How had her life turned upside down in a few short days? "I can't believe I need someone to distract the press. I was never Maddox's mistress."

Gabe's eyes narrowed as he considered her. "All right. Let's say I believe you. What was your relationship with him? Were you doing work for him outside of the office?"

"Not officially, though we did discuss work. The first time he showed up at my loft, he claimed he wanted to go over my plans to convert to a new cybersecurity system. But after a few minutes, he changed the subject and we ended up talking about other things. We were just friends." She wasn't sure how else to put it.

"Mad didn't have female friends. He had lovers and employees."

Frustration threatened to boil her blood. "Before our weekend together, I hadn't been to bed with anyone in a year and a half. Maddox and I didn't have anything romantic or sexual going. When he started coming to my place, he seemed . . . lonely. Sad."

"He always came to your place? Sorry, I didn't realize Mad knew how to get to Brooklyn."

Everly grinned. Sometimes he'd been a terrible snob. "Apparently he learned. His driver dropped him off. He certainly didn't take the subway."

"So you're trying to tell me you've never been here before?"

"Not once." He'd never invited her here and she'd never asked. He'd seemed to like her cozy loft.

"Did he ever spend the night?"

Maddox had been quite the night owl. He would often keep her talking until two or three in the morning, but he'd usually gone back to Manhattan. "Only once. He was drunk and he showed up at my place without calling. When he rang the buzzer to come up, I could tell that he wasn't himself. He kept talking about some woman. I worried about him that night."

"Do you remember the name of the girl he talked about?"

"He never mentioned it. I didn't pry. He only said he loved her and he'd lost her."

"How long ago was this?"

"A couple of months ago." She tried to remember an exact date, but couldn't. "Anyway, all I did that night was put him to bed. I slept on the couch. The next morning, he apologized for any inconvenience and swore he'd take the couch next time. I asked him if there would be a next time and he gave me one of his wry smiles and a shrug. Do you think he was upset about your sister?"

Gabriel was quiet for a moment. "The timing fits. If he felt guilty about what he'd done to Sara, he had good reason. But I seriously doubt Mad ever loved her. He couldn't have and still treated her the way he did. Honestly, I don't think Mad knew how to love just one woman. How did you come to work for Crawford? Who recruited you?"

That was another mystery, too. "A headhunter contacted me and hired me away from my former employer. I was working as an IT department team leader in a company of about a hundred—much smaller than Crawford—when the guy called. He offered me a job on the spot. It took me a few days to actually wrap my head around the fact that the offer was genuine."

"You weren't an executive at your last job?"

She shook her head. "Hardly. I'd recently been moved up to project manager. I was on an executive fast track, but it still would have taken years to reach the level I'm at now. I got lucky."

"That seems like a whole lot of luck," Gabriel remarked. "And this headhunter represented Crawford? Would you recognize his name?"

"Of course." She couldn't forget the name of the man who had effectively changed her life. Her father had passed a few weeks before she'd gotten that call. She'd been depressed, and this had been an open door to a brighter future at a time she'd needed it.

He nodded toward the laptop. "Hack into Mad's e-mail and look for any messages he wrote the headhunter about you."

"Why?" What did this have to do with solving Maddox's murder?

"Because I don't think your new job at Crawford had anything to do with luck. Mad never used headhunters. He had a solid HR department and preferred to promote from within every chance he could."

"He wouldn't have dealt with the headhunter directly, I'm sure. As you said, he had an HR department. Maybe they couldn't find a candidate with the right skill set in their own organization, so they went outside."

"Indulge me. I have a hunch and I'd like to see if I'm right."

Was he trying to prove that Maddox had hired her in order to sleep with her? She knew it wasn't true, but she was worried about giving Gabriel anything that he could twist. "What makes you think Maddox would be so invested in hiring a security project manager? That's the position I was initially hired for. A month later, a new, even larger team was being formed around international cybersecurity threats. The team needed a director, which was a perfect position for my skill set. Five months after, the previous VP of cybersecurity retired, and I was promoted into his job."

"No doubt, other people in the department had worked for Crawford longer and were just as qualified."

She could think of a few. "Maybe Maddox wanted someone younger, more versed in electronic means of security than my predecessor and his cronies."

"Even so, an executive position like that should have taken you years to attain . . . unless a very powerful person handpicked you for the role."

Gabriel was wrong. He had to be. There was zero reason for Maddox Crawford to have taken an interest in her before they'd even met. "That doesn't make sense."

"I know how Mad's mind worked. Please check." He pointed to Maddox's laptop.

"I've been through his business e-mail already. We're lucky the IT folks hadn't nuked the account yet. I didn't see anything like that."

That made Gabriel pause. "What about his personal e-mail? Did you look through that?"

Everly sighed and reached for the computer. He was like a dog with a bone. "I'll do it now."

She opened her former boss's private e-mail but found it password protected. She could get around that, but the first and easiest solution was to figure out the password. A truly smart person selected a random set of numbers and letters, but most people picked something personal. What would Maddox choose? He didn't seem like the kind to get sentimental or obsessive about anything—with a singular exception. The night he'd come to her loft shitfaced he'd been absolutely focused on one subject.

"What's your sister's name?"

"Sara." Gabriel spelled it for her.

She typed the name in, and Maddox's e-mail popped up. "I'm in."

Gabriel sat forward. "*Sara* was his password?"

"Yeah. I know you think otherwise, but she must be the woman he talked about loving and losing that night. You know, he never seemed the same again. He hung around me a lot more, but he still seemed awfully alone."

Gabriel raked a hand through his hair. "I don't understand. He broke things off with Sara. They were happy—at least I thought so." He huffed. "Bastard. Sara had dolled herself up to go to a reception with him. They'd been planning to take their relationship public. While she was waiting for him to pick her up, he sent her a kiss-off text. How could he care about Sara and treat her like that?"

Everly had no idea.

She stared at the computer screen, clicking her cursor into the search field to type in the headhunter's name. It popped up immediately, displaying a few messages. That surprised her. "You're right about the e-mails. But why would a man as powerful as Maddox Crawford deal directly with a headhunter?"

"What do you see? Was he looking for a specific set of skills?"

She had to stop because what she read didn't make a lick of sense. "No. He was looking for *me*. Why would he ask for me by name before we'd ever met? He gave the headhunter all my personal information—no idea where he got that—and said to hire me, regardless of my demands. I should have asked for more money."

Gabriel stood and walked around the desk to peer over her shoulder. When he leaned in, Everly felt the heat of his body. "Open the attachment Mad sent."

She clicked and got another shock. "It's a complete file on me. My driver's license, social security number, school records. What the hell is going on?"

"I'm not sure, but he was definitely interested in you." He moved away, pacing across the floor. "None of the e-mails spell out why Mad wanted to hire you?"

She skimmed the rest of the messages. "No. Maddox simply told him to get it done and that there was a bonus if he could get me on board within six weeks."

"But he only wanted to be your friend," Gabriel said, his disbelief evident. "Who the hell are you, Everly Parker?"

"No one," she whispered back. "I was raised in the middle of nowhere by a cop. I went to a state college and worked almost full-time to put myself through. I got a decent job when I graduated but it's not as if I know any classified secrets."

"Maybe not but you know how to hack a system."

"Anyone in my business can hack a system." Though secretly, Everly suspected she was a bit better than most. Lots of practice had ensured that.

"Have you hacked any systems you shouldn't have? Besides ones involving Peter Jackson trailers."

"Not in years. I will admit I've hacked into some places that could get me in trouble, but that was in college. Why would Maddox care now? I never did it to hurt anyone, merely to prove to myself that I could."

"Maybe you saw something you don't realize is important."

Maybe she had, but she didn't see how any of this helped them figure out who had killed Maddox and why. If someone who worked at Crawford felt slighted that they hadn't been promoted when her predecessor retired, sure, they could have killed him in rage. But it made far more sense for the disgruntled employee to off her and hope that Mad chose him or her to backfill the position. Besides, she'd come here with Gabriel to get some answers—and he'd begun asking all the questions. She was a little sick of feeling interrogated.

"I don't think so," she told him. "Let's come back to that later. Tell me what you didn't tell the police."

He stopped pacing, and his face went stony and blank. "I told the police everything relevant."

"So that's how this is going to go?" She sighed in exasperation. "You only brought me here to figure out my role in all this. You had no intention of sharing what you know."

"I don't know anything."

She stood and headed for the stairs. Destination: front door. "Then I don't think we have anything else to say to one other. I'll take my chances with the press."

Everly didn't care that there were reporters in front of her building. She would find a hotel. Or better yet, she would take a few days off and get out of the city. She had college friends scattered a few hours away. Her father's sister lived in Connecticut. She could visit her father's grave and figure out where to go while she decided what the hell to do with her life now.

Gabriel wrapped his arm around her middle, hauling her back against his steely body.

"Don't go," he whispered against her ear.

With those two low words, he transported her back to the intimacy of their weekend together. She remembered how it felt to be under him, his body working to bring them both to climax. She also remembered how safe she'd felt in his arms. When he'd held her, he'd surrounded her, kept her breathless.

Why couldn't she stop thinking about that? Damn him.

"Don't touch me like this," she insisted. "You're my boss now. That's it."

He wrapped both arms around her, holding her tight. "When I hold you, it's like a balm. You're the first person to make me feel good in so fucking long. Don't make me stop."

It felt good to her, too. But she knew this heady sense of intimacy only lasted as long as the arousal. Later, he would push her away again, and she would be devastated. No matter how much she loved being with him, the pain wasn't worth the momentary pleasure. She'd let him talk her into coming here because he'd promised to be honest with her.

"You have to. I'm not going through this with you again, Gabriel. If you can't trust me, then it's time to walk away."

"I was at the airport that day."

She stilled in his arms. No wonder he'd been reluctant to spill that. "You're telling me you were at the airport when Maddox flew off?"

"Yes." His gruff breath ruffled her hair.

"Why?"

"I had to talk to him again. I went there to try. I'd walked through the park for hours. Once I'd cooled down, I knew I couldn't leave things the way they were between us. We'd been friends for most of our lives. I realized I had to salvage what I could and hope he would eventually seek some kind of relationship with his child." He sighed behind her, the action pressing them closer together. "Mad would have been the first of us to be a father. That day, I couldn't imagine him not knowing his own kid. We . . . how do I put this without sounding like a poor little rich boy?"

"I know your parents weren't around much." Everly couldn't help but empathize. Even before her mother had left she'd always felt distanced from the woman and it had hurt. So even if it made her stupid, she also responded to Gabriel's sadness. Something inside her wanted to comfort him.

She clasped his arms, which he still had wrapped around her, and allowed him to draw her closer.

"Creighton Academy was my parent most of the time. That's where I met all my friends. Sometimes I think I spent my childhood alone until I met Mad. A lot of who I am today is because of him and his constant friendship."

Gabriel seriously mourned Maddox. The grief hollowing his tone tore at her heart. In some ways, he hadn't simply lost a friend, but a man he considered a brother. And he'd lost Maddox on the ugliest of terms.

"Gabriel . . ."

"Let me get this out." The way he grabbed onto her told Everly that only sheer will kept him going. "That day I sat in the park after I'd threatened to kill him, I thought about what it meant to have kids. These five men were so instrumental in shaping my life. I couldn't imagine a world where our families didn't know each other. I couldn't imagine all of us not getting together with our kids to relax, laugh, drink, and yell at them, the way our parents hadn't yelled at us. We were supposed to be better, damn it. Our children were supposed to have a real childhood."

Everly nudged at Gabriel. He sighed reluctantly, then eased his grip. But she didn't leave his embrace. Instead, she turned into him, without bothering to remind herself this was a bad idea. That didn't matter now; only the desolation in his voice did. It took her right back to the time they'd spent together at The Plaza before names and reputations had come into play. Whether it was smart or not, she cared about this man, and he was hurting. She wrapped her arms around him. He hesitated for a moment, then brought her against him tightly. They shared a silent moment of succor. Gabriel seemed to draw strength from her.

Finally, he rested his chin on her head. "I thought you were going to push me away."

"I should." But she could feel him bringing her closer, as if he'd never let her go. In the moment, she wanted to believe whatever they had together could work.

"Don't. Please let me have this moment." He raised his hand to her face, cradling her cheek. The gesture bespoke affection more than sex, and felt so achingly tender. If he had dragged her to the desk and started tearing at her clothes, she would have been able to resist him. Maybe. But the sweetness of his touch utterly disarmed her. The need to protect herself crumbled under her need to comfort him.

"It's all right, Gabriel."

"It isn't. I don't know if anything will ever be right again. I only know that, for all his faults, I miss Mad. I also know that I want you. You think we can go back to something professional, but I can't. Because I can't stop thinking about you. I haven't gone five minutes without thinking of you since the moment we met."

She hadn't, either. Every second of her life seemed to be consumed by thoughts of Gabriel. "I think about you, too."

He pulled away just enough to stare down at her. "We're in this together, you know. I've felt guilty about dragging you into a mess, even though the rumors about your relationship with Mad would have surfaced eventually. But I'm glad you're here. I'm not sure you could have handled the press on your own."

That was true. She could handle a lot by herself. She was very competent. Her father had taught her self-defense and how to use a gun. She felt comfortable making the decision about when to flee or fight. But she had no idea how to handle a mob of insistent journalists. If she'd been left to her own devices, she would have headed home, never realizing there was trouble until it was too late. "This is your world. I don't really understand it."

His eyes turned serious. "I'll take care of you, Everly. I'll keep the press off you. Hopefully, once we figure out what happened with Mad, they'll stop writing about you and move on to the next juicy story. Then you can get back to your life. Will you trust me?" He slid his hands up to frame her face. His thumb traced her lower lip. "Can you stand beside me and try to solve this crazy puzzle?"

Could she stay with him for days yet still hold herself apart? Everly couldn't imagine how. Even now, she stood in his arms, barely two hours after she'd vowed to keep things professional between them. She'd be lying to herself if she denied the fact that she felt connected to him. Still, she had to try to resist the temptation of him. Nothing lay down this path except great sex—and heartbreak. But she was a big girl. She could handle it.

"If you're honest with me, then yes." Everly eased away from him, leaving the comfortable circle of his arms.

Guilt nagged at her. She was asking for honesty, but she wasn't ready to tell him about the texts or the pictures yet. She needed time to be sure that what she'd received was actually relevant. Now that she was involved, all her investigative instincts were kicking in. She had a part to play in this and she got the feeling that, if Gabriel really understood, he would stand in her way. Whether he would do it to hide something or to protect the "little woman," she wasn't sure, but she knew he would try.

He sighed. She got the feeling that he was only giving her a bit of space for now and would be more persuasive later. "All right. I've told you my secrets. You know enough to go straight to the police and give them cause to arrest me."

She wasn't going to do that. Maybe she was an idiot and her hormones were affecting her judgment but she believed that he hadn't gone to the airport that day with any ill intent. "Why haven't they seen you on the surveillance footage? Surely they have cameras at the airport."

"It's a small, fairly exclusive airport. They're also very private. It's one reason we fly in and out of airports like that. There are cameras but the security is not as tight or in-your-face as a public airport. Maybe none of the surveillance caught me. I don't know. It was certainly the last thing on my mind that day. But eventually, the police will run the toll tags on my car and figure out where I went. The logic that if I'd planned to kill my friend, I would have covered my tracks better, will be lost on them."

Most likely. "Then you'll have a hard time explaining why you lied during your interrogation."

"But if I'd told Detective Johnson, he would have arrested me on the spot. I had to buy time to see if I could figure this out. I know Dax or Connor could have done the same, but they didn't know Mad as well as I did. If someone killed him in such a premeditated fashion, they had a motive and I need to find it. It also had to be someone with the means, who knew about bombs and knew that Mad intended to fly to DC that night." He crossed back over to the desk. "I thought I would find something in here. His desk is a mess. Mad never was very organized. It will take me most of the night to go through the rest of this stuff. I don't even know what I'm looking for. I wish he'd kept a damn diary."

"He wasn't a teenage girl," she returned. "I think we need to figure out why Maddox wanted a meeting with the president. I doubt he was going there for a beer. Who did he ask you about in that video? He mentioned a name when you were talking to him at lunch."

"Sergei. It's Russian. He didn't mention a last name. That would have been helpful. I don't know a Sergei. Never met one. And merely because the name is Russian doesn't mean the person who uses it actually is. He could be as American as apple pie."

"If Maddox was going to the president, maybe Sergei was someone the president knew."

"It's possible. Since Zack's father was an ambassador to Russia for years, he spent a lot of time there," Gabriel mused. "His parents sent him back here to attend some boarding school. He started Creighton in the seventh grade. When he went to visit his father in Moscow, I know he was very sheltered from that world, but it's worth a shot. I'll talk to Roman tomorrow and see if we can arrange a call or something. Until then, I'll keep looking."

He sat back down at the desk, his shoulders slumped as he looked across the mountain of paperwork.

She couldn't help but watch him. "You know, I think Maddox was worried something bad would happen to him. He wasn't just sad the last few weeks, but anxious. Maybe that's why he broke up with your sister."

He looked down with a shrug. "If he'd been worried, he should have come to me. He should have done anything but crush and humiliate her. Mad and I have been through a lot together. Hell, the six of us made promises. I know they were made when we were children, but we've stood by them for decades. So don't try to justify anything he did to Sara again."

A chill seemed to settle over him, and Everly knew now wasn't the time to reach him. Despite their intimacy a few moments ago, he was right back to looking at her like he had in the office. She had to remember that his resentment of her relationship with Mad was always there, always bubbling with suspicion under his gorgeous surface. "I'm going to go and see if there's anything I can make for dinner."

"I would appreciate that."

She looked at Gabriel for a moment, but all of his attention was now on the haphazard slips of paper littering the massive, masculine desk in front of him. He'd closed her off, and that was probably for the best. The more distance they maintained between them, the more they could concentrate on what was really important. She turned and walked out, leaving him to his thoughts.

As she did, her cell pinged, signaling she had a text. She pulled it out of her pocket and glanced down.

Don't get caught in Bond's web. Meet me tomorrow instead.
3PM. Parking garage. I'll answer your questions.

Everly stared at the screen, her heart racing. He was moving the date of their meeting forward. Meeting this person alone in a parking garage was undoubtedly dangerous. But what if he knew something about Maddox's murder that might solve the mystery and exonerate Gabriel? Something that could help her get her life back?

Tomorrow. She had until then to find everything she could about Maddox's death and decide what she would do next.

Two hours later, Gabe sat back and wondered why he'd gotten so wound up. Between the food Everly had put on his plate and the half a bottle of Mad's ridiculously good Pinot Noir he'd consumed, he didn't want to remember why the world was a shitty place. Their fare— chicken, potatoes, and frozen peas she'd somehow made amazing— had been simple, entirely tasty, and all the better because Everly had made it with her own two hands.

After they'd consumed the food and drink, the evening hush turned to a still night. Darkness fell over the room, and Mad's desk light did little to illuminate the space between them. The air quietly hummed with tension. She looked so lovely, so close. Gabe didn't want to go back to Mad's desk and try to unravel a murder. He wanted to forget it all and spend the evening inside her.

"I should clean up." She started to gather the dishes.

"Stay."

If she went back up to the main floor, he wouldn't likely see her until morning. Perhaps a wise thing since he had pressing problems and he still wasn't sure what her role in Mad's life had been. It probably didn't matter now, but Gabe couldn't stop wondering why Mad had handpicked her to head up Crawford's cybersecurity. Or why his old friend had given her his time and attention if he wasn't sleeping with her. Everly could absolutely be lying about that, but Gabe wasn't sure it mattered now. He wanted her too much to care.

The question was, how to get her to trust him enough to go to bed with him again? With most women, he could whisper a few pretty words or offer her some baubles. Or he could simply explain that no one would believe they weren't sleeping together, so they might as well. He was pretty sure none of those tactics would get him anywhere with Everly.

So he needed to find another reason for her to stay close to him. "Why don't you help me look through some of Mad's notes?"

"I've been thinking . . . what if he left something important in his office at the Crawford building?"

Gabriel shook his head. "After a corporate espionage case about a decade ago, Mad stopped storing anything relevant there except a box of condoms and some lube."

Now that he thought about it, he really wished his pal had used those freaking condoms a few months back.

No. He couldn't think of Sara's child as a mistake. The baby was a blessing—and all the flesh and blood he'd have left of Mad.

"I don't remember him working much from home."

"Probably not, but I'm betting he kept his secrets here. Mad believed that information is power. So he *knew* his enemies."

"Enemies?"

"You accumulate them in our world. We had enemies in school, in college, and definitely in the corporate world. So I'm sure he kept something on everyone he considered a potential enemy. I wouldn't even be surprised to find files on myself and the rest of the guys."

"Shouldn't we start looking? Most anyone he's hoarding information about could be a potential suspect. You've already been through this desk and you didn't find anything. So where would he have put that kind of sensitive information?"

"No idea. I only know he would keep it someplace safe."

"Did he have an actual safe?"

Gabe nodded. "It's up in his bedroom. I found the combination taped inside his desk drawer down here. I checked inside already, but I didn't find anything except some cash and a gun I would be shocked if he actually knew how to use."

Guns had scared Mad. Gabe and some other guys had talked about hunting once, and Mad had wanted nothing to do with it. In fact, he'd tried to talk Dax out of joining the navy because he'd been sure Dax would get shot. But something had scared Mad enough to make him put aside his qualms and buy a firearm.

Everly looked around the room. "He might have another hiding place down here. How old is this building?"

Gabe shrugged. "Pretty old. Mad's family has been in the city for over a hundred years. His great grandfather was one of the railroad barons. He purchased the big family house on Fifth, close to the Vanderbilt mansion. Mad moved into this place after college. He said he couldn't stand how stuffy the mansion was."

"How long has this place been in the family?"

Gabe had heard this story a few times. "A couple of generations. This is where the Crawford men kept their mistresses. Mad suspected that even his father had kept a woman here at one point."

"Doesn't everyone have a place for their trysts?" she said, more absently than acidly as she glanced all around the room, scanning, studying.

As she circled the room, Gabe wondered what the hell Everly was up to. She paused in front of the fireplace.

He frowned. "Where do you think this hiding place might have been?"

She took her time answering. "Well, this is the only part of the house that doesn't look as if it's been remodeled significantly in the past few years. Paint, yeah. But the rest of the house feels updated and has modern conveniences, like recessed LED lighting. For some reason, he kept this office looking far more original."

"I asked Mad once—when he crashed in my guest room during renovations—why he hadn't gutted this part of the house, like he had the rest. He claimed he liked the historic feel in here. At the time, I thought he'd simply gotten tired of having people crawl all over his place and dust spewing everywhere."

"Is it safe to say this house was around during prohibition?"

Shit. Why hadn't he thought of that? "This was a speakeasy. It was one of the ways Alfred Crawford made up for losses in the stock market after the crash. The booze money kept him afloat until his legitimate business was in the black again. You think there are hidey-holes?"

"I think it would fit the period of the house and explain why Maddox never had this lower level remodeled. He told me once he knew where all the skeletons were hidden because he'd found their hiding places. Of course, he was drunk when he said that."

Gabriel didn't look surprised. "I can only speculate what he meant, but I'll bet he had more secrets than I imagined."

She started to knock along the fireplace surround. She was methodical, moving over the wood inch by inch until the rap sounded hollow. "Something's here."

Everly felt along the wood, brushing her hand near a seam in the paneling. He heard a soft snick, then a panel opened, revealing a little compartment shrouded by utter darkness.

"Holy shit." He stared. "You were right. What's in there?"

She eased her hand inside and began feeling around the wall. "Well, I was right about the hidey-hole. But I'm starting to think Maddox really did use this library for its intended purpose because I was wrong about him hiding secrets in here." She pulled out a bottle of Scotch. "Wow. This looks old. Macallan 1926."

Son of a bitch. "They auctioned that fucker off at Sotheby's last year for seventy-five K. He swore he wasn't the asshole who outbid me."

She handed the bottle to him. "Well, it's yours now. Unfortunately, it's not going to help us prove anything except that Maddox valued alcohol far too much."

He cradled the bottle like the precious angel it was. "This is worth every penny. But there has to be more space in there, some other hidden compartment." He set the bottle down on the desk because it definitely wasn't going into hiding again. "A speakeasy would have needed a bigger area to stash liquor. There has to be more behind that compartment door."

Everly shrugged. "Maybe." As she made her way around the room again, she seemed to study the walls. "It stands to reason there'd be a hidden door somewhere around here . . ."

The west wall was dominated by the fireplace, but there was plenty of space on either side. She ran her fingers along the wainscoting.

Gabe glanced around the mantel, too. Mad had settled a few pictures on there, including one of the six of them on their graduation day at Creighton. They looked so damn young, except maybe Zack, who stared at the camera as though he'd known what kind of weighty responsibility the world had in store for him. Gabe still saw that same seriousness on his face when Zack gave a press conference.

Forcing his attention to the rest of the area around the mantel, Gabe studied a pair of sconces mounted on either side more closely. They matched the motif of their surroundings, but they were ancient. Mad had swapped out all the other fixtures in the room for something that looked vintage but ran more efficiently. These had never been touched. In fact, he'd never seen them lit.

With a frown, he reached up and flipped the switch. The small bulb inside one fixture lit up, but nothing else happened.

"Try the other one," Everly said, pointing. "It seems to have its own switch."

"Okay." He moved to the left and flipped that one on. The lightbulb illuminated, but he also heard a distinctive click.

Everly's eyes lit up. "There's a tiny crack in the surround now. I think the whole mantel moves."

Sure enough, the left side of the mantel had eased ever so slightly away from the wall. He reached along the seams, shoving at the now-exposed door. It was heavy but moved with a little force.

"How big is the space inside?" She crowded in behind him.

"I can't tell. It's pretty dark." He activated the flashlight app on his phone and shined it around the entrance. "Mad must have been in here recently. No cobwebs." He looked down. "And no dust on the floor where the mantel meets the wall." He studied the wall to his left. "There must be a light switch."

Gabe hoped he was right about the recent use of the place. Otherwise, he might be walking into a bug-filled haven. He didn't mention that to Everly. She seemed tougher than he'd originally given her credit for, but he didn't know any woman who actually liked insects.

"Here it is." He found the light switch and flicked it on.

A small light illuminated in the ceiling. When he entered, he discovered a hallway. As they followed it around, he found a long, narrow room with ceilings covered in a dark-stained wood and low lighting. Mad had the secret space filled with comfy seating. A sturdy wooden bar sat at the back with a big mirror behind it, affixed to the exposed brick of the brownstone.

Gabe couldn't help but grin, both in humor and sadness. "Mad must have loved this place. Wow."

There had been hidden layers to the man he'd called his best friend for more than two decades. In that moment, he wished they could have shared this discovery together.

But it was damn comforting to share it with Everly, too. He took her hand in his, tangling their fingers.

"This is amazing," she breathed. "Can you imagine what it must have been like back in the day? New York's wealthiest men coming here for a drink. Everything looks authentic, even the barstools." She scanned the room with wonder in her eyes.

Clearly, Mad hadn't told her his secrets, either. Gabe was as cynical as could be, but even he didn't believe anyone could fake that expression. God, she was beautiful. She practically glowed. It was damn near impossible to imagine Mad keeping his hands off her. It had only been a few days since Gabe had made love to her and he was dying. Mad had not been a patient man.

She walked over to the bar and stepped behind it. "The next

ridiculously expensive bottle of liquor I find is mine. I'll sell it and pay off my college loans."

"He's got a record player in here. How crazy is that?" He looked at the antique thing sitting on a shelf behind the bar. He'd seen something like it in movies before. The base looked like an old record player, but there was a funnel-like appendage attached.

"It's a gramophone," she explained. "Turn the handle and see if it plays."

A vinyl record sat on the machine. He found the handle and gave it a few turns. Louis Armstrong's "Body and Soul" played through the room.

"That is really incredible." She gaped, listening with reverence. "It's like we've gone back in time eighty-five years."

"Is that right, doll?" He did a James Cagney impersonation that was best described as terrible.

Clearly trying not to laugh, she bowed her head, lips pursed together. Then something behind the bar caught her eye.

"Look at this." She grabbed a metal box and set it on the polished wooden surface. The metallic sheen glimmered in the low light. "There's a combination lock securing it shut." She glanced Gabe's way. "Any idea what this is?"

He shook his head, drinking in her excitement. Then his logic kicked in, and he frowned. Mad had barely kept anything locked in his safe. Why would he stash a metal lockbox in a hidden room, especially when all someone had to do was pick it up and cut off the lock? Mad's mind had worked in mysterious ways, so he couldn't be sure . . . except Gabe wondered if his friend was trying to tell him something from beyond the grave.

"Are you thinking what I'm thinking?" she breathed. "We may have found something."

He liked the way she said *we*. He knew he should jump all over her find—and he would—but he couldn't let this moment by without touching her.

"Yeah." Gabe held out his hand. "Come here, baby."

She stopped, her full attention focused on him. "Gabriel . . ."

"Dance with me, Everly. Just one dance. How often are you going to get to dance in a real speakeasy?"

She pursed her lips for a moment, but then they turned up into a smile. "You know how to motivate me, Bond."

She joined him in the middle of the room.

"I like it when you call me Gabriel." He drew her lush body to his, closing his eyes at the perfection of her curves against him.

As he began to lead her around the floor in time to the romantic jazz tune, he was thankful for all the stupid dance lessons he'd been forced to take and the cotillions he'd endured. It made this moment so much easier to sway to the music with Everly, bringing her closer and closer.

She sighed, resting her head on his shoulder as if it was the most natural thing in the world. As if she belonged there. "But everyone else calls you Gabe."

"Some people call you Eve," he argued.

"Mostly my dad. Now that he's gone . . . it makes me a little sad."

"Even when I called you Eve during our weekend together? It felt right to say it because you were so perfect, like the woman God must have modeled all others after."

She stiffened but didn't withdraw from his embrace. "This really isn't a good idea."

Of course it wasn't, but he was done fighting his need. "Dance with me."

She settled back down, relaxing a bit against him. "This place really is incredible. How did Maddox keep it secret from everyone, even you?"

He could smell the citrus of the shampoo she'd used and a hint of her peachy-soft skin. "I have no idea. This place would have been a playground for him. I'll ask Sara if he ever mentioned it."

He stopped when he would have gone on. It seemed natural to talk to Everly, but it wasn't right to discuss his sister with her until he was sure what Everly's relationship with Mad had truly been.

But she didn't seem upset or jealous—or have any reaction at all—to Sara's name.

The music played and they swayed together. Everly's head came up. Her eyes gleamed as she stared at him. "This is crazy."

"Yeah. I've never met anyone like you."

She scoffed. "You've met a lot of women. It was hard for me to date when I was a teenager. My father would meet any potential boyfriend at the door in full uniform, gun included."

His parents hadn't met the first girl he'd fucked. Or the second. Or the third. "Your dad sounds like a smart man."

He had a sudden vision of the daughter Everly would surely have one day. The girl would have her strawberry-blond hair and sweet smile. And the boys would be all over her. He could do one better than her dad. He could hire bodyguards to protect her virtue.

Damn. He'd thought about having kids with Everly Parker. He was in way, way too deep.

"I didn't have a real boyfriend until I was in college. Do you know how he met my dad? When we were driving home for the weekend so I could introduce him, Dad pulled him over for speeding. Did a pat down and everything. I swear, I think the only reason Bryan stayed with me was fear that my father would hunt him down if he made me cry."

"I would like to have met your father. He probably would have been better than the cops I dealt with today."

"Oh, he would have been so much harder on you. But I think he would have liked you, too. You're not what he would have expected."

He was fairly certain what people expected of him. "He would have thought I'd be immature and entitled?"

Her cheeks flushed and her gaze slid away from him. "Pretty much. But you're not. I think you're like the rest of us, just trying to hold it together."

He was trying to hold on to her. For the first time in his life, he'd found someone he couldn't let go of. "Everly, I need you."

She rose up on her toes, her head tilted back. "I don't want to but I think I need you, too."

It was as close to an invitation as she'd likely give him, and he wasn't going to question or refuse her. He also wasn't going to rush this time. He'd been out of control with her this morning. It was time to remind her how well he could take care of her.

He cupped her face, his body never losing the rhythm of the dance. Her hands drifted to his waist, holding on to him. She exhaled, closed her eyes, and offered herself up.

His lips met hers in a sensual brush. As their feet kept time to the music, he led her lips in a dance as well. He sank his fingers into her hair and gave over to the deep need to surround himself with this woman. He slid his tongue along her lower lip until she drew in an aroused breath. Then he invaded.

Everly opened for him, her tongue seeking and gliding along his, teasing and playing. She pressed her body flush against his chest. As the kiss deepened, they lost the dance, primal need taking control.

He slid his hands down to her spectacular ass and dragged her fully against him, letting her feel the hard stalk of his erection, so ready to pleasure her. He'd been surprised at how readily she responded to him, but he reacted to her with equal enthusiasm. When she walked in a room, his body prepared itself for sex. When he even thought about her, he got tense and needy.

"Gabriel, how do you do this to me?" She whispered against his lips as her hands began exploring his body.

This was chemistry at its finest, but there was a little piece of him that thought it might be something more. He didn't say it. He could barely think it when he wasn't sure where she'd come from or who she'd been to Mad. "We fit. We're good together."

There was a very nice couch only steps away, and Gabriel backed her toward it. He didn't want to wait. Didn't think he could stand to.

She sank down to the couch and looked up at him, the softness in her eyes slamming into him like a runaway freight train.

He might always need this woman. God help him, it made zero sense, but he might be in love with her.

She held a hand up, beckoning him to join her. He leaned in to do just that when, over the music from the gramophone, he heard what sounded like a door shutting, followed by footsteps on the floor above.

His adrenaline started to flow.

They weren't alone anymore.

NINE

Everly sat up as Gabriel crept across the room, switched the gramophone off, then eased toward the little hall that led to the secret door. "What's wrong?"

Suddenly tense and alert, he pressed a finger to his lips to silence her and nodded at the ceiling. Something was going on above them. She wasn't sure what, but she'd been too lost in the moment to hear. Though she prayed he was mistaken or being overly cautious, she went on high alert.

Following Gabriel, Everly rose on shaky feet and tiptoed across the hardwood floor, praying it didn't creak.

He grabbed her hand and pulled her to the secret door, which was still slightly ajar, as he whispered into her ear. "Someone's upstairs."

The words had barely cleared his lips when she heard it, too. A door slammed. Footfalls clomped.

"Didn't you set the alarm when we came in?" she asked.

"Yeah. Whoever sneaked in apparently knew the alarm code and turned it off."

She breathed a little sigh of relief. "Then it's probably the house-keeper or Dax."

"Dax would have texted first to warn me he was coming." He held his phone, and she watched him text Dax and Connor at once to tell them trouble had arrived.

"What if the housekeeper forgot something?"

"Then she's about to get the scare of her life." Gabriel looked down at her. "You stay here. I'm going out there to grab a few items from Mad's desk."

She shook her head and gripped his hand. "We're safer in here."

But he'd already slipped free from her hold and was easing back into the library. Everly tried to see out, but the view from behind the hidden door was limited.

More loud footsteps resounded through the otherwise deserted house. Something else—a drawer, maybe—opened and closed. The sound repeated a multitude of times from the direction of the kitchen. Then she heard what sounded like furniture being overturned. Glass shattered.

"What the fuck?" a man from somewhere above cursed. "This was supposed to be easy."

Closer. The voices were getting closer. That last squeak had been above her head. They were on the stairway and it only led to one place. Right here. Her heart pounded in her chest. It was probably kids look-ing for money or drugs, or the reporters had been quicker than Gabriel had given them credit for.

But they wouldn't know the alarm code. Dread pooled inside her because there was another explanation.

Whoever had killed Maddox had come back to find or cover up something. Whoever was on those stairs wouldn't be swayed or run from the idea that they'd called the police. Someone had gone to great pains to kill Maddox and he wouldn't hesitate to kill her and Gabriel, too.

She pushed the door open a little farther and peeked out in an attempt to warn Gabe that they had incoming. He stood at the desk, opening the drawer with quiet precision, then extracted something.

Frowning, Everly peered, trying to discern what he thought was important enough to risk his life. The glint of metal gave him away. A gun. And he didn't fumble with it at all as he checked the clip and flicked off the safety. He knew exactly what he was doing.

"Lighten up. It's easy. Focus." Another stranger's voice floated through the lower level.

"Nothing in this part of town is easy. Did you get the money up front like I told you?"

Based on their deep voices, the two men drifted ever closer. Gabriel lifted his head to the sound. He was trapped on the other side of the room. He zipped his gaze at her and motioned her to shut the door.

She wasn't about to leave him out there. The door to this secret room didn't open easily. If he had to trip the switch to release it again so he could hide in this adjoining space with her, it could cost him critical moments.

"I got half up front. Cash," the first one said.

"Do you smell that?" the second asked, sounding as if he had nearly reached the bottom of the stairs.

"What?"

The floorboard creaked as they reached the library. They were coming too fast. In seconds, they would round the corner of the room and see Gabriel.

Fear gripped her, and she looked around for anything she could use as a weapon. She spotted the fireplace tools outside the secret doorway. A poker leaned against the marble surround. She snatched it up and gripped the thin but sturdy column of metal.

Gabriel glared at her from across the room. It wasn't hard to read his lips as he mouthed a warning to her. *Don't you dare.*

She wasn't about to cower and hide when she could help. She'd been raised by one tough cop and still trained with the security guards who stood sentry around Crawford's building.

"This dude has been dead for days, but it smells like someone was cooking recently," said one of the men as he rounded the corner into the library. "If we're not alone, we need to get this shit done fast. There can't be any witnesses."

Gabe crouched under the desk and hit the screen on his phone three times. 911. Within seconds, he began whispering to the dispatcher.

"Damn. We should have waited to light up the top floor. This place looks ripe for the picking." They crossed the library floor with all the subtlety of elephants.

Everly shrank back. Two men. All in black. The tallest glanced around the room, looking under the sofa, tossing books from the shelves onto the floor, then heading for the desk, holding a bag in one hand and a bottle in the other.

"There's no time for that. We need this place to go up fast. One more room, then we get out of here."

Gasoline. She could smell it faintly but every second seemed to bring it closer. Oh, god. They'd torched the top floor. While she and Gabriel had been dancing, these men had set the house on fire.

The intruder stopped in front of the desk, lifting papers and nosing around before leaning over to sort through the drawers. With a curse, he shoved everything on the floor. What the hell were they looking for? Everly didn't get to think much about it before the tall one pounded a fist on the desk, then ignited his lighter and held it to the rag poking out of the bottle's neck.

Molotov cocktail.

From up above she heard the shriek of fire alarms.

Gabriel stood up from under the desk, pointing the gun with confidence. "Stop right now. The cops are already on their way."

The man with the bottle cursed and immediately threw it at Gabriel.

As he ducked behind the desk again, Everly bit back a scream. The curtains behind Gabriel immediately went ablaze.

The sound of gunfire ricocheted through the room. Everly's heart chugged with fear, especially when the second man pulled a gun from a holster at his side and started creeping toward Gabriel.

"Leave it, man. Let's go. Bastard's as good as dead." The first man darted up the stairs once more.

"Les . . ." the man called to no avail.

Chaos seemed to take over. The library was on fire. The sound of glass breaking cracked through the space, but she couldn't tell where it was coming from. And the second man hadn't been as eager to leave as the first.

A dark figure moved past her, stalking Gabriel.

She couldn't see him, couldn't tell if Gabriel had been hurt. She had one shot at saving him.

She slipped out from behind the secret door and immediately felt the heat. Flames licked the wall as smoke filled her every sense. Biting back the need to cough, she moved in behind Gabriel's attacker.

Everly didn't think twice. Hesitation killed. Her father had taught her that. *Don't ever raise a weapon you're not willing to use, baby girl.*

She raised the poker and whipped it down on the man's head as hard as she could. A dull thud rose above the crackling, hissing sound of the spreading flames. Their assailant stumbled forward, falling to a heap on the floor. His gun clattered out of his limp hand.

Gabriel popped up over the desk, pointing that gun right where the thug had stood. Unfortunately, Everly was rooted there now, frozen, poker still in hand. Her fingers shook and went numb. She let the poker fall to the floor.

Gabriel's face flushed as he lowered the gun. "What are you doing? I could have killed you."

"Are you hurt?" Her hands were shaking, but she was pleased her voice was still solid.

He scowled. "I'm fine."

Heat began pouring off the curtains. The smoke burned her lungs. "We have to get the fire out."

Gabriel shook his head. "It's too late for that. They must have left themselves a path out. We need to find it."

"Shit," a deep voice said. Les stood in the middle of the library, his eyes on his fallen friend.

Gabriel raised the gun again and aimed. "Don't move."

But the man dropped the bottle he'd been holding and ran. A crashing sound split the air and the area rug under his feet burst into flames.

There was no way out now.

Everly looked down at the man on the floor. He wasn't moving at all. Gabriel picked up the arsonist's gun and pocketed it. He grabbed the file folder he'd been organizing.

"Is he dead?" It was a stupid question because the man's eyes were open and unseeing.

Gabriel shook her lightly, bringing her back to the moment. "You did what you had to do. But we're going to join him if we don't get moving and find a way out of here."

Everly stood, jittery yet numb. What was his name? Did he have a family who would miss him? What had he come to Maddox's house searching for before he set the place on fire?

"C'mon," Gabriel shouted over the crackling din of the growing fire. "I'll try to find a blanket or something to cover us. We need to protect our skin from the flames. Grab that box we found in the secret room."

When she looked around, the blaze had grown to something fast approaching a conflagration. Fear slammed into her. It helped her focus on escaping . . . but only to a point. She had to decide that she wanted to survive. And that took bravery. Her father's voice played in Everly's head. *Make the decision, Eve. Always choose to live.* Shaking away her shock and terror, she nodded. If she made it out of here alive, she'd have time to sort through everything else later.

"Okay." No matter what happened, she would fight to find a way out. With Gabriel.

She slipped back into the secret room and quickly grabbed the lockbox from the bar. The temperature felt much cooler in this brick room. While the fire was already doing damage to the house around them, she could barely smell the smoke in here. A cool breeze hit her face.

She'd found the way out.

Gabe forced himself to stay calm. He'd done it through the hour it took them to find their way to the surface. Everly had found the series of tunnels Mad's great grandfather had used to store and transport his hooch. His secret supply route had become their way to safety.

He'd been perfectly reasonable as he'd called Connor to pick them up after they'd emerged from the tunnels. He was fairly certain he'd shown no outward signs of the rolling tension that had overtaken him the minute he realized someone was coming after them. Even through his second police interview in less than twenty-four hours, he'd maintained a level of sanity he didn't feel.

"I'm going to get cleaned up." Everly stood at the bottom of the stairs in Connor's apartment. "Are you sure I'm not intruding? I can find a hotel."

"Stay. Your room is through the second door on the left, Everly." Gabe's tone was perfectly normal. He wasn't barking orders and marking his territory the way every primal instinct inside him wanted to. But he knew the adrenaline crash was coming—and fast. "There's an en suite connected to the room. You can use that shower. In the morning, Dax will find us both some fresh clothes."

"Thanks," she murmured, then climbed the stairs, her weariness evident in her slow ascent and slumped shoulders. She stopped halfway up and turned back to him. "For everything, Gabriel. Are you sure we shouldn't go through the things we saved from Mad's house tonight?"

"Get cleaned up. We'll deal with it tomorrow." The order came out a little harsher than he'd meant it to, but his tone did the trick. She turned and trudged her way up the stairs.

As soon as she disappeared, Dax whistled beside him. "You're in bad shape, brother."

Roman shook his head as he closed up his briefcase on the nearby coffee table. "I don't think I've ever seen you wound so tight. Is this about the cops?"

The police suspected he'd set that fire himself to cover up some clue to Mad's murder. They were still trying to identify the man's body inside the brownstone and figure out how he played into the scenario. The other man had apparently escaped. But that wasn't what upset Gabe. "I'm fine."

Connor shoved a glass of Scotch in his hand. "Sure you are. You need to calm down before you deal with her. Do you have any idea what those men were looking for?"

Gabe gratefully took the Scotch and knocked it back in one swallow. "None. They left everything of value, as far as I could tell. They seemed more interested in papers and files and books. It doesn't add up."

"With one thug dead and the other missing, we can't get any answers."

"Exactly. And Everly didn't see or hear anything I didn't, so she can't provide any clues." He sighed. "I have no idea what to do with her."

"What do you mean?"

"She damn near got herself killed tonight. Once those assholes figured out we were in the house, they tried to kill us. She took one of them out before I could do it. I damn near shot her."

Connor led him to the sofa and slid into the chair across from him. They were in the apartment he'd bought five years before. Gabe wasn't exactly sure when or how Connor had come into his money. Sparks had come to Creighton on a lacrosse scholarship. He'd been brought in to captain the ailing team and he'd turned it around fast. His own family had consisted of a single mother who'd spent her life waitressing in a bar. She'd thanked God Connor was athletic and happily shipped him off to boarding school. All too often, she hadn't picked him up for holidays. The rest of the group had split time taking him home on vacations.

But this place, while understated, bespoke wealth. It was the penthouse of an exclusive building on the Upper West Side. Clearly, his buddy was doing all right for himself.

"She isn't the type of woman who will hide when she can fight. I've been studying her, asking around." Connor had his own Scotch in hand. "Her employees really like her."

"She honestly saved your ass tonight?" Roman asked, handling the old bottle of booze they'd saved from Mad's house, along with the files and the metal box. Thankfully, Connor had turned up before the police so none of what they'd escaped with had been confiscated as evidence. "And this Scotch? She should get a medal for saving this. Let's open it."

Gabe moved the bottle of vintage alcohol out of Roman's reach and passed him the much more reasonable twenty-five-year-old bottle. His buddy was missing the salient point. "Yes, but only after she took a crazy chance that could have ended with me putting a bullet through her heart."

He still couldn't get that moment out of his head. He'd crouched behind that desk, every sense he possessed focused on one thing and one thing only: those footsteps creeping closer across the floor.

Gabe had held his breath, waiting, waiting . . . He'd timed it just right and darted to his feet, more than ready to pull the trigger. He'd visualized taking the man out moments before he'd stood. Except as he began applying pressure to the trigger, he'd registered Everly standing there with her hair mussed, a fireplace poker gripped tightly in her hands.

He could have killed her. He could have accidentally put a bullet in her, and she would have ceased to breathe. To exist. He would never have been able to hold or kiss her again. And now he wanted to strangle her because he was still so angry. Scared, he acknowledged. The thought of never seeing her again terrified him. He didn't like the feeling.

"Go easy on her, man," Dax said as he stood. "You owe her. She was smart as hell to figure out that place had escape tunnels."

Connor frowned as he set his now-empty glass down. "It makes me wonder what else Mad was hiding."

"I have no idea." He turned up to Roman. "You really don't know why he wanted to talk to Zack?"

Roman shook his head. "Mad didn't tell me. He called and asked me to schedule a meeting. I told him Zack was too busy because he was pissed at Mad at the time. You know he always had a soft spot for Sara. After the way Mad treated her, he wasn't in the mood to reminisce. I think he feels incredibly guilty about refusing now."

"But Mad was coming to DC anyway?"

"He told me he'd camp outside the Oval Office if he had to." Roman shrugged.

"Does Zack know a man named Sergei?"

Roman paused to think for a moment. "I can see if he's met with anyone who goes by that name lately, but I don't recall that he's spent time with a Sergei. Honestly, since Joy was killed, he works day and night."

"Mad's last words to me were a question about that man. Dig for me, okay? Ask Zack." He tapped the metal box they'd smuggled out. "I saved as many of the files from Mad's desk as I could, along with this box we found hidden in the secret room. Can you get that open?"

Connor studied the lockbox. "One way or another. It's deceptively strong. Also fire resistant. He wanted this info to survive. I'll have it open by morning. It's late tonight. Why don't we all head to bed? There's not a lot we can do until I get this sucker open and the police have more information. Once they ID the dead guy, we can try to figure out who hired him. Maybe then, we might piece together who's behind this crazy shit, maybe even who killed Mad."

Gabe had been thinking the same thing. And the waiting added another layer to his untenable mood. He glanced back, his gaze climbing the stairs to where he knew Everly would probably be showering, water sliding down her bare body as she got ready for bed. Damn, even though exhaustion and worry weighed him down, one thought of her and he was beyond ready to climb inside her again.

Roman clapped him on the shoulder, bringing him out of his reverie. "Go to her."

With that advice, his friend headed back to his hotel. Dax waved to them both before climbing the stairs to the other guest room.

Gabe hesitated.

Connor shifted his stare from the lockbox and met his gaze. "I didn't bother to make up the sofa bed."

Gabe tightened. He wanted Everly, but she needed sleep more than his lust. "Maybe you should."

He scoffed and poured himself another Scotch. "Be honest with yourself. You're not going to sleep on the couch." He winced Gabe's way. "How's Sara going to handle Everly? She must have seen the gossip sites by now."

Sara was a reasonable woman, but her anger toward Mad hadn't abated much. Though she'd been quiet during the funeral, his death seemed to have sharpened her fury to something approaching hate. Some of that transferred to the women Mad had flaunted to the press since he'd left her. Sara needed time to heal and bury the bitterness now that she'd buried the man. "I'll tell her the papers have the relationship between Mad and Everly wrong."

"So you'll lie to her."

"I don't know what went on between those two. She swears nothing. Even Dax believes her." He raked a hand through his hair. "Hell, I don't know exactly what's going on between the two of us. Either way, I don't think I need to drag Sara into it. It could be weeks before she comes back to the city. If—and I mean if—Everly and I are still seeing each other then, I'll ease Sara into it."

"Or you could choose to believe Everly and tell Sara to deal. You've treated your sister like she's made of glass and she isn't. She knew who Mad was when she got involved with him. She knew damn well how it could end."

"Do you believe there's any way Mad and Everly weren't involved?"

"Not a chance, but then I'm not the one who's crazy about the girl. Sometimes happiness requires a certain suspension of disbelief, especially the romantic kind. If you wanted my advice, I would tell you that you can't blame her for who she dated before she knew you. Maybe it's best if you forget any relationship she had with Mad. She doesn't seem to be yearning for him, but the way she looks at you is awfully interesting." He shrugged. "If you want her, take her. And don't look back."

"I guess it's good I didn't ask for your advice." He didn't like how Connor's words made him feel. Eager. Reckless. Desperate. "Are you going to bed?"

Connor's head shook. "Nah. I'm a night owl. Besides, I think I might have figured out who our nasty little blogger is. I caught her scent this afternoon and I've exchanged two e-mails with her. I'm pretending to be a crazy conspiracy theorist. She thinks I've got a scoop. We'll see if I'm right in the morning. I gave her some information. If it shows up on Capitol Scandals, we'll know I'm close."

"Her?"

"Yes." Connor's face was illuminated by the light of his computer screen. "I was surprised, too. Her name is Lara Armstrong. She's Senator Armstrong's only daughter, and she really tears into her father's party a lot. Lucky for me, I'm a sucker for a rich girl with daddy issues." He laughed. "Go to bed. I'll get the box opened first thing in the morning. For now, I'm going to see if I can find a way to crush this earnest little blogger."

"After you told me to go easy on Everly?"

"I'm not emotionally attached to Lara Armstrong and I don't intend to be," Connor explained with all the heat of an exterminator talking about a bug he intended to eradicate. "By the way, there's a box of condoms in the nightstand."

From what he could tell, Connor might not be emotionally attached to anyone but his childhood friends. But that couldn't matter right now. Gabe needed to take care of his own issues before he helped his buddy.

He stalked up the stairs, well aware that his cock already throbbed for Everly. He needed to make a few things clear to her. They'd decided they were in this together for the duration. Partners of a sort.

She was about to find out who the senior partner was.

He opened the door to the guest room. She'd been smart enough to not lock it.

Her purse looked out of place among the masculinity of the antique paneling, dark iron-frame bed, and gray linens. Whoever had decorated Connor's home believed in austerity. The only thing that saved the room from being oppressive was the white ceiling, with its intricate moldings and details common in prewar buildings.

That droopy black purse was all she had since she couldn't go home. She really couldn't now that every major news outlet in the country was spewing her name and digging into her past. Everly was alone in life . . . and he was the only person who could take care of her.

Gabe turned the bed down, not wanting to bother with it later. When he opened the nightstand drawer, he found the condoms right where Connor said they would be. At least something was predictable today.

After grabbing one, he opened the pocket door between the bedroom and bathroom. Steam floated out from the shower. Her clothes were neatly folded and placed on the countertop along with one of Connor's T-shirts for sleeping. Apparently, he didn't have the same wardrobe of women's castoffs Mad had collected.

The thought of Everly wearing Connor's clothes disturbed him. She didn't need to wear anything to bed. He intended to make sure she didn't put that T-shirt on.

He pulled off his own clothes with none of the care Everly had put into doffing hers. They fell to floor, then he stroked his cock twice before rolling the condom on. All the while he envisioned her in the shower, her soft, curvy body slick with moisture.

Unable to wait a second longer, he stalked to the shower opening. She stood under the spray of the rainfall head with her back to him. He drank in the graceful line of her spine, the exaggerated curve of her waist, and the perfect globes of her ass. Her hair reached halfway down her back when it was wet, a gorgeous tangle of blond and red. Itching to touch her, he felt so hard it hurt.

She froze, her back stiffening. "I knew you would come sooner or later."

At least he hadn't scared her. He stepped in behind her, giving in to his instincts, his need to possess. He cupped her shoulders and ran his hands down to her breasts. "I couldn't stay away. I'm not even going to try. I want you."

"It's a mistake." Even as she said the words, her head fell back against his chest and he felt her sigh.

If being with her was a mistake, it was one he intended to make over and over. "Do you want me?"

Her hand drifted back to touch his hip. Her palm flowed down against his ass as she wriggled her own. His cock found the seam of her pretty backside and he nearly lost it.

"You know I do," she muttered.

Everly didn't sound happy about it. Honestly, he wasn't thrilled with his obsession, either. But he knew whatever feeling flowed between them was bigger than they were. Fighting it would be futile.

"Then stop thinking and let it be for tonight. Everything else will sort itself out."

Her breasts filled his palms with a sweet weight. He ran his thumbs across the nipples. The little nubs were already hard. Gabe loved how she squirmed against him and how her breathing picked up when he tweaked those pearls.

"We're safe here," he murmured. "We probably should have come here in the first place, but I wanted to see what we could find at Mad's."

Her every curve pressed against him, teasing and taunting him. "We had to go there. We have to figure out who killed him or we'll never be safe again. I can't let you go to jail."

He wrapped an arm around her waist and pulled her against his body. "You don't worry about that. Keeping me out of jail is Roman's job. But we need to get one thing clear, baby."

He turned her around, walking her back until she reached the shower wall. He gripped both her hands in one of his and forced them high over her head, leaving her vulnerable and open to his stare, his touch.

"What's that, Gabriel?" Her tone had gone husky.

"The next time I tell you to hide, you do it." He loomed over her, intending to imprint his will on her.

She shook her head. "I couldn't leave you."

"I almost killed you."

Her soft, velvet curves were distracting him from his very reasonable lecture. By the way her nipples puckered, despite the warm water, Gabe knew she wasn't really listening anyway. As he crowded her, he felt the hard points against his chest. Between the water at his back and her skin blanketing his front, he was engulfed in warmth.

"But you didn't," Everly replied. "You wouldn't have. You have to know how scared I was for you. I couldn't leave you out there alone."

"Never again, Everly." He couldn't hang on much longer—to his temper or his need. He couldn't lecture her when all he wanted was to be inside her. He let his hand slide down her body, teasing its way to the cleft of her sex. "Tell me you want me again."

"I want you so much." Her words came out in a sexy groan.

"Tell me you need me." He slid a single finger against her clitoris. She was already wet, her needy bud standing hard. His cock jumped at the sensation of her arousal coating his finger.

"I need you." Her hips wriggled as though she couldn't stop herself from seeking more of his touch.

"What were you thinking about that made you this wet?" Yeah, he didn't give a shit about a lecture now, only about how slick she was, how tight she would be around him. He rubbed her clit in rhythmic circles, just enough to coax her whimpers.

"I was thinking about you. I wish we'd never left that hotel. I wish we'd stayed there, that I was still Eve and you were Gabriel. I don't want the rest of it. But I want you."

Her words cut through him. He ached for the same thing. He wanted her without all the doubts and suspicions and danger.

He slanted his mouth over hers and kissed her with everything he had. Why wait? Everly had known he would come after her. She was focused on the pleasure he could give her. No doubt, she was ready for him now. She'd known damn straight she wasn't sleeping alone tonight. Gabe didn't intend to let her down.

"If you want me, then take me deep. Forget about everything else. All that matters is we're alive and here with one another." He kissed her, stroking his tongue against hers before he lifted her and shoved her flat against the wall.

Everly gasped as she wrapped her arms and her legs around him. His cock was so close to the slick heaven he felt desperate to be inside. Her breath sawed in and out of her chest. Her pupils dilated. Heat seared him. In that moment, he felt as if he had been cold all his life until he'd met her.

"Hold on tight," he demanded.

She clasped her hands behind his neck and locked her ankles at the small of his back. Gabe shifted his hold, grabbing a handful of her ass and lifting her, aligning their bodies. Then he let gravity do the work.

She slid onto the head of his cock, then began enveloping his staff in her tight, blistering grip. He groaned, the sound magnified by the small, enclosed space. As he penetrated deeper, she gasped and her head fell against his shoulder, her nails digging into his skin.

"Gabriel," she breathed. "It feels so good."

She was the one who felt good. Every inch of her he claimed made his head spin more. As she lowered onto his cock, he nipped at her neck. Her pulse pounded against his tongue. He held her tighter.

For a long moment, he remained still, letting her get used to the feel of him filling her up entirely. Everly surrounded him. Saturated him. Intoxicated him. She was everywhere as he tasted her skin, drowned in her moans.

His next thrust was an exquisite fight through her tight clasp. She gripped him as if she'd never let go before he slid back into her like a finger through melted chocolate. He sank in again, plunging farther, faster, harder into her sweet depths. Thinking went out the window. Hell, breathing wasn't far behind. Right now, there was only her.

This was more than sex. It was pure connection. He was bound to Everly in a way he'd never been to another woman, in a way he'd never imagined being to *any* woman. And right now, the fact that he couldn't join their bodies in every way possible simply wasn't acceptable. Gabe wanted her as affixed to him as he felt to her, knowing she was utterly with him in the moment.

"Kiss me," he demanded gruffly.

She lifted her head. Their gazes collided. Her chest rose hard and fast with every breath as she wriggled on him. With a cry, she surged closer, and her lips crashed over his.

As he drank Everly in, he lifted her until he'd almost withdrawn completely. Then he shifted his grip to push down on her hips, impaling her. "So fucking good."

She groaned against his lips, and he thrust his tongue into her mouth. She surrendered, opening to him and letting him have his way. She gripped his nape, her fingers trying to sink into his severely short hair, silently entreating him to give her more.

With pleasure.

Gabe started to thrust in earnest. Damn it, he wasn't going to last, but at least he could feel her beginning to tighten around him. He smiled in savage satisfaction. She wouldn't last, either. If he timed this right, they could find mind-blowing satisfaction together.

With a little mewl, her eyes drifted closed.

"No. When I'm inside you, you're my Eve. You look at me while I'm fucking you." He refused to let her drift—to mentally be anywhere else with anyone else.

Her lashes fluttered open and their stares locked. Beautiful hazel eyes. Sometimes amber, sometimes warm brown, sometimes—like now—so green. Her eyes were warm and giving, almost embracing him. When he looked into those eyes, he couldn't imagine she was anything but innocent. "I'm here. I'm with you. I need you."

Primal desire rolled through him. This act was beyond pleasure. Gabe intended to use it to make certain that she was every bit as attached to him as he felt to her. They had to share more than flesh and bliss. They needed honesty. And burying himself inside her while he stared down into her goddamn soul felt as starkly honest as he'd ever been.

This was also about trust. They were in a dangerous situation, and she needed to trust him to do more than give her an orgasm. She needed to trust him with her life if they wanted to survive.

He crushed her against the wall, slamming his cock in deeper still. He shoved in, tilted out, thinking of nothing beyond making her eyes widen with pleasure. When he submerged completely again and ground against her pelvis, she parted her lips to scream.

He covered them with his own, drinking down the sounds of her release. He wanted those sounds for himself. Always. He'd rip apart any fucker who tried to take her from him.

As she shattered and convulsed, her slick flesh spasming around him, a tingle zipped down his spine. Ecstasy spiraled out of control, poleaxing him. Gabe felt utterly lost, as if some part of him would now and forevermore be a part of this woman. With a hoarse shout, he came, pumping deep inside her. He hated the condom in that moment, wanting absolutely nothing between them.

As the pleasure subsided, his muscles turned to mush. Slowly, he withdrew and let her slide down the shower wall until her feet touched the floor. But she didn't look much steadier than he felt. His whole body pulsed, replete—for now—but he couldn't quite make himself move away from her. Gabe didn't want to stop touching her.

He reached for the soap and turned her so she faced the wall. She leaned back against him, utterly trusting him to not let her go.

"I need you, too," he whispered against her ear. He moved his hand over her body, worshipping her the way she deserved. The first time might have been rough and quick, but he had the whole night with her. He wasn't about to waste it.

TEN

I need you, too.

Everly knew they were only words he'd uttered in the aftermath of passion, but everything feminine inside her responded.

As they'd made their way out of the tunnel following their escape from Mad's house, Gabriel had gripped her hand, leading the way to safety. They'd had to wend through dank, dark tunnels with only one light to make their way through the gloom. Everly had never once worried he would leave her behind.

At Connor's penthouse, she'd climbed into the shower, trying to hold herself together—not to crave his nearness and protection so much—but she'd been shaking. Every time she'd closed her eyes, she could still feel the flames licking around the room, threatening to consume them. The realization that they had almost died hit her. Then Gabriel had come to her, touched her, wiped all that away with his furious possession. He'd proven why she needed him.

After their hurried coupling, he'd washed her from head to toe, his hands sliding across her skin with tender care. Her adrenaline had finally crashed. And Gabriel had held her while she'd cried. He hadn't spoken, merely let his touch echo his earlier words.

In that moment, he really did seem to need her, too.

Now, she relaxed in his arms, replete and lulled, as he carried her to the bed. He laid her on the mattress, across soft linens.

Giving herself to Gabriel Bond tonight, however, put her in uncharted territory. She couldn't pretend that whatever they shared meant nothing but simple pleasure and a way to forget her troubles. They'd admitted they needed one another. If he left her tomorrow morning, she would likely mourn him for the rest of her life because she was absolutely certain she was falling in love.

He opened a drawer in the nightstand and pulled out a box of condoms. Thankful he was ever prepared, Everly blinked at him as he stood above her, raking his hot stare over her splayed body. He paused at her breasts and the juncture of her thighs. That intent gaze should have rattled her, but his blue eyes held such warmth that she couldn't be anxious, much less gather the will to cover herself. What, exactly, did he see in her? When he looked at her like that, she felt beautiful.

"God, do you have any idea what you do to me, Everly?" His voice sounded thick, raspy.

She had an idea, since his erection stood thick and tall again. No escaping the fact that he aroused her unbearably. A little smile flitted across her lips.

"Of course you do." He grinned ruefully in return. "Damn, you have the most beautiful breasts I've ever seen. Tomorrow morning, call Hilary and tell her to let everyone know that you're taking the rest of the week off."

She blushed at the compliment, then realized what the sneaky bastard had done. "I have to go to work, Gabriel. With Mulford on vacation, I'm in charge of all of security. And I'm the executive on duty since Tavia is probably buried with spinning Mad's death in the press and putting the finishing touches on the upcoming foundation gala. She's only got Valerie to help, and it's a lot of work. Besides, after my name has been tossed all around the press, I'm not going to give the people I work with any more reason to gossip that I'm sleeping with the boss."

She turned over. If they were going to have an actual discussion, she couldn't do that spread out and naked on the bed. She had to get at least somewhat dressed. Connor's T-shirt would do.

Before she could reach for it, Gabriel's hands wrapped around her ankles. He flipped her back over and joined her on the bed, planting one knee between her spread legs. He hovered above her.

"You are sleeping with the boss, and it's none of their business. I wasn't joking. Call in tomorrow and take vacation." He smoothed his hands up her legs. "I like these, too. Every single inch of you is gorgeous."

"I have responsibilities at work, and last time I looked, seeing to the needs of your penis isn't part of my job description."

"I'll appoint someone else to be the executive on duty. The place can run for a few days without you. Damn, even your toes are pretty. I was never a toe guy until you." He nipped at the flesh around her polished nails.

It sent shivers up her spine. "Gabriel, I can't allow this . . . whatever we're doing together to completely disrupt my professional life. Buttering me up with compliments won't change my mind."

"I wasn't buttering you up. I was gloating because all this pretty flesh is mine." He kissed his way down her leg. "All fucking mine. By the way, the company is mine, too. You might have forgotten, but I'm not only *the* boss, I'm *your* boss. I say you're taking time off. You won't be leaving this apartment for a while."

But she had a date tomorrow to meet the informant who supposedly had the scoop about Maddox's murder. Of course, this mysterious stranger had also warned her not to get caught in Gabriel's web, but Everly knew she was fully ensnared. Yes, they'd agreed to be partners in all this, but she still hesitated to tell him about the meeting. Gabriel would disapprove. In fact, he'd probably leave her here with his watchdogs and make contact with the informant himself. That couldn't happen. She'd been instructed to come alone and didn't want to risk losing this source in case he had vital information. Everly intended to find out what this person knew, especially if it explained who'd killed her friend, and it exonerated Gabriel.

He had to be innocent. She couldn't think otherwise, but she also couldn't give him everything she had. If she did, he would remove her from the investigation. Everyone knew two heads were better than one. He needed her.

He kissed her kneecap, and she couldn't hold back a shiver. Who would have guessed a person had so many sensitive nerve endings there? As he cradled her hips and breathed over her skin, he derailed her train of thought, which had likely been his plan all along.

"I have a department to run and it doesn't run itself," she argued, though her voice sounded a bit more breathless than she'd like. "I can't disappear indefinitely."

He dropped to his knees, positioning his mouth right over her pussy. "You're going to have to because the minute the press finds out you're in the office, they'll be all over that building, stirring up trouble. No one will get anything done."

"I know a thing or two about securing a building. I think I can keep a bunch of nosy reporters out of our workspace."

"You're in charge of cybersecurity. And you can't monitor every maintenance worker, deliveryman, and temporary office assistant who comes on the premises. Anyone could slide in under false pretenses. Even if you could manage to keep the pesky paparazzi out of the office, they would only hunt down other Crawford employees during their off hours and want to know what sort of on-the-job duties you're performing. Guess what those folks would say."

Everly already knew, and none of it was complimentary. She sighed.

"You and I staying away from Crawford's headquarters right now actually helps productivity and morale."

Gabriel had a point, damn him. But she needed to get that SD card from her safe. She hadn't managed to view all the photos and she wanted to study them. "All right. Then I'll work on things from home. I'll need someone to pick up my equipment and—oh . . ." She gasped as he leaned in and breathed over the tender mound of her sex. "I can't think when you do that."

With a smile, he did it again. "I don't want you thinking about anything but me."

As if she could. Since the moment she'd met him, he'd overtaken her every waking thought. If she let him, he would dominate her life. And they'd butt heads because he needed that control. Everly hadn't allowed anyone to tell her how to live her life since childhood.

He held her down with a firm grip and spread her legs wider, opening her up for his delectation. "This is a beautiful pussy. I wonder what I should do with it."

How the hell could she answer that when she could barely hold in a plea?

Gabriel could be so powerful and passionate. She loved that about him. But she also adored his teasing side. He was a very complex man—and a frustrating one. Despite the orgasm she'd had barely fifteen minutes earlier, he'd reawakened her body so quickly, so easily. She needed to feel his tongue on her, diving deep. His mouth lingered right above her most needy spot, and she ached. Everly couldn't hold in a whimper.

She knew he was distracting her from the real issues, but in that moment she simply couldn't focus on anything else. He had her right where he wanted her.

"I can think of a few things," she managed to eke out.

"I can, too. Don't move." He released his grip on her legs and gently parted the petals of her sex. "Such a lovely pink. And look at that cream. Is that for me?"

"You know it is."

He didn't look convinced. "I need to be sure this is all mine."

"It's yours," she wailed.

With his fingertips, he traced against her flesh lightly, just enough to tempt her. Lord, he was killing her.

"Say the words, Eve. Tell me what I want to hear."

She knew exactly what he sought. "I belong to you."

Had he wanted her to admit that for his pride . . . or his heart?

"Yes, you do." And he sounded very satisfied about that.

He licked her, his tongue plunging into her furrow. A shock of heat flushed through her body. Everly gripped the sheets with a high-pitched hitching of breath. It took everything she had not to squirm.

"Show me this pussy is mine." Demand rang in his low voice. "That all of you fucking belongs to me. No one else."

Gabriel was definitely possessive. Even that first night he'd given off a covetous vibe. Now he seemed intent on proving that she was his—and his alone. But he didn't have anything to worry about.

"I'm not interested in anyone else. All I can think about is you."

He softened slightly. "Good. I don't share. I'm definitely not sharing this." He rubbed little circles around her clit before he took another long, slow swipe at her with his tongue. "Hmm. Do you have any idea how good you taste?"

She shook her head. "I do?"

He held a single finger up as if to ask her to give him a second. He settled back between her legs and covered her with his mouth. Another rush of heat scorched her system, especially when he settled in deeper. His tongue plunged her depths, penetrating her as his cock had earlier. Over and over, he speared her deep, invading and arousing her until he had to pin her to the sheets to stop her from wriggling with every moan.

Once he'd subdued her, he lifted one hand, thumbing her clit in light, teasing circles. His tongue worked her opening at the same time, driving her out of her mind.

"This is mine." The words rumbled against her folds. "Your orgasms are mine. Give me one now. Come against my tongue so I can taste you."

Everly couldn't hold back a second longer.

The pressure surged between her legs, then exploded in a white-hot burst. She cried out, calling his name as he hurtled her into a blaze of satisfaction. It flowed through her veins, making her blood hum. In that moment, Gabriel felt like the center of her universe, as if her very world revolved around him.

He crawled up her body as he covered it with his own and crushed her to the mattress. "This is what you taste like. It's heaven."

He slanted his mouth over hers and probed deep. Instantly, she tasted her own tangy-tart flavor on his tongue. He wasn't satisfied with a peck or even a short mating of mouths. Not Gabriel. He dominated her with his lips, imprinting himself on her, telling her without another word that he owned her all the way down to her soul.

She was breathless when he finally released her. With a swift move, he rolled to his back and lifted her.

"On top of me, Eve. Now. Fuck me."

His commanding growl sent a fresh jolt of heat sizzling through her system. She eased off his body just enough to straddle him, shockingly eager to join with him again and feel the consuming pleasure only Gabriel could seem to give her.

The first night they'd spent together, Gabriel had been in charge, leading her to sweet oblivion as he'd taken her over and over. Now, as she stared down at him, Everly realized he'd finally put her in the driver's seat.

He looked so gorgeous with his blue eyes burning in his flushed face, like a big predator lying in wait for his prey, plotting his next move. She had a feeling she'd better enjoy her chance to call the shots because it wouldn't be long before he snatched control from her again.

Everly brushed her palms across the corded muscles of his shoulders and his chest, reveling in the hard feel of his flesh, his accelerating pulse. She leaned in to press her lips over the beat of his heart, loving the way he closed his eyes. When she licked at one masculine, brown nipple, he groaned.

His eyes snapped open, the thunder there matching his glower. "Are you teasing me?"

She shifted across his wide chest to lick the other flat disc, enjoying the game. "Turnabout is fair play. And maybe I want to know what you taste like, too."

He cursed. His whole body went tight. "You're going to kill me, baby. Just understand that I will take back control. And then . . ."

His smile let her know she'd be in all kinds of trouble. Everly loved that idea.

She continued her long exploration of his lips, neck, and chest, her head swimming with his scent, his fingers roaming her back, every moan resounding in her ear.

Slowly, she kissed her way down his body, the muscles of his abs tightening as she drew closer to the stiff part of Gabriel that had brought her so much exquisite pleasure. Until him, sex had been all right. She'd enjoyed it the few times she'd had it previously, but she'd never experienced anything like the incredible heights she'd found with him.

"Are you going to suck my cock?" He watched her, a hungry stare darkening his face.

"Yes." Her voice sounded so throaty, almost foreign.

"Lick every inch. Take my cock between your luscious lips and drag your tongue all over me, baby."

Everly stared down at the flesh in question. Gabriel's cock looked engorged, angry at being denied, and beyond ready. She grasped it gently in her hand.

"Harder," he spit out between clenched teeth. "You don't have to be gentle. I won't break."

She tightened her grip and dragged her palm down his length, loving the soft skin that covered his rigid erection, the way he tensed and hissed at her touch. As she leaned over to kiss the distended head, his length pulsed in her hand. He turned even harder as she held and stroked him.

Gabriel smelled of the soap they'd used in the shower. She inhaled the fresh scent that mingled with his own musk as she dragged her tongue over the sensitive tip of his erection. Salty and masculine, Everly tasted the slightest hint of dewy arousal and lapped at him for more.

He growled, and a deep satisfaction spread through her. She did have power over him. She could open herself and feel for him, since he felt something for her, right? Falling for him wasn't dangerous if he cared, too.

The idea that she could have lost him in that fire rolled over her. She closed her eyes and let herself feel a wave of concern, huge relief, and something that felt suspiciously stronger than attraction. She was afraid to examine how much more. Love?

But Everly knew she'd spent too much time being afraid to invest in people. Maybe she'd been more impacted by her mother's desertion than she wanted to admit. Perhaps she'd feared winding up like her father, loving a ghost who'd left long ago. Everly knew that could happen with Gabriel; he could very well leave her alone and yearning. But she refused to lose the beauty of this moment to her fear.

If Maddox Crawford hadn't come along, she'd still be at her old job and working like a dog, never venturing out of her little neighborhood, only dating the fish in that small pond. Her bit of time with Maddox had shown her a thing or two about living large and pursuing her dreams. He'd given her the courage to go for what she wanted—and there was nothing in life she wanted more than Gabriel Bond.

She tossed away every fear about him. If she truly meant to seek a relationship with this man, she had to open herself up. She had to trust him.

"Jesus, do you have any idea how good that feels?" He tangled his fingers in her hair.

She knew how much she enjoyed it when he licked and sucked and ate at her. So Everly fitted her tongue into the little groove under the head of his shaft and rubbed there. He was too big to fit in her mouth all at once, so she sucked the head while she pumped his shaft in time.

"Oh, yeah. Oh . . . baby. Damn." He tugged gently on her hair.

"Everly, stop. I want to be inside you. Put the condom on me and ride me now."

She knew by his tone that he wasn't in the mood to bargain. Hopefully, she'd have time later to toy with and tease him, suck him until he couldn't last a second longer. She meant to lavish and bestow on him all the pleasure and attention he gave her so he knew exactly how good it felt to be wanted that way. Someday.

For now, she grabbed a condom from the box and tore the package open. She'd never actually performed this service, but she shoved that out of her head. With a minimum of fumbling, Everly managed to roll the condom over him, stroking his length as she covered every inch. Her excitement built.

Once she'd finished protecting them, she let her gaze wander up his body as he laid himself out for her taking. In that moment, Everly found it so easy to believe that he belonged to her, that his body had been made to give her pleasure, that his heart beat with devotion for no one but her.

"I'm crazy about you, Gabriel." She couldn't say anything more. Not yet. But she couldn't remain silent, either.

A sexy smile tugged his lips up. "I'm crazy about you, too, baby."

Relieved and almost giddy, Everly straddled him, aligning his cock to her opening, ready to take him deep inside her body. He raised his hands to clutch her hips and guide her down.

"Like I said before, we're in this together. You and me." His whisper made that sound far more intimate than merely the sharing of some danger and passion. He made it sound as if he meant something emotional and lasting. "We have to trust each other. I'll take care of you, I swear. I'll never let anyone hurt you."

Gabriel was right. To have any sort of real relationship, they had to try. She couldn't keep secrets from him anymore. They'd left the police station after his initial interrogation, intending to lay all their cards on the table. Everly didn't want to wait anymore. If they were going to work, she had to be all in.

Because right now, he was about to be all inside her.

As she sank down, taking him inch by inch, she gasped. He was so big. Every time he filled her, he stretched her until she couldn't breathe. He crowded all the empty spaces inside her and made them sing. Not her sex, but her head, her heart . . . Damn, she was in so deep.

Everly inched her way down, not wanting to rush the moment. Gabriel's stare jumped from her face to the place where their bodies slowly joined.

"It's amazing." He gripped her hips, smoothed his palms up to her waist, then plumped her breasts as he urged her down.

The instant he filled her completely, he caressed the length of her arms and tangled their fingers together. Everly closed her eyes, letting the moment sink in. Still. Silent. Almost reverent. No way to escape the feeling of connection. She found an intimacy she'd been missing her whole life. This man meant something to her, so much that it scared her. But with their bodies fused, hands joined, and stares locked, Everly found it easy to believe that she meant something to him, too.

Gabriel tugged her down to his chest. "Kiss me."

She found his lips with her own, brushing softly and reveling in their closeness. She swore she could all but feel the boundaries around her heart crumbling. Yes, it terrified her. *He* terrified her because in a couple of short days, Gabriel had proven how empty her life was without him. He'd shown her how good it felt to be adored.

Determined to give him the same in return, she licked along his sensual bottom lip. A shudder went through his powerful body, and she loved it. God help her, but she didn't see any way of avoiding the truth.

She loved him.

They would share pleasure and sleep tonight. Tomorrow, she would tell this man everything. She would show him the e-mail and texts she'd received. Together, they would figure the problem out. They were a team. Partners. She was no longer alone.

Everly was too aware of the world not to know that she could be headed for heartbreak, but loneliness sucked, too. After all, it was better to have loved and lost than never to have loved at all, right? On the other hand, now that Gabriel had worked his way into her heart, she had no idea how to cast him out—and didn't want to.

At his urging, she began to move her hips, following the rhythm of her heart, heeding the needs of her body. She let go of every thought in her head except for him and the pleasure they shared.

Gabriel cupped her waist as she lowered herself onto his erection again. As he nudged her up faster, she sighed, then immediately canted down once more, allowing him to fill her utterly. Over and over she rode him, loving the feel of him swelling against her flesh. His hips bucked up, fighting her for control, but it only increased the sweet friction that threatened to send her over the edge again. Little pulses of sensation sparked from her core, forcing the rhythm faster and faster. He cupped her breasts, his breath sputtering as he pumped his way deeper.

Almost there. Almost there . . . He changed the angle of their thrusts, generating a friction against that magic spot inside her that had her gasping, clawing at his chest, ready to chant his name. Ecstasy was so close.

As he pushed inside her once more, she cried out in a keening wail and found it. Pure perfection exploded between her legs, inside her womb. She clutched him. Gabriel was her lifeline in this drowning pleasure—just as she hoped he would be in life.

As she found bliss, he went taut under her and held tight, forcing his cock higher inside her body, as if determined to leave his mark. With a hoarse shout of satisfaction, he pumped out his orgasm.

Repletion drugged her veins. Everly fell against Gabriel, her body utterly exhausted, her mind blessedly clear. He enfolded her in his arms. She felt protected and loved in a way she never had. Tears stung her eyes. It might be too soon to tell him all of her feelings, but she'd poured them out through her touch. The way he'd gripped her in answer . . . he must know or sense how she felt. Given the way he growled her name as he shattered, it didn't seem to scare him off.

Snuggling in deeper, she listened as the thundering beat of his heart slowed. She breathed with Gabriel—in, out, endlessly—and didn't move off of him. She wasn't ready. That moment would come soon enough. Until then, she'd maintain their connection as long as possible.

Their first night together, she'd given him her body. Tonight, she'd shared her heart. Tomorrow, she would reveal her secrets.

Y ou look like hell," Gabe commented as he jogged down the stairs the following morning.

He felt unexpectedly cheerful for a man who might be arrested for murder at any moment. He knew damn well the situation warranted him being more serious, but after an amazing night with Everly, he couldn't work up the will to frown.

Unfortunately, Connor didn't look as if he'd had a similarly fantastic experience.

His pal flipped him the bird. "I was up all fucking night investigating for you."

The dining table was covered in stacks of papers. It looked as if Connor had pried the lockbox open without too much fuss. The lid gaped wide, the contents ready for further study.

Gabriel would rather study how beautiful Everly was in the morning light. He'd woken up beside her, her body tucked close to his. He'd thought about lying in bed with her all day, taking her again and again.

Instead, his cell phone had vibrated, and he'd cursed the real world intruding. He hadn't wanted to wake her so he'd rolled out of bed and tiptoed into the bathroom. He'd answered several texts, canceling meetings at Bond Aeronautics while ignoring probes from the press, then he'd gotten dressed and come downstairs.

"Is Everly still sleeping?" Connor asked.

He nodded. "Yes, she needs rest. Yesterday was hard on her, especially the fire at Mad's." His guess was that she'd been bottled up for a long time. Gabe had encouraged her to cry, to let her emotions out and share them with him. He'd been so gratified that she'd trusted him enough to comply. Had she ever cried with Mad? The question disturbed him. "Besides, the longer she sleeps, the longer it takes for her to figure out we're stuck here."

He didn't want to be the one to tell her their hideout had quickly become their prison.

"No way around that truth." Connor sighed. "Roman's in the kitchen making coffee. Warning: he's not in a good mood. There are so many members of the press milling around the building—even someone from *People* magazine, I'm told. Roman had to slip in using the supersecret celebrity entrance created for the famous blowhards who inhabit this place. Two movie stars, a Broadway legend, and three producers who are convinced that people will recognize them in hoodies and sunglasses." He scoffed. "Puffed-up douchebags."

A little of Gabe's shiny mood faded. If Roman had been forced to sneak in, the press presence must be worse than he'd hoped. "Shit. How did they find us?"

Roman strolled into the living room, his face set in a fierce frown. He held two mugs of coffee and handed one to Connor. "Probably the cops. Since we had to tell them where you'd planned to stay last night before they'd stop questioning you about the fire, I'm sure word got around the precinct. Someone who didn't mind taking a little kickback for tipping off the press likely ran his mouth. So Dax is downstairs working with security to make sure no one slips up here."

He'd promised to protect Everly. He needed to do a better job of it.

"Any chance they'll go away if I make a statement?"

"You going to go hunting for unicorns next?" Roman shot back. "Of course not, and anything you said could be twisted in the press or a court of law. You're better off keeping your mouth shut. There's an underground garage with a tunnel that leads to the building next door. But I'm not sure it's uncommon knowledge. We'll try taking you in and out that way if necessary."

At least they might have an escape route. "I don't want those reporters getting anywhere near Everly."

"No, but you sure like getting near her yourself," Connor said with a knowing grin. "She's a screamer, by the way. Any time I nodded off, she'd start making noise, and I'd be wide awake again."

Gabe scowled. Everly would likely be horrified to know Connor had heard her cries of pleasure. Gabe wasn't thrilled to know that his buddy had heard them, either.

Roman set his mug down. "Are you sure sleeping with this woman is a good idea?"

He didn't like the way Roman said *this woman*. He scowled. "Her name is Everly."

"All right. Are you sure sleeping with Everly is a good idea?"

"Everybody already thinks I am," he replied. "I don't see how it hurts anything at this point. I could go out and make a statement that we're not together. No one would believe it."

"You're likely to hurt her. I've done some checking. She's not like the women you usually date."

"I'm not really dating her." But no denying he was involved—deeply. And what he felt for her was so new and fresh, he wasn't ready to discuss it, not even with his best friends. He sure as hell wasn't letting them dictate when and how he spent his time with her.

"I think she would disagree, and that's why it's a bad idea to continue sleeping with her," Roman countered.

"He's not going to listen, man. He can pretend all day long, but he's really falling for her." Connor redirected his attention to his computer screen, hitting the button to refresh. His eyes flared. "There she is. Oh, yeah. I've got you now."

"Has he finally gone feral?" Gabe asked Roman, tossing a thumb in Connor's direction, more than happy to change the subject.

Roman glanced at the screen. "Shit! Is Senator Armstrong's daughter really running Capitol Scandals?"

"Probably." Connor sipped his coffee. "Or she's shacking up with whoever is. Either way, she's up to her pretty neck in trouble. But my hunch is that she writes the blog."

"Damn it. Armstrong is Zack's ally in the senate." Roman scowled. "Tread carefully, Connor. If this comes out, it could be damaging to our administration. That blog is full of crap challenging Zack's policies."

Capitol Scandals was the tabloid of choice for the DC crowd, but . . . "Isn't it a rag?"

"The front pages are, but dig a little deeper and you'll find a lot of commentary on policy. She completely disagrees with almost everything Zack and the senate have done in the last two years," Roman explained. "Of course she backs it up with crazy conspiracy theories that seem to contain just enough fact to scare the shit out of people. But if it came out that one of Zack's closest allies has a dissenting daughter bent on destroying him, it wouldn't be good."

A predatory gleam lit Connor's eyes. "I can shut her up."

Gabe didn't like the look on Connor's face. "You can't kill her for expressing her opinion."

But the CIA "analyst" smoothed over his expression, that nasty gleam in his eyes suddenly gone. "Of course not. I meant I'll explain that continuing to run this 'clandestine' site is no longer a viable career choice. She blew her cover by falling right into my trap. Look at the headline on Capitol Scandals this morning, boys."

IN THE MIDDLE OF DANGER, PLAYBOY SAVES BOOZE

Gabe sighed. Had the blog mentioned how he'd evaded the two armed men who had tried to kill him? Or talked about his willingness to sacrifice himself to save Everly Parker? Nope. Everything in black and white revolved around the fact that he'd saved Mad's wretchedly expensive Scotch. "Well, this is going to help my image. Really, how can I thank you?"

Frowning, Connor snatched the computer back. "I would have saved that Scotch, too. Leaving it behind to die tragically in that fire would have been a terrible crime." When Gabe slanted him a warning glare, Connor sighed. "Look, I had to give Lara Armstrong something no one else knew to see if she'd run with the story. You passed that bottle off to Dax when we picked you up in Harlem. The cops had no idea you ever had it, so this 'leak' proves beyond a shadow of a doubt that she's either running Capitol Scandals or talking directly to whoever does. She's the only one I told, the only one who could have known."

Gabe understood the reasoning, but wished Connor had passed on a more positive angle. "You couldn't make up a story, like I bench two-twenty or something?"

"I'm not that creative." Connor rolled his eyes. "Besides, I had to give her a tidbit up her alley, and she loves to run pieces that make the rich look entitled and stupid. It's a theme with her."

"We need to shut her down." Roman took a seat and ran a hand over his tired face. "Before her identity comes out."

"Once I figure out what she knows," Connor promised. His voice had taken on that stony, I-know-something-you-don't quality he used when he no longer thought it was prudent to talk.

"What's up?" Gabe couldn't let him keep secrets. "What do you think she knows?"

Connor's jaw tightened, his whole face becoming a stubborn mask.

Roman sat up, pinning Connor with a stare. "Don't hide shit from us. I know you're used to dealing in secrets and you play close to the vest, but we're not agents and there's no need-to-know basis here. We need to know everything."

Connor's shoulders slumped, and Gabe knew whatever was about to come out of his mouth would be bad. "I didn't want to even mention it until I found out if she's trying to make money or waves by tearing Mad apart. She says she's heard rumors that he was a pedophile."

Gabe felt his jaw drop. Mad had loved sex—no doubt—but no way had he ever touched a child. "Are you fucking kidding me? If Lara Armstrong runs that story, I'll sue her. I don't care what it will do to Zack. He's a big boy and he can handle it. But I won't let her spread lies."

Lies Sara and her child would be forced to read and endure for a long time because stench like that lingered. No. That wasn't happening as long as there was a breath in his body. His sister had already been through enough.

Roman shook his head and reached across the table and over the box Everly had found in Mad's secret room the night before. He bypassed the piles of papers and plucked up three photos. "We know that's not true, but we did find some weird stuff in that box. Do any of those girls look familiar to you?"

Gabe took the pictures from Roman. Each showed a smiling girl of no more than thirteen or fourteen. The African girl in the first picture looked innocent, dressed in a school uniform, standing outside her classroom and waving. The second photo looked much like the first, though this Indian girl wore a pretty red bindi on her face and a different uniform. A third girl was in a hijab, signaling that she'd reached puberty.

"Why would he keep pictures of random girls from around the world?" Gabe refused to believe Mad had any sexual interest in these children. Hell, until Sara, Mad had preferred older women. Even when they'd been teenagers, the idiot had hit on everyone's mom. Gabe was grateful to this day that his mother had turned the douche down. That would have been awkward.

"Good question." Roman shrugged. "But it's not the only one. I have more difficult questions after talking to the police early this morning. From dental records, they were able to identify the body you left behind at Mad's. His name was Jason Miller and he was from Brooklyn. Brighton Beach to be exact. He had a nice long rap sheet.

Did two short stints in prison for robbery and assault. According to the cops, he was a known thug-for-hire."

Connor smiled, but there was no humor in the expression. "In fact, they said he worked quite a bit for the mob. Since he grew up in Brighton Beach, I assume they meant the *Bratva*."

The Brothers, something the Russian mob called themselves. They ran illegal gambling rackets, along with other criminal ventures around the city. "So the person who hired him might be our elusive Sergei?"

"Possibly," Roman replied. "I've got an investigator looking into the man's background and known associates. He's going to ask around over the next couple of days. Hopefully, we can piece together some ideas about who else was involved. I've got to head back to DC in the next few days, but I'll keep my ears open."

They would all have to resume their lives soon. Dax's leave would probably only last another couple of days. He had no idea how long Connor had before he needed to be overseas again, engaging in his cloak-and-dagger existence.

"Do they have any line on the identity of the second guy, the one who ran away?" Gabe asked.

"They caught a glimpse of him on a security camera around the corner from Mad's. The NYPD is flashing it all over Brooklyn, but they're fairly certain it's one of a group of men Miller hung out with. They'll find him eventually," Connor explained. "And I have zero idea what the rest of Mad's crap in this box means. Some of it seems to be in code. Or he was really freaking drunk when he wrote it. There's only one thing that might be helpful. Mad jotted down the name of a private investigator he'd hired, some guy named Wayne Ferling. It's too early to visit his office for a chat, but I'll go down later this morning and figure out why Mad hired him."

"I'll try to identify these girls." Gabe could work with Everly. He was kind of eager to see her in action.

"Speaking of private investigators," Connor began with a grim stare. He slid a folder Gabe's way.

"What's that?"

"You remember how you asked me to hire a PI to look into Everly Parker's past so you could dig up dirt on her? Well, that's the dirt. Not that there's too much of it, but no one's completely clean. They worked fast. I especially liked the rumors that her father was a dirty cop. He claims they're utterly unsubstantiated, but he says it's something you can work with. There's also a cousin in prison and something about her mother. Naturally, the majority is about Everly herself and Maddox. Everyone was willing to talk about them. Shall I tell him to keep digging?"

Gabe opened the folder and shame swept through him. God, he couldn't even look at it. "I ordered that before I knew who she was. Tell them to send me a bill. I don't need their services anymore."

Connor nodded. "First sensible thing you've done."

Gabe's cell trilled. He yanked it from his pocket, then winced when he saw the caller's name. Sara. God, in all the craziness he hadn't called her to explain what was happening. She'd likely found out he'd been questioned by the police and nearly been killed in a fire from TMZ or an Internet news blast. Damn it. He closed the folder and set it on the table. He'd ordered it in anger and he wasn't going to read a word of the damn thing.

"I'll be right back." As the guys nodded, he ran his finger over the screen to accept the call.

He stepped into the living room, leaving Roman and Connor at the dining table. Like the rest of the apartment, the living room was decorated in clean, masculine lines and lots of dark leather furniture. He wondered what Everly's place looked like. He imagined it was a lot brighter and more feminine.

He took a deep breath and held the phone to his ear. "Hey, sis. I'm sorry I haven't called."

"Tell me you're not sleeping with his whore." Even with a hundred miles between them, he felt the chill in her voice.

"Excuse me?" He'd never heard his sister say that word. She rarely ever cursed. She certainly didn't curse at him.

"You heard me, Gabe. Did you think I wouldn't see? Her picture is plastered all over the Internet."

"You can't believe everything you see," he placated, not liking the anxious fury he heard in Sara's voice. The doctor had told her to relax. A few weeks ago, she'd experienced some spotting and cramping. Her OB had explained that she had to keep stress to a minimum. "Calm down. You know getting upset is bad for the baby."

"You want me to calm down? Based on everything in the press, I'm almost positive he left me for her, Gabe. He walked out on our future— our baby—for her. I can't stand the thought of you even talking to her."

"Sara, listen. I have to talk to her. If she was involved with Mad, she might know something. You do understand that Mad was probably murdered."

"I've heard that speculation. If it's true, the list of suspects is prob-ably a mile long. That doesn't mean you have to sleep with all of them." A muffled sound didn't quite mute Sara's cry, and that tore at him. "Are you sleeping with her? Never mind. I already know the answer."

What the hell was he supposed to do? He couldn't let Sara get so upset. If she lost the baby, he wasn't sure what she would do. Sara was the last member of his family. Their mother and father were gone. He was all she had in the world, and material shit aside, this baby was Mad's last legacy. "I am spending time with her, but it's not what you think."

Because how the hell could he tell his overwrought, hormonal sis-ter that he was crazy about the woman who might have been Mad's last lay?

Sara wasn't capable of being rational at that moment. He had to deal with her the best he could until he figured out the whole truth. Then he'd sit down and explain.

"What is it, then?"

The way Sara felt now, he could never turn Crawford over to her while Everly still worked there. He'd have to find a place for his pretty computer nerd, maybe at Bond Aeronautics. Hell, he had the connections to get her a job nearly anywhere she wanted to work. After Sara had taken the reins at Crawford, he would gently ease Everly into his sister's life. But for now, he had to do whatever necessary to keep Sara calm.

"She's somehow involved in all this." No lies there. Surely Everly had information. Until he solved Mad's murder, Gabe had to keep both of the women in his life safe. "I have to stay close to her because I think she knows more than she's saying." Or more than she understood. "Mad dug himself ass deep into some shithole I don't understand, but she's the key. I've got to stay on her and tell her whatever she wants to hear in order to keep her close to me."

"So the press is wrong? You don't love her?"

Love her? The very word sent a little shiver up his spine. Being in love would mean diving into something he didn't really understand. His parents had been friends but hadn't shared any spark or passion. They'd been more like business partners. The way he felt about Everly was entirely different. When he looked at her, a flipping inferno raged through his system and threatened to engulf him. Was that love? Maybe . . . but he wasn't ready to go there yet.

"Everly Parker is the means to an end. I'm going to find out what she knows and then I'm going to deal with her. I already have a plan in place."

His plan was to placate his sister and figure everything else out later.

"Yes, I can clearly see that you do have a plan in place, Bond."

That hadn't been Sara. Gabe felt his heart drop to his knees. He whipped around.

Everly was still flushed and slightly mussed, dressed in yesterday's clothes. He watched her face turn utterly white. A sick feeling roiled in his gut. She held the folder containing the PI's report in her hands.

"You're going after my dead father's reputation? That's very classy of you. You'll forgive me if I don't stay around to help you out anymore than I already have, you bastard." She darted away, racing for the penthouse's front door, her heels clattering against the hardwood floor, echoing the pounding of his heart.

"Sara, I'll have to call you back." Because he couldn't let Everly get away. God, not like this. She now thought the absolute worst of him. "Take care of you and the baby."

"All right. I'm sorry, Gabe. I shouldn't have yelled at you. I'm being selfish. I love you." Then she gasped. "I just saw online about you being caught in a fire last night? Are you all right?"

That was the Sara he knew, the sweet girl he'd played with during his childhood summers. "I'm fine. I'll explain later. You have to trust me. I'll call you soon."

He hung up, resolving to ring Sara back as soon as he could, then took off after Everly. She must have heard the worst possible part of the conversation and coupled it with that fucking report he'd ordered. Now he had to find a way to make her understand. At this point, he hoped she'd even talk to him.

As he dashed to the front of the penthouse, he found Roman staring out at the private elevator door that only opened here and on the ground floor. Guests needed a code to come to Connor's place . . . but anyone could go to the lobby. "What the fuck happened?"

"Shit. She ran off?" Gabe had expected her to be angry, upset. He'd suspected he'd be dealing with tears. He'd never imagined that she'd be impulsive enough to run. His whole body went into a deep freeze. "How the hell did she get that report? Where's Connor?"

Roman's eyes widened. "She saw the PI report? Fuck me. She must have walked in after Connor went to take a shower. I was trying to hunt down some breakfast. Shit. It was sitting on the table."

Gabe didn't reply. He was already out the door.

ELEVEN

Everly willed the elevator to move faster. The folder in her hand practically shook with her rage. God, he must think she was so stupid. The whole time he'd been telling her how much he needed her, he'd had an investigator pulling up all the worst parts of her past.

And those rumors about her dad. She knew who they came from—an ex-con her father had put away. He and his lawyer had tried every dirty trick they knew to get the conviction overturned.

While these rumors are likely untrue, the subject has a soft spot for her late father, according to many sources. Threats of ruining his reputation might silence her on the subject of her relationship with Maddox Crawford.

Or it might have the effect of her shoving something so far up Gabriel Bond's ass he could never see straight again.

She'd climbed out of bed all but humming and come down the stairs with a satisfied smile.

After the night she'd spent with Gabriel, she'd been on top of the world. Cloud nine. Nothing would get in her way. She'd walked downstairs, ready to work. She needed to see if the receipts from the coffee shop had yielded any leads on her mystery informant. The text from last night had been a bust. She'd already traced it to a burner phone.

She'd gone downstairs, ready to give Gabriel every shred of evidence she had. Connor seemed to know a lot about hacking. He might be able to help her, too.

Unfortunately, she hadn't found Gabriel. She'd found this file.

She wasn't going to cry, damn it. She promised herself. No tears. No moaning and wailing. In some ways, she'd earned this betrayal and pain by being so gullible. After all, what did a sex god like Gabriel Bond really want with her? But she refused to let him beat her down. Everly would not sit home alone with her doors locked, wondering where everything had gone wrong. She would pick up, move on, become even stronger.

But right now, the thought of shooting Gabriel Bond in his very talented man parts certainly appealed.

The elevator doors slid open. Through a watery film of her tears, she looked across the dark, private lobby. Crap. So much for not crying.

Trying to suck it up, Everly stepped out of the elevator. She had nothing with her except her purse, that folder, and her pride. She refused to need anything—or anyone—else.

She grabbed her cell and quickly dialed a familiar number.

Scott answered on the first ring. "Everly? What the hell is going on?" His shock was obvious. "Everything is insane here at the office. Did you really almost freaking die?"

She didn't have time to explain last night or her private hell to him now. They could do that over cocktails at his place. "Can you pick me up?"

"Pick you up?" He hesitated for a moment. "I thought you were with Bond."

She started across the lobby, eyeing the doorman ahead as he stood sentry in front of the lone door, its glass darkly tinted. "That's done. I need help, Scott. You usually drive to work on Wednesdays, right?"

"Yeah, I've got my car here. Where are you?"

Somewhere on the Upper West Side. Last night she'd seen them drive past a couple of familiar landmarks. It would be best to walk to one of them. Everly had little doubt that Gabriel wasn't done trying to control her, so he'd be hot on her heels. "Meet me at the Museum of Natural History. I'll be waiting in the lobby. Text me when you arrive."

"It'll take me a while."

So she'd get some overpriced coffee in the basement cafeteria and hang out with the blue whale until then. "That's fine. Thank you so much."

Everly hung up and bit her lip, glancing at the doorman guarding the exit. She marched toward him. No indecision. No hoping she'd misunderstood Gabriel. When he came down here, she didn't want him to find her wringing her hands and waiting. She needed to be gone.

Everly didn't have any cash with her or she'd simply hop into the first cab she could find. Yeah, she could use a credit card, but Gabriel would find her in two seconds on the grid. If he couldn't track her, then Connor would.

Drawing in a deep breath, she pushed aside the pain in her chest. She'd deal with her broken heart later. For now she had to figure out how to counter everything in that damn report.

When she reached the doorman, he didn't move a single tassel on his uniform, much less step aside so she could leave. "Miss, I don't think you want to go out that way."

"Yes, I do. Thank you very much."

Reluctance crossed his face as he shrugged, opened the door, and stepped back. When she heard a ding behind her that sounded too much like the elevator, she dashed outside into a usual crowd of New Yorkers clogging up the sidewalk.

Suddenly, flashbulbs popped and a roar of shouts with the sound of her name startled Everly. These weren't typical corporate drones walking to work. These people shoved video recorders, still cameras, and more than a few audio devices in her face, all barking for her attention.

Crap, they were reporters, and they were everywhere.

Everly couldn't move, couldn't turn back around to the safe haven of Connor's lobby again. They'd blocked her escape route and invaded her personal space. She felt panicky and sick, as if she'd either throw up or pass out.

"Ms. Parker, who's the better lover? Gabriel Bond or Maddox Crawford?" A blond reporter thrust a microphone in her face.

A man with a camera elbowed the blonde out of the way. "Are you bitter that Maddox Crawford didn't leave you his estate since you were his last mistress?"

"Is that why you're sleeping with Gabriel Bond now, for the money?"

Everly tried to pull back, to push her way out of the crowd, but they circled her like hungry sharks refusing to be denied a long-awaited meal.

"Were you in on the plot to kill Maddox Crawford?"

"Did you set fire to the brownstone yourself? Or did Bond?"

"Did Bond and Crawford fight a deadly brawl over you?"

"Are you in love with Gabriel Bond?"

Her panic ratcheted up, threatening to overwhelm her. She couldn't breathe or think with all of them in her face, hollering personal questions at a rudely impatient clip, as if the public had a right to know about her sex life and her feelings.

The tabloid journalists continued to hover. More cameras flashed in her face, their lights blinding her. Once more, Everly tried to backpedal, but the horde had closed ranks, creating an even tighter cage around her. She felt like a trapped animal. She couldn't breathe.

Suddenly, strong arms encircled and lifted her.

"Get back or I'll have the cops arrest all of you," a deep voice shouted behind her. Dax.

He'd come out of nowhere, but Everly sagged against him in relief.

She could handle herself in a one-on-one fight, but this was a mob. She was willing to do almost anything to escape this terrible harassment. She'd believed she would be safe here, but apparently that was another lie Gabriel Bond had told her to keep her compliant.

"Are you having an affair with Ms. Parker, too, Spencer?"

"Back off," Dax roared, throwing a few elbows.

Finally, the vultures moved, parting reluctantly for his powerful body and insistent shoves. The doorman held the portal wide, and Dax hauled her into the dark lobby seconds later. As soon as the doorman pulled the opening closed, the overwhelming buzz of the reporters' shouts receded.

Dax spun her around and studied her upturned face with a frown. "What the hell did you think you were doing?"

Gathering herself, Everly straightened her hopelessly wrinkled skirt with shaking hands and told herself to use her head for once. She still faced the same problems she'd had before blindly walking into that mob. Dax might have been nice earlier, but he was Gabriel's friend. He would always side with his pal. For all she knew, he'd helped put together the report on her.

"Leaving," she answered finally, satisfied with the confident note in her voice. "You can't keep me here against my will."

Dax sent her a long sigh. "What the hell did Gabe do now?"

"Everly!"

She turned at the sound of Gabriel barking at her across the lobby. In that moment, she hated him with every cell in her body, and she still couldn't help but think he was the most gorgeous man she'd ever known. When he stalked her way, her heart ached all over again.

She decided to talk to Dax. He looked like he would be infinitely more reasonable. Even though he would side with Gabriel, he wouldn't break the law to do so. She hoped.

"I want to leave here."

Gabriel huddled in beside her. The instinct to move away pressed down on her. She refused to give him the satisfaction. Instead, she focused on Dax. "I want nothing to do with that man. If I can get out of this building, I already have a ride out of the city."

It was a little bit of a lie, but she didn't care. Gabriel had apparently told her many. What did her one hurt? She could easily take a bus if Scott couldn't drive her that far. She would head to her aunt's house in Connecticut. Let the press try to find her in the 'burbs. She wouldn't leave the house. In fact, she could hide for weeks, maybe months. Her widowed aunt would be thankful for the company. Then Everly would move somewhere else. The West Coast sounded good.

"What did you do to make her run?" Dax demanded, sounding pissed off. His eyes went to the folder in her hand and he cursed. "I told you that was a mistake. Why the hell does she have that report?"

"Connor left it on the dining room table and then she overheard a conversation I had with Sara," Gabriel began. "My sister was upset, so I told her what she wanted to hear. She's already come close to losing the baby."

So Gabriel meant to play it that way? Really? She wasn't buying a word. Sometimes the best way to win an argument was not to engage. If she meant so little to him, then she needed to treat him similarly. People only fought for something if they cared, and Everly wouldn't allow Gabriel to think she did.

"I want to leave. If you don't allow me to do so, then I'll call the police and explain that you're holding me against my will."

Dax gestured toward the door. "There's the exit. Good luck."

"Everly, you can't go out there. They'll tear you apart. Come upstairs with me, baby. Please give me a chance to explain. What you heard wasn't the truth. I was trying to keep Sara calm. She's in a bad place emotionally. And I can explain that report, too. Please come with me."

She turned away and considered the door. She'd been shocked and overwhelmed when she'd first stepped out there. Maybe she could handle it now that she knew what to expect.

"I won't save you this time," Dax explained. "If you get stuck, you'll have to get yourself out."

So she knew where he stood. "That's very gentlemanly of you."

"I'm not a gentleman when people I care about are getting hurt. You aren't thinking straight." Dax shot Gabriel a dark glare. "Neither one of you is."

The elevator doors swooshed opened. Roman and Connor stepped out.

Roman heaved a big sigh as he spotted them. "Thank fuck you caught her before she darted outside."

Dax shook his head. "Nope. I was too late to prevent that. I was getting a cup of coffee—that's now cold, I'm sure—because I thought my responsibility was simply to keep people out. No one mentioned that we'd have to keep them in, too."

Connor frowned at her. "What were you thinking? Have you forgotten that barely twelve hours ago someone tried to kill you?"

She would never forget last night's terror. She would likely go to her grave remembering her relief at taking her first smoke-free breath, and how good it had felt afterward to sleep in Gabriel's arms. Too bad that amazing feeling would always be entwined with this morning's humiliation. "Somehow I think I'll be safer the farther I get from Mr. Bond. This is about him. Not me."

"I disagree, Ms. Parker. And this is a conversation better conducted in the penthouse. So, if you'll come with us . . ." Roman gestured to the elevator.

She shook her head. "I'm not going anywhere except away from here and Mr. Bond. If you won't help me, I'll take my chances with the reporters."

She turned away from them all. The last thing she wanted to endure was a lecture from these four men. They didn't have anything close to her best interests at heart.

Someone caught her elbow. Everly glanced over her shoulder to see Gabriel with his hand on her and determination stamped across his face as he started to haul her back.

She had to stop treating him like her boyfriend. It was long past time to shut all the girly love shit down.

"Get your hand off me." She forced every word out between clenched teeth.

"You can't go out there. It's dangerous," he insisted.

"Last warning. Let go."

"Everly, listen to me, baby . . ."

No, she was done listening. Instead, she plowed a fist right to his gut. Her street-smart dad had taught her how to defend herself. The time to be her father's daughter again instead of Gabriel Bond's stupid sex toy had definitely come.

Gabriel groaned and staggered back, clutching his stomach.

"Touch me again, and I'll make it hurt worse," she threatened.

Dax chuckled, looking almost impressed. "That must have stung, buddy. She's had training."

"Don't let her leave," Gabriel eked out as he hunched over.

"If Dax tries to stop me, I'll give him the same treatment," Everly shot back, then sent Spencer a warning glance.

Dax frowned. "Come on, Parker. Be reasonable."

Roman held a hand out as though placating the lion he found in his midst. "Let's talk this out. There are things you don't know, Everly. You really are in danger."

"As your friend there so recently found out, I can handle myself." Besides throwing a mean right hook, she had a permit to carry concealed. She hadn't carried since Maddox's funeral, but as soon as she got out of here, she would grab her Beretta and defend herself if necessary.

"Come upstairs and listen to what Gabe has to say. If you still want to leave after hearing him out, I'll escort you out of the building undetected and get you where you need to go," Roman vowed.

"She can't leave," Gabriel argued, still clutching his sore stomach.

They were giving her a choice, but she couldn't allow Gabriel another chance to deceive her. Roman and Connor both lied for a living. Dax maybe not as much, but to navigate military politics, he'd probably told a fib or two. And Gabriel . . . Don't get her started. The whole lot of them were excellent at getting exactly what they wanted. She was too straightforward to play this game. She said exactly what she meant. There was no way she could play games with these men and expect to come out on top.

"I'll take my chances alone." She turned to leave.

At some point, Connor had worked his way behind her and now blocked the exit.

"Get out of my way." She was done being intimidated. And honestly, Connor was leaner than Gabriel. If she could incapacitate him, she doubted Connor would be any harder to take down.

"Connor, don't hurt her." Gabriel held up a hand, his face and voice projecting calm, as if he placated a wild animal.

Connor's face was perfectly bland. "So you want me to let her go?"

She really didn't like the look on his face. Instinct told her to take a step back, but she had already proven that she had terrible instincts. "Get out of my way. I'm not staying here. If you want to detain me, you'll have a fight."

His smile wasn't pretty. "It won't be much of a fight."

A prickle of fear snaked up her spine.

"My father was a cop. He taught me how to defend myself." Adrenaline pumped through her system. She had to stay confident. After all, she sparred regularly with the Crawford building's guards. They'd learned very quickly that if they went easy on her, she handed them their asses. After she'd taken out a couple of the big ones, they'd treated her like an equal.

"He didn't teach you how to fight me."

"Connor, buddy. Be gentle." Gabriel sounded downright worried.

She was done playing. Hell, she was done altogether. Most men just talked a good game, and she was no longer in the mood to chat.

Everly pivoted to walk around Connor. When he reached for her arm, she would twist it out of his grasp, then she'd either go for his solar plexus or aim a little lower and make him wish he hadn't been born a man.

Unfortunately, Connor didn't reach for her arm. Before she could even take another breath, he hooked his arm around her neck and braced his free hand against her temple. She tried to figure out what he was doing, but that didn't give her a spare second to fight.

"I think you need a time out," Connor rumbled. "Nighty-night."

Damn it. He meant to perform a sleeper choke hold. Everly squirmed and fought, but he was too strong, holding her immobile as he pressed on her jugular, stopping the flow of blood to her brain. Her vision blurred. The folder slid from her hand, all her dirty secrets on the floor for everyone to see.

"Let her go!" Gabriel dashed in front of her, concern swimming all over his face.

"She's all yours, buddy."

Gabriel caught her in his strong, secure arms. Then the world blinked out.

You nearly fucking killed her. You didn't have to do that," Gabe gritted out as he settled Everly onto the sofa.

She looked so pale as she lay there unmoving. Jesus, maybe he should call a doctor. Then kill his friend.

"She's fine." Connor waved him off. "Do you know how often I use that move? I haven't killed anyone yet."

"Yes, you're an expert because the analysis you do is so deadly," Gabe shot back. He was tired of Connor pretending he sat behind a desk all day.

Connor shrugged, obviously unwilling to explain further. "Danger is everywhere these days. And she really was going to walk out. Do you know what the press would have done with her? They could help her fuck you seven ways from Sunday if she chose to play the woman scorned. All she'd need is one national interview where she implies that you killed Mad in a jealous fit, and you'd find yourself indicted by a grand jury and being held without bail."

"Connor is right. He had to stop her," Roman seconded.

Dax grinned down at him. "Well, I'm glad Connor was there because after what she did to you, Gabe, I think I'll avoid pissing her off. That was one mean move she pulled. You're lucky she didn't try to take your balls."

"The day is still young," Gabe replied with mock enthusiasm.

But once the silence fell, a thousand thoughts crowded his head. If Connor hadn't stopped her, she would have gone. Would she have ever given him a chance to explain? Had he really touched her for the last time? Everything inside him rebelled at that thought. He'd never been denied much in his life, especially a woman. Gabe hated to think that his luck had run out when it finally counted.

Swallowing, he knelt beside her and brushed a lock of reddish-blond hair from her face. Despite her pert nose and stubborn chin, she looked so fragile. Gabe knew that appearances could be deceiving. Her anger certainly hadn't been a delicate thing.

"How long until she's conscious?" he asked Connor.

"She'll be awake and fighting you in a couple of minutes. Be prepared."

Roman paced, raking a hand through his hair. "That doesn't give us much time to decide our next move. How the hell are we going to keep her here?"

"Lock her up." Connor pointed to the floor above them. "The third bedroom is small. The window is sealed shut so she can't do anything stupid. There's one way in and one way out, and it happens to lock solely from the outside."

Gabe stared at him. "Do I even want to know why?"

"No. You do not."

Dax shook his head. "We can't lock her up."

"Sure I can," Connor replied.

"We are not going to put her into some sort of prison." Gabe wouldn't give Everly another reason to hate him. "I'll talk to her when she wakes up, make her see reason. She has to understand that I requested that report before I knew who she was. And what I said to Sara upset Everly, but she'll calm down once I explain my logic."

Everly's eyes fluttered open. "Wha . . . what happened?"

Maybe whatever Connor had done to her had induced short-term memory loss. Gabe sat on the edge of the sofa beside her and cupped her cheek. "Hey, baby. How are you feeling?"

She sat up and shoved his hand away, then surged to her feet. He moved in to balance her in case she hadn't quite recovered. She let him hold her arms in a steadying grip for a moment, but the minute she seemed stable, she jerked away.

"Everly, please let me help you."

She shook her head, her strawberry waves brushing her shoulders decisively. "You've 'helped' me enough, Bond. Now I'm feeling like a walking, talking bitch on wheels. I think the police would be interested to know that your friend almost killed me."

Gabe winced. Obviously, the short-term amnesia had been wishful thinking. She remembered everything.

"Why doesn't anyone have faith in me?" Connor asked no one in particular.

"I have faith that you're an asshole," Everly muttered. She strode to the other side of the room with a pissed-off glare that nearly dropped him.

"How's your head? Your vision?" Gabe asked, easing closer. "Do you need a doctor?"

She held up a hand to stop him. "Don't pretend you give a shit. I read enough of that report to know you don't. Now someone said something about a back way out of this place. A friend is coming to pick me up."

"Scott?" Roman asked. "He called while we were in the elevator. I told him you no longer needed a ride."

Her expression iced over even more. "And my day is complete. Are you sure you all went to Creighton Academy and not Douchebag prep school? I'll take my phone back and find a cab."

"Will you please listen to me?" The desperation icing Gabe's veins surprised him. The thought of Everly walking out of his life made him physically sick. In that moment, he wished he'd somehow managed to keep his heart untouched . . . but no such luck.

"Well, you boys have given me no choice." Her gaze zipped over to Connor. "Are you former military? My father could do that move. He learned it when he became a SEAL."

"Something like that," he replied with a bland smile. "We'll leave the two of you alone. Come on, Roman. We should be able to contact the PI by now."

"The PI who told you how to damage my dead father's reputation? You need more out of him?" She looked from Roman to Dax— seemingly at everyone but Gabe.

"Not that one. When we got Mad's lockbox open, we found an investigator's card inside," Dax explained. "We suspect Mad hired him. Since Mad's gone now, we're hoping that this PI will divulge what he was hired to investigate."

"I'd like to see the contents of that box. As long as I'm here, I intend to examine the evidence I nearly died to find. At the moment, I'm still temporarily in charge of Crawford's security." She flipped a stubborn hazel stare Gabe's way. "Any chance you'll send me on my merry way to the unemployment line?"

"None." Gabe spoke the word like a vow.

"So, given Mulford's absence and your stubbornness, figuring out who killed the boss falls under my purview. So why don't you show me what you've uncovered."

"Baby, let's talk first about what you saw in that report and over-heard me tell Sara. I didn't—"

"It no longer matters. I'm only here for the case. Who's the PI?"

She was going to be mulish obviously, and he worried that could be permanent. "Give me five minutes. After that, I won't say another word on the subject. We'll focus on the case. I'll show you everything we've found. Please."

She sat again, crossing her arms over her chest. "It won't work. I'm done playing the fool for you."

Clearly, talking to her was going to take longer than five minutes. Even if he had five days, Gabe wasn't sure he could find the right words to rekindle the adoration he'd seen on her face last night.

He cast a troubled glance at Roman, Dax, and Connor. They nod-ded, then filed into the dining room. Gabe was alone with her and he wasn't sure what to say. What the hell was he going to do if he couldn't make her believe him?

He sat on the sofa beside her, attempting to respect her space. "My parents are both gone, and I'm the only family Sara has now."

She held a hand up. "I'm going to stop you there, Bond. Let me guess what happened. Your sister saw the press concerning us and flipped out because now you're sleeping with the woman who took her baby daddy away."

"I wouldn't put it that way, but she wasn't pleased."

"She was angry because like everyone else in the world she thinks I'm a money-hungry whore out to find myself a sugar daddy. Stop." She put a hand up when he tried to talk. "You thought the same thing in the beginning. Hell, you might still think it."

"I don't. I don't think you were after Mad's money."

She huffed a little, a dissatisfied sound. "I suppose I should be glad you now only think I was sleeping with him for pleasure. Let me talk, Bond, and you'll get your turn. I get why you said what you said to Sara. It was harsh, but you had to come up with some way to explain my presence."

"Yes," he said quickly. "That's exactly what I was trying to do. I was trying to calm her down. I don't want her to lose the baby because she gets overly emotional."

"Somehow I think she's stronger than that, but I'll leave that to you. I'm not upset about what you said to Sara. I'm pissed as hell about that report. You had a private investigator dig up dirt on my life. On my family. How am I supposed to forgive you for that?"

At least he had a way to explain this. "I ordered that report the morning I took over as CEO of Crawford. I didn't know you were Everly Parker. I found out Mad had been having an . . ." *Shit.* This kept coming between them. "I learned the rumors about Mad having an affair with one of his VPs. I was angry and I worried that this woman would potentially come after a part of his fortune or start talking to the press and putting more pressure on Sara."

She chuckled but there was no humor behind it. "So you decided to destroy me before I could do any of that."

"I made the decision to gather some ammunition in case a woman I didn't know came after my family. Once I knew who you were, I would never have used it against you."

She shook her head. "I don't believe you. You would use it if you had to. You would do anything to protect your sister and your friends, including sleep with the enemy. Just like they would risk going to jail to spare you the potential of me saying something to the press. At the end of the day, blood is thicker than water, isn't it?"

He'd stepped into a minefield. "I did not sleep with you to keep you close."

"So the sex was an added bonus?"

He had to force down his frustration. She was deliberately misunderstanding him. "No. It was attraction and chemistry, and you felt it, too."

She jerked her gaze away, stubbornly staring at the wall in front of her. "Yes, but that doesn't make us compatible. Even if you never used that report, you're the type of man who gathers ammunition on your enemies in case you might need it. You're the type of man who threatened to kill his best friend."

What the hell was he supposed to say to that? "I wouldn't have done it."

Her gaze was blank as she looked at him. "The same way you wouldn't have used the report. You say all the right things, Gabriel. Can you be honest with me for two seconds?"

"I've been honest with you all along."

"Are you going to fire me when this is over? You want Mad's holdings to go to Sara. You're going to give her the company. I assume you won't want me there when she takes over."

At least he could answer that question. "I won't fire you. I won't hurt your career. If I have to, I'll find you a new job."

"If you're not firing me, why do I need a new job?"

"Everly . . ." He knew he was pleading with her, but he had no idea what else to do. "I can't leave you in your current position. You're right. Sara is eventually going to take over Crawford Industries. I can't run two companies at once, and Crawford is her baby's inheritance. When she takes over, you can come with me to Bond. I'll move my head of online security to Crawford. It will work."

In fact, the plan was perfect. He could keep her close. Bond had different security issues than Crawford. Maybe she would see it as a challenge. When he had to travel for business, he could take her with him. It could be good for them as a couple. Win-win.

"Bond is smaller than Crawford with significantly fewer cybersecurity needs," Everly replied with a shake of her head. "You don't exactly have a big retail wing, so you don't need the sort of Internet security I specialize in. That position at Bond is a fluff job. So I would be taking a step down. I'll pass."

He felt his fists tighten, along with his temper. "Sara can't work with you. You have to understand that."

"Why not? I'm good at my job. I would think she would like having other female executives around."

"You can't expect her to keep you on." He was happy with how reasonable he sounded when all he wanted to do was scream. Couldn't she see he was trying to keep them both out of harm's way?

"Why not?"

He was going to have to lay it out for her. "Because she thinks Mad left her for you. She thinks you're the reason her baby doesn't have a father."

"Ah, so the would-be wife doesn't want the whore around. Excellent. Tell her she doesn't need to fire me. For the first time in my adult life, I'm going against my word, Gabriel. I quit. Once I can clean out my office, I'll be gone forever, and your precious sister doesn't have to sully herself with my presence."

"You're not listening to a word I'm saying."

"I've heard everything," she shot back. "In fact, I hear you so much better now that I know where you're coming from. I'm willing to accept that you really had no idea who I was that first night. But every single second since the moment you realized Maddox spent time with me after he left Sara, you've plotted and planned to humiliate me in the worst way possible."

"That's not true, damn it." He didn't exactly sound coaxing now, but he wasn't going to let her rewrite history to suit her mood. "I admit I didn't handle our first meeting well, but I sure as hell haven't tried to humiliate you."

"You say you didn't know who I was when you ordered that report, but you didn't cancel it. You didn't call off the PI. You've still got your ammunition in case I ever turn against you. Why would I want to live in that world, Gabriel?" She waved him off. "It's irrelevant. All of this talk is completely useless because I know the truth. Tell me one thing: Do you believe me when I say I didn't have anything beyond a friendship with Maddox?"

He sighed, deeply sick of this argument. "It doesn't matter anymore. Everly, I don't care who you slept with before me. I want you. I want you now, and whatever went on in the past is in the past.

Eventually Sara will accept you in my life. She'll come around. She's a smart woman, and you'll win her over."

She stood again, this time steadier than before. "No, I won't because we're through. You see, it might not matter to you, but it's everything to me. I won't be with a man who thinks I'm a liar."

Everly walked away, and Gabe was fairly certain he really had lost her forever. He'd never felt more desolate in his life.

TWELVE

Everly fought her instinct to go back to Gabriel and accept whatever he would give her. It was weak, but she really wanted to believe he was telling her the truth. A friend in her neighborhood had recently miscarried after a very stressful reorganization at work, and it had been heartbreaking for her family. So Everly understood why Gabe might have thrown her under the proverbial bus to calm his pregnant sister. But she also hated the thought that she might become one of those stupid girls who made excuses for a boyfriend's bad behavior because she couldn't stop loving the jerk.

All that aside, by his own admission, he intended to force her out of her job before his sister assumed Crawford's helm because he believed she'd been Mad's mistress. And she couldn't get that report out of her head. Now she wished she'd been able to hold on to it. How much more had he found out besides the crap about her dad? Shouldn't she know what he could come at her with? Maybe she should do her own digging. She wouldn't need a PI. She could find out everything about Gabriel Bond. She could hack into his banking records and make it look like he was laundering money. . . .

Oh, god, this was what life with a man as ruthless as Gabriel Bond would be like. Warfare. She was prepping for a war with a man she'd fallen in love with. Her heart sank. Even though she'd liked Maddox, he'd been the same. Always prepared to take down his enemies.

She couldn't live this way.

"Are you two good?" Dax asked as she walked in the room.

"As good as we're going to get. Now what did you find?" Everly saw no reason to vomit out the details of her relationship with Gabriel, especially to his friends. Instead, she headed for the table. What she needed was to lose herself in work and figure out the mystery in front of her. Then she and Gabriel could go their separate ways.

Connor glanced up from the papers he'd been studying. "You knew Mad pretty well, right?"

"I think so." She wished Mad was here now so she could get his opinion on how to deal with Gabriel, who'd behaved this morning like a complete douchebag-asshole-idiot. She bet that Maddox would have given her some crazy-sounding advice, which, under the punchline, would have been terribly sage. Or he would have offered to find her a male prostitute. Really, it was a fifty-fifty proposition with him.

"Do you have any idea why he would be looking for two women?" Connor asked.

Roman sighed as if the answer was obvious. "You're talking about Mad. Ménage à trois, you moron."

Connor rolled his eyes. "I don't think he would have spent ten grand merely to find a threesome. Fine. He might have, but I doubt he would've hired a PI. He knew a fair number of high-class escorts. He would have just called them."

"I'll give you that," Roman conceded. "So who did he hire this PI to find?"

Connor looked down at his notepad. "According to the PI's daughter, Mad hired her dad, Wayne Ferling, to find two women over the last two years. The first was named—"

"Why talk to the daughter, rather than the man himself?" Everly interrupted. "Could you not reach him?"

"Mr. Ferling was killed by a mugger two months ago," Connor explained. "Right in front of his house, in fact."

"That's suspicious," Dax said with a whistle.

"Yes, it is, considering the fact that Ferling lived in a safer part of the city," Connor admitted. "I checked and his was the only murder in that vicinity in the last two years."

"So Mad's dead and so is the PI he hired under mysterious circumstances," Gabriel posited, strolling into the room.

Everly tried to act as if he was nothing more than another cog in the wheel of this mystery. "Sorry I interrupted you earlier, Connor. Carry on."

He nodded. "Ferling's daughter said that Mad first hired her father to find a woman in her fifties, Deborah Elliot. That was a little over nine months ago. She's alive and living in Florida. Then more recently, Mad sought a woman named Natalia Kuilikov. She was a Russian immigrant who came to the States almost fifteen years ago. Apparently, she disappeared a while back."

"We keep finding Russians in the middle of this shit." Dax paced the floor, his face thoughtful. "First, Sergei, then the *Bratva*, and now Natalia. That's awfully coincidental. But Deborah Elliot doesn't sound remotely Russian. How does she fit in?"

Suddenly, Everly wasn't thinking about Dax's question or her problems with Gabriel. "Maddox was trying to find Deborah Elliot? You're sure about that?"

"Yeah." Connor nodded, looking quite certain.

A wave of dizziness rolled through her head. She braced her hand on the table, trying to process the possible implications. Now more than ever, she wished she could lean on Gabriel.

"Everly? What's wrong?" He moved behind her and pulled out a chair.

She sank into the seat. Deborah Elliot. He'd been looking for

Deborah Elliot. The idea made Everly's head spin again. "Deborah Elliot is my mother."

The room stopped, and every eye suddenly turned to her.

"Are you kidding me?" Roman asked.

She shook her head. "No. I mean, that's my mother's maiden name. I'm sure there are plenty of Deborah Elliots out there, but for this to be another coincidence . . ." She finally looked at Gabriel. "Maddox searched for my mother. Once he found her, he apparently went out of his way to find and hire me. Why? And what made him go looking for her in the first place?"

"With Mad gone, we may never know," Gabriel answered. "But I think I remember your mother's name listed in the financial records I found on his desk last night."

"Are they in that folder you saved from the fire?" Connor asked, looking around the table for said file.

"Yeah." Gabe pointed to the plain manila folder at the far end of the table. "That's it. When I studied it, everything inside seemed so random. Mad had shoved a ton of receipts into that folder, along with old payment records to a Deborah Elliot."

"Payments? How did Maddox even know my mother?"

Connor flipped through the files Gabriel had saved. "He didn't. His father did. These payments were made some twenty-odd years ago. Is there any way to pull up Crawford Industries' archived HR files? I have a hunch. I happen to remember Benedict Crawford really well, since I spent a bunch of holidays with Mad and the old bastard."

Before she could clear the shock buzzing through her brain to volunteer for the task, Gabriel grabbed Connor's laptop and started typing, his face grim. "I remember, too. Do you think—"

"Yeah, I do." Connor's face tightened with thought. "These payments totaled north of two hundred thousand over the course of six years. What else could this be about?"

"Sounds like hush money to me," Dax put in.

All four men studied one another, as if looking for consensus. They conducted a whole conversation through raised brows, facial tics, and half sentences. Feeling completely left out, Everly's head spun faster.

Hush money? Why would anyone need to hush her mother? She could easily see the woman accepting the money. It was what she'd always wanted. Her mother hadn't hung around long, but Everly could remember her talking about a time when her life had been better and it had all revolved around money and social position. She couldn't help but look at Gabriel. He had both. She would do well to remember that. People who lived in this world—or had fallen from it like her mother—would do anything to stay in it or get back to it.

None of her morbid thinking answered the question of why a man as powerful as Maddox's father would have given her mother so much money.

"I don't understand," she demanded finally. This was their world. Surely they did. "Someone explain this to me."

"As soon as Gabe finds what we're looking for," Connor promised.

"Got it. Yes, she worked for Crawford briefly twenty-eight years ago. She left the firm, married Everly's father, and gave birth all within a few months. Benedict Crawford continued the payments until Everly was six."

The implications were immediate and staggering. If she hadn't been sitting, Everly would have fallen over.

"My parents both had blue eyes. I-I never knew where I got my hazel green." The thought hit her from nowhere and she murmured that fact to no one in particular.

"Maddox had green eyes," Gabriel said softly. "So did his father."

Everly closed her eyes. Oh, god. She was a Crawford. The knowledge made her sit back and gasp for breath.

Gabe turned to her, concern glowing from his blue eyes. "Everly?"

She nodded. "Benedict Crawford would only have had one reason to shut my mother up. Deborah Elliot wouldn't have cared enough to be a whistle-blower, but she was definitely the kind of woman to sleep with her boss and use her illegitimate child for financial gain."

"Damn . . ." Dax muttered. "You're Maddox's half sister?"

That revelation answered some questions but raised others. Why had her mother never bothered to mention that her dad wasn't really her father? Had he even known? Why had no one told her that she had a sibling, especially Maddox himself? Obviously, he'd known. He'd hired and mentored her, offered his friendship, and made her laugh. He'd simply never given her the truth.

"Now that I think about it, baby, you actually look a little like the Crawfords. Besides the eyes, you have their chin. Be happy you didn't get the old man's nose." Gabriel was actually smiling at her. "Well, now we know why Maddox didn't touch you."

So many years. So many lies. So many questions. Everly knew that dwelling on this revelation wouldn't help with the job at hand. Still, the weight of this information staggered her. Froze her. How was she supposed to feel? Betrayal and anger were sure to set in soon, but at the moment . . . just shock. Her head told her that being an illegitimate Crawford didn't change who she was as a person, yet how could it not change her perception of her past—and her future?

Everly dragged in a deep breath. Later. She'd examine this when she had time, when she could be alone. No way she wanted to show Gabriel another ounce of her vulnerability.

She forced herself to focus and turned her attention to Connor. "That's all fascinating, but how does it have anything to do with the reasons for Maddox's murder? Do we have any idea who this Natalia is? Have you run a skip trace on her yet?"

Gabriel went down on one knee beside her. "Hang on. You understand this changes everything? I can tell Sara the truth now. Do you know how much better she'll feel that Maddox wasn't sleeping with you? That he merely spent time getting to know his sister?" He smiled. "She'll be so happy that her baby will have an aunt."

Everly gaped at him. Did he really think uncovering this secret made everything somehow better? In his head, probably. But Sara wouldn't accept her any more now than she would have while believing her to be Maddox's lover. Sara would likely see Deborah Elliot as a whore, and Everly as an illegitimate something far beneath her. "It doesn't matter."

"Of course it does." Gabriel put a hand over hers. "This changes everything."

She pulled away. "It merely means that since you have some proof Maddox didn't sully me, you're finally willing to believe I wasn't lying. So *now* you feel like having a relationship. It's too late, Gabriel. I ended it twenty minutes ago when you proved that I can't trust you. We'll try to figure out who killed Maddox, see if this Natalia person had any possible connection to my mother, and determine if any of this was relevant in Maddox's death. Then we're done." She directed her attention to Connor without missing a beat. "Did the private investigator find a phone number for my mother? I haven't spoken to her in years. I would greatly prefer not to now. Can one of you call? I'm sure if you offer her cash, she'll answer your questions."

She couldn't stomach the idea of talking to her mother, especially after the way this morning's revelation had shaken her. If she actually found herself on the phone with Deborah Elliot, Everly knew she'd probably yell. The selfish bitch had split with her hush money and left her daughter to be raised in near poverty by a man with whom she didn't share a drop of blood. Despite all that, George Parker had raised her as his own. He'd been a dad to her—far more than the sperm donor who had been her biological father.

Dad had never told her that she wasn't his daughter by DNA, but maybe he hadn't known. And if he had, she loved him all the more for being the best parent a girl could have. He'd given her everything he could, especially his affection and support—unlike the other men in her life. Benedict Crawford had paid her mother to be rid of his responsibility. Maddox had withheld the truth and manipulated. He could have told her they were siblings at any time, but he'd remained mute. And Gabriel . . . she didn't even want to think about Gabriel.

"Everly?" Gabriel searched her face. "Baby, that's not true. It doesn't have to be that way."

She stood because she didn't have anything else to say to him. Everly needed to make an exit, but she wasn't sure where to go. She turned back to Connor, Roman, and Dax, all watching her quietly. She was ready to argue that she should leave when some pictures caught her eye. Among them, a trio of familiar faces sat on the table. "Where did you get those?"

"They were in the lockbox," Roman supplied. "We're concerned about the reasons Maddox was hiding these pictures. If anyone finds out he kept photos of young girls hidden, especially the woman who runs Capitol Scandals, they'll use those against him."

With a shake of her head, she let out a little huff. "These aren't sexual images. Maddox might have been a playboy and a pervert, but he wasn't the sort to prey on children."

"I agree," Connor seconded.

Everly picked up the photographs and glanced through them again. At least she could shed some light here and maybe put this vicious rumor to rest. She pointed to the photo on top. "This girl is missing. She was taken from her village about a month ago. In fact, they're all missing. They were girls attending schools sponsored by the foundation. Maddox must have been helping the effort to locate them. I believe that far more than him having some sick fascination. Besides, these kids were from separate continents. How could he have had any sort of inappropriate relationship with them from thousands of miles away?"

"I'm glad we have another scenario to work with." Connor's eyes narrowed. "Tell me about this foundation."

"The foundation has actually been around for close to fifty years, I think. It's Tavia's pet project now, but everyone at Crawford has a hand in it."

"Tavia isn't even old enough to have run the foundation for a decade," Dax pointed out.

"Her grandmother started the program. After she retired, her mother assumed control." Everly studied the photos again. "After they both passed away, Tavia took on the leadership role. She's been growing it since and brought it to Crawford about six years ago when she was first hired as a junior executive. I've heard the family was once wealthy, but they'd invested heavily in dot com startups that failed not long after the September eleventh attacks. So when she took control, she sought corporate sponsorships to keep it afloat. Given Maddox's reputation with women, the foundation bought him and the company good publicity he needed. It sort of countered the nasty rumors about Crawford men and made Maddox look more like a lovable scoundrel than a douchebag."

"Crawford puts a lot of money into this thing. I've even helped out, too. I suspect Tavia has benefitted," Gabriel mused.

"Sure. The foundation helped her rise up the ranks quickly. More recently, she brought her buddy, Valerie, along with her. Maybe that's why Maddox never dismissed her from her job. Because he had no trouble firing women he'd slept with in the past if he had just cause."

"We'll probably never know for sure." Roman didn't sound as if he liked that possibility.

"Unlike Tavia, Val would never get her nails dirty with the actual kids. But Maddox really believed in the work the foundation did. So maybe he kept her around because she helps to organize the annual gala." She frowned. "But we all pitch in, really. My friend Scott, who you were probably horribly rude to on the phone, donates a lot of his spare time to handle the foundation's marketing and promotion. I've volunteered on several school supply drives. It's fun and makes us feel like we're doing something good."

"You know we could be chasing our tails," Dax mused. "These photos could be completely unrelated to the women Mad hired the PI to find. And all of that could have nothing to do with his murder."

"But we've got no other clues," Connor pointed out.

"Yeah." Gabriel sounded low, as if the worry they'd never solve his friend's murder weighed on him for more reasons than his potential prison sentence.

Everly tried not to be swayed by his grief.

"It's obvious that Mad found the checks to Deborah Elliot, which prompted him to find Everly," Dax went on. "We can gather that he has pictures of the girls because they're missing and someone likely asked him to help find them. Maybe Ferling had contacts overseas? Maybe this Natalia is another missing girl."

Everly shrugged. "I know Crawford's overseas offices are working hard. Tavia has urged them to all but move heaven and earth to find those girls, I'm sure. They're like her family. And I haven't heard anything about a Natalia being missing. We get updates."

"Maddox stored all this information together in a lockbox. I think every bit of it is connected somehow. We're simply not seeing it," Connor surmised. "I'm going to run the name Natalia Kuilikov past some people I know."

"He's talking about spies." Gabriel moved his chair closer to Everly's and whispered in her ear. "Though I'm sure he would call them *fellow analysts* or something."

Everly forced herself to hold her ground, not be swayed by his attention, by the way he'd invaded her personal space. "Why don't I sneak into the office and talk to Tavia, see if she gave Maddox the photos? If so, maybe we can cross the missing girls off the list in terms of having anything to do with Maddox's murder."

"I'll go with you. We'll take the chopper," Gabriel offered.

Dax shook his head. "The chopper was on top of the building that burned down last night."

"My helicopter? They took out my helicopter?" Gabriel pounded his fist on the table. "Fucking assholes. Now I'm pissed."

So nearly being killed hadn't poked the bear like losing his precious helicopter had?

"Maybe you should stay here and deal with the insurance company on that," Everly suggested. "I'll head to Crawford on my own. All I need is a car."

He shook his head. "If we go to Crawford Industries, we go together."

"I don't think that's a good idea." Dax crossed his arms over his chest.

"Everly is right. We can't hide out here indefinitely. Maybe our best bet is to bring some of the truth to light," Gabe suggested. "Let's out Everly as Mad's half sister, then our relationship looks a bit more pure."

"We don't have a relationship," she reminded him. "So outing me to the press is pointless."

"That's not true," Roman contradicted her. "If they know your biological relationship to Mad, they're more likely to stop speculating about wild ménages and that Gabe killed him in a jealous fit."

"Agreed," Connor said. "Talk it over while you both get cleaned up. You'll come to the conclusion that this press conference is a good idea. If you're going to face the media, you'll need to look polished and professional. Roman can have a new suit for you, along with a dress and shoes for Everly, shortly. By the time you're showered, the clothes will have been delivered."

"I think you're right." Gabriel stood and held out his hand to her.

She didn't take it. "I don't want to give the press anything new to chew on."

Roman was already on the phone, talking in animated language to someone. He pulled the device from his ear and sent her a questioning stare. "Shoe size?"

"Seven but—"

He didn't listen to anything else she was poised to say. He merely shoved the phone against his ear again and strode from the room.

"Let's go." Gabriel grabbed her arm.

"You go. I'm not," she protested as he started to lead her away.

Though the thought of wearing clothes that didn't reek of smoke tempted her, the last thing she wanted was to be alone with Gabriel.

He wasn't listening. Instead, he led her to the stairs. "You can't think this conversation is over. I know I screwed up, but I won't stop talking because it makes you uncomfortable."

"It makes me angry, Gabriel. And I'm not going into that bedroom with you."

He turned, and those gorgeous eyes of his narrowed. "Why? Are you afraid I'll take advantage of you? Or are you afraid you'll let me?"

Everly glared at him. He was wrong . . . mostly. She was way too hurt and angry to desire him now. In thirty minutes? An hour? After one of his toe-curling kisses? She didn't want to take that bet. "Think what you want."

Gabriel simply smiled. "If anything happens upstairs, you'll be the one to initiate it. You have my word I won't lay a hand on you unless you want me to. Do you want me to, Everly?"

When his voice dropped, turning low and sexy, she couldn't help but respond. It was a purely physical reaction. She could ignore that. She wasn't going to fall into his trap again, right? She held on to the image of that report and of that information going into some system where Gabriel Bond kept dirt on the people in his life—just in case. She couldn't help but remember Maddox had done the same. Gabriel had even admitted Mad likely kept files on him and all their friends, too. She would always be waiting for Gabriel to turn on her. "No. I don't and you should know I'm not going to change my mind."

"We'll see." He let her hand drop and started up the stairs.

"Are you that convinced no woman can resist you?"

"No. I don't think we can be in the same room without touching one another. You're mad at me now but how will you feel in a week when I've treated you like a princess and indulged your every wish? How will you feel after I've shown you all I can offer you?"

"I'll feel like you only offered me those things after you got proof that I wasn't a whore. I'll feel like you still have a file on me, ready to turn against me the minute you think I've betrayed you."

"First, I never called you that, not once. Am I happy you didn't have a relationship with Mad? Damn straight. It would have been messy. But I was way past caring. I wanted you, regardless." He opened the door to their room for her. "As for that report, I've explained it and I've gotten rid of it. I didn't even read the damn thing. You have to believe that I ordered it before I knew who I was talking about. I asked the PI to look into your family, Everly. But I knew damn well from our weekend together you didn't have one. I was protecting my sister and her baby from some faceless woman who might come in and demand a portion of Mad's inheritance."

Everly walked into the bedroom, ready for a fight. "Have you even thought about the fact that I actually have a claim on Mad's inheritance?"

Now he would turn on her. Now she would really see Gabriel Bond.

He sighed and sat on the bed, still rumpled from their lovemaking. "Of course you do. I think Mad would want you to have some. We can talk about it. We'll sit down, you, me, and Sara, and discuss what we should do. I think having something from your brother might make you feel more welcome in this world."

She stared at him because that was not what she'd expected him to say. Not at all. "I don't want anything from Crawford. And this is not my world."

It didn't matter. Everly walked into the bathroom and started the shower. Tears streaked down her face as she tried to take it all in. Why hadn't Mad told her? Had he ever meant to clue her in?

Was she always going to feel like the little girl whose mother hadn't wanted her? Now she knew her biological dad hadn't wanted her, either. Gabriel wanted her, but for how long?

Twenty minutes later, her heart wasn't aching any less but she did know how much she was going to miss Gabriel. It seemed crazy to be in love with a fling she'd known a handful of days. Even worse, learning she was Maddox's half sister had thrown her for a loop, and her first reaction had been to turn to Gabriel for support and comfort. But if he'd given it, would he have followed that up with a stab in the back? She wanted to trust him—probably more than she should. She simply didn't know if she dared.

When she emerged from the big shower, she found a whole new cosmetics case on the basin, filled with amazing goodies from Dior and Chanel, all in her colors. Everly was under no illusion; this stuff had been expensive. But putting on some makeup would make her feel more together, and if they did have this press conference to announce that she and Maddox had been siblings, she needed to look her best.

She finished and blinked into the mirror at her polished image, then tightened the belt around the robe she'd borrowed from a nearby hook and emerged into the bedroom, ignoring Gabriel's stare.

"Your clothes are in the closet," he said.

Roman had apparently brought them up, along with the cosmetics, while she'd been in the shower. A pretty aqua-colored sheath hung from the rod. A pair of gorgeous beige heels that would likely be hell to wear rested on the hardwoods below. A lacy bra and a pair of matching panties, still with tags, sat folded neatly on a shelf.

Despite being an attorney-turned-political bigwig, Roman knew how to dress a woman. The outfit was chic yet professional and would suit her perfectly. She caught a glimpse of the label. Prada. No wonder it looked so good.

"I hope you don't expect me to pay you back for this dress. I can't afford it, especially since I won't have a job soon." She took the hanger off the rack, picked up the underwear, and started for the bathroom. She wasn't about to change in front of Gabriel.

"The dress is yours. Stay here, Everly. I've seen it all," he protested.

She closed the door nearly all the way. The spare inch she left was only so she could hear him. She wanted this conversation over as soon as possible. "You don't get to see it anymore. Now give me this grand and logical reason why I should face the press with you."

She caught a glimpse of him moving around the bedroom. He was taking off his shirt, revealing all those pretty muscles. *I will not stare. I will not stare.*

"Well, first off, telling the press that you're half Crawford will change the optics of the story. Suddenly you're not the woman caught between two men. You're the woman with one man who cares for you very much and you recently lost your brother. It's infinitely more sympathetic."

He had a point. Again, the desire to believe what he was saying welled up inside her. She was afraid to trust it. Everything she'd learned about his world scared her. Even if he felt this way today, how could she be sure he would be there tomorrow? He went through women like water. How did she know he didn't treat them all exactly the way he was treating her, right up to the point when someone newer and shinier came along?

She pulled off her clothes, placing her old skirt aside. Hopefully, the dry cleaner could remove the smoky stench. "Wouldn't I be more sympathetic if I was facing this tragedy alone?"

"No. Because then you're the girl who had a crazy weekend fling with a guy she met in a bar, rather than the one having a relationship with her brother's best friend and bonding with him after the heart-wrenching funeral."

Damn if he wasn't right again. If she didn't reveal her relationship with Mad to the press, they would comment on Gabriel's sexual antics, but it would be a blip on the public's radar. Basically, he'd get off scotfree, while she would probably be labeled a slut for the rest of her life.

And as much as she wanted to be angry, Everly had to think about the fact that Sara was having Maddox's baby. That child would be the only family she had left in the world. Was she willing to drag the family name through the court of public opinion, taking an infant with her, simply to avoid Gabriel and salvage her pride? No. Crap, she hated being backed into a corner.

Everly finished donning the dress, then glanced at herself in the mirror. Other than the fact that she needed some heated implement to tame her hair, she looked pretty damn good. The dress did amazing things for her figure. The color illuminated her skin and made her eyes appear greener than normal.

She was as ready to face reality as she'd ever be. It wasn't fair that the gossip rags would smear her name if she didn't go through with this, but no denying that walking out with Gabriel on her arm would go a long way to quelling ugly rumors. If the tabloids thought they were a boring couple, they would lose interest.

"Fine. We'll do the press conference. I'll play nice for the camera—but I have conditions."

"Anything." He stood at the door, bare-chested, staring at her through the one-inch opening. "Tell me what you need."

She needed him for more than the tabloid situation, but that wasn't going to happen. Better to accept that now. "First, I can't zip this dress by myself."

With a hungry gaze, he pushed the door between them fully open, and she tried not to gawk at how fine Gabriel truly was. "Turn around and I'll get it for you."

She lifted her hair and spun around, grateful for the excuse to avert her eyes. Maybe someday she'd find it easier to look at him. For now, it made her ache so badly she could cry.

"This dress is beautiful on you," he murmured as he dropped one hand to her waist. The other began to lift her zipper. Slowly. So slowly, as though he was reluctant to cover her bare flesh. "Tell me your other conditions."

"I want to talk to Sara when this is over. I want a place in my niece's or nephew's life."

He stopped lifting the zipper. When Everly glanced up, she found him staring at her intently in the mirror. They looked like a couple getting ready for another normal day at the office.

"I promise that Sara and I won't turn our backs on you. I know you don't believe me, but that was never my plan. I placated her earlier to defuse her anger, so she could be in a good emotional place to accept you later. I wasn't plotting to shut you out. I don't think I can. But if the only way I can have contact with you is through the niece or nephew we share, then I'll take it. Maddox Crawford was a bastard and he was my best friend in the world. He wanted you taken care of. That's obvious to me. So know that no matter how angry you are, I will take care of you. I would have done it because we were lovers, but I'll do it because Mad made us family."

Family. The word filled her with longing. She hadn't realized how much she missed her father until she learned she'd had a brother—and she'd lost him before she'd ever known all he was to her. She wanted more than anything to belong to a family.

Though she would be smarter to dispel the notion that she would be in Gabriel's, Everly nodded and stepped away from him. "Thank you. I don't need anyone to take care of me, but I would like to know the baby."

"Done. Any other conditions?"

"You'll keep your hands off me." He had to. She might be able to have a civil relationship with him in the future, for the sake of Sara's baby, but nothing more. No matter how much they would both love their niece or nephew, that would be the extent of their connection.

"I can't promise you that."

Everly tried to put a lid on both her temper and the inconvenient zip of thrill rolling through her. "Don't worry. I'll make sure of it. Are you going to shower and finish changing?"

"I showered in Connor's bathroom while you bathed in here." Without turning away or giving her a chance to escape, he wriggled out of yesterday's pants.

Underneath, Gabriel was stark naked.

She sucked in a breath and tried not to look, but that was like giving a junkie a full syringe and telling him to stay away. The hard bulges and sinewy dips of his body displayed the fact that he was all man. The expression Gabriel sent her way said that he knew it. Smug bastard.

While she tried to keep her tongue in her mouth, he managed to change into a clean pair of boxer briefs, charcoal slacks, and a snowy white dress shirt. The crisp cotton lay open at the throat, showing off several inches of tanned chest. She could still feel him under her palms, warm and smooth. She itched to touch him again and curled her fingers into a fist so she wouldn't.

With a deft grace, he stood in front of the mirror above the dresser and donned a red tie. "It would be best if we walked in and out together. Ignore any questions you don't want to answer."

"I don't want to answer any of them."

"Then leave it to me. Roman called for a limo. He's going to Crawford with us. Roman Calder being photographed at our side will lend an enormous amount of credence to the seriousness of our relationship."

"Fake relationship." Damn. She sounded stubborn even to her own ears but she needed boundaries between them or she would weaken. Gabriel certainly wouldn't put them up himself. He seemed determined to use every trick to coax her back to his bed.

Why? That was the one thing she couldn't figure out. Perhaps if she could answer that question, she'd have a better idea how to sort out this whole mess between them.

He shrugged. "Whatever you want to call it. Roman being seen with us suggests that Zack approves. It means the press will believe we're serious. You can stay with me at my place. In a few weeks when the heat dies down, we can quietly break up, if that's what you want. But you should know that I'm going to do everything in my power to make you want to stay."

She couldn't stop the way tears suddenly formed in her eyes. "I don't belong in your world, Gabriel. I don't even want to. I know that eventually I'll forgive you for that report. I won't be able to help myself. But the price I would have to pay to be with you is too much."

He softened, moving toward her to take her hand. She allowed it, needing comfort at the moment. "What are you talking about, baby? The press?"

She shook her head. "It's not just the press. It's all of it. Mad didn't tell me. You say he wanted me taken care of, but he didn't tell me. For all I know he was gathering intelligence on me so he could fight in case I ever found out and wanted a piece of the pie."

Gabriel sighed and tugged her closer. "I don't think so."

"And you. I won't ever really fit, you know. I don't know which spoon to use or who the power players are. I like computers because they don't lie to me. Code doesn't bend the truth. It does what I tell it to do. I'll always be a nerd from a small town. You can put me in this dress, but you'll never forget where I came from and neither will your friends. Before you know it, you'll see me as a liability and you'll go right back to those supermodels and actresses you love so much."

His arms went around her and he held her close. "Baby, you can't think that."

She let him hold her. It might be the last time. "I do. Can't you see how much better it would be if we parted civilly? I can't be what you need and I don't even want to try to fit in. I can't stand the backbiting and the manipulation."

"If you don't like my world, it's only because you haven't seen how you're changing it. Everly, since the moment I saw you at that bar, something shifted inside me. I don't like how my world works, either. So change it with me. We don't have to play by anyone's rules but our own. And as for you not being enough for me . . . you are my amazing nerd goddess and I am in awe of you. I am fascinated by the way your mind works and enthralled by how strong you are. You're a mystery to me and I'll go to my grave trying to solve you." He stepped back, his face flushed with emotion. "So listen and listen good, Everly Parker. I'm going to seduce you. I'll be beside you constantly, holding your hand and kissing you every time you'll let me to remind you how good we are together. You might sleep in another bedroom tonight, but I assure you, you'll be thinking about me and how much pleasure I can give you. You'll lie in bed and remember all the ways I put my hands and mouth on you. I'll be a few feet away, thinking about how good you feel and taste. I'll wish I could hold you close and show you how much I want to be with you. I'll keep looking for a way to make that happen and I'll be completely ruthless about it. When you're ready, all you have to do is walk down the hall. I'll be more than happy to make everything up to you and show you what we've been missing."

He stepped away, leaving her with shaking hands.

Everly was fairly certain she wouldn't think about anything else tonight.

THIRTEEN

G abe opened the door and gestured for Everly to enter first. She
was still a little pale from the impromptu press conference they'd
held in a nearby hotel, but he thought it had gone well. By tomorrow,
everyone would know that he and Maddox hadn't been embroiled in
a love triangle with Everly. The public eye would still be on them, but
the frantic throng of hungry paparazzi would likely dwindle now that
they'd introduced Everly as Maddox Crawford's long-lost sister and
Gabriel Bond's love interest.

At most, he had a few weeks to convince Everly to stay with him
and see if they could build any sort of future. Right now, his chances
of winning her back weren't looking good.

The receptionist's eyes widened as they walked through the double
doors of Crawford Industries' lobby. Jennifer stood, her professional suit
crisp. Her face, however, looked both stunned and haggard. "Mr. Bond."
She nodded. "Everly, I'm so glad you're back. The press keeps calling. I
tell them we have no comment, but they only dial us again immediately
and ask the same questions. The system wasn't designed to handle this
many calls. What should I do? The whole office is in chaos."

In the background, the electronic ring of the phone trilled nonstop. Beyond the reception area, Gabe heard voices raised, doors slam. This wasn't the cool, professional lobby he'd seen yesterday. Apparently, none of the other executives had handled this crisis. He smelled blood in the water, and the sharks were circling. Damn it, Everly had been right. With Mad gone for good, they both needed to be here until the fervor died down. Without a firm hand, all sense of order would implode.

"Call Amanda and Hilary and ask them to handle the traffic." Everly was calm and cool, as though being presented with a problem to solve actually helped focus her. "The extra phones plug into the system and I can reroute all calls from numbers not stored as one of our contacts. That way, you can manage the regular clients while the other ladies can handle the reporters. Has anyone in PR written a script they can follow? Has legal blessed it?"

The woman handed her a lone page over the counter. "I received it ten minutes ago."

Everly scanned the document, then nodded. "Crawford Industries won't comment on the private lives of its executives. Perfect. Copy this, then pass it to Amanda and Hilary. Tell them to recite the script verbatim, then hang up. Nothing more."

The phone kept ringing, an insistent drone.

"One moment." Jennifer dispatched the call quickly to another department in the building, then sent Everly a grateful smile. "Will do. I've still got calls on hold. Nearly every line."

Everly nodded. "Well, now we've got a plan. It'll be all right. I noticed the guards are on the doors downstairs. Are they being rotated regularly?"

"Yes. Scott already volunteered to handle that and posted a schedule."

"Thank goodness. Let me know if you need anything else."

Everly turned away. She didn't even look at Gabe before pushing through the frosted glass doors and striding through the sea of cubicles, heading toward her office.

Luckily, she couldn't walk very fast in those heels. He needed to thank Roman for that later.

"Everly, you know, this isn't going to work if you can't look at me."

She turned back and frowned. "What are you talking about? I can look at you."

He very deliberately took her hand and brought it to his chest, urging her closer. "If the employees don't buy that we're having a real relationship, they'll talk to the press and we'll be right back where we started."

"Gabriel, I'm a female executive. A young female executive. Do you know how hard it is to get people to take me seriously? I wasn't trying to ignore you. I was trying to be professional." She extracted her hand from his. "We shouldn't have to give them PDA in the office to convince them. And I don't want chins wagging that we're being inappropriate here, especially since you're my boss."

Gabe leaned closer. He could see her point and wondered how hard it had been for her. He would try to make sure she had it easier in the future. "I won't be your boss for long. I'm merely a caretaker for Crawford Industries. And I'm your boyfriend, according to that interview we just did. You lost your brother. I lost my best friend. No one expects us to be cold and professional." He tugged on her hand, drawing her closer. "Besides, everyone is watching."

Everly glanced around and finally noticed all the eyes on her. She cursed under her breath, but laid her palm against his, tangling her fingers in his own. "I don't like subterfuge."

He was used to it, having been exposed to it for a good majority of his childhood and his whole adult life. But to Gabe, they shared nothing pretend. "That will be over soon."

They made their way to her office where Everly locked up her purse and sorted through her messages. Gabe looked around at her multiple monitors and all the other assorted devices. He wondered briefly if he could ever measure up to her love of all things electronic.

"Don't you want to go to your office and check in?" she asked with a raised brow.

"Sure. I would love to work in my office. At my company. But I need to get a functional knowledge of this operation." That gave him an idea. She knew Crawford Industries and loved it. Managing the corporation until Sara could take over might bring them closer together. "You can start filling me in over dinner tonight. We've got reservations at Le Cirque."

She frowned a little. "I suppose you chose someplace public for show."

He didn't want anything about their relationship to be an act, but she wasn't ready to believe that she could fit into his world. Until she was, he would take whatever time with her he could get. "No, I like the food, but we'll make it a working dinner. You can fill me in on the management structure here. You know, what's working, what needs to be changed."

"I suppose this has really disrupted your life, too. You know, you could go back to Bond Aeronautics for the afternoon. I'll talk to Tavia about the photos. I assume she gave them to Maddox but I'll verify."

"Not happening." Gabe wouldn't budge on this point. Between the fire and the swarm of press, the idea of leaving her here made him more than uneasy. "Someone tried to kill us last night. I'm not letting you far from my sight. Whether you believe me or not, whether you think you need it, I will protect you."

"Those two men didn't come to kill us. We merely happened to be there when they tried to burn down Mad's house. I think they meant to destroy some evidence, cover something up."

"Yes, but they were willing to kill us to do it," he pointed out. "One of them got away. We don't know that he won't return to try to finish the job here. So you're stuck with me."

"Fine." She frowned as she booted up her laptop, then turned to the screen beside it, her eyes narrowing.

That was not her thinking face. That was her pissed-off face. He tried not to find it attractive but failed. "What's wrong?"

She leaned forward and her fingers worked over a different keyboard that appeared to be connected to a mega-sized monitor. "Someone tripped the security."

"For the building?" Entering or leaving the premises required magnetic security badges. Everyone had to wear them inside the building, too. The plastic rectangles showed their picture and contained codes that dictated what floors and sections the employee was authorized to access. Before the security guards had buzzed him in yesterday, he'd had to prove he was the new CEO of Crawford Industries.

"No. For my computer. Someone tried to access my desktop." Her fingers flew across the keys. "It's my main system. Both this and my laptop are hooked up to my backup system and my monitors, but this has way more power and storage than my laptop. Someone tried to get on it, but the system shut them down after three unsuccessful attempts at my password." She stood again and reached for the phone. "Henry? Hi. Thank you, it's nice to be back. Can you pull the security cameras around my office for the last thirty hours or so? I need to know everyone who went in and out of my office. I know it was secure. I unlocked it when I arrived yesterday morning, but clearly someone tampered with it since. Thanks." She hung up. "He's going to review the tapes. Someone was in here but what were they looking for? Company secrets?"

Gabe shrugged. "You're a hot property right now. Most likely, one of the employees tried to break into your system to look for torrid e-mails or dirty pictures they could sell to the tabloids for a buck. If they gained access to your computer, they could gain access to your cloud account, too, right?"

"I do *not* have a cloud account. And why would I have pornography on my work computer?"

Oh, she was so naive. "I wasn't talking about porn. I was talking about naked pictures. Of you. Of us."

She blushed prettily. "I wouldn't have those, either. That's ridiculous."

He would love to have a couple of pictures of her all soft and naked and flushed from orgasm. "But it happens. You've heard about celebrities who store those shots on their phones or computers."

"I hate this. I hate all of it. How do you live under a microscope?"

He wanted to put his arms around her, but she'd probably protest since they were alone now. "People are always watching and judging. We all encounter that in life. It's the scale of the scrutiny that's new to you." He shrugged. "I'm used to it, having lived with the press for years. I don't have it as bad as Mad did, though he often seemed to court the attention. And Mad didn't have half of what Zack endures."

There were days Gabe turned on the news and wondered why Zack didn't shoot himself. Being the president was one of the world's most difficult jobs. Everyone had their opinion and no one hesitated to tell him what it was.

"I don't think I can function like this. It's impossible to walk down to the corner market or hop on a subway without attracting attention."

Yes, she'd made it plain that was a wall between them. "Believe it or not, it won't always be this intense. The paparazzi loses interest once a man like me gets married, pops out a couple of kids, and starts spending his evenings at home with family. Of course, some of the perks go away, too. When I'm not so interesting, the maître d's at the hot spots aren't as willing to slip me a prime table."

"When you have little kids you'll be lucky to choke down a burger at a fast-food place."

Oddly, the thought didn't scare him the way it used to, not when he pictured kids who looked like her. It would be nice to go home to his family each night. He'd raise children differently than his parents. He would be there to tuck them in, to listen to their worries, and provide guidance. He would never send his babies away for their education. As much as Gabe loved his friends, he wanted his kids to rely on their parents for love and comfort.

"I'll probably want to eat at home a lot, actually. It's not something I've done much of in my life. I think it would be a nice change."

"Please." She rolled her eyes. "You'd be so bored."

No, he wouldn't. "I'm not the playboy the tabloids have made me out to be. I'm ready for something low-key and steady. Let me take you out to the Hamptons. We could grill and walk on the beach, spend time together. We'll start there. It's beautiful and quiet this time of year."

She hesitated for a moment. "I'm sure it is, but this whole cozy picket fence thing isn't possible in your reality. I don't think I fit in your five-star world."

"Everly, baby . . ."

"Stop. You think I'm going to be so dazzled by your jet-setting life that I'll change my mind. But I'm not built for the spotlight. I don't want to worry about someone photographing me if I trip on the sidewalk or I go to Duane Reade for tampons."

At least they were talking about a potential future. Right now, her logic wasn't leading the discussion, just fear. Gabe did his best to soothe her. "This scrutiny really will let up. I know all this attention seems overwhelming now, but it will pass. Then we can make our own future. No matter what happens, you will be a part of my family. I'll always be here for you, and Sara will, too. My sister is a wonderful woman and she'll need all the help she can get to raise that baby. You're the only family from Mad's side. She'll want you around, like I will."

There was a sheen of tears in her eyes as she looked up at him. "Neither of you has anything to worry about from me. You get that, right? I really won't come after Mad's money or the company."

"That concern never crossed my mind," he softly assured. "Not once I knew who you were."

"Good. Crawford Industries belongs to Maddox's child."

He nodded. "Yes. And we'll keep it safe for him."

"Or her." She was very firm about that.

"Or her."

God, he was crazy about Everly. He couldn't help himself. He leaned over and brushed his lips across hers. She stilled. Her breath caught. But she didn't move away. Her breasts brushed against his chest and he could feel his cock jerk in his slacks. All he had to do was get in the same zip code as her and he couldn't think about anything except how good she felt, how much he needed her.

Gabe took advantage of the moment to kiss her softly, doing his best to convey his adoration. He wouldn't give up or leave her. It occurred to him that she'd been alone since her father's death. She was the type of woman who needed a family, and he would give it to her. That was his real way in. Not money or fancy trips or gifts. Family. He could give her a place to belong, a place where she was valued and loved for the unique woman she was.

As he deepened the kiss, she wound her arms around his neck. He could inch her onto the desk. Given all the computer equipment on the surface, he wasn't sure he could sweep it away to lay her out, step between her legs, and find his way home—but he'd give it a hell of a try.

Hungry and aching, Gabe started to maneuver her back.

The door burst open.

Everly jumped away, her whole face flushing.

Tavia stood in the doorway, blinking and pressing a hand to her chest. She blushed every bit as much as Everly. "I'm so sorry."

Gabe knew they'd come to Crawford to talk to her, but right now he wanted to throttle the woman because Everly looked horrified. And clearly, he'd lost his chance to seduce her for the moment. Already, she was stepping away from him, putting distance between them.

Everly shook her head, brushing her hands down her skirt. "No, it's fine. You weren't interrupting anything."

Tavia's wide mouth pursed as her face fell. "I obviously did, but when I heard you were here, I couldn't help myself." She rushed forward and threw her arms around Everly. "I was so scared for you. I saw the news this morning. Oh my goodness, a fire? You almost died, sweetie."

Everly hugged her back stiffly. "It wasn't that dire, but it also wasn't pleasant."

"That sounds awful." Tavia jerked, her shoulders moving as though she cried.

Everly patted her. "I'm fine. Everything's all right now." She looked at him over Tavia's heaving shoulders. Her eyes were wide and she looked a little like a deer caught in the headlights.

He frowned, wondering if Tavia was always this emotional.

Everly looked a bit lost, too, while she comforted her friend. She'd nearly died, but Tavia needed consoling. His sweet Everly provided it. That was how she worked. She couldn't help but give people what they needed. If he played his cards right, she would give him everything he craved: her body, her affection, her tomorrows.

Gabe braced himself to say and do whatever it took to win.

Twenty minutes later, Everly sat in Tavia's office and accepted a mug of coffee from Gabriel. She needed it. In the chaos of the morning, she hadn't gotten more than a couple of sips at Connor's penthouse and she was a three-cups-a-morning kind of girl.

Gabriel allowed Tavia to cry a bit more before he'd taken control and herded them to the woman's office, ostensibly to make her more comfortable. Everly felt sure it had more to do with not wanting to talk about what they'd found in Maddox's house in an office someone had recently broken into.

"Thank you." She couldn't help but be grateful that Gabriel had put a stop to Tavia's emotional display. She'd been a little surprised at the woman's reaction to her near-death experience. They were friends, no doubt. Tavia had been the first woman to befriend her when she'd come to Crawford, but she hadn't realized how close Tavia considered them.

Everly owed her right now. Tavia had saved her from making an idiot of herself because about ten seconds more of Gabriel's kisses, and she might have surrendered to him right on her desk. She might have laid back and spread herself out and welcomed him inside.

She'd been moved by his nearness, by the thought of always being in the baby's—and therefore Gabriel's—life. It would be smarter if she walked away . . . but she didn't see how. They would meet up every few weeks or so, and she would have to watch his life play out. How was she going to spend years close to that man and not give in to him? Worse, if she managed to keep her distance, how much would it tear her apart to watch him fall in love and marry another woman?

"So you said you found some pictures?" Tavia had fixed her makeup and looked like herself again, though her nose still appeared a tinge red. Pacing behind her glass and metal desk, she looked every inch the modern female executive as she gave Gabriel a brilliant smile and accepted a mug from him as well. "Thank you so much. I'm really sorry I interrupted you two earlier." She regarded Gabriel. "I have to admit I warned Everly about you. I thought you were using her for sex."

"Not entirely. I'll never turn it down but . . ." Gabriel sent her a smooth smile. "You can't believe everything you read in the papers and see on TV. We're quite serious."

Everly chose not to comment. She'd promised to keep the secret that they weren't really a couple and she intended to honor it. "Tavia, those photos Maddox had hidden? They were pictures of some missing girls. He kept them in a lockbox with his most private documents. Did you give those snapshots to him? I recognized the girl we discussed on Monday. The others you showed me at lunch a few weeks ago. I couldn't get their faces out my head."

Tavia nodded and seemed on edge again. "It's hard to even talk about this. I get so attached to these girls." She shot a glance Gabriel's way. "You have no idea how much. They're young and they should have their whole lives ahead of them. The world is a nasty place." She paced the room again, her steps quickening. "The truth is, Maddox was going to pull the plug on the foundation. He came to me a month ago and threatened to defund the entire project."

Everly set the mug down with a shocked clatter. "He did?"

Tavia held a hand up. "I talked him out of it. He was concerned about a pattern of overspending on the fundraisers. He brought a bunch of receipts into my office."

"For catering and liquor for the last two years?" Gabriel leaned across the desk.

"Yes." Tavia looked surprised that he knew such details. "You have to understand, I don't have a lot to do with the ins and outs of the actual party anymore. That's been Valerie's role for the last two years. I'm embarrassed I didn't pay more attention to what she was doing. From what I can tell, she skimmed roughly a hundred thousand dollars during her tenure. She has a network of caterers who are probably splitting the money with her. I managed to persuade Maddox not to fire her. He wasn't happy but he agreed."

Everly looked Gabriel's way. Tavia's intervention explained why Valerie still had her job.

"How did you persuade him to forget about being scammed?" he asked.

"I didn't. All I did was ask him to wait until after this year's gala so we can get a better paper trail. We weren't looking for fraud last year, so we don't exactly understand how she stole so much."

Gabriel stared a hole through Tavia. Everly didn't know how the woman held up under that stare without buckling. It nearly made her squirm in her seat.

"What would have happened if Mad had yanked his funding before the upcoming fundraiser? Would the foundation have gone under without Crawford support?" he quizzed.

"Not at all. I have plenty of corporate sponsors who would love to take over. I take calls from cosmetic companies and feminine product producers all the time. It would be great promo for them," Tavia explained, then sighed. "I'll be honest, I could likely find a better corporate sponsor. I've been offered enough money to quit my corporate work and spend my time exclusively on the foundation."

"Why haven't you?" The foundation was Tavia's obsession, her passion. She barely slept, it seemed, working nearly twenty-four seven to make these girls' lives better.

Tavia shrugged. "I felt as if I owed Maddox. He took me in and funded the foundation at a desperate time. Besides, my mother had a fondness for this company." She raised her gaze, looking a bit sheepish. "Apparently, your mom wasn't the only one seduced by Benedict Crawford."

"Tell me you're not my half sister." Apparently her biological father had gotten around.

Tavia's laughter filled the room. "No. I look like my dad, actually. My mother had her affair with the elder Crawford in his later years."

"What about you and Mad?" Gabe asked. "I know you two were lovers and—"

"Eons ago," Tavia interrupted. "It was a fling. He wasn't any more serious than I was. We realized we were better off being colleagues and friends, so we left it there." She smiled at Everly. "Your press conference this morning shocked me. What a bombshell. Now I understand why Maddox was so crazy about you. He wasn't having sex with you; he was getting to know his sister."

The whole subject of Maddox made her a little teary. They'd agreed in the limo not to mention the fact that she'd only learned that day that she was related to him. Everly simply nodded.

"Maybe that will calm Val down some," Tavia mused.

"What do you mean?" Gabriel asked.

Tavia flushed. "Um, how do I put this delicately? Everly, there's a reason she hates you."

"Mad was sleeping with her." Gabriel's jaw tightened. "And thought you were, too, baby."

"They were very quiet about it," Tavia confirmed. "He stopped seeing her after he started seeing Sara."

"You knew about Sara?" Everly asked. She thought that had been a closely guarded secret.

Tavia nodded. "Yes, but I would never talk about it. That was their business. After Mad broke things off with Sara, Valerie made herself available to him again. But he chose to spend all his time with you, and you know what the rumors said."

So Valerie thought Maddox had moved on with her, all but discarding his old lover. No wonder the accountant had been so full of venom lately.

"Valerie had to know that Maddox was never serious about her."

Tavia winced. "She's always had a thing for him, though I suspect it was more about his money than his heart. And the fame. She wanted that, too, and was very upset he wouldn't take her out in public. I tried to warn her that Maddox wasn't serious about her, but she wouldn't listen."

Gabriel rolled his eyes. "Mad couldn't do anything that wasn't messy."

"That's true," Tavia said. "We agreed that if Valerie took even a cent this year that I'd help him put together a tight criminal case against her. I'd planned to see that through after this year's gala, provided I haven't been fired by then." She gave Gabriel a pointed look. "But Maddox took the paperwork with him. My hands are tied without that. Did you say you found it?"

"Yes, but I'm not as worried about that as I am about the pictures of those girls," Gabriel admitted. "I'll bring in a forensic accountant and figure out everything Valerie's done. We can proceed from there. Trust me, I won't hesitate to fire her. Now did Mad mention why he wanted pictures of your missing girls?"

"I gave those to him," Tavia explained. "I asked him to hire mercenaries to find them. Um, a group with a very distinct set of skills. He was reluctant, and I gave him the girls' pictures because I hoped that having faces with the names would motivate him."

"Mercenaries?" In foreign countries, they could be a necessary evil, but Everly wasn't aware that Crawford Industries had ever needed to use them.

"Yes." Tavia continued pacing. She never sat still. "When I asked, Maddox said he knew some. After I shared the pictures, he promised to think about it. But before he could get back to me, he . . ." She sniffled, looking as if she tried to hold herself together. "God, what a mess." There was a knock at her door. Tavia looked at her watch and stiffened. "It's Valerie. We have a meeting."

Gabriel stood and straightened his jacket. "I'll handle her."

"You can't," Tavia whispered. "Not until you get a solid case together and fire her. If you tip her off now, you'll give her time to cover her tracks. I know her well, Mr. Bond. She'll cause trouble if your ducks aren't in a row."

Everly nodded at Gabriel in agreement. But even looking at the man threatened to split her heart open. Less than an hour out of his arms and already she ached. Grabbing a few minutes to herself seemed like a good idea.

"We'll get out of your hair, Tavia." She turned to Gabriel. "Why don't you go to your office for a while? I'm sure you still need to meet with the other VPs. And have Connor bring you the files. You can make some phone calls to start the investigative process. I'll go to my office and tackle my inbox. We'll meet back up at five. After all, appearances would be better if everything looked normal this afternoon."

He slid his hand into hers, locking their fingers together. "All right." He glanced Tavia's way. "Will you be okay with her?"

Tavia was already striding to her office door. "Of course. I promise you, I can handle this. She won't suspect a thing." She swung the door open and gave Valerie a huge smile. "Hey, come on in. Have you had lunch?"

Valerie barely ate at all, from what Everly could tell.

The stick-thin woman looked past Tavia to stare at her. An expression Everly could only describe as one of distaste crossed her face. "I think I lost my appetite."

Gabriel's hand tightened on hers. His face was perfectly bland as he led Everly from the room and turned to Valerie. "I'll see you later."

Those four simple words might have sounded innocuous, but Gabriel managed to turn them into a threat.

"I thought you were going to let Tavia handle it," Everly murmured as the door closed behind them.

She didn't want to admit how much she enjoyed holding his hand, how safe she felt. She knew every eye in the office was on them, but at that particular moment she didn't care. Touching him settled her, and she loved showing off her guy.

And that was why she needed space. It would be far too easy to forgive and forget that he really wasn't hers at all. Despite his words otherwise, she didn't know that he ever could be.

"I didn't like the way that woman looked at you." He steered them toward her office. "I'll have her escorted off the premises as soon as I can."

She wouldn't miss Valerie at all, but something felt off. "If she really took that much money, she deserves it. She might have been smart enough to steal and she was probably plenty pissed off at Maddox, but I don't think she killed him."

"I don't know about that. I'm more interested in her for her obvious infatuation with Mad than I am for her stealing. She would have been fired, but I doubt he really would have prosecuted her. It would hurt both the company and the foundation's reputation. Any case he was compiling was likely in an effort to force her to keep her mouth shut." Gabriel stopped in front of Everly's office. He stared down at her. "However, she wanted him, and there are women crazy enough to kill rather than let their obsession go. We still have a lot to figure out, but I think it's safe to say that woman had motive to murder Mad."

Absolutely, and Everly didn't think Valerie was rowing her boat with both oars, so she might have wanted to kill Maddox. But being capable of his murder was something else. "I've worked with her for a while. I'm a little surprised she managed to swindle a hundred grand. I definitely don't think she's smart enough to blow up a plane."

Gabriel frowned. "Maybe her stupid is an act or she found greed motivating enough to get smart. Either way, I want the police to investigate. I'll put together some information, then let them ask her questions. But I want you out of this as soon as possible." He sighed and brought her closer. "I'd feel better if you came with me."

"I'm perfectly safe in the office." She still wasn't convinced Valerie was anything but a bitch. Besides it wasn't long before she was supposed to meet with her informant. She was fairly sure she'd be safe there, too. The parking garage was never empty before nightfall. Employees would be driving in and out, and there were plenty of security cameras. "Go. Do what you need to do. I'm fine."

He leaned in and brushed his lips against hers. God, that felt good. "I'll see you in a few hours. Don't leave the building."

She wouldn't. Technically, the parking garage was attached. She glanced down at her watch. She had time.

Her office was blissfully quiet.

She went to the safe and pulled out the SD card she'd locked up previously. She sat down again and began downloading the photos. She wanted them on her laptop. Clearly, her desktop was no longer secure.

She stared at the third photo. She could see Mad through the window of her loft. He was smiling and he had a glass of her crappy brandy in his hand.

Her brother. What would her life have been like if she'd grown up with him?

She downloaded two more photos before her computer popped up a message that the destination drive lacked adequate space to store the files. Something was eating up her hard drive. She'd known she was having issues with this damn system.

Everly moaned. She hadn't had the chance to fix or rebuild it, as she'd intended. Because her laptop had been having issues, she'd planned on wiping the system and starting over clean, hoping it would clear the problem. She'd spent hours on Monday backing up her files to the external hard drive in preparation but hadn't been able to finish the next step.

She hadn't planned on spending her day performing computer CPR, but she suspected this evidence was important, and she needed to make another copy of the photos that she'd keep close—just in case. With grim determination, she double-checked that she'd captured everything she needed on her hard drive before she proceeded to wipe her system clean and reformat the drive. Once all that was done, she could finally reinstall the operating system but it was going to take her all freaking day.

Scott came by about thirty minutes later with a sandwich in hand. They talked about inconsequential things as though Scott knew she couldn't discuss Gabriel. He kept it light. She dealt with a myriad of issues, the day flying by.

Hours passed before she looked up and realized it was time to meet her mystery contact. A little thrill of excitement zipped through her. Finally, something she could do. She'd felt so helpless the last few days, as if events were happening to her rather than her making them happen. The chance to be active was a relief.

She ejected the SD card. Backing up these pictures would have to wait until she could get her laptop running again. She wasn't about to take the chance with this evidence, so she tucked the disc and her laptop into her safe, then withdrew her gun. She'd felt naked without it these last few days, but she hadn't felt right carrying a firearm to a meeting with her new boss or the police precinct, so she'd left it behind. Now, she checked the clip and tucked it in her purse. The parking garage should be safe, but she wasn't an idiot. If she couldn't bring anyone with her, she must have some sort of backup.

Finally ready to get some answers, Everly called down to the security office and got one of the guards on the line. He would watch over her from the cameras and send a sentry in if she got in trouble.

Now she had someone to watch her back. Everly could watch her own front.

It was time to figure out who her informant was and what the hell he knew.

So you're telling me Mad was murdered over money?" Dax shook his head. "I always thought he'd fall off the roof while trying to sneak out of a married lady's house. Or be shot by some jealous husband."

Gabe looked at the receipts Dax had brought with him. It had taken his friend a few hours to gather the evidence they needed, discuss the situation with Connor, and cross town. He wished Everly would have made time to eat lunch with him, but she'd claimed she had too much to do. He'd spent a few hours organizing the receipts and Valerie's HR file. Tavia had been right . . . and wrong. The purchase orders and receipts in the file looked damning but weren't solid enough to convict Valerie if Mad had decided to threaten her with prosecution. But he may have found an ace up his sleeve. He had so much to wrap his head around but he'd been glad when Dax showed up.

"I don't know if I would say it was entirely over money, but money was definitely involved. He apparently fucked Valerie at some point, before he dated Sara. I suspect he discovered that she was skimming money from the budget Crawford donated to the foundation's galas. I found more information this afternoon. He'd gathered a pretty solid case against her. His secretary gave me a backup of his computer. According to her, he handed it to her in a sealed envelope the evening he died, just before he left the office."

"Like he knew he was going to die?" Dax frowned.

"Hilary said he often did that before he went out of town because he'd lost or dropped more than one laptop during his travels. He refused to use the same backup system as everyone in the building because he didn't want anyone having access to his sensitive files. So he'd often backup to a thumb drive and seal it up in an envelope. When I asked Hilary where I should start figuring out how Mad ran this place and what plans he might have had, she handed me this thumb drive."

Dax shook his head. "So you can piece together his case against Valerie?"

"Yeah. I found a whole folder about her. He'd compared the last three foundation fundraisers. Valerie handled all the ordering and catering for the last two. Between the year before Valerie stepped into this role and last year's gala, the expenses went up nearly a hundred and fifty percent."

Dax whistled. "Didn't she think that would attract attention? Unless she's stupid, she had to know it would."

Gabe nodded, pondering Dax's words. He was right; Valerie hadn't been at all subtle. Everly had claimed the woman wasn't smart. She'd managed to steal money, but not quietly. She had, however, shown enough creative accounting to make tracking her difficult. And that took brains. Still, if she'd been the one to blow up Mad's plane, that would require more than passing intelligence. If she didn't have much, wouldn't there be some lingering clue? A smoking gun somewhere?

"I don't know. Mad knew more than I first thought. I found some additional files, but he had them password protected. I need Connor to break in."

He'd tried all the obvious passwords. He knew Connor could hack in, however. Since he wasn't sure what he would find, he didn't want Everly involved.

"Pressing charges against an employee for theft could give that foundation some bad press."

"I don't care." He'd considered it and decided it was worth the bad publicity to make sure that woman went to jail. If he was right, then she'd killed his best friend.

And he really hadn't liked the way she looked at Everly. He knew a jealous woman when he saw one. Some women would merely be catty, but others—like Val—would go the extra mile. "The money was taken from Crawford Industries, not the foundation. It was an abuse of the company's largesse, and as long as I come out with a firm statement of support for the foundation, it should be fine."

Gabe didn't worry about that. But what the hell was he going to do to keep Everly close to his side if the imminent danger passed? He could buy a couple of weeks at most because of the press. If he couldn't change her mind by then . . . He cursed under his breath. He needed more time because he did not intend to become friendly strangers with her. He didn't intend to be someone she said hello to at the kid's birthday parties or at business meetings.

"I texted Connor. He's already working up a dossier on Valerie. Roman has a couple of his associates compiling files on all of the workers here. And by the way, I talked to Everly's mom this afternoon. She's a real peach. She confirmed the information Everly gave us. I know your girl doesn't want any more exposure than she's already got, so I threatened her if she went to the press, just in time apparently. She was poised to make money off her daughter's new fame."

"If she speaks a word, I'll ruin her."

Dax chuckled a little. "I thought you'd feel that way. I spent some time with Everly's employees. They're really loyal to her. A couple admitted to being wary at first because she . . ."

"Has breasts?" He could imagine what some members of the cyber-security team had thought about reporting to a petite female.

"Yeah. The last head of cybersecurity was an older guy, former military. Everly must have been a massive change for them. She proved herself very quickly. They now call her the queen of the geek squad. They like the hell out of her. They're worried about her. You should be prepared for them to give you a hard time. You need to face facts, Gabe. She's happy here."

Damn it, he'd rather have her with him at Bond. A working relationship would help foster their personal one, but she wouldn't switch jobs for him. He respected that, even as he found it irritating. But she hadn't given him much choice; he was going to have to deal because she was smart and competent and deserved her own career. Sara would likely back Everly up on this, so he would find himself outvoted.

"What else did you learn?" He wasn't worried about any skeletons in her closet.

"She's a hard worker. Everyone in her group likes her."

Because Everly was the sort of woman who excelled. Unlike him, she hadn't had a multimillion dollar company to fall back on. No inheritance. No cushy job or trust fund waiting for her. She'd had nothing but her own grit and she'd worked her ass off to succeed.

His heart constricted. He'd dated a lot of girls, but she might be his first real woman.

What was he doing with her? Playing around? Protecting his temporary turf? Because nothing they shared seemed that way. It felt so damn serious.

"She is exactly what she says she is," Gabe said.

Dax nodded. "Yeah. You're an asshole."

"I know. I should have believed her when she said she hadn't been another notch in Mad's bedpost. But I can't take it back now. And I can't let her go."

Regret weighed on him. He wished he'd had more time to convince her they could be great together. He would have come to the right conclusions about her platonic relationship with Mad on his own, but now he wouldn't have the chance.

Dax nodded in complete agreement. "No. You can't let her go. You need her. She makes you halfway decent to be around, man."

"Asshole." But he was smiling because it was good to have his friend's approval. Dax liked Everly. Mad had loved Everly. Yeah, that mattered, too. He wondered why Mad hadn't trusted him with the knowledge that he had a sister.

His intercom buzzed. With a long sigh, he picked up the receiver. He recognized that he didn't have the same enthusiasm for Crawford business that he had for his own company. He loved building planes and helicopters. As a boy, he'd been obsessed with anything that could fly. Bond had been his birthright. Crawford Industries might make him more money, and he just didn't care. But Everly had a passion for this place. He couldn't coax or force her to go to Bond Aeronautics with him, no matter how much he wanted to. She belonged here.

"This is Bond."

"Someone from security is here to talk to you. He says he has information about security tapes."

Shit. "Send him in."

Dax's eyes widened. "What's going on?"

"Someone broke into Everly's office since she was here last. She asked the security guys to roll the footage to try to figure out who could have done it. Apparently, they found something." He crossed the room and opened the door.

An older gentleman dressed in his Crawford Industries blue uniform stepped inside. He held a laptop and wore a frown as he nodded Gabe's way. "Mr. Bond, I thought you would want to see this."

Gabe sent the older man a grave nod. "Did you find footage of someone entering her office?"

"I definitely did. The door was locked, but apparently the woman had a keycard. Now, on the janitorial staff, the floor workers have cards that open almost every door, but they only clean the locked offices twice a week. This wasn't Ms. Parker's night, and the head janitor is a man."

"What woman?"

The guard lifted the lid to the laptop and hit a key to start the video feed. The footage was black and white but showed the hallway outside Everly's office clearly. The janitor, a short man wearing earbuds, moved in front of the lens, sweeping his vacuum across the beige industrial carpet. He danced a little while he worked.

And then Gabe saw her. She'd tucked her hair up in a ball cap and she wore a blue janitorial jumper, though it hung off her thin frame. She started to look around, clearly nervous, but whipped her stare down, as though she knew exactly when and where the hall cameras would be aimed. But then any halfway decent burglar would know that.

"Who is she?" Dax asked.

He had a hunch, but it was hard to be completely certain. There were plenty of skinny, tall women working for Crawford. It was New York City, after all. The police would argue it could be any of them. Gabe leaned in, trying to discern anything definitive.

Then she lifted her hand to Everly's doorknob and revealed something no real janitor would wear on the job: a delicate white watch. Chanel, if he wasn't mistaken. Sure, it could be a knockoff, but why would anyone who immersed their hands in cleaning solution routinely as part of their job description wear jewelry that wasn't waterproof? He'd noticed that same watch earlier when she'd done her best to stare Everly down.

Now he had some proof that Valerie was up to no good. Forcing her way into Everly's office was a form of B&E. Gabe didn't need more proof than this.

"That's Valerie from accounting and she's fired. Let's escort her to the lobby now. Make sure she takes nothing with her except her personal belongings. Then we'll hand her over to the police." They could hold her until he could scrape together the rest of the proof necessary to make embezzlement charges stick.

"Yes, sir." The guard nodded.

Gabe felt better being able to get rid of the woman. Something about her screamed *crazy bitch* to him. He'd met enough to know. Some women talked a good game, while others would happily cut their enemies. Gabe bet that Valerie fit into the latter category, and he wanted her as far from Everly as possible. His girl might know how to defend herself, but he didn't want her to have to. "Dax, could you come with us, in case—"

"She goes pyscho on your ass? Yeah." Dax was right behind him.

Gabe took off. He didn't give a damn if everyone stared and wondered if their new CEO had gone insane. He only cared about ensuring Everly's safety.

As he reached Valerie's office, dread spread through his chest. He had no specific reason to think she'd already acted or harmed Everly—except a terrible gut feeling. With his heart chugging, Gabe threw open the woman's office door. Empty. Gone.

He turned to Valerie's assistant. "Where is she?"

The woman clearly heard the urgency in his voice. She immediately turned, flustered, and stammered. "I-I . . . well, she, um . . . Ms. Richards is gone for the afternoon."

Gabe had a bad feeling he knew what Valerie's plans were.

He turned to the security officer. "Find Valerie. Now."

FOURTEEN

Everly scanned the empty level of the parking garage, then glanced nervously at her phone. Ten minutes past three. It felt as if she'd been waiting forever. Her nerves stretched tight.

Maybe the secret e-mail and texts she'd received had been a terrible joke. Maybe whoever sent them was a prankster. Or a sick individual.

Three levels belowground, each sound was magnified as it echoed off the concrete. Every squeal of tires or sudden slam of the brakes from above as cars navigated the structure amplified underground. The tense moments buzzed with anxious anticipation.

So when Everly heard the echo of footsteps against the cement behind her coming down the ramp toward her, she nearly jumped out of her skin.

She reached into her purse to reassure herself her firearm still lay inside, then stepped away from the bank of elevators that had brought her down. She searched for the source of the footsteps. Her mysterious contact obviously liked drama and wanted to keep her on edge, so he'd walked down the parking garage to reach her. Regardless, he seemed determined to make an entrance.

If this man turned out to be a reporter, she would take out her frustrations on him and give him the tongue lashing of his life. If he was for real . . . Everly didn't know what she'd do.

When she caught sight of the man, she had zero doubt he was the one who'd contacted her so mysteriously. He walked toward her, his polished wingtips clicking smartly. His face was barely visible under the brim of a fedora. Despite the unseasonably warm day, he wore a trench coat with the collar upturned to better hide his face.

Though his film noir getup made her stop just short of rolling her eyes, Everly remained on guard. Yes, he stood roughly half a foot taller, but she couldn't take him seriously when he was dressed so Hollywood for the part.

Though she had a hard time seeing his face, especially given the dim lights overhead, she pegged his age at roughly fifty. The guy looked surprisingly fit, so he'd probably hold his own in hand-to-hand. He could be carrying, but then so was she. Given the lack of a telltale bulge in his coat pocket, she'd draw her weapon far faster than him since he had to get through the voluminous trench to a shoulder holster.

His gaze was steady as he closed the distance between them, but he remained mute until he stepped onto the concrete pad near the elevators, just beyond the security cameras. "Miss Parker, it's good to see you can follow instructions."

So he was impressed by her ability to read? Fabulous. "Why am I here?"

He raised a brow. "No small talk, then?"

She didn't have time. Gabriel would come for her before long, and she would rather not have to explain this meeting to him. "I prefer getting to the point."

He nodded. "I was pleased you made it out of Crawford's brownstone alive last night."

"So was I. And your point is?"

He acknowledged her impatience with a sly grin. "If you haven't already, I believe you'll discover the man killed at the site was hired muscle for the Russian mob, someone they used when they didn't want close ties to a crime."

"We've already figured that out." The man's knowledge didn't prove anything except that he'd read online news sites or gotten ahold of the police reports. Anyone who understood the way the Russians work would be suspicious of a criminal from Brighton Beach. "The police are looking for the second man. He got away."

The informant gave her a regretful frown. "They'll have to work fast or they won't find Mr. Hall alive."

"Mr. Hall?" As far as she knew, the police hadn't identified the second assailant yet. They had captured some grainy footage of him on a CCTV as he'd fled, but they hadn't yet put a face with a name.

"If my information is correct, you'll soon learn that the second man involved in the crime is Lester Hall."

She froze. The assailant who'd perished in the fire had called his accomplice Les. How could this man possibly know that?

"He's a known associate of the *Bratva* and a childhood friend of Jason Miller," her informant went on. "I'm sure he thought he could go into hiding, but I firmly believe the men who hired him would much prefer that he never have the opportunity to speak of the incident. They likely hired both men to torch Crawford's house and planned to kill them afterward. Those Russians know how to keep secrets. In a few days, Hall's body will surface, and the police will likely chalk up your near-death experience to an isolated case of arson and close the file."

Everly didn't like what she was hearing. "Why would two men without ties to Maddox randomly torch his brownstone?"

She didn't mention that she and Gabriel had seen the thugs looking for something—whether to swipe or destroy it, she didn't know. She wasn't here to give her informant information.

The man shrugged. "It won't matter to the police. They're petty criminals. No one will mourn them. They're easy to mentally convict and forget."

She recoiled. "That's harsh."

"But true. Miller and Hall brought no value to society, and the man whose house is in ashes is dead now, so there's no true victim. As long as the police and public can assign blame and say the crime has been solved . . ." He shrugged. "Almost everyone will be happy."

"But not all?" Everly asked. She hadn't quite decided if he was a total crackpot. Maybe. Probably. But what if he really did know the identity of the second arsonist? What else might he know?

"Well, *you* shouldn't be happy. In the next few hours, the authorities will close the case on Maddox Crawford's death, too. They'll either rule that it wasn't a homicide after all or name a patsy. Either way, they will close every avenue of investigation and sweep it all under the rug."

The man sounded like a conspiracy theorist . . . but did that necessarily make him crazy? "Why? He was murdered, right?"

"Of course," he shot back as if it was obvious. "He knew too much and he couldn't be allowed to live."

"Knew too much about what?" When the man hesitated, Everly glared at him. "Your e-mail and texts indicate you have all the answers. If that's true, tell me what Maddox died for."

He bent his head and looked at her from under his brim as he spoke. She couldn't see his face, but his low growl was unmistakable. "Good. You are smart, wanting to get to the heart of the matter. Everything else is background noise and distraction. Did pilot's error kill him? Or was it a bomb on the plane? And what about the sudden appearance of that video showing Bond's threat to kill Crawford? It makes your boyfriend look awfully guilty and will keep the public speculating. But all that merely scratches the surface of what's really going on. You're digging, but you've barely clawed a fingernail into the glossy coating yourself."

"What do you mean?"

"You're starting to get information, but the clues seem unrelated, like they don't quite fit together, right? Don't give up. The evidence gives false impressions when laid out in pieces as simple, individual truths. When you put everything together and look deeper, you'll see."

She really wanted to write this man off as a loon. But even if everything he'd said so far had been outlandish, she had a gut feeling he might be on to something. "Stop speaking in riddles and tell me what the hell is going on."

"I don't have tangible proof. You'll have to find that for yourself. But believe me, if I laid the whole truth out, you'd call me a liar. Or you would panic."

"I'm not a damsel in distress."

"You're not," he agreed smoothly. "But these are huge stakes. Almost unimaginable. You may not believe me about that, either, but try. Your life might depend on it."

Everly wished she could call bullshit on that, but after Mad's murder and the intentional fire at his house, she didn't have trouble believing it.

"Do your own investigation," he went on. "If you uncover the layers as I have and keep asking questions—even if they seem crazy—you'll figure it out."

Why would the stakes in her half brother's murder be so ridiculously high? And how was she supposed to know the right questions to ask?

Everly frowned. "I don't understand any of this. I know why a jealous husband or a scorned lover might have wanted to kill Maddox, but they would probably have wanted the satisfaction of killing him with their own hands, not rigging his plane to go down."

"Think bigger, Ms. Parker." He scoffed. "Much bigger. Who benefitted most from his demise?"

"If you're suggesting that Gabriel Bond killed him to inherit—"

"I'm not. This is bigger than simple greed." He glared at her. "Who has the power to cover up a murder like Crawford's? Research that and think really outside the box about why. I won't say more now. It's too much to lay on you at once without documentation. But I won't leave you without resources. You can trust one person."

This dramatic speech hadn't made much sense, but Everly finally got a glimmer of where this was heading.

"You?" She raised a cynical brow at him.

He laughed, a deep chuckle. "Oh, heavens no. I wouldn't trust me at all. No, I'm talking about Lara Armstrong. She's in DC. Find her. Compare notes. She's tugging on a few threads, but she hasn't figured out which ones to yank yet. When she does, she'll be in danger because no one wants this information revealed, as our friend Mr. Crawford discovered the hard way."

Frustration bubbled up. Why couldn't he simply tell her what he knew? "I don't have time to investigate, and it's not exactly my skill set. Just tell me who killed my brother."

Even as he shook his head, his grin grew wider. "I was surprised you discovered that information so quickly. Tell me, did it make Mr. Bond feel better to know he hadn't slept with his best friend's mistress?" He sobered. "He might not be guilty of murder, but whatever you do, don't trust Gabe Bond."

Everly suspected she shouldn't. She would always wonder what would have happened if he hadn't learned about her true relationship to Maddox. Would he have ever believed that she hadn't warmed Maddox's bed? Or would he have decided that he couldn't handle his friend's leftovers and dumped her? Despite all that, she didn't like this stranger talking badly about Gabriel.

"I don't think my relationships are any of your business."

"If your relationships get in the way of the truth, they are."

Who the hell did he think he was? "You called me here to give me information—"

"No, I called you here to give you direction. So far, you're not taking it well."

He was talking in circles and it was irritating the hell out of her.

"Say what you came to say and be done. At this point, I'm ready to write you off as a meddling conspiracy nut."

"Ah, finally the feisty girl comes out. So you don't like me bad-mouthing Gabe Bond, do you? You're in deep with him."

"Again, that's none of your business." Once they figured out who killed Maddox, she and Gabriel would only see each other occasionally, for the sake of Sara's baby. She could resume her work and her thriller-novel-a-week habit. He could go back to his former life as a Manhattan manwhore.

Why did that thought hurt so much?

"I don't object to Gabe in general. He's simply involved with people who need to bury this information so deep, it never sees the light of day. Several factions are competing to come out on top, and some don't even realize other teams exist. Once they do and you start putting the pieces together, you'll be in danger. Trust me, this picture is only starting to come into focus. What you know is one corner of a much larger puzzle."

"Does this have anything to do with the missing money?"

He frowned. "Missing money?"

So her mystery informant didn't know everything. Maybe he didn't really know anything. Everly shook her head. This guy was probably a nut job after all.

"All right, what's the scam? Do you work for Lara Armstrong, whoever she is? You know what? It doesn't matter. I'm done listening." She turned to leave.

"Wait. I'll prove my knowledge to you. Tell me, did you find the pictures of the missing girls in the lockbox in the hidden room?"

She froze. Not even the cops knew about the lockbox. She and Gabriel hadn't wanted it taken into custody as evidence—or to start any speculation about Maddox's predilections by turning it over. "How did you know about that?"

He smiled. "It was very clever of you to find your way out of the fire." He knew he had her, and she could practically sense his satisfaction. "Don't look so shocked. I know a lot of things I shouldn't. That's why you need to listen to me."

"Why don't you go to the authorities yourself?"

He shook his head. "I'd be discredited and discounted. Like I said, I know what I know, but I have no tangible proof. You, Ms. Parker, have that young, earnest thing people will believe. And I have no doubt you'll find the proof to back it up. I'll steer you in the right direction."

"Why me?"

"Because you were his sister," he explained. "Because you have the talents necessary to solve his murder. Because he would want you to be safe and happy."

She had so many questions, but she doubted he'd answer any of them. "Who are you?"

"That doesn't matter. I'm a minor player in this game. I've hidden my identity to save my neck. You won't be able to discover it. Don't waste valuable time trying. Just know that I'm sympathetic to your brother and to you."

"But not to Gabriel."

His head shook slightly. "I wouldn't say that. I admire all of Maddox's friends. I merely don't think it's in your best interest to trust them. Those boys take their friendships seriously. Don't think you'll come between them—not for a second. If Gabe has to choose between you and his childhood brothers, he will choose them. He might regret cutting you loose, but he will."

The garage suddenly seemed colder than before. Yes, Gabriel had powerful friends, but she wasn't sure what her mystery man was trying to say. "Why would he have to choose?"

The man's features turned steely, his eyes hardening. "Because they're in deeper than even they realize, and that's another reason I can't simply tell you everything I know. Even if I had all the proof and everyone believed me, they'd attempt to cover it up in order to protect their own. The truth must be revealed."

"I don't understand." She heard the sound of a car rumbling above her.

"I know it's a lot now. I sent you the information you need to begin." She heard frustration creeping into his tone. "Start there."

The revving of the car's engine sounded louder suddenly. She felt the ground move as someone zipped by in a white sports car. Everly frowned. Not many cars parked this far down. Even in the middle of the workday, there should be plenty of spaces above. True, some people were freaky about parking next to other cars, but she hadn't noticed the vehicle parked on this level earlier.

She turned back to her mystery man, hoping he wouldn't be spooked by someone else's presence in the garage. She had more questions, but the most important one needed an answer now. "Are you talking about the e-mail and texts you sent? Because you didn't send any information in those."

The sound of screeching tires echoed somewhere behind her. Whoever sat behind the wheel of that vehicle was driving like a maniac.

"Not that. The information." When she sent him a blank stare and shook her head, the man's eyes widened. "I sent you a ton of information. It's the only copy. Everly, if that falls into the wrong hands, we could lose everything. Shit!" He looked frantic. "You'll never find Sergei without that data."

Sergei, the man Mad had mentioned in his video with Gabriel right before her brother's ill-fated flight?

"Who is Sergei and why would I need to find him?" she asked as the nearby elevator dinged. The doors began to part, and she turned to see who would come this far underground in the middle of the workday.

Before she could discern who occupied the elevator, a more ominous sound filled the garage and snagged her attention. An engine revved loudly. Tires squealed. Then she caught sight of the white car tearing back down the aisle toward her. As the car zoomed closer, Everly waited for the driver to step on the brake.

Instead, the person behind the wheel gunned the engine—and steered the vehicle directly toward her.

"Everly!" Gabriel shouted over the racing car.

She had the briefest glimpse of a woman driving. Valerie.

The accountant wasn't stopping. Or even slowing. And she wasn't turning to go up to the next level. No, Valerie was headed right for her, wearing a murderous look on her face.

As Everly stared at the woman, a flood of fear paralyzed her.

Suddenly, she was flying through the air before landing with a hard thud, tangled with Gabriel's solid body on the hard cement. As she heard a male grunt, the car whizzed by her, so close she felt a cold rush of air zip across her skin. Then she heard the sounds of metal colliding with concrete slam through her brain and she whipped her head around to see that the vehicle had slammed into the wall she'd been standing in front of only moments ago.

If Gabriel hadn't tackled her, rolling her away from the car's path, Valerie would have killed her.

His arms tightened around her for a long moment. As he disentangled himself and rose to his knees above her, his face appeared ashen. "Are you all right? Did I hurt you?"

She was a little banged up, but there was zero question in her mind that Gabriel had risked his life to save hers.

Though out of breath, she managed to sit up. "I think I'm fine. Thanks."

Dax raced over, holding a semiautomatic in his hands, his stare glued to the car. "The Mustang hit the wall pretty hard, but I think it's safe to say the building won that battle." Dax looked down at her. "You need a bus?"

Ah, the comfort of a man who knew the lingo. She moved her arms and limbs experimentally, relieved that all felt well. Everly was pretty sure she wouldn't need an ambulance. "No, but if Valerie is still alive, she'll need one."

Dax nodded.

"Get out of the vehicle and put your hands up." A strong masculine voice rang out through the now-quiet garage.

Everly saw one of the guards drawing down on the car. From what she could tell, the vehicle's front end had been crushed. Smoke billowed from the hood. The airbag had deployed and, given its movement, she'd bet Valerie was behind it trying to breathe or find a way out from under it.

After a glance around, she didn't, however, see her mystery man. He'd gone, probably deciding that the turn of events was either a reason or a smokescreen to get the hell out. He was hiding. Hell, he'd probably find some other conspiracy to run down for kicks.

But how had he known about the lockbox?

"Come out slowly," the guard repeated, attention directed at the car.

Very slowly, the woman opened the door and stepped out on shaky feet, holding her hands in the air. "I wish I hadn't missed, you bitch. You took everything from me."

She was still in her designer clothes and her five-inch heels, but mascara smudged her face and blood stained her blouse. She looked somehow polished and vicious at once.

Everly had to ask. "What did I ever take from you?"

"Maddox. He was supposed to love me. He swore that he wanted me, but in the end, he went to you. Always to you. Why did you steal him? I hate you."

Apparently, Valerie hadn't seen her morning press conference. And Everly was tired of explaining herself. "Maddox wasn't my lover. He was my *brother*. You tried to mow me down to avenge the romantic loss of a man I never once touched."

Her eyes flared. "That's not possible. You're a liar. A corrupt whore trying to destroy me because you wanted Maddox to yourself. That's why you planted documents to frame me, but I'll prove that you're the guilty one or I'll take you down with me if it's the last thing I do."

Everly heard the sirens from above. She was about to see the NYPD for the third incident in less than forty-eight hours. She winced. How terrible was her afternoon about to get?

Gabe watched as Everly shook the officer's hand. His soft, curvaceous female had handled the situation with strength and grace. Most women would be crying and shaking and looking for someone to comfort them. Even Valerie had been hauled off, hysterically screaming her intent to get even. But Everly had merely moved on to the next task. She'd been perfectly calm as she talked to the officers, even laughing and joking at one point. Seeing this side of her was a bit of a revelation. She was so competent, so in her element.

She'd ignored him for the most part except to ask if he needed anything.

At the moment, he'd said no, but he'd lied. Gabe needed to get her naked and underneath him. He needed to get his hands on her so he could assure himself that she was alive. Damn, he was the one who needed some comfort.

"You all right?" Dax crossed his arms over his chest as he looked over the mess of the parking garage.

Absently, Gabe thought they'd have to bring in a structural engineer to ensure that batshit crazy bitch hadn't made the entire building unstable.

"Not really. I want to know everything about that woman."

Dax nodded. "After the questionable catering receipts, Connor started working on it. He pulled Valerie's records and found that she failed to disclose some time she spent institutionalized for emotional issues."

"Are you kidding me? How the hell did she get hired?"

"C'mon, Gabe. You know that, by law, HR departments can't ask about certain personal issues. She apparently tried to have that period sealed off, but Connor found it easily enough. Rumor is, she was also known around the office for being very willing to accommodate her male bosses."

So she slept around. "I still don't understand what she meant about Everly planting evidence against her."

Dax's brows rose as he thought. "I suppose she's trying to persuade everyone that she didn't embezzle any funds. It should be easy enough to prove. It's a lot of money. If Valerie is guilty, I doubt she buried it in coffee cans in her backyard. We'll figure it out, but I think it's safe to say that attempting to murder Everly will likely carry a longer sentence."

His heart rate ticked up again. "That's not funny."

"Too soon to joke. Got it. Sorry, man." Dax patted him on the back. "Why was Everly down here?"

Gabe hadn't thought about her reason for coming down here, only about getting to her so he could ensure her safety.

Luckily, one of the guards had seen her striding toward the parking garage. It had been simple enough to check her progress through security cameras and discover she was on the bottom level. What—or who—the hell was down here? Not her car. According to her, she usually rode the subway into work, and Dax had brought them here this morning in the limo.

"When the elevator doors first opened, she was talking to someone," Gabe observed. "A man, I think. I thought he was just someone she knew. The asshole didn't stick around to make sure Everly was all right. He might have been scared, but now I wonder. Most people would assume Valerie had simply had a car accident. They would make sure no one needed medical attention and give a statement to the police. Not this guy."

"You thinking he knew otherwise and ran?"

"Something like that. Except he didn't run away, he walked. Now that I think about it, he was surprisingly calm."

"Sounds like Everly arranged to meet clandestinely with this guy. Gabe, have you stopped to think that she might have been meeting a reporter?"

He shook his head. "She wouldn't do that, at least not knowingly."

"A lot of women would enjoy the attention."

"Believe me, not Everly." Gabe wouldn't believe that unless he caught her sitting in a newsroom and wired with a microphone, ready to go national.

He stopped. He trusted her. The realization stunned him. He really trusted her. He would believe whatever she told him because he knew this woman deep down to her soul. Oh, he might not know every detail about her—how she liked her eggs or her favorite things to do on a lazy Sunday—but he damn well knew her character.

"You're sure?" Dax quizzed, but his smile made Gabe think his friend trusted her, too, and just wanted him to admit it.

"I'm sure. If she met with someone, then she thought that person could help. I'll ask her about it." He raked his hand through his hair, aware that he seemed to be doing a lot of that lately. "It's past five-o'clock for her, as far as I'm concerned. She's been through enough today. Why don't you bring the limo around? I think the police are finishing up here, and the last thing I want to do is remain at the office."

He needed to be alone with her. Seeing her almost die today, knowing he could have lost her irrevocably, had changed something inside him. Yes, last night had been harrowing, but he'd been a part of it, with her every step of the way. Today, he'd barely been able to do more than watch Valerie try to mow her down. He was furious Everly had put herself in a position to be the crazy woman's target, but he knew damn well his girl hadn't come here for selfish reasons.

Gabe knew he'd screwed up. He should have believed her when she'd sworn she and Mad hadn't been lovers, but he'd been so sure she'd been lying because he hadn't believed someone like Everly Parker existed. His cynicism might cost him the one woman he could love.

Shit, he'd thought about love again. He could definitely love Everly if he could break past her walls and earn her trust. She'd had them before he'd come along, Gabe was sure, but his idiotic comments to his sister and that damn report had turned her little garden partitions into a mighty fortress around her heart. And his lifestyle. He couldn't discount that.

Goddamn it, he really needed to be alone with her, find out what she'd been doing here, who she'd been talking to, and how sweet she'd taste now that he knew his feelings.

Then he had to figure out a way to earn her trust again.

After a nod at the policeman she'd been talking to, she turned and walked back in Gabe's direction, her fully restocked purse hanging at her side. The new dress she wore had a tear in the skirt and a giant smudge of dirt on the shoulder. She still looked so gorgeous he could barely stand not touching her. Even in the gloom, she practically glowed.

"The EMT cleared me. I don't have any signs of concussion, so I won't need any tests at the hospital. I think they're done with the paperwork for the evening. I'll have to go down tomorrow and they'll need witness statements, but the security cameras should pick up most of the incident. I think it will be very hard for Valerie to say she missed that turn." She put a hand on one hip, and her eyes narrowed. "I'm going to assume you found me using the security cams. You didn't LoJack me in the middle of the night, did you?"

No, but Gabe was thinking he might try that next. He hadn't liked not knowing Everly's whereabouts. The damn woman so rarely stayed where he put her.

Was it wishful thinking to hope that he wouldn't need measures that drastic? That the danger would finally stop? It looked as if Valerie was the bad guy in this mystery Mad had left behind . . . but Gabe wasn't totally convinced. "The guards helped me track you."

"All right. I'll roll with it because I really am happy not to be a corpse. Any particular reason you decided to track me down in the middle of the afternoon?"

How did she manage to make him feel slightly guilty for invading her privacy instead of like a hero for saving her life? "We found proof that Valerie was the one who broke into your office. Then I . . ." How could he explain this without sounding like a loon? "I got a feeling you were in danger and that I should find you."

"It didn't help that no one could find Valerie, either," Dax added.

"That makes sense. She clearly had it in for me—for all the wrong reasons." She sighed. "I think the cops are assuming Valerie was the one who hired the Brighton Beach boys to torch Maddox's house because he was obviously investigating her."

"It's logical," Gabe admitted. "I'll feel better once we find the money she embezzled."

At least it would prove that she was guilty, not merely unhinged.

"Yeah." Everly sent him a contemplative stare. "I'll look into her financials as soon as I can, but I'm still not sure she'd know how to blow up a plane."

Dax cleared his throat. "Um, that's not an issue anymore. While Everly was talking to the police, I got a call from Roman. The FAA has reversed its position on the crash. They say the chemicals found at the site were the result of cross contamination and not actually on board the plane. Apparently, there's a chemical plant in the area that's being investigated by the EPA for illegal dumping into the area's waterways." He swallowed. "They're ruling the crash pilot error."

Though he no longer apparently had the threat of a murder charge hanging over his head, a cold chill swept over Gabe's skin. "Bullshit. Mad couldn't possibly have erred so badly that his plane crashed."

Everly looked frozen as well. "Are you sure? There was a storm that night."

Gabe shook his head. "Mad has flown in the worst of conditions. Not long after we got our pilot's licenses, he experienced an equipment failure in heavy fog and came out perfectly fine. He wouldn't have let simple weather derail him. And if he thought the plane was going down, he had the know-how and equipment to parachute out. There was no distress call. No call at all."

"You've also forgotten more about planes than most people ever know, and Mad knew almost as much. This sounds like a pure cover-up to me." Dax's face tightened.

"I want to look at the black box data. I can tell you everything Mad did from there, but he was a good pilot. His plane was equipped with cutting-edge safety and navigation features. The thing practically flies itself. I don't get why else the FAA would suddenly change their findings."

"Someone has something to hide," Everly whispered, so white she looked as if she'd seen a ghost. Then again, it had been a long day for her.

Just in case, Gabe sidled closer. "Money. Bad shit like this is usually about money, and I'm the only person who benefitted from Mad's death."

"That we know of." Everly's gaze turned thoughtful.

"None of this makes sense." He shrugged. "Who else would want Mad dead?"

Everly hesitated, obviously reluctant. "Gabriel, you have very powerful friends who could convince the FAA to turn a blind eye."

He stilled, his feet seemingly planted in the ground as her words sank in. "You think I had Zack strong-arm the FAA?"

"I think if anyone could do it, the president could. Or maybe Roman. I doubt a commander-in-chief does his own dirty work." She gently bit into her bottom lip as she considered the problem. "You have the support of the White House, and your friend, Connor, is obviously very good at his job, which I suspect has something to do with intelligence. Between the three of them, they could likely cover up anything."

He stilled and stared at her. Everly thought he'd killed Mad?

"Gabe would never do that." Dax's voice sounded like a hard warning.

Everly couldn't possibly want him if she thought he was a killer. She couldn't ever trust him if she thought he could do something so heinous to a man who had been like a brother to him, the man who'd been *her* brother.

Everly raised her gaze to meet Dax's. "Of course he couldn't. Don't be ridiculous. But he's the chief suspect. Everything leads right back to Gabriel. Would your friends cover that up for you? Would they try to protect you?"

Relief swamped him, and he no longer cared that they were standing in a parking garage with three of New York's finest, two security guards, an EMT, and a crime scene photographer. He closed the distance between them and sank his fingers into her hair, drawing her face up.

"What are you—"

He didn't let her finish the question. He covered her mouth with his. He needed to be close to her, needed the feel of her body against his. He took her mouth in a long, slow brush. The moment she relaxed against him, he invaded. He caressed her tongue with his own in a sensual slide. He found comfort in the way she curled into his body, the grip of her hands at his waist as she melted into him. At least she was honest with him when he kissed her. Her trust issues and his stupid mouth didn't rule them here.

Being this near her was arousing him, and it had more to do with the chance to brand himself on her than simple sexual desire. His need for Everly was so much more complex. All-consuming.

But he couldn't satisfy his craving for her here. He couldn't claim her in the way he needed if he wanted any chance to keep her. With a growl of frustration, he pulled back, allowing himself one more brush of his lips against hers before setting his forehead against her own and letting himself breathe her in for a moment.

"You thought I was accusing you of something?" Everly asked, her hands still on his waist.

"I'm so grateful that one of us in this relationship is very smart." He needed to grovel. He would get down on his knees and beg if he had to—whatever it took to earn her forgiveness and convince her that he cared deeply.

She chuckled. "I know you wouldn't have hurt Maddox. Well, I think you might have kicked his ass, but you wouldn't have killed your friend. You wouldn't kill anyone."

She was wrong about that. An hour ago, he'd wanted to wrap his hands around Valerie's throat, not stopping until she could never threaten Everly again. When he thought about the people who had nearly murdered her over the past few days, Gabe felt savage and perfectly capable of killing. "I definitely didn't end Mad and I'll find out if Zack and Roman are worried that someone's trying to set me up."

He kissed her one last time, then stepped back and sent a questioning glance Dax's way.

Dax shook his head. "I don't know a damn thing about it. And you can leave Connor out, too. He would have simply confronted you. I'm not saying Connor wouldn't cover it up, but he would find out the truth first, and that would include putting you through a very uncomfortable interview."

Everly looked up at him. "You're not going to let this rest, are you?"

"Not as long as I have breath in my body. Mad's death wasn't an accident." He knew that. Maybe his conviction made him sound naive or mental, but Gabe refused to back down when he could help the people he loved. Just because Mad was gone didn't make their bond less real. "I owe it to him."

Dax nodded. "We all do."

Everly looked his way with a resolution he'd never seen on her face. "He's wrong about you. The man I met earlier, I mean." Her jaw firmed, and she slipped her hand in his. "Since before the funeral, I've been getting messages from an individual who claims to know what happened to Maddox. So I met him earlier this afternoon."

He let that wash over him. She'd been hiding information from him. He'd been honest with her and she'd been hiding. "Damn it, Everly. That was dangerous."

He was going to let it go because he couldn't afford to get his back up. That wall of hers now had a chink in it and he wasn't going to give her any reason to fix the sucker. She was being honest now and that was all that mattered.

She shrugged. "Calculated risk. I had a gun. I'd like to look through the security footage, but I doubt we'll get a great shot of this guy. He wore a hat and kept his head down. If we did capture an image of his face, I know some facial recognition software that might help us ID him. I'll have to hack the FBI . . . unless one of your friends wants to help."

Thank god. She'd found one thing about his lifestyle that might be beneficial. He had friends who could help her hack major government websites. Yeah, his life might have been easier with a girl who only wanted a Tiffany bracelet. Not his nerd goddess.

"I swear I'll talk to Roman and get you whatever you need. Now tell us everything you can." Gabe vowed to protect her. He didn't want some crazy bastard texting her, convincing her to meet him. It was too dangerous. Even the thought of it made him insane.

"Not here," she murmured. "I don't have enough proof to bring the police into this. And I'm worried whatever we tell them will be leaked to the press. I think we should conduct our own investigation until we have a firm grasp of who's hiding what and possess solid evidence."

She was right; this wasn't the place to talk about it. "Dax, can you bring the limo around? We should get out of here."

Everly shook her head. "I need to go upstairs and get my laptop."

"No. Valerie isn't coming back. We'll have security lock your office. It will be safe." He refused to let her argue that point. After she'd nearly been killed again, no way was she walking back upstairs and calmly strolling into her office. Time to talk about her taking a short leave of absence while they figured out who was pulling what lethal strings.

Her shoulders lifted and fell with the force of her sigh. "I really need that laptop and some other items from my office."

Gabe crossed his arms over his chest. "No."

Everly shook her head. "Fine. At least it's in my safe, so I know no one will make off with it. And we need to talk about where I'm sleeping tonight because I think it's time we took a step back."

He moved closer so she would hear his whisper. "That's not what it felt like when I kissed you a few minutes ago. In fact, space felt like the last thing you needed."

"Just because I respond to you sexually doesn't make us a good match out of bed, Gabriel. There are still a lot of issues between us that can't be solved with sex. I'm going to finish up with the police." She walked over to the lieutenant, her heels sounding against the concrete.

Grimacing, Gabe watched the sway of her hips. She turned, and he could see she was tired, too. Of fighting him? Of being forced to bend to his wishes when that so obviously wasn't her nature? If they'd had a proper dating relationship, he would have indulged her every whim. He could have proven how patient he could be with her, but it seemed as if he'd spent half his time knotting her up in a state of stress and anxiety, trying to protect her and fighting the urge to rail when she resisted.

The other half of their time together, when they were alone, he'd found both an ease and a craving he'd never known possible, one that had been missing from all his other relationships.

If he pushed Everly too hard, he would lose her.

"I'll go get the car, but I'm not taking us directly to Connor's," Dax said. "You need some alone time with that woman. She's not happy with you, brother. You need to grovel. And by grovel, I mean you need to spend some serious time making her scream. I've found women are way happier after I've given them a couple of orgasms."

Gabe wasn't sure he should listen to Dax's relationship advice. "So says the man whose wife left him."

"Yeah, well, I was on a ship for a year, so I couldn't give her any orgasms. Not surprising she dumped my ass." Dax slapped him on the back. "Trust me, I know what I'm talking about. You need to settle things with that woman, Gabe. She's good for you."

He nodded. She was the one. In a million years, he'd never imagined he would find her, much less in the midst of death, chaos, and danger. Gabe wondered, however, if he was good for her. Even if he wasn't . . . he didn't think he could let her go.

FIFTEEN

Everly stood in the lobby of the Crawford building and waited for Gabe to join her while Dax brought around the limo. She thought seriously about marching out of the building and getting on the subway. She could be home in no time. She'd lock every door and let her phone ring so she wouldn't have to deal with Gabriel Bond at all. She could hole up, turn on a Doctor Who marathon, and veg with her computer. She could gather everything she knew about Valerie and try to connect her to those two thugs. She could try to find her informant's identity because, despite his warning, of course she was going to do that.

Then she wouldn't have to think about Gabriel or worry about melting for him. She could hide away and try to get back to the woman she'd been before she met him.

Except he would have his superscary, probably worked-for-the-CIA spook friend break in. Then she would really be in for a lecture.

No. She wasn't going to run from him. Maybe she should. But she refused to dash away like a timid rabbit. Instead, she'd talk to him until he understood that she needed time to process everything that had happened.

The problem was, she didn't actually want time away from Gabriel. No, she wanted to be with him—in every sense of the word—especially after yet another brush with death.

"Oh, hell. Your dress! It's ruined. Are you all right?" Scott dashed out of the elevator and over to her side, his expression concerned.

She wondered what he'd heard about the incident with Valerie. "A few bumps and scrapes, but otherwise, I'm fine."

"Thank goodness. The rumor is that Val tried to kill you." His voice shook slightly.

Oh, the gossip mill at Crawford really annoyed her. She wished it hadn't chosen now to be so accurate. "Valerie had the wrong idea about my relationship with Maddox." Everly shrugged. "But I survived."

"It's my fault." Scott's shoulders slumped. "I knew she didn't like you. I should have said something."

"Everyone knew she didn't like me, Scott."

His stare bounced up to hers, and she couldn't miss the guilt there. "I knew *why* she hated you."

That confused Everly a bit. "You knew she'd had a fling with my brother?"

"It's still so weird to think of you as Crawford's sister, but yes. At one point, Val was what a lot of straight dudes would call his *convenient pussy.*"

She winced. "Okay, you don't have to be so graphic."

"Sorry. Early this year, Crawford hooked up with Val every now and then. She often waited around the office to see if he wanted her. He wasn't serious about her. Once, I was out with Tavia and Val at happy hour, and Crawford called her."

"Like . . . a booty call?"

Scott nodded. "Just like that. He said that he was drunk and to meet him at some hotel if she wanted to fuck. Apparently, she didn't care how desperate accepting made her look. She jumped up and left the bar. Tavia said that whenever Crawford beckoned, Val ran."

"So when he started spending a lot of his evenings at my place more recently, she assumed I was her competition."

"Oh, you weren't even in the same league. He cared about you. He barely spoke to her during the day. But she'd deluded herself. Tavia said she'd go to lunch and tell her friends that Crawford was going to marry her. She talked about what a whore you were for trying to steal him."

Well, the day wasn't complete if someone didn't accuse her of prostitution. "I hope she gets some help in jail." And a nice long sentence. "It's not your fault. I probably wouldn't have told you if someone was being horrible behind your back and there was nothing you could do about it. Val and I weren't friends. I knew she didn't like me."

"I never imagined she would go so completely crazy on you."

"Well, she did. I'm trying to look on the bright side. At least now it will be much easier to go through her records and figure out where she hid the money she embezzled. You did a turn in accounting, right?"

He stood up a little straighter. "Sure."

"You any good at it?"

Scott grinned. "I find accounting easy."

Relief wound through her. Finally, she might get some concrete answers about why Maddox had been killed. "Could you look into the accounting on the foundation gala for the last few years? I would really love to get a big picture of exactly what Val did. If you could find out how and where she funneled the money, that would be insanely helpful."

"Sure. I can certainly take a look. Most likely she worked with caterers to overcharge and then split the extra money with them, but I'll tell you if I see anything else."

"Thanks. I would love your thoughts. I have to know what happened. This might be the reason my brother was killed." But the idea that emotionally unstable Valerie could manage to kill Maddox by tampering with his aircraft kept bugging her. It didn't compute. If Valerie had wanted to kill Maddox, it seemed far more likely she would have chased him with a knife or tried to run him over, not put a bomb on his plane. And why would anyone cover up the crime for her?

Unfortunately, Everly didn't have another suspect. Her mysterious contact hadn't given her much to work with. Oh, she'd find the information he'd mentioned and look up Lara Armstrong, see if she dug up any more clues or proof, but she couldn't fathom that it would lead to anything more than a dead end.

Scott stared at her for a moment before nodding. "Sure. I'm on it."

"That's a relief. Gabriel has a forensic accountant coming in, but I need answers now. Even a quick-and-dirty look would help."

"A forensic accountant?" Scott's eyes went a little wide. "Okay. Yeah, I'm not that good, but I'll have a report ready for you as soon as I can. It shouldn't be too hard."

That was one problem taken care of. "Thank you. Call me as soon as you're done, okay?"

"You got it." Scott looked to his side and Gabriel was striding toward her. "Looks like your escort is here."

She gave Scott a quick hug, feeling eyes on her. When she turned back, Gabriel stood, watching. Pure possessiveness blazed across his face before he seemed to force himself to relax. He gave Scott a smile before his hand found hers.

Moments later, he led her through the lobby doors and ushered her toward the limo. Only a few reporters loitered outside. Gabriel had been correct. Between the announcement that she wasn't Maddox's mistress and the FAA ruling the crash pilot error, she and Gabriel weren't much of a story anymore. She breathed a little easier as Dax pulled away from the curb.

Then she noticed someone had raised the partition between them and the driver. It made the big, beautiful stretch limo feel very intimate. She was alone with Gabriel—and so aware of him watching her intently.

"What's going on?" she asked, her voice not quite steady.

He stared at her from across the seat, his brilliant blue eyes threatening to pierce her. A sexy five-o'clock shadow clung to his jawline. "You and I should talk."

Gabriel was right, but she didn't want to discuss the subject most likely on his mind. "I don't know. The man I talked to this afternoon said I shouldn't trust you because you'll side with your friends when all of this shakes out."

He sat up straight, his expression turning serious. "We're on the same side. So what is that supposed to mean?"

At least he wasn't looking at her like she was a little bunny he was about to eat in the sweetest of ways. "You tell me."

"Baby, I don't even know what this asshole told you. Apparently nothing good about me. How does he know anything at all? How do we know he's not some reporter?"

She'd asked the same questions herself. "He asked if we'd found the pictures of the girls inside the lockbox in the hidden room."

That shook him. "How did he even know we found a hidden room or the lockbox, much less what was inside?"

"I have no idea."

He blew out a breath. "Mad had cameras installed throughout the house. For . . . security." Something about the way he said *security* gave her pause. "I assumed they were destroyed in the fire, but maybe not."

"Security, huh? More likely Maddox had cameras around the house so he could make sex tapes." She knew her brother. He'd been a great friend to her and a complete pervert to all other females.

Gabriel's lips curled up slightly. "Fine. He might not have always used them for security. But I can't think of any other way this guy knows about that room or the lockbox. But how could he have been in the house with us?"

This was her area of expertise. Back in college, she'd managed to catch the school streaker by hacking the security cams of her dorm. She hadn't turned him in or anything. She'd just wanted to prove she could do it. The dude had been surprisingly well hung, and after a while, everyone looked forward to his monthly runs.

"He didn't have to be in the house with us. If he remotely stole the feed, he could have watched us. He could have been watching us the whole time."

His furious expression told her he didn't like that thought. Truth told, Everly didn't like it, either.

"But that doesn't explain how he knew about the pictures inside the lockbox," she pointed out. "We didn't open the box at Maddox's place."

He leaned over and checked the small control panel on his side of the limo, ensuring Dax couldn't hear him. "The only other way your guy could know is if he's talking to Dax, Connor, or Roman. But I don't believe any of them would betray us."

She didn't, either, but was surprised he'd considered his friends as suspects for even a moment.

"Unless my informant has been watching Maddox's 'security' feed for days or weeks and saw him load the box."

"And why would he do that unless this guy's interest in Mad preceded his death?" Gabriel cocked his head, leveling her with a stare rife with suspicion. "Unless your informant was involved."

Everly saw his point, that maybe her mystery informant hadn't just been a spectator in Maddox's murder, but she saw another possible angle. "Maddox was a subject of interest in life, too. Maybe this guy had been monitoring him for potential tabloid/sex tape fodder and simply kept watching the feed to see what happened in his murder investigation."

Gabe froze, then blew out a breath. "Any idea who this guy is?"

"No, but he knows plenty. He claims he sent me some information that might help me understand Mad's murder. So far, all I've received from him is one e-mail and a couple of cryptic texts. He claims he sent me some information. He called it data, but I haven't gotten anything like that. I did have someone send me a camera, but it's got pictures on it, not data. I downloaded some of the pictures off it before my laptop crapped out on me. If you had let me go get the damn thing, I could load the pics on Connor's computer."

Gabriel sighed. "I'm sorry. I was trying to protect you. I promise we'll get them first thing in the morning. Valerie won't break into your office from jail. Now explain this to me."

Valerie being in custody was the only reason she hadn't stormed back up and gathered her evidence. "It looks like someone was watching me and Maddox before his death and sent me a camera with a memory card inside. That memory card contained photos." She held a hand up because Gabe looked ready to blow. "I'll remote access my system tonight and let you view the pictures I was able to download. I promise. Tomorrow we can look at the rest. Take a deep breath."

Gabriel squared his shoulders, and they seemed to grow broader. She was starting to pick up on all the signs that he was angry or concerned. "He took pictures of you before Mad died?"

Yep, he was going to flip out. "I think he knows a lot about me. Really, about everything. He said there's more to Maddox's death than we're seeing. Far more. I got the idea that he meant that whatever's happening went beyond a murder. He mentioned the name Sergei. We're supposed to find someone with that name."

He ground his teeth together. "The day he died, Mad asked me about a Sergei, but I don't know one. Did your mystery informant say how we're supposed to find him?"

"Not we. Me. I'm supposed to find Sergei alone. The informant said I couldn't trust you." But she felt as if she could. Or was that simply because she really wanted to believe her heart wouldn't lead her so astray?

"I swear to god when we figure everything out, I'm going to beat the shit out of this Sergei guy—and your cloak-and-dagger informant."

That probably wasn't such a great idea. "I suspect we're looking for a man with ties to the Russian mafia. I wonder if he has anything to do with that other woman Maddox was trying to find. Natalia, wasn't it?" The connection had been playing around in her head all morning. "I want to hire an investigator to find her."

"The last one died under questionable circumstances, Everly." Gabriel turned stern. "You're out of this. Now that Valerie's been caught, your part in all of this is over."

"No." She shook her head emphatically. "I'm the one this mystery man is willing to talk to. He suggested I make contact with Lara Armstrong, whoever that is. I'm going to do that and start feeling out what she knows."

He'd gone a nice shade of pale. "Absolutely not. She's the one running Capitol Scandals. Connor will handle her."

Yeah, with the finesse of a sledgehammer—kind of like Gabriel now. "Be reasonable about this. I want to find out who killed my brother. I get it. You didn't like the whole me-nearly-getting-flattened thing, but you need me."

"I know how competent you are, but you're still out. I can't risk you again. God, I know you're going to hate me, but I won't let you put your life on the line."

Did he really mean what he was saying? He looked terrified and resolute at the same time. Was he really so afraid he might lose her? How did she deal with that? Stomping her foot and screaming hadn't gotten them anywhere. "Gabriel, you can't put me in a box. I know that seems like the safe thing to do, but it won't work. You say you want me."

"I do. God, I do."

"But you don't want me the way I am because I'm not the woman who can walk away from this investigation."

Frustration melded with worry in his tight expression as he surged into her personal space. "Damn it, Everly. I didn't want our conversation to go this way."

Being so close to him made her heart trip. Sorrow threatened to shred her because they were still so far apart. "You want some sweet little thing who will do whatever you tell her. Who will let you put her in a nice cage, and I'm sure there are plenty of women in this city who would be more than happy to do your bidding and never question you once. I hope you find her because I'm not that girl."

"I don't want them." He grabbed her shoulders, his stare pinning her to the seat, his intent plain. "I want you."

"I don't think you really do or you wouldn't ask me to give up." Tears threatened. "Maybe it's time to admit we threw ourselves into this without thinking."

His eyes heated as he leaned forward. "I'm only trying to protect you."

"That's what I'm trying to make you understand. I don't want to be protected. I want to be your partner. If you knew me at all you would know that if you cut me off, I'll conduct my own investigation. I'll do it even if you fire me."

"You have no idea what I can do when I put my mind to it, baby. If I want you under house arrest, you'll find yourself locked down twenty-four seven."

A little zip of fear went through her because he sounded serious. "You wouldn't dare."

"I wouldn't take that bet if I were you." He moved into her space, forcing her to shift toward the door. "If I give him the word, Dax will take us out of the city, and you'll find yourself in a safe house with four bodyguards paid not to listen to reason. They won't let you slip away. They'll keep you there until I say you can go."

She pushed at him, the very act of touching him setting the inevitable clash in motion because she wasn't leaving here until she'd proven to him that she wasn't a soft, acquiescent little thing. Up until this point, she'd let him take the lead in their relationship. There hadn't been any reason not to and it felt right, but now she needed to show Gabriel that she could handle him.

"Have you listened to anything I've said?" She countered him, moving into his territory and shifting her dress so it bared her thigh. His stare immediately dropped there, and she couldn't miss the way his slacks tented. She had power in this relationship, and she wasn't above using it. "You have to take me as I am or let me go. I'll be honest, I'm not ready to decide what I want, but I know I won't be in a relationship where you think you can lock me up and only take me out when you want me."

"I always want you." His hand drifted to her knee before sliding up the skin she'd exposed. "Always."

The minute he touched her, her clothes felt too tight, encumbering. Only Gabriel did this to her—and she feared only he ever would. If they couldn't work out their differences, she would likely be alone for the rest of her life.

"No, you want some woman you made up in your head, one who purrs for you on command and hangs on your every word." She was pleased with how even her voice sounded, despite the fact that her heart pounded like a drum.

"No. I want the woman who's smart enough to find a way out of a burning house. I want one who's brave enough to stay behind and rescue her lover when she should be fleeing. I want one who challenges me at every turn." He caressed his way up her waist, and she suddenly found herself sitting in his lap, the length of his erection pressed against her backside. "I want you every minute of the damn day. I can't think straight for wanting you."

"You're able to think enough to boss me around."

"You may not believe this, but I've never been this possessive. I'm not the asshole who demands his woman does everything he says." He wrapped his arm around her waist. "I let her go her way and I go mine. Usually."

Yeah, nothing between them had been like that. "Maybe we should go our separate ways, too. With Valerie in custody, I doubt I'll have a problem going home."

"Fuck that. I can't let you go." His jaw tightened. "Show me your breasts."

The minute he used that deep, dominant tone, Everly ached to comply, but doing that had gotten her into trouble in the first place. "I don't have to do a damn thing you say."

"Like you ever have," he growled. "You knew I wouldn't want you to meet that man alone so you sneaked out. You put yourself in danger."

"I had a gun and I know how to take care of myself." She dismissed his accusation.

"That man could have had accomplices, just waiting to off you. Or he could have taken you." His hands tightened as though he was afraid to let her go. "Anything could have happened to you. If I hadn't figured out where you were . . . I don't even want to think about it."

The male scent of his skin mixed with the sandalwood notes of his aftershave and teased her nose. Any time she caught a whiff, Everly flashed back to moments he'd covered her body with his, working and straining between her legs to give her the greatest pleasure she'd ever experienced. He was so near, and to feel that again, all she had to do was move a few inches closer until their lips met. He wouldn't need more enticing than that.

"I can take care of myself." She eyed his beautiful mouth.

"Not against these people, you can't. Damn it, Everly. Tell me, am I the only one who's in deep? Would you not care if I walked into what could be an ambush? Would it mean nothing to you if I died?" The words sounded like a desperate growl.

She hesitated. Everly hadn't imagined he felt the same deep attachment she did. Not really. She'd known he wanted her and, protestations aside, assumed his possessiveness stemmed from his alpha-male personality. But now he wasn't talking about her safety or even just sex. Could he really be falling for her? Could she trust that she wasn't yet another woman this billionaire with movie-star charisma would adore completely for a few weeks or months before he moved on?

Could she be the woman he truly wanted to settle down with?

Probably not. But even if she wasn't, holding back the truth might keep her heart safe, but he'd made himself vulnerable to her, and she couldn't return his honesty with lies.

"Oh, Gabriel. I would be devastated," she whispered. "If something happened to you, I would want to die. But I also can't live in a safe bubble."

He fused his stare to hers, as though trying to imprint himself on her. "And I can't let you go."

"I'll always do my best to stay safe, but I can't stop living to do it."

"Damn it, woman," he cursed. She was right. He knew it and he obviously didn't like it.

"Kiss me," he demanded. "Fucking kiss me now."

Giving in might not be smart, but her recent brushes with death made her need to seize this moment. If she didn't drink in every second she had with him, she would regret letting this chance to touch him slip through her fingers.

Everly suspected she was only putting off their inevitable parting, but she'd choose him—and living life to the fullest—every chance she could.

Leaning in, she layered her lips over his with a little catch of her breath. If she had only one more night with him, she would take it.

Soft. His lips were so soft and sensual for a man. She gripped the sides of his jaw, feeling the rough beginnings of his beard. She loved the way he felt, the contrast between his soft skin and rough masculinity. That dichotomy mirrored the man himself. His alpha exterior hid a wealth of tenderness he'd probably only ever shown to his five closest friends. Everly felt blessed to see it now. She might not have the luxury of sharing all her remaining tomorrows with him, but she had right now.

His hand glided up her thigh as their tongues tangled together. She parted her legs to give him access. Here, they fit together perfectly, as if they were made for each another. In his arms, the world fell away. No mysteries to solve. No reporters to elude. No danger to fight. No grief, loss, or uncertainty. Just her and him and a sense of rightness.

She ran her tongue over his bottom lip, and despite the strength of his big body, he shivered.

"Show me your breasts, Eve." His hand moved restlessly up her thigh, climbing higher. He skimmed his fingers so close to the place she needed his touch most. Instead, he seemed content to tease her. Time and again, he stopped short of covering her needy flesh while he claimed her mouth.

She kissed him back, eager to tease him in return. She kissed his nose and both cheeks, rubbing their faces together with sweet affection before she ran her tongue along the edge of his ear. "What will you give me if I do?"

"My hands touching them. My lips and teeth worshipping them. I want to lick them and suck on them until you're so aroused you can't think or breathe." He maneuvered his hand back up her leg, his fingers teasing the edges of her panties. "Are you getting wet for me? Are you aching for my cock?"

"You know I am." In fact, she had to bite her tongue not to beg for the pleasure he always delivered.

"Then show me your breasts." That damn hand moved away again, making her moan with frustration.

"Get the zipper for me." She couldn't reach it. She'd needed his help with it this morning. Then, it had been a sweet intimacy. She'd almost been able to forget their fight and pretend they were merely another couple getting ready for the day. Since he'd zipped her in, it seemed only right that he tug it down and help her out of the clothes that kept them apart.

He glided his hand up her thigh and torso, grazing the side of her breast until his fingertips brushed the back of her neck. Sensation sizzled down her spine. Then slowly, he dragged the zipper down with a muted hiss.

"I love undressing you. It's like unwrapping my favorite gift." He leaned in and nuzzled her neck. "Every time I see you, all I want to do is get you naked and claim every part of you."

Biting back a little gasp, she let him drag her dress down her shoulders. She leaned back, giving him space to drag the sleeves down her arms. The dress fell to her waist, baring her bra. His stare fell to her chest, his breathing now ragged. He tugged at his tie, pulling at it as if he couldn't quite breathe.

His reaction made her feel so powerful. If someone had told her last week that today she would be stripping in a limo for the most beautiful man she'd ever met, she would have told them they were crazy. She wasn't some sexy thing. At least she'd never felt that way. But Gabriel had changed that. Changed her. She couldn't help but feel beautiful because he looked at her with such desire in his eyes. He never let her hide behind her insecurities—and she had no need in the face of his honest passion. Even if they parted tomorrow, she'd be forever grateful that he'd helped her find a new confidence.

Everly unhooked the clasp of her bra and let her breasts bounce free. The minute she bared them, he licked his lips like a wolf scenting prey. He was ready to make her his meal.

"Put your arms behind your back."

"You're bossy."

He jerked his head from side to side. "I'm desperate. Put your arms behind your back or I'll be forced to do something drastic and ruin these very nice slacks."

Gabriel was usually in control. Everly liked knowing she could make him come so close to losing it.

Biting her lip, she grasped her hands behind her back. Her breasts thrust out and her nipples peaked as though anticipating his touch.

"Do you know how beautiful you are to me?" He palmed both breasts, his big hands cupping her.

"I know you make me feel that way."

"I want to be with you, Everly. And I don't mean only right now. I don't want this to end." He looked up at her, his face filled with a question she didn't know how to answer because she wasn't sure quite what he was asking for. He surely couldn't be asking for a real commitment. She couldn't possibly think about that now.

"Don't make me wait," she murmured instead. "Please."

He leaned in and kissed her breast, licking the turgid peak. He primed the sensitive tip, swirling around and up, flicking it with his tongue before he nipped the end with his teeth. The sensation shot straight to her sex. She gasped.

"You don't believe me," he murmured. "You think I'll discard you, but I won't, baby. I intend to protect you, Everly. I choose you. I'll stand by you. Even if you try to leave me because you think it's best for us or whatever, I'll come for you. I'll convince you."

Easy to say in the heat of passion, but could things actually work out between them? She could eventually forgive the stupid things he'd said to his sister. But he was still the glamorous boy, and she was the ordinary girl falling for him. So she found it hard to trust that the words he spoke now were any more real than what he'd told Sara. Everly understood that Gabriel's life experiences had taught him to be wary, and she understood why he hadn't trusted her in the beginning. She wanted to believe she truly meant something to him, that they could grow together. How did she simply believe this stunning man wanted her beyond sex? Could they overcome all the issues between them and possibly build a future?

And then she couldn't think anymore because he sucked her nipple between his lips and pulled her close. He tugged on her, sending jagged pleasure racing through her system.

"I need more." He eased her down on the seat. She could feel the car rolling over the road underneath her, the rhythm somehow soothing.

He pushed her dress up, and before she could protest, he whisked her underwear off her hips and down her legs. Tossing them aside, he shoved the dress farther up and stared between her legs.

Her hungry wolf had become hungrier.

"Won't Dax be stopping soon?" The question came out in a breathless rush. "Maybe we should wait until we get back to Connor's place."

But she didn't want to wait. The minute they stopped and the limo door opened, the world would invade again. They would have to debrief Connor on everything that had happened, and it would be hours before they could be alone again.

But she also didn't want to appear in tomorrow's tabloids with her dress around her waist and Gabriel between her legs.

He didn't seem to have the same concerns as he crouched down and kissed his way up her thighs. "He won't stop until I tell him to. I wanted to be alone with you. I want to taste you again. Did I ever tell you how fucking good your flavor is on my tongue?"

His mouth hovered over her pussy, and all thoughts of stopping slipped away. He nosed her, rubbing his face right against her most sensitive parts. Everything he did felt so good, so right. It was a bit forbidden and so intimate it made her heart swell.

"I love it when you taste me."

His head came up, his eyes flaring. "Do you?"

A little smile played at his lips before his head disappeared between her legs again, teeth scraping over her inner thigh.

"I think about you touching me all the time." Everly gasped, her fingers raking into his short hair.

He pulled back and cupped her thigh, his fingers whispering over her clit. "Like this?"

She moaned, her whole body tensing. "More."

"Then tell me what you want. Tell me what you need. What does this sweet little pussy want from me?"

"Kiss me."

"Oh, I can do that." He laid a little kiss right above her clit. "See. I'm very good at kissing you."

Bastard. She didn't miss his smirk. He was enjoying the chance to torment her and intended to make her work for it. "No. Lick me."

He ran his tongue along one side of her labia, then the other, in a slow slide that drove her mad. "Your wish is my command."

"Damn it, Gabriel. I want your tongue everywhere. Devour me. Make me ache and scream and come." She stared at him. "No one else can make me feel like you do."

"That's what I wanted to hear."

He lowered his mouth to her, and she gasped at the first long drag of his tongue. Her head fell back, and Everly could do nothing except surrender. She'd yearned for the pleasure, the give and take, the moments when she surrendered to him. But it would mean so much more if they had a future. She wanted to be his partner—in pleasure, in business, in life.

Her thoughts scattered as his tongue worked its magic. "Gabriel . . ."

"Spread wider, baby." He shoved her knees apart, wedging his shoulders in between.

Panting, she drowned in the exquisite bliss. One of his fingers parted her folds, breached her. It felt so good, awakened a whole new hunger in her. She pressed against it, trying to coax him to penetrate deeper, move faster. But he continued that steady, driving rhythm that made her body tighten, made tingles form, made breathing almost impossible.

He hurtled her toward the pinnacle of desire. Everly scratched at his scalp, tried to wrap her legs around his shoulders—anything for the extra bit of sensation that would drive her over. He refused to be rushed or alter her slow, maddening slide into insanity.

When she whimpered, he tongued her clit, then glanced up at her. His lips glistened with her arousal. "You want more."

It wasn't a question.

"You know I do."

"Then ask me for it."

"More, Gabriel. Now." She wanted to shout her demand at him. She'd been so close to falling over the edge. "Give me more . . ."

He seemed determined to torture her. "More of what? More of my fingers or do you want my cock?"

There was no doubt in her mind what she wanted. "I need you inside me, Gabriel. Hard. Fast. Fill me."

His face lit with dangerous satisfaction. "Absolutely, but I want you to work for it, baby. I intend to make this ride last awhile."

He lowered his lips to her again, and Everly gasped, every muscle tensing as he drove her toward stunning pleasure again.

In this, they were in synch. Like him, she wanted this magic to go on forever.

Gabe reveled in everything about her. As he stroked his tongue along her tender flesh and thrust a second finger deep inside her, he couldn't help but take in everything. She smelled so good. Womanly and sweet. He was fairly certain he would die still remembering the taste of her arousal on his tongue. Her skin was so soft that he was worried about leaving a mark on her thighs from his damn whiskers, but he hadn't had time for an afternoon shave.

Everly didn't seem to care. She spread her thighs wide, presenting her gorgeous sex to him without hesitation or inhibition. She opened for him like a flower that had gone far too long without the sun. He licked the pearl of her clitoris. The little jewel poked out of its hood, begging for his attention. He was going to lavish it. She might fight him everywhere else, but here they were of the same mind, had the same needs.

He shoved his fingers high into her pussy and sucked her clit, establishing a rhythm that soon had her wriggling on his hand, desperate for relief. The sight, sound, and scent of her arousal alone fueled his desire, but with every moment, she grew more desperate, nails clawing his scalp, thighs tightening around his head. God, he loved her unabashed enthusiasm for sex, the way she never held anything back.

He felt her clench around him and heard her keening cry. She writhed on the supple leather, her body riding out the orgasm he gave her. Her scent filled the car—and his nostrils—until he ached to tear at her clothes, claw out his zipper, and fill her with every inch he had.

When her storm slowed, the waves softening, she sighed. "How do you do that to me?"

He didn't answer her because he wasn't sure what to say. Sex with her was simply better. It had been from the first moment he'd touched her. It had also been different than the countless times with the blur of faces and bodies he'd known before. What he shared with Everly was somehow . . . more.

If another woman had complimented his sexual prowess, he would have grinned and proven himself worthy, but her words made him feel oddly vulnerable. He didn't want to merely be a good lay to her. He didn't even want to only be the best sex she'd ever had—not if that was all he meant to her.

Gabe wanted to be her only lover. He wanted to be the man in her heart.

The thought rolled over him, and he sat back in the seat with a stunned sigh. Everything below his waist urged him to open his slacks and shove his cock inside her waiting flesh, but he needed more than pleasure from Everly.

He, who was rarely unsure and never hesitated, sat frozen. What if she didn't reciprocate?

Even with the doubt and fear tumbling in his head, Gabe couldn't take his eyes off her. She looked so lovely and wanton with her dress all gathered at her waist. All her gorgeous curves and most intimate parts were on display for him. He loved that about her, too.

Her skin was flushed a rosy pink and her mouth was slightly open as she took a long breath and opened her eyes to look at him. "What's wrong?"

He shook his head. "Nothing."

Her flush deepened. "Don't you want me?"

"I want to know if you want me." God, that sounded stupid. He should take her. She wouldn't fight him, but he needed something far beyond her acquiescence and an exchange of flesh. Getting her into bed wasn't the question; getting into her heart was.

"Of course I want you. I thought that was pretty clear." She tugged at her skirt, trying to right her clothes. "What's going on? Is Dax just going to keep driving?"

Shit. He'd lost her. The disappointment was more than crushing. "I'll tell him to head home."

Though they wouldn't really be heading to his home, that word seemed right because, for him, home had become wherever she was. When the hell had that happened?

Gabe dragged air into his lungs and tried to not punch out the windows of the limo. How he was going to get through the rest of the night he had no idea, but he shouldn't have expected more after the way he'd treated her this morning.

He didn't even want to think about what he was going to do for the rest of his life.

Staring out at the Manhattan street, he watched Midtown pass by. The lights of nearby Times Square illuminated the early evening. Tourists thronged through the square, gawking at the multitude of flashing signs for everything from Broadway shows to sneakers as locals rushed by and ignored them.

Gabe winced. He was putting off the inevitable, but he wanted to make something clear before he gave Dax a final destination. "Everly, I'm going to do whatever it takes to make you forget what I said this morning. You should know that. I realize this is a horrible time to start a relationship, but I can't let you go because the timing isn't right. I screwed up. I should have believed you. I can only promise that I won't make the same mistake again. You might think I'm a complete pig for being so stubborn about your safety, but I promise I won't shut you out."

She gave him a wary glace, clearly not sure she believed him. "Are you still going to lock me up?"

Yes, that had been a reaction to her pushing him—one he regretted. He closed his eyes for a long moment, listening to her rustle back into her dress and wishing he could have a do-over on most of this day.

"Of course not." He opened his eyes, ready to explain himself, and all the fine words he usually used to charm and coax a woman stuck in his throat when he saw her. "You're naked."

She was beautifully, gloriously naked. She hadn't straightened out her clothes at all. Instead, she'd taken them off and knelt on the floorboard.

A sexy smile curled her lips up. "You're stating the obvious, Mr. Bond."

His cock was suddenly jumping with excitement. His heart wasn't far behind. "Eve . . ."

She moved between his legs, hands gliding up his thighs. "My turn, Gabriel. I think that's been our problem. I haven't demanded equality from you. I can't be this perfect princess you lock away and only take out when you think it's safe. The world is a big bad place and you need someone you can count on. So do I. The man today told me that when the chips are down, you'll pick your friends over me."

He would really like to have a talk with that guy. "It's not true."

She held a hand up to stop him. "I think it might be, but I'm not sure what I can do about it so I'm going to choose to live in the moment for now."

He didn't want to live in the moment. He realized that as he stared at her. He was a man who constantly lived for the now. After his father passed, he'd been forced to take care of the business, his sister, now Crawford Industries, and a niece or nephew. He'd bucked at the responsibility, but Everly made him want to be better. She made him long for a future.

His playboy days were past and it struck him squarely in the chest that he wouldn't be that carefree boy again. Maybe it had all been an illusion anyway. Those days of running around the world with his friends were gone. He'd remember them fondly, but meeting Everly had been the catalyst for his true shift from boy to man. Her man.

And she very likely wouldn't believe a damn word he said.

That made him feel so fucking helpless. He could fire her and try to force her to work for Bond, where he would make sure she was safe. Then two paths would lie ahead of them: She would either hate him for what he'd done or she'd go along with it and, slowly, all the life in

Everly would dim, her unique spirit ground down by his need for control.

Gabe didn't know what to do next, how to find his way out of this corner he'd maneuvered himself into. He only knew he wanted her so desperately he would take anything she gave him.

"What are you planning to do, beautiful?" He settled back because she wanted control, and he had to give it to her—for now. He would take over again, but after he'd let her have her way for a bit.

His Eve skated her hands on top of his slacks, over his cock, making him writhe and seek more of her touch. "Tempt you."

"All you have to do to tempt me is exist."

She eased his zipper down carefully. "I don't know about that. You seem a little hesitant tonight."

His cock sprang free. It seemed to strain her way as though it knew exactly where it wanted to be. He didn't like being called hesitant, though. It looked like it was her night to push him. "Hesitant? Baby, I was trying to give you the freedom you seem to need."

She was staring at his cock, her fingers coming out to brush against his flesh. "I don't need freedom. But I could show you I want you. I could lick you and suck you, but I've been thinking about something. The last few days seem to have taken a toll on you. Maybe you should lie back and let me take care of you."

"I did that this morning, for all the good it did me."

"Well, it might have gotten you further if you hadn't told your sister I was just your convenient whore." She sat back on her heels.

Oh, she was spoiling for a fight. He might give her one. "I didn't say that."

Everly shrugged one perfect shoulder. "Maybe not word for word, but close."

"You're not going to listen to anything I say." It ate at him. She'd only left him one avenue. "Well, baby, giving up control doesn't seem to be working so maybe I should take it back. Come here."

Gabe couldn't miss how her nipples peaked the minute his voice got rough. She enjoyed sex when he took over. He had no doubt she liked to be on top from time to time, but she was in a tough spot, too. He was asking her for an awful lot of trust, given his past and what he'd told Sara, not to mention what her informant had said. Sure, they could try to talk it all out now, but he rather thought it was time for some action. Maybe he could express his feelings for her more eloquently without words.

"What do you want?" Everly ran her tongue over her lips as her breath hitched.

"What do you think I want? You. Like I said, I always want you. I definitely want the Everly who was brave enough to get out of her clothes and on her knees in a car in the middle of Midtown on one of Manhattan's most crowded streets. I think I want to fuck that Everly right now."

The limo had hit the typical traffic around Times Square. They were stopped in the lane closest to the sidewalk and Everly turned her head. Her eyes widened as she glimpsed the hundreds of people walking all around them. She raised her hands to cover her breasts.

Gabe refused to have any of that. Instead, he pulled her into his lap. "Don't you dare. You undressed for me. You wanted to show me how gorgeous you are. You're not hiding now."

"But, Gabriel . . ." She gestured to the window.

He wouldn't let her use that as an excuse. "The windows are heavily tinted. No one can see in. No one can see how fucking pretty your breasts are. Except me."

He cupped one. He was never going to get over how perfectly she fit in his hand or how soft she was. She shivered in his arms, and he was fairly certain it wasn't out of embarrassment or fear.

Did the idea of sex with a crowd so nearby arouse her? Oh, he could get dirty if that got his girl hot. He held a breast in his hand as though showing it off to the people on the street. "If they could see you, they'd all stop and stare, transfixed. That's how beautiful you are. They would watch you. They would worship you."

A shaky laugh came from her throat. "I hardly think so."

"Stop seeing yourself through your eyes. See through mine. See how gorgeous I think you are." Even if she left him, he wanted her to know that. He wanted her to look in the mirror and see how amazing she was and never question it again. "Spread your legs."

"I don't know." But her knees were falling to the sides, revealing her pussy.

His cock jumped at the sight. Her sex was swollen from her recent orgasm but it already looked wanting and needy again. He touched her, sliding his fingers through her cream and coating them. "And this is so lovely. They would watch while I rub you, letting my fingers fuck in and out. Like I will in a moment."

"Oh . . ." She arched her head back. "Do it, Gabriel. Touch me."

"I will, but in my time. First, I'm going to let the people out there watch the show. It's better than anything on Broadway. It's prettier than the lights." He could feel her writhing, trying to get closer to his fingers. "They'll watch how your mouth comes open when I do this."

He gently pressed on her clitoris. Exactly like he'd imagined, she gasped and her mouth opened in a surprised O as though she was truly caught off guard. He wanted to teach her to expect that pleasure from him, to demand it. He wanted her to know that when his hands were on her body, she would always be satisfied.

Her back arched, breasts thrust forward, and she was such a sexy sight. She was laid across his lap, her legs spread for his pleasure. Though he was absolutely certain no one could see inside the limo, he could imagine the world admiring how stunning Everly was. But the sight of her naked and in ecstasy was only for him. He would play at exhibitionism, but he would never be able to show her off. Her body belonged to him, and he wasn't about to let another man see it.

The car moved but only another few feet. Someone brushed against the limo as they crossed the street.

Everly's eyes sprang open.

He circled her clit again. There was only one way to make her lose her inhibitions and that was to overwhelm her with pleasure. "Get on your knees."

He helped her to the floor. She dropped to her knees, and then all he could see was her gorgeous ass in the air. He reached out and put a hand on her cheeks, stroking her.

"Please, Gabriel. I can't take much more."

"You'll take as much as I give you." But he wasn't going to wait. He needed her. He got to his knees behind her, letting his slacks fall. He didn't take the time to get out of them. His need was far too urgent and he loved the fact that he was mostly dressed while she was deliciously naked. There was something decadent about all her skin on display.

He stroked himself before gripping her hips and aligning his cock. Yes. This was what he'd needed. The whole day would have gone differently if he'd kept her in bed.

He winced. That was exactly what she was trying to avoid. She didn't want to be his little sex toy. She wanted to be respected. Did she want to be loved? By him?

Gabe was fairly certain that boat had sailed and there was nothing he could do about it. He loved her and he had to find a way to prove it. Sometimes the simplest way was the best. He'd learned that a long time ago.

He pressed inside her, her body surrounding him, her heat pulling at him. "I love you."

She cried out and pushed back against him. He could feel how the words affected her. But she didn't say anything in return.

"I love you." Maybe he would just say it until she believed him. He pressed deeper, every inch a pure pleasure. "I love you so much."

Her head shook, but she pressed back, taking more of him. "Gabriel, I can't."

Everly had been through so much in the last forty-eight hours. Hell, only a couple of hours ago she'd nearly been mowed down. He couldn't ask more of her now.

Even if he lost her, he would love her. That fact hit him squarely in the chest as he held her tight. "You don't have to, baby."

He let go, shoving his cock deep. So good. She felt so perfect, her silken flesh clamping around him. He pounded into her and she fought back. For every thrust, she matched him, fierce in her fight for pleasure.

He pulled her up, keeping himself deep. Her hands flattened against the window with a thud as she tried to balance, her breasts close to the glass.

"What would they see now if they could? A gorgeous woman being fucked by a man who can't live without her. They would see you but they would see me, too. I wouldn't be able to hide from them, and I won't hide from you. Not one second more."

He looked down, watching his cock sink inside. Their joining was such a beautiful thing. But he needed to see her face, damn it. He didn't care about the fantasy anymore, only her.

He withdrew and dragged her down to the floor, grateful for the soft carpet beneath.

As he flipped her over, her eyes were sleepy with desire. "What?"

She was everything he'd never even known he wanted. Needed. The restless yearnings he'd had all of his life seem to vanish when he was with her. It made him nervous because this woman had so much power over him. She could ruin him in a heartbeat. A few cruel words from her, a betrayal, and he would never be the same. He'd seen it so often. Marriages in his world weren't happy. They were unions of money, ambition, and sex. And he wanted more.

He wouldn't get it by backing down now. He lined up again and thrust home once more.

This time, her legs wound around him and her arms enveloped him as she sighed. "That's better. It always feels good, but I like this. I like when you can kiss me."

He held himself still, his cock deep inside, as he leaned in and kissed her. It was a sweet thing, a mingling of mouths. "I want to see your face. I want to see your face when I tell you how much I love you."

Tears filled her eyes as she looked up at him. "Gabriel, I can't. I told you."

He pulled out and slowly filled her again. "You don't have to. You don't ever have to tell me, but I need you to know. I love everything about you, Everly Parker."

He held her focus, looking into her eyes as he made love to her. She made him a better man. He wouldn't hide or shrink back from it. Everly's love was important. He would do anything to earn it, but feeling this love for her meant the world to him, too. His love for her had changed him in so many ways.

He kissed her again, letting her off the hook for now. He would try again and again—as often as he could. He would never give up.

For the first time, he fought a real-life battle. Sure, he'd fought on athletic fields, in schoolyard scraps, and in boardrooms, but winning Everly Parker would define his future. He would be ruthless in his pursuit of her.

Gabe let her take his weight, wanting their skin connected everywhere. Chest to chest. Mouths kissing. Arms tangling.

Over and over he thrust into her, wanting the moment to last. She clenched around him and came twice before he couldn't hold out another second. His spine tingled and his balls drew up. He thrust in hard and gave her everything he had, the pleasure overtaking him.

Breathing hard, he fell on her, reveling in how close they were, the way their hearts beat together, the way their breaths aligned.

The car picked up speed as they moved through Midtown.

"Gabe, I hate to be the bearer of bad news, but I need to head back to Connor's. I'm afraid there's been a development." Dax's voice came over the speaker.

At least he had good timing, but Gabe's heart sank. The last thing he needed was another problem.

He looked down at Everly. "Are you okay? Can you come with me? I know you want to go home, but if Connor's found out something, I want you there."

She nodded. For the first time since he'd fucked up, she gave him that same soft smile she'd had when they met. "Yes. I'll be with you."

He pushed back onto his knees and helped her up. He touched the speaker that connected him to the front of the stretch limo. "All right. Turn us around."

He was about to reach for her dress when she curled up in his lap. "We've got a few more minutes. That traffic was bad. Just give me a little longer."

Gabe wasn't about to refuse her. He held her as they drove through the Manhattan streets, the bright lights and masses of people still at bay for a few moments more.

SIXTEEN

Everly tried to smooth out the sadly wrinkled fabric of her designer dress as she walked into the kitchen of Connor's condo. Gabriel was right behind her, but his suit seemed to have survived their limo romp much better than the Prada dress.

Romp? Was she really trying to fool herself? What they'd shared hadn't been some random sex act. Yes, it had been hot and crazy sex, but Gabriel Bond had said "I love you."

And she hadn't returned the words.

They had been right there on the tip of her tongue. Replying in kind would have been so easy, natural even. But as much as Everly cared for him deeply, she was afraid of his affection not lasting, of his glittering paparazzi world, of how badly she could be hurt if she stayed. Gabriel scared her because she didn't recognize herself when she was with him. She wasn't the sexy girl who made love in a limo, her naked body mere feet away from a crowd of random people walking up and down the streets. But Everly had to admit, she liked who she was when she was with him.

She wished she knew exactly what to do about him. About them.

"You okay?" Gabriel's fingers brushed against hers as though asking to be held.

She stepped away because holding his hand often led her to discard her brain. "I'm great."

She was a little walk of shamey, but other than some soreness that had come from almost being murdered, she was surprisingly fine.

Because he'd saved her.

She glanced up at Gabriel. He didn't even try to hide the hurt that her pulling away from him had caused. He locked his jaw and stared, his eyes burning with misery. Her stomach twisted as he frowned and walked into the room ahead of her.

Dax stepped around her and joined Gabriel, putting a hand on his shoulder, as though giving him comfort. When the navy captain looked back at her, anger fueled his glare.

She was the bad girl in this scenario.

Everly squared her shoulders and walked into the dining room where Connor stared intently at his computer. His close-cropped hair looked like he'd been scrubbing a hand through it.

He glanced up at Gabriel, his lips firming before he spoke. "The police found the second man from last night. Lester Hall. He's dead. One bullet between the eyes and two to the chest."

Dax's eyes closed and he groaned. "Shit."

So her mystery man had been right again. "Sounds as if he was executed. Most likely by the *Bratva*, if my information is correct."

"Why do you say that?" Gabriel asked. "We don't know for sure the Russian mob is responsible."

Connor sat back. "I think Red's right. Two to the chest and one to the head is the mark of a pro who wasn't taking any chances." He turned to her. "I'd like to know what information you have. When you left this morning, you didn't have much."

She shrugged. "This afternoon I met with a man who's been sending me mysterious texts and seems to have cut into the camera feeds in Maddox's house."

Connor's jaw dropped, and she was fairly certain she'd surprised him. She would bet not many people surprised Connor Sparks. "You met with a Deep Throat?"

"That sounds a little like a porn film," Gabriel replied with a shake of his head. "She met with a man who seems to know some things."

Connor sighed. "Excuse him. He slept through the second half of American history. He apparently missed the lesson about the shadowy figure during the Watergate scandal who led Woodward and Bernstein to the truth and eventually brought down Nixon's presidency."

"I knew that." Gabriel rolled his eyes.

Something about the Watergate reference scared her. "Well, my Deep Throat was definitely playing the part to the hilt. He showed up in a trench coat and fedora. I almost walked away, until he proved that he knew some surprising things. He kept reiterating that what's happening goes far deeper than Maddox's murder and reaches further than I could imagine. Maybe it's because you mentioned Watergate . . . but my mind goes to one place."

"Zack," Gabriel said, his eyes grave.

"You think this man is after Zack?" Dax asked.

"I don't know. He was purposely vague."

Connor rubbed a hand over his eyes. "Again, I think Red's right. And she's way smarter than I gave her credit for. The minute there's a hint that Zack is involved in anything slightly scandalous, this will explode."

"Did he shut down the FAA investigation?" Everly asked.

"I don't know." Connor stood and stretched. "If we're quick, we can catch Roman at that fundraiser at The Plaza in twenty minutes. He's got to head back to DC tomorrow. I say we corner him and find out what the hell's going on. Roman has always been an excellent liar, but we know his tells. If he's hiding something, we'll figure it out."

"And do what?" The mystery man's words haunted Everly. He'd said they would cut her loose to protect their own. How did she know they wouldn't do that and leave her without knowing what had happened to her brother?

"We'll figure it out," Connor assured.

"Zack wouldn't do anything criminal," Dax insisted.

"But he might cover up for someone." Gabriel stroked his chin.

"Who?" Connor asked.

Gabriel simply shrugged. "Maybe he thinks I'm guilty. I don't know. And what about Roman? You know he would have done anything to get Zack elected, especially after Joy's death."

So maybe he'd cover up for another one of his dear friends, too?

A grimness settled around the room at the mention of the president's late wife. Everly remembered the news coverage of her taking a bullet meant for Zack Hayes at a campaign rally days before the election. Zack had covered his wife's body with his own in the ensuing chaos but it had been too late. An image of the young, handsome politician covered in blood had been in every newspaper, on every TV.

Of course, she'd never met the president, just seen images of a serious, even grim executive officer whose smiles were so rare they caused flashbulbs to burst. She didn't know him or how ruthless he might be. But she had met Roman Calder and had a very good idea the lengths he'd go to for a cause he embraced.

Gabe sighed. "If Zack wanted something swept under the rug, Roman would cover for him. Hell, he'd arrange it."

Connor paced. "We need to talk to him. I don't see the connections. I've looked all damn day and I don't see anything in this whole clusterfuck beyond the fact that Zack's father was the ambassador to Russia for years and the *Bratva* seem to be involved. Zack hasn't been back to Moscow in decades. Maybe Roman knows something."

"And he's not telling us?" Dax demanded.

Connor slammed his laptop shut and shrugged. "Maybe. And it gets worse because the only person we might have been able to talk to died in jail about an hour ago."

The whole room seemed to still. "Valerie is dead?"

"Yep. The police found her unconscious in her cell, and she flat-lined on the way to the hospital. They're theorizing she had drugs in her system when she was arrested and it took that long for them to work. The officers said she seemed a little out of it when they brought her in," Connor explained.

"Or someone dosed her in jail because they didn't want her to talk," Everly mused.

Connor's eyes met hers over the table. "Or that. I wouldn't be sur-prised if they found a needle mark somewhere on her body. It would be easy enough to do at any point in the process. God knows the *Bratva* owns a couple of cops."

"So we're right back where we started." Something dangerous was still lurking out there and they were a step behind.

Gabriel approached, taking her hands in his. She didn't pull away this time. "Everly, I know this is frustrating, but I swear I'll do any-thing I can. For now, you can't go home alone."

As if she would do that. "I'm not fighting you on this, Gabriel. There's a real threat. We have a whole bunch of dead bodies piling up. I didn't tell you about Deep Throat because I didn't want to scare him away and I knew you'd balk at me going to that meeting."

"True enough," he conceded. "If he calls again, I'll let you manage it. You dealt well with him today, but you didn't handle the car that nearly killed you. I'll agree to let you meet with him if you agree to let me watch over you."

He was trying. She could, too. "Okay."

Maybe they could work out their differences after all.

Connor nodded. "All right, then. I've got to get dressed for a ten-thousand-dollar-a-plate dinner. Gabe, I grabbed your tux a little while ago. It's upstairs."

"How did you get in my place? You don't have keys."

The man simply smiled. "You need to come with me to this shindig.

Everly is your cause, and you need to have this out with Roman. Dax can stay behind and guard her."

"He doesn't have to fight my battles," Everly pointed out. "Let me go. I'll do it."

Gabriel squeezed her hand, then glanced at Connor. "She's got a point. I'll call a shopper and get a dress sent up here right away. It won't take more than an hour."

Of course. She couldn't go dressed as she was. They weren't trying to block her out, just get the ball rolling. At some point she had to decide if she trusted Gabriel Bond or not. If he loved her, as he said he did, she had to believe he would talk to Roman and wouldn't screw her over.

"Go," she assured him. "Dax and I will be fine here. I might do a little hacking of my own if someone will loan me a computer. Gabriel made me leave mine behind. I think it's time I looked into the foundation."

"Good. I've spent all day digging into Crawford. The foundation was my next stop," Connor admitted. "I've got a system you can use."

"Don't believe him," Dax said with a mischievous grin. "He's spent a good portion of his day flirting with Lara Armstrong over the Internet."

Connor actually flushed a bit. "It wasn't flirting. I'm building a relationship with her so I can find out what she's doing."

Boy, did she have some scoop for him. "Lara Armstrong is the one person Deep Throat told me I can trust. He says she has information."

"Really?" A predatory smile lit Connor's face, and she suddenly felt bad for Lara Armstrong.

"He also said he sent me information and I haven't found it. I need to comb through my e-mail again to look for it. I suppose he could be lying." She didn't think so, but she had to look at every angle.

"Not about Lara's involvement. She's up to her pretty blue eyes in this mess, and I'm going to find out what she knows. I'll be ready in fifteen." Connor stalked toward his bedroom.

"Someone needs to pray for that woman," Dax said under his breath.

Everly agreed. Connor looked like a hungry wolf when he talked about Lara Armstrong.

"He's either going to fuck her or kill her," Gabriel murmured, staring after Connor. "I'm leaning toward the former."

"I don't think he'll kill her." Dax shrugged. "I hope."

Gabriel smiled down at Everly. "You sure you're okay staying? I really will take you with me."

His earnest attempt at including her did wonders to settle her concerns. "It's okay. And if you need Dax, I will promise not to leave this condo."

"Neither of us will be leaving." Dax had his arms crossed over his massive, hard chest.

"I could stay with her." Gabriel looked reluctant to go.

"Gabe, you know Connor's right. Get a move on. I'll watch after your girl. How tight do you want the leash?" Dax asked, completely ignoring her.

Gabe looked down at her, reaching for her other hand. "I shouldn't be gone too long, but if something happens, shadow her. She's good. She knows what she's doing. I want her to have backup." He leaned over and brushed her lips with his. "I love you, Everly."

Those words threatened to break her. And all she could manage was a breathy, "Thank you."

He sighed, and his hands tightened on hers before he stepped away. "Be good."

As Gabriel mounted the stairs, she felt more hollow with every step between them.

"*Thank you?* He says I love you and you thank him?" Dax shook his head, obviously disgusted. "I need a beer."

He walked away, and she was pretty sure she'd lost him as an ally. Rubbing at her forehead, Everly wandered back into the living room. The big bay windows showed the beauty of the Upper West Side and the Hudson in the distance.

What was she going to do? She knew what she wanted—Gabriel. She merely wasn't sure she should keep him. She'd made her decision to trust him. Despite what Deep Throat had told her, she'd given all her information up. She'd told Gabriel and his friends everything because she trusted him.

When he came back down, he was dressed in a tuxedo that made him look even more like a Hollywood star on his way to a red carpet premiere. Should she judge him on his looks? Should she be afraid because he was so beautiful? Or should she remember that he was a human being who needed the same things everyone did—love and affection? She could be the woman who provided them if she'd open herself up.

"I'll be back soon." He kissed her gently as though slightly afraid to deepen the contact, despite all their intimacies.

She wanted to kiss him back, wanted to promise him everything would be fine, but all she could manage was a nod.

Everly wanted to say a lot more, but Connor entered, glancing at his watch with impatience.

With a nod, he and Gabriel left. She hoped Connor had some food in the place because she was a little afraid Dax would let her starve.

"I'm ordering pizza. You like mushrooms?" Dax's big body took up most of the entryway.

"If you slap some pepperoni on it, too."

An hour and one pepperoni and mushroom with extra sauce later, she pulled up the three photos she'd managed to download and turned the screen toward Dax. She'd used the system Connor had left for her to remote dial the laptop in her safe. It was connected to the small network of computers she kept for her use. Now that she'd accessed her system, she could see the pictures. She kind of wished she'd left the SD card in its slot. She might have been able to find a way to view the others without downloading them.

He frowned down. "And someone sent these to you. Any chance Deep Throat was referring to them?"

She had to shrug. "I don't know. It's not exactly information, is it? I hate to think there's more than one creepy stalker following my every move, but I don't see how it fits. Deep Throat is a conspiracy theorist. He was talking about Mad's death being bigger than we realize. So why would he send pictures of me and Maddox?"

"No idea. This looks like it was taken from the building across from yours."

"Yes," she admitted. "The building across from mine has roof access so I assume that's where the photographer was."

"He had a nice telephoto lens on that thing." Dax stared at the screen. "And you said there are more of these?"

"Yes," she replied, but something Dax had said made her stop. "I'm having trouble with my laptop. I've had issues for about a week. Something's wrong with my hard drive so my storage capacity is screwed up. I need to strip the thing down, but every time I try someone attempts to kill me. Sorry, it's been a rough few days. The camera I received didn't have a telephoto lens. It's one of those little digital things."

He shook his head. "This was taken with a telephoto lens. No question."

Everly's cell trilled. She looked down, hoping it was Gabriel.

Unfortunately, it wasn't Gabriel's name that popped up on her screen but Scott's. He usually called her at least once a day and twice on the weekends.

"I need to take this." She rose from her plush chair.

Dax nodded her way. "I'm going to look through these if you're okay with it."

"Sure." She wouldn't have been yesterday, but she was rapidly coming to like Gabriel's friends. She'd had a nice dinner with Dax. The navy captain had regaled her with hilarious stories about his childhood and some of the trouble he and Gabe and the rest of the gang had gotten into. Sitting and talking to Dax had made her realize that, for all their wealth and privilege, they had been little boys alone in the world. Now, they were men. Like any other man, Gabriel could leave her. He could walk away, the same way her mother had. Any man could do that, but Gabriel might be the one man worth risking her heart over.

Everly dashed from the living room into the kitchen and swiped her thumb across the screen. "Hey, Scott. How are you?"

"Are you okay, Everly? I'm a little scared." His voice was low, almost a whisper.

"I'm fine. What's going on?" She headed back to the living room.

"I looked through those records you asked me to. Did you know that for a couple of years there was a secondary sponsor for the foundation fundraiser?"

There were always secondary sponsors. There was a whole list of corporations who donated money to the foundation. "Of course."

"Everly, I talked to Tavia a few minutes ago and we're both scared for you. She didn't bring it up at the time, but after what happened to Valerie . . . I don't want him to hurt you. Please, you have to get to safety."

He was being awfully dramatic. "What are you talking about?"

"Gabriel Bond is in this up to his eyebrows. Bond Aeronautics handled the catering two years ago, and I found some e-mails between Valerie and Gabe Bond. They were lovers, running some kind of scam together and embezzling from Crawford. You have to meet me at my apartment so I can show you the evidence."

A little chill swept through her.

Gabriel involved with Valerie? She'd been an attractive woman, and he'd never once given the impression that he knew her. On the other hand, Valerie might not have been smart enough to plot and execute a plane crash, but Gabriel certainly was. In fact, that was right up his alley.

But if they'd been in some sort of scam together, why would he have brought the receipts for the foundation galas to her attention? Why would he have saved her from Valerie's homicidal madness? If they were involved, Everly couldn't picture him allowing Val to be arrested if he had any suspicion she'd die in jail.

"I don't know, Scott. I probably shouldn't. Maybe I can get away tomorrow."

"You have to come now," he argued. "Bond could hurt you. He's the one behind this. You realize that, right? God, Everly . . . Valerie wasn't my pal or anything, but I think he set her up to take the fall for everything. Get away while you can." He hesitated, and his voice dropped again. "Tell me you're not with him right now."

That was an easy one. "No. He's gone."

"Then leave. Right now. Come to my apartment, and we'll figure out what to do, how to keep you safe."

Indecision twisted in her gut. Maybe Scott had read everything wrong, misunderstood, but she hated to worry him. Besides, if she didn't say yes, he'd only keep calling. "All right. I'll grab my bags and I'll be there in an hour."

"So you'll be here by eight?" Scott asked, insistence in his tone. "Promise?"

Her grip on the phone tightened. "Yes."

"All right. I'll be waiting. He's a criminal mastermind who doesn't balk at murder. Be careful."

She hung up the phone with a stunned frown and paced.

What was going on? Who the hell could she trust? She only had two choices: Gabriel or Scott.

Her friend was prone to a bit of drama and embellishment, but calling Gabriel a criminal mastermind? That didn't sound like the man she was falling for at all. And Scott had been so insistent that she come to see him right now. If he really thought she was in danger, why didn't he come to rescue her? Or even ask where she was?

On the other hand, was Gabriel telling her that he loved her his ultimate lie simply to control her? Was she a sitting duck in Connor's apartment?

Trying to bury emotion and sift through facts, she trekked the hall and stopped in the living room where the laptop screen illuminated Dax's harsh features.

"I have a question."

He didn't look at her, but kept his eyes on the screen. "Shoot."

"Did Gabriel know Val?"

"Who?" Dax reached for his soda.

"Valerie. You know, the would-be murderess who died in lockup a couple of hours ago? Any chance Gabriel knew her before this week and had been doing her?"

Now she had Dax's attention. "What the hell are you talking about? There is zero chance Gabe was having a fling with that crazy bitch."

She didn't know Dax. She'd met him a few days before. She didn't really know Gabriel all that well, either. On the other hand, she'd known Scott for a long time. He'd stood beside her. He'd been her friend.

"First"—Dax went on—"Valerie wasn't his type at all. Second, he never once mentioned her to me, even as a piece on the side."

"You don't know everyone Gabriel has . . . dated." She really hated to think of him having sex with another woman.

"No, but if he'd seen her more than a couple of times, the paparazzi would have picked up on it. And third, why does it matter? I've never once heard him tell another woman that he loves her. Ever."

Everly stared Dax down. He didn't flinch.

She really had only one choice at the end of the day.

"Then we have a problem. I think my friend Scott is involved in this thing. That was him on the phone. Maybe he's simply mistaken about what he found, but he could also be trying to set Gabriel up. Scott tried to convince me that Gabriel wants to kill me."

"And you don't believe your friend?"

In the end, the decision had been simple. She'd done what her father had always told her to. She'd looked in her heart and she'd followed her gut. Gabriel Bond wasn't a criminal. He was actually a horrible liar. When he'd said he loved her, he'd meant it. It hadn't been a ploy. It had been his truth. She was betting her life on it.

"I don't."

Dax sat up. "Who is he?"

She sank to the couch. Sometimes a girl had to take a leap of faith. "Scott Wilcox works with me at Crawford. I asked him to look into the last couple of years of receipts for the foundation fundraisers. He said he has proof that Gabriel is involved in the embezzlement and that I should come to his place right now to see it." She took a deep breath. In for a penny, in for a pound. "Clearly, he's trying to lure me away from here and feed me a plate of bullshit. It would be a good play if someone wanted Gabriel and me separated, for whatever reason."

Dax stood. "You would be a very good pawn, especially if he wanted to use you as leverage against Gabe. My buddy would pretty much do anything to keep you safe. And we would help him. Maybe Scott's figured that out."

And there it was, the confirmation of her gut feeling. Deep Throat might have been spot-on about the lockbox and the investigation into Mad's murder, but he'd been wrong about Gabriel. He and his friends would stick together. All five of them had one another's backs, but that included their women, too. And she was Gabriel Bond's woman.

She was going to be his wife, and it was time to follow her loyalties and take her place.

"We need to think smart. Like you said, I'm a pawn. I think it's Gabriel they need. He had plenty of motive to want Maddox dead, and Scott, along with whomever he's working with, is using that to their advantage."

Everly refused to let Gabriel fall into danger. He wasn't going down on her watch.

"Or they want to create chaos, keep us so busy watching our backs we're not catching what's really happening." Dax scrubbed a hand through the dark stubble over his scalp. "I don't like any of this. If Mad really thought Valerie was stealing, why wouldn't he have fired her ass? Why all the subterfuge?"

"He wanted to gather enough evidence to prosecute her?" She answered in a question because now that she thought about it, that logic didn't make sense. "Except . . . I happen to know that we haven't prosecuted an employee in forever. Earlier this year, when an employee was found trying to sell proprietary documents, he was simply fired. Most corporations don't prosecute because of the bad publicity."

"The stock can take a dive over something like an embezzlement scandal. The Mad I know would have fired her and cut his losses."

But the receipts hadn't been the only things they'd found. Actually, now that she really thought about it, the receipts hadn't been locked up at all. They'd been sitting on his desk with a bunch of other papers. Mad hadn't been hiding them.

What he'd kept hidden and safe were the pictures of the girls, as well as her mother's and the Russian woman's names.

What had Deep Throat said? Sometimes she couldn't see the forest because of all those distracting trees.

Calm down. Think. You have pieces to the puzzle. Now see how they fit together.

Her father had adored puzzles. They would often eat on TV trays because the kitchen table had been covered in whatever puzzle he'd been working on at the time. He'd always told her that putting together a puzzle taught a man patience. He would stare at the individual pieces and slowly a pattern would form.

Maddox Crawford had been a man who almost always chose the direct path. She'd seen him fire an executive for getting an investor report wrong. Maddox hadn't carefully built a case. He'd been judge, jury, and executioner. He'd certainly dismissed more than one woman he'd slept with who proved herself troublesome.

He was a man with a multibillion-dollar fortune at his fingertips.

He wouldn't have truly missed the money. He would have been more worried about the impact to the company and the foundation than he would have been concerned about getting that cash back.

The important things had been in the lockbox, carefully concealed. The pictures of the girls. Her mother's name. Natalia Kuilikov.

What had Tavia said about the missing girls today? That Maddox had been considering hiring mercenaries. But the morning after she'd slept with Gabe, Tavia had told her Crawford Industries' own team was searching for the girls. Everly hadn't really been involved with the case because it wasn't a cyber threat. Besides, Tavia had known the girls and their families, had the necessary information.

She needed to look something up. "Can I see that computer again for a minute?"

He shrugged and scooted to the side, pushing the laptop in her direction. A few keystrokes later, she was into Mulford's files regarding this investigation. And she didn't like what she saw.

"Weeks, sometimes even months, have gone by and my counterpart who handles the physical security, Joe Mulford, hasn't received any sort of update or request for reimbursement from any member of the Crawford security team overseas." She frowned as another thought occurred to her. Suddenly, so many things weren't adding up. "This is going to sound like an odd question, but did Maddox know any mercenaries?"

Dax laughed. "Hell no. Mad knew sommeliers across the globe, but not mercenaries. He would have come to me or Connor if he was looking for someone with that skill set in a farflung part of the world."

"Would he have gone to Zack? After all, he was flying to DC when . . ."

"No. He definitely wouldn't have asked the president for a reference on a soldier-for-hire. Besides, as you know, Crawford has divisions across the globe, each with their own security team. Mad would have started there."

"If Mad had decided that wasn't working?"

"Wasn't working?" Dax stared at her as if she'd gone crazy. "You know they're top-notch. They know the locals. They know their terrain. I dare anyone to do a better job in those territories. But if they weren't getting the job done, he'd fire them and hire someone better. Not hire someone who could be bought off."

Dax was right. "So there are girls missing from foundation schools. At least three. There are likely more, but Maddox thought those three were important. I know two of them were from Africa, one from India."

She pounced on the computer. Dax helped her with passwords. It was a simple thing to look up the names and locations of the schools. Two were within fifty miles of a Crawford subsidiary.

"You're right. They shouldn't have needed mercenaries." She frowned. "After Tavia contacted the overseas teams directly, Mulford should have been asked to approve their expenditures. But I looked at his reports. Zilch. Zip. Nada. Not one request for reimbursement filed for on-the-job expenditures. When I told Tavia I'd follow up on his behalf, she told me not to do anything to distract them." A nasty feeling settled in her gut that Tavia was somehow in on the scam, too. "What if those girls didn't merely disappear?"

Dax shook his head. "How would we prove it?"

"I think . . . I need to figure out why those damn pictures were sent to me. Maybe I'm thinking too literally. Deep Throat was insistent I should have received his information. I've been thinking it would be out there in the open, but what if he was sneakier than that? That camera is the only thing I've received that wasn't about work. If my laptop wasn't malfunctioning . . . Oh, damn it." The truth hit her like a ton of brinks. How had she been so stupid? She raced back into the kitchen. "I would have figured this out in a heartbeat if my laptop hadn't been giving me trouble already. How could I not have seen it?"

Dax was right behind her. "I don't see it at all, darlin'. How about illuminating me?"

She needed to be sure first. She pulled up the folder containing the photos. The last few days had been so chaotic, she hadn't thought to question why the photographs were taking up so much space. She had thought the trouble was with her system, but what if it was all about the photos themselves?

The menu popped up along with the file sizes. She pointed at the screen. "Do you see those file sizes? They're huge."

"Are you fat shaming the pictures?" Dax asked, his eyes narrowed. "Why does the file size matter? Aren't pictures big files?"

Her hands were moving, flying across the keys because she knew what she had now. "They are big, but these are enormous. These took up almost all of the available space on my hard drive and there is a very good reason why. There's something hidden in here."

"Hidden how?"

She pulled one of the photos onto Connor's computer. His system wouldn't have the same capacity issues hers had. Again, she wished she'd left the card tucked into her laptop. She would have been able to remotely download everything to Connor's laptop. "It's called steganography. You bury important information under something that seems innocuous. Typically, the culprit codes their hidden material in a photograph. A huge file size is always the tip-off when someone tries that. And there it is."

The photograph morphed and became something different.

"Whoa. What did you do?" Dax took the seat beside her. "Is that Russian?"

A thrill went through her. "I cracked the code. I can do it very easily now that I know what's here. And that is definitely Russian. It's all in Cyrillic. Unfortunately I have no idea what it says, but it looks like someone scanned it in. Those are handwritten pages."

"I don't know a ton of Russian, but I do know the alphabet. Zack is fluent and we used it almost like a code." He pointed to the screen. "That's a name. Do you see how it almost looks like an entry and then it's signed. Over and over again. Like a diary. That's feminine handwriting, I think. She signed her diary entries."

Everly stopped. "So this is a woman's journal. Dax, please tell me her name is. . . ."

"Natalia."

"Oh god." She still didn't understand it all, but she knew one thing: She had to get back to those other photos. "We have to go to my office. The rest of this journal is on that SD card. That's what Valerie was looking for, I'll bet. She must have been involved or they used her as a patsy. This will lead us to the mysterious Natalia who hopefully knows a dude named Sergei."

"Agreed, though I'm not sure what this has to do with embezzlement of Crawford funds used for the galas. I feel as if we're still missing pieces of the puzzle." But he was putting his boots on.

"I do, too, but we have to grab that SD card before Scott and whoever else is helping him does. That might tell us what we're missing. If they steal that information, we'll lose any chance we have to figure out what really happened to Maddox."

"Gabe's going to kill me." He pulled out his cell and dialed a number. "Shit. I got his voice mail. Gabe, get your ass to Crawford. We think we've figured out a big, missing piece of this puzzle. It's the package the informant sent, which is in her office. I'm taking Everly because she has access to the building and I don't, but hustle there as soon as you can. Call me." Dax frowned as he hung up. "All right. You lead the way."

Everly practically raced out of the building and into the night.

feel naked without my cell phone," Gabe grumbled as they worked their way around the crowd.

"You know why Roman does it," Connor said.

Because there had been one too many scandals involving people taping speeches that were then played out of context or showed the politician in a bad light. Those tapes of politicians speaking to their bases had unhinged more than one campaign, so Roman had declared cell phones out of bounds inside the banquet halls for fundraising events, even the ones Zack wasn't supposed to attend.

"I know, but it's a pain in my ass." He strained to see through the crowd as they were finally allowed into the ballroom. A familiar face caught his eyes. "Hell. Is that who I think it is?"

Connor followed his gaze until it caught on a pretty blonde. "That's Liz. Shit. Why wouldn't he tell us?"

If Liz Matthews was here, then it followed that Zack was here as well.

Gabe's gut twisted. Roman had lied to them. "I guess we should be happy he didn't ban us from the ballroom."

Connor held a hand up. "Stop. Those are our best friends. Give them a chance to explain."

He scoured the crowd, looking for Roman. Now he understood all the security he'd been forced to go through.

"Mr. Bond?"

Gabe turned to find one of the Secret Service men he'd met a few days ago. *Shit.* "I need to see Zack."

He stood his ground and wondered if they would haul him out kicking and screaming or if they would simply quietly tase him and dump his body somewhere.

"He would like to see you both. He and Mr. Calder are waiting in a private room upstairs. They saw you come in on the security cameras. I'm supposed to tell you that speaking to the tabloids about any incidents that might or might not have resulted in him earning the nickname 'Scooter' is an offense punishable by time in Guantanamo Bay."

"Is he joking?" Gabe asked.

Connor's lips had curled up. "I don't think the Secret Service is allowed to joke."

They followed the big guy in the dark suit to a private elevator.

"I think that was Zack's way of telling you he knows you're going to be pissed," Connor whispered as the elevator started up.

"Yeah, well, no amount of joking is going to stop me from being pissed, but I'm not stupid. I'm not going to punch the fucker until he leaves office."

"He's joking," Connor said, rolling his eyes as he turned back to Gabe. "They really don't joke about threats to the president, man."

The doors opened, and Roman stood inside, wearing a perfectly pressed tux. He held his hands up. "It's not what you think."

Gabe thought seriously about throwing a punch anyway, but the Secret Service guard stood with his sunglasses on, looking badass, and Gabe decided to keep his head on his body. "Then explain what's happening. I want to know who shut down the FAA investigation. I want to know why Mad was really on his way to see Zack. I want the truth this time because someone is coming after the woman I love and I won't let Zack's politics get her killed."

After a short ride, they reached their floor. Connor followed Gabe out, and the guard took up a place in front of the elevator doors as they closed again.

Roman started talking. "First off, I was trying to keep Zack's appearance tonight a secret. That's why I didn't tell you. The tabloids have been following you and Everly everywhere."

"Not anymore."

"I'm glad to know that plan worked."

"Roman, bring them in. I think we should tell them everything." Zack's weary voice sounded from around the corner.

Gabe strode into the suite's large living area. Zack sat on the plush sofa, and it looked as if he hadn't slept the night before. Though he was dressed to the nines, an air of exhaustion hung around him.

Zack looked behind Gabe and Connor, then nodded. At once, the Secret Service retreated. "Is Dax with your girl?"

Gabe nodded. "Yes."

"I was so sorry to hear about the harrowing incidents. I'm glad neither one of you was hurt." Zack reached out and picked up a glass of what looked like Scotch. He downed it, then got up to make another. He glanced back, offering them a glass. "Anyone else?"

"No. I'd really just like the story. I need to get back to Everly." He didn't like seeing Zack so tired, but Everly was his first concern now. He didn't care if exposing FAA irregularities started a scandal that rocked Zack's presidency. Not if it meant getting Everly out of danger.

"I know this probably won't help, but he asked me to bring you in." Roman took a seat. He had a glass of his own. "He was going to tell you everything over breakfast tomorrow. He didn't even realize that the plot leading to Mad's death may be about him until earlier today when I told him what we'd found. We still don't understand what it means."

Zack turned. "You have to know I wouldn't want you to endure the hell I went through for anything."

Losing his wife. Gabe and Mad had been the ones to sit with Zack in the hospital that first night. He hadn't been injured but after the reporters had gone, Zack had lost it. The doctors had sedated him. He and Mad had watched over him while Roman made arrangements for Joy's body.

Gabe softened slightly as he sat. "I know you wouldn't." These were his closest friends. He needed to have a little faith. "Tell me what you know."

Zack shrugged out of his jacket and laid it over the chair he sank into. "I know the head of the FAA swears to me his people tell him it was pilot error. I had nothing to do with it, but I would like to have Connor check into everyone involved in the investigation. I know you're not supposed to work on American soil, man."

Connor shrugged. "I've done worse things. I'll get on it."

He would find the truth. Oh, Zack might not act on it if he thought he had good reasons, but Connor would find it. That was one worry gone. "Why was Mad coming to see you?"

"He wanted to ask me about a woman named Natalia Kuilikov." Zack took another drink. "He told me he'd been contacted by someone who had found her diary. He wouldn't tell us who had contacted him, but he said Capitol Scandals was actively trying to acquire it. Apparently there was a bidding war for the book on the Deep Web."

Gabe shook his head. "The Deep Web?"

"It's like the dark alley of the Internet," Connor explained. "There are addresses that you can't get to through the regular means. A lot of criminal activity takes place on the Deep Web. Who was she? An old girlfriend of yours? Is she dead?"

"I don't know," Zack admitted. "I thought she was still in Russia. And she certainly wasn't my girlfriend. I've talked about her with you. Nata."

"Your nanny?" Gabe thought back. Nata was the nickname Zack had used when he'd been too young to pronounce Natalia. Zack had spoken fondly of the young Russian woman who had taken care of him for the first seven years of his life in Moscow.

"Yes." Zack groaned. "You can see where I'm a bit confused. I was seven the last time I saw her. He and Mother employed an American woman who watched me during the summers when I wasn't at boarding school. By the time my mother was killed in a car accident, Dad decided I was too old to need a babysitter. What could Nata have said that was so vital or secret that people would kill to know?"

"Did your father have an affair with her?" Connor asked.

"I already went down that road." Roman paced the floor. "Even if his father had an affair with his childhood nanny, that's not scandalous enough to touch Zack. His approval ratings are ridiculously high. Everyone knows his father had problems with women and booze, but the man is way out of the public spotlight now. A discovery like that is a footnote in a biography."

"Have you asked your father?" Gabe knew Zack wasn't close to his dad, but if he could shed some light on what was happening, it was worth the attempt.

Zack sighed. "I can try, but he's in early stage dementia, I'm afraid. And he didn't like to talk about the past even when he could remember it."

"Then there has to be something more. We have to find that damn diary ourselves," Gabe said. "I want to put some investigators on the video feed from the parking garage. Maybe we can catch the man who was talking to Everly. He seems to know way more than he should. I also want to see the wreckage of Mad's plane. My company built that plane. I taught Mad how to fly it. I want to do an independent study."

Zack nodded. "I'll see what I can do. Is Everly really Mad's half sister?"

"Yes."

"Wow. I wish I could have seen how that bastard would have handled having a sister. God knows he hit on all of yours. It made me happy I was an only child. Do you remember when he hit on Roman's cousin when we were teenagers?"

Gabe was able to laugh. "She broke his nose. That was one of the best days ever." He sobered a bit. "I wonder how he would have handled having a kid."

"I hope Sara knows that we're all behind her," Zack explained. "Anything we can do."

"You can get my cell phone out of jail," Gabe requested.

"Already done," Zack said. "It should be up here any minute. When we spotted you coming in, I tried to catch them before they took your phone, but I missed."

"I want to call Everly and let her know I'm on my way back. I think we're going to stay with Connor for a while. His place is better protected than mine. I have to very quietly watch over her."

"Or he could be the one with the broken nose," Connor added. "Everly is not the debutante type. She's a cop's daughter and she lets you know it."

"You and Mad's sister." Roman's head shook as though he couldn't quite believe it.

"I'm going to marry her." He was going to try anyway, but he had to work on their relationship, on building her trust.

"Never thought that would happen." Zack smiled and stood, holding his hand out.

Gabe took it, but brought his old friend in for a hug. These were his brothers, his family-by-choice. He could count on them. "We're going to figure this out. We'll put a stop to it."

"Damn straight we will." Roman had a hand on Zack's back.

"And we'll take out anyone who threatens us," Connor promised.

Their circle was incomplete, but Dax wasn't the only absentee. They would be forever diminished because Maddox was gone.

Grief sprang up in Gabe like a bottle had been uncorked.

"I miss him, too," Zack said. "I hate the fact that I wouldn't meet with him. I thought he was trying to get me to smooth things over with you. He told me he had something important to talk about, and I blew him off. Maybe he wouldn't have gotten in that plane if I hadn't hung up on him."

"You can't think like that," Roman said as they broke apart. "Mad was always reckless. I'm going to miss him forever, but we had a right to be pissed at him. All we can do now is try to figure out who killed him and why."

The elevator door dinged again, and another agent entered carrying Gabe's and Connor's cell phones. Liz Matthews was right behind them. She was dressed in a fashionable black dress that gathered at her small waist and flared over womanly hips. He'd heard her say she was too heavy to be on camera, but television couldn't capture her brilliance, the way her eyes sparkled with life. Gabe was grateful to her for saving Zack from the brink of despair. She was lovely inside and out.

And it was lucky no camera was around to catch how the president of the United States looked at her with hungry eyes.

"The crowd is getting restless, Zack. There are only so many Beltway jokes a girl can take." Her smile widened as she took in the room. "Gabe and Connor. It's nice to see you both. How is your sister doing?"

Liz never forgot to ask about family. She was a good Southern girl. "She's good. She's taking a little time off to relax." He had his cell in hand and it looked like they'd gathered all the information they could here for now. It was time to get back to Everly. "Zack, thank you. We'll contact you as soon as we know something."

"I'll get you the information you need. And I'll make sure you get to examine the plane." Zack reached for his tuxedo jacket, pulling it on. Liz was right there, smoothing it down and straightening his tie.

"Thank you." Gabe looked down at his cell. Dax had called. He checked his voice mail. Dax's low voice came in loud and clear.

Gabe had to get his ass to Crawford now.

He intended to marry her—if he didn't kill her first. Damn it. Dax knew he didn't want her out there.

And he was going to take a deep breath and deal with it. She was walking into a well-guarded building. She could handle herself. Because if he wasn't careful, he would push her away with his protective instincts.

"Connor, have them pull the limo around. We have to swing by Crawford and pick up Everly and Dax." He dialed Dax's line.

"Hey, don't yell at me. She's very persuasive," Dax said.

At least they were all right. "Wait for me. I can be at Crawford in fifteen minutes."

"We're walking through the doors now. Everly figured out that she's got Natalia Kuilikov's journal on an SD card in her safe. She's also decided that her friends here at Crawford are dirty and I think she likes you. Like-likes you."

That was Dax, always joking. "Well, I like-like her, too. Keep her safe. I'm on my way."

"I'll call you when we're leaving, and you can pick us up. We took the subway since you and Connor hijacked the limo, and he wasn't kind enough to leave me the keys to his Porsche."

He glanced at Connor. "You couldn't leave him the keys?"

Connor snorted. "As if. He would strip the gears in a heartbeat."

"Hurry up. We'll meet you in front of the building." Gabe hung up, a thrum of adrenaline starting. "Everly thinks she's got the information."

"Is there something I should know?" Liz asked.

Zack gave her what Gabe thought of as his politician smile. "Just some information on an old friend. Nothing for you to worry about. Let's go downstairs. Election day is only, like, six hundred days away. Are you sure I can't quit now?"

The elevator arrived, and they shuffled in, followed by the Secret Service agent, who pressed the button for the ballroom and the lobby.

Liz fussed over Zack. "Nope. Let's go, Mr. President. If you quit, I'm out of a job and I need shoes. You can play with your friends later. Roman, I need you to run interference. If anyone lets Senator Baxter too near the gin, you know how that goes."

The door opened, and Liz and Zack exited.

"I'm coming." Roman stopped in front of Gabe. "I'll be at your place as soon as I can. Be careful."

The doors closed again.

"They need to do it in the Lincoln Bedroom," Connor said with a shake of his head.

Gabe wished those two would do it anywhere. Sometimes he was fairly certain that Zack had the worst job in the world.

They finally made it to the lobby.

"I'll have them bring the car around." Connor stepped toward the valet, and Gabe wished they'd taken the Porsche. He couldn't get to Everly fast enough.

One way or another, he was going to settle things with her tonight.

SEVENTEEN

Everly pocketed her keycard and wondered who was getting fired in the morning. No one was sitting at the security desk. The place was empty and eerily quiet.

It had been a hell of a night. As soon as they'd gotten off the subway, she'd received a text from a neighbor saying the door to her loft had been standing open and someone had trashed her whole place. She'd briefly called the elderly woman, who said it didn't appear as if anything had been taken but someone had definitely been looking for something.

Deep Throat's information, no doubt.

"Gabe is coming, but he's got to make his way through traffic, so we have a few minutes. Are you sure we shouldn't go over to your place first?" Dax asked.

She shook her head. "Nope. I had my neighbor lock up. We can deal with that later. We know what they were looking for."

"This place is creepy at night." Dax looked around, frowning.

She was getting used to being around him, and it felt right to tease him. "Aren't you some sort of naval hero? Should you get the creeps?"

She pushed the button for the elevator.

Dax followed her on and touched the button to take them to the fortieth floor. "I am a captain in the U.S. Navy, thank you very much, and that means I'm used to having people around me twenty-four seven. This empty shit is creepy. Give me a big-ass boat with a few hundred men who all carry guns and answer to me, then I'm happy."

"You're spoiled, Captain Spencer." She gave him a smile, but her chest felt tight. Once they had this piece of information, it was possible the rest would fall like dominoes and she wouldn't have a reason to stay with Gabriel . . . except that she wanted to. Panic threatened when she considered not being in his life. Despite all their fights, she couldn't imagine not seeing him.

She had to shove those thoughts aside and focus on the issue at hand. She needed to figure out why Scott was involved in this mess and exactly what Tavia was guilty of.

Everly suspected the foundation was at the heart of the mess somehow. Tavia *was* the foundation. Her family had founded the charity. Tavia's life and career were all about running it. She had to be involved. It would have been fairly simple for her to manipulate documents to incriminate Valerie.

The question was why would Tavia need the money? Was the foundation in financial trouble? Or was something more sinister going on? And had Valerie been offed to keep her from talking?

"We're going to get in and get out," Dax said. "Grab that card thing and we'll leave. We'll look at it when we get back to Connor's."

Maybe she could still be vital to the case. Even after she turned over the information, they might still need her. "Agreed. I'll let Connor deal with the document and I'll start looking for Deep Throat. I'll e-mail him back and hopefully get him to go to another Internet café to reply. I can figure out where he likely lives if he keeps going to the same spot or one close to it. I suspect the sucker uses cash because I haven't been able to match up credit cards to the times he's written me."

"You're kind of scaring me now, Parker. You can really do all that on a computer?" When she nodded, he whistled. "You're a dangerous little thing and I'm sorry. Deep Throat needs a new name because Gabe was right. All I can think about is porn." Dax stood at least a foot taller than her and had another hundred pounds of muscle, but he made her smile. He was a little like a big, gorgeous chocolate lab.

The elevator doors dinged open, and she led the way out and onto the familiar floor.

"Something's up. I just lost all my bars." He stared down at his phone.

"Maybe something is wrong with the cell tower." She looked at hers. Nothing. "I'll hurry."

She hadn't taken more than five steps when Dax put a hand on her. She turned. "What?"

Dax put a fist up. From years of being around ex-military men, she knew it was a signal to go silent.

She stopped and listened, hoping it was the guards doing a walk-through or the janitors.

Dax pointed ahead of them.

Everly's stomach turned as she realized what she was looking at. A pair of sneakered feet poked out from behind the bank of cubicles in front of her. A vacuum was lying on its side.

"Back to the elevators," Dax whispered. "Someone's here and they've got a cell jammer in place. I'm getting you out."

"He could have had a heart attack." Everly started to walk toward the downed man.

"No. Something's wrong." Dax pulled her back before they heard someone moving in the hallway to their right.

"It is unfortunate for you that the diary seems to be gone, *myshka*. You know I can't return home without it."

Her whole body went cold. Russian. Whoever was speaking had a thick Russian accent and she could hear his boots thud against the carpet.

"Uncle Yuri, this has all been a terrible mistake." Tavia's voice shook as it got closer.

Dax dropped to the ground, pulling Everly with him. They were coming from the opposite side and would block the elevators soon. They would have to cross the Russian's path to reach the stairs. So she followed Dax as he crawled into the cubicle maze and ducked into one in the middle.

He pulled her close, his voice against her ear. "Don't scream."

When she turned, she understood what he meant. She shoved a hand over her mouth to stop the shriek that threatened. The body of one of the guards had been shoved against the side of the cubicle, his lifeless eyes open below a gaping hole in his forehead. He seemed to stare at nothing. Her stomach churned. The other guard was almost certainly dead as well. That was why the lobby had been empty of security.

"A mistake?" It sounded as if they'd stopped right in front of the elevators. "It wasn't a mistake, *myshka*. You got greedy. It wasn't enough for you to run girls. You wanted to blackmail the boss. Where did you find the diary? Natalia has been missing to us for many years."

"Maddox Crawford found the diary. The best I can figure out, his father came into possession of it back when he was sleeping with my mother. Maybe she gave it to him for safekeeping, but somehow Mad got hold of it. He's the one who wanted to force me to blackmail Ivan. I would never do such a thing. I'm loyal to my family. I only want to run my foundation. Didn't I come through for you this summer? I managed to get the arms shipment through when no one else could."

"But you couldn't cover up your own human trafficking ring."

"I've sold hundreds of girls. Only three have ever been publicized as missing. I think my record stands on its own."

Everly's stomach turned again. Tavia hadn't been trying to educate girls in poor countries at all. She'd been plucking them from their families and ensuring they had short, miserable lives so she could make a few bucks. She'd duped everyone. Had Mad figured out the truth before his death? Was that why he'd been killed?

"Your record could get us all . . . how do Americans say? Knee-deep in shit. I told you this would only continue until you got caught."

"I haven't been caught," Tavia argued. "And I won't be. We need to focus on your problems. We don't have to kill the girl. My brother is wrong. If we kill her or kidnap her, the police will be all over us."

"I was not sent here to stand by and hope nothing goes wrong," Tavia's uncle replied in a deep, rumbling voice.

Tavia seemed to ignore that. "All I'm saying is if we can find the diary before she does, there's no need to kill her. The little idiot has no idea what's going on around her. If she did, she would have gone straight to the press."

"How can you be sure?"

"Because I know her. She's a do-gooder. If she understood what that diary meant, she would go straight to the authorities. Trust me. When things cool down, she'll forget about everything but her new boyfriend's big wallet. Everything will go back to normal and all our plans can continue on."

They were talking about her, Everly realized with a shiver.

"We have to find that diary," Tavia continued. "Now, it's obviously not in Crawford's office. We've checked everywhere. There's a chance it was destroyed in the house fire."

"Jason and Lester searched Crawford's house first. *Nichego.*"

"Nothing? Okay, m-maybe he took it on the plane and it went down with him. After all, he was on his way to see the president."

"Which is why it was so necessary to kill the man. Everything could have fallen apart if he'd made it to DC with that diary, you dumb bitch. Do you know how many years this plan has been in place? How many people have died so we have this chance?"

"I know what's at stake."

"Yet you decided to make a quick buck off it." Another voice joined them, this one familiar. *Scott?* "I found proof that she's the one who sent the blackmail e-mails. She's also been skimming from the foundation to the tune of about a half a million a year. Tell me, did it all go up your nose, sis?"

Scott was Tavia's brother? His smooth tones were gone, and he sounded far angrier and more ruthless than Everly had ever heard him.

"What is this?" the Russian asked.

Scott gave a sinister chuckle. "Tavia has a small cocaine problem. I believe you'll find she skimmed from Crawford and set up poor Val to take the fall, but that wasn't enough. When the diary fell into her lap, she saw another way of making money. Unfortunately, Crawford found the fucking thing when he was investigating the missing funds. Hence, the situation we find ourselves in."

"How much did Crawford know before he died?" the Russian asked.

"He figured out enough to realize that Zachary Hayes is in real trouble," Scott replied. "He'd started asking questions about Sergei."

A crash echoed through the room, along with what sounded like a whole lot of Russian curses.

"Calm yourself," Scott soothed. "We're not done yet. Everly Parker is late for our meeting. I have to hope she's running behind. I have a man in place in case she shows up, but we have to deal with the possibility that she's thrown her lot in with Bond and his crew."

"Uncle Yuri, you have to believe me." Tavia sniffled.

"I don't have to do anything, my niece, and you've forgotten who the boss is here. Let me show you."

A cracking sound split the air, and it was all Everly could do not to scream as she heard a thud. Dax's arms tightened around her.

They'd killed Tavia. That sound had been a gun discharging and Tavia's body hitting the floor. How many bad guys with guns were there? How were they going to get out of here?

"You know I didn't want to do that. She was family," the Russian said, his voice low. "I can't have her skimming money from corporations and exposing us. Her habits made her ineffective, and she had to be put down."

"I know," Scott replied. "She was threatening our operations. I haven't lived most of my life in this godforsaken, piece-of-shit country for my sister to blow everything over cocaine."

There was a long pause. "Find me the diary."

"I told you, I think the Parker girl has it," Scott explained.

"Tavia said she was nothing but a stupid whore."

Scott huffed, an arrogant sound. "Tavia has a bullet through her brain, so maybe we shouldn't listen to her. I'll search Parker's office thoroughly. It wasn't at her apartment, so it has to be here."

"Why would Crawford trust her with it? It makes more sense that he would have taken it with him," the Russian mused.

"I watched him and I've gotten close to her. It took me a while to figure out how to do it, but once I knew she was important to Crawford, I played gay. It earned her trust. I think Crawford would have sent his long-lost sister a copy. For all his quirks, he was careful. Even if the original had gone down with him on the plane, he would have had a backup. Now I can't get into her system. I tried. She's got it locked down. We'll have to steal it and hire a hacker, but I would feel better going through her office again. We need to go through her desk and then start looking for a safe. And I'll pull every piece of hardware I can. It's got to be there."

If they got the safe open, they would find the SD card. It might take them a while to figure out the information was embedded in the photos but they would do it. And the information would be lost to her, Gabriel, and all his friends.

Factions. Deep Throat had talked about factions being after the diary. If Scott got that card, the intelligence would be lost to her faction, because she was choosing sides and it damn straight wasn't the Russians.

None of the obstacles between her and Gabriel mattered now. Not the press or the women who had come before her. Not even that stupid report he'd had compiled on her. None of it mattered stacked up against the possibility of never seeing him again. She loved Gabriel Bond and if she survived, she would never let him go.

"How will you take care of everything?" the Russian asked.

"You forget I did a rotation through security. That's how I knew where to place the cell phone jammers so the guards and the janitorial staff couldn't call out. I'll wipe the computers so it looks like only Tavia swiped in. No one will have any idea what really went on. I can have us out of here in twenty minutes."

"All right, then."

Everly moved closer and whispered to Dax. "We have to get to my office."

"No, we're not doing anything until it's safe," Dax whispered against her ear. "They don't know we're here. They'll leave soon. If they get the SD card, then we'll have to steal it back, but not until I'm sure you're safe."

The elevator dinged open, and Everly felt a sick slide of dread that the possibility they would all die had just skyrocketed.

The building was silent except for the sound of Gabe's and Connor's shoes against the floor. The guards seemed to have taken a break, but Gabe was focused on Everly. He'd almost made it to the elevator when Connor stopped him. "I lost service on my phone."

Gabe looked down at his cell. Sure enough, he had no bars. "That's weird. There must be something wrong. No wonder they're not answering. I bet their phones aren't working, either."

At least he knew where they were going. The doors opened and he started to step inside.

Connor grabbed his arm. "You don't understand. I had service out on the street. I think someone's got a cell phone jammer on the building. A very powerful one. Whoever it is, they don't want anyone to be able to call in or out."

Everly was upstairs. And she likely wouldn't know what she was getting into. She could have walked into an ambush.

Gabe made the decision in a heartbeat. He stepped into the elevator. "Go and get help."

"Gabe! Get your ass back here." Connor started toward him, but Gabe pressed the button to close the doors.

"I'm going to kick your ass," Connor growled as the doors banged shut. He could hear the reverberation of Connor's fist against the metal.

Connor was the only one who could get help now. Gabe couldn't stay downstairs and hope for the best. The floors ticked by, his adrenaline spiking with every inch closer. Someone was up there and they wanted Everly.

Had whoever killed Mad caught her? Was she already dead?

His heart clenched at the thought of her being in pain, in fear. He would have done anything in that moment to change places with her.

He'd always thought that a husband wanting to die before his wife was a protective thing, but now he realized it was selfish at the core. He didn't want to have to live without her. He didn't want to feel the pain that would come from knowing she was gone.

Please. Please. Please, let her be alive. It had been years since he'd prayed, but he would have begged anyone he must to spare her life.

The elevator stopped and the world seemed to slow. The doors opened so sluggishly, and the first thing he saw was a woman on the ground, her body crumpled in unnatural angles. Bile crept up his throat, but then he realized the woman in front of him had silvery blond hair, not Everly's sweet reddish hue.

Tavia.

Not Everly. Tavia was dead.

"Nice of you to join us, Bond," a dark voice said. "Please to step out of the lift."

He put his hands up and stepped out of the elevator. The man in front of him was a giant bull with broad shoulders and a barrel chest.

He had tattoos slithering up from under his T-shirt and covering his neck. His dark hair was cut in an almost military style so there was nothing to detract from the jagged scar that ran down his face.

Those tats told the tale. Even in the low light, Gabe could make out the ones on the man's arms. There was a church and weeping angels. He'd spent some time on the Internet earlier in the day and he'd seen those tattoos on Russian mobsters. They detailed their crimes and the punishments they'd survived.

He made sure his hands were visible and hoped Connor could summon the police in time. "What's happening?"

"You're going to play dumb?" The younger man beside the Russian was Everly's friend, Scott. It looked as if Everly and Mad had been surrounded by betrayal. Scott held a semiautomatic with the ease of one long used to the feel of a gun in his hand.

Playing dumb was his only option. He let desperation creep into his voice. "If you're looking for money, I can get you plenty of it."

Where was she? Had Dax figured out the situation and hidden with her?

"He is the plane builder?" The Russian stepped forward, looking him over.

"Yes, uncle. And he's loaded. What are you doing here this late, Bond?" Suspicion crept across Scott's face, and he looked around as though trying to decide if they were alone.

If they didn't know Everly and Dax were up here, then he wasn't about to give them away. He needed to give Dax a shot at getting her out of here. "I left some paperwork. I need it for the lawyers. God, why would you kill Tavia?" Because she was obviously involved. He didn't say that. He looked down at her and shook his head. "She did so much good in the world."

"My sister was a coke head who liked to sell little girls to the highest bidder," Scott said. "How would it affect the old bottom line if everyone knew that Crawford Industries has been a front for human trafficking for years?"

Mad had been looking for the girls. Mad had figured out some-thing was wrong. Despite the situation, one worry eased in his chest. Mad had been trying to do some good of his own. "I don't believe it."

"You don't have to." Scott stepped forward. "All you have to do is get Everly Parker up here."

"I'm not supposed to see her tonight. She told me she was going back to her place," Gabe lied.

"Step away from the elevators, Bond." Scott moved around the last line of cubicles and started to trek the rows, looking down each.

Was Everly there?

"Why do you want Everly?" He had to keep them talking.

"That is none of your business," Scott's uncle said. "If you don't get the Parker woman up here, I will kill you. You're no use to me, and our plan to clean up this mess is now blown, no?"

Scott's jaw tightened, showing his anger. "Yes, it is. Still, you might want to leave him alive. I think he might be very useful in getting Everly to talk. I don't think she'll come if I call since it appears she stood me up." He regarded Gabe. "She's hot, as you know. I tried to hit on her when we first met. I guess she's only willing to give it up for a billionaire."

"Why were you stalking Everly at all?"

"We figure out that she's Crawford's sister long before he does," the Russian said. "We use Crawford Industries for many years. His father was easy man to deal with. The son, not so much. I think you will be easier, though. You seem like reasonable man."

"He has a sister, too. I could always send the boys to find her. You didn't think we were alone, did you? I have several of the most sadistic criminals the brotherhood has ever seen going through Tavia's office even as we speak. I think you'll like them." Scott pulled out a walkie-talkie. It would work despite the jammer because it would be tuned to a frequency of the user's choice. "Niles, come in. I have a new job for you." Scott smirked Gabe's way. "He'll be more than happy to enter-tain your sister until you take me to Everly. I'll ride along with you to make sure you don't get lost. If you and Miss Parker give me what I want, your sister won't be damaged. Too much."

Gabe's heart stopped.

"Are you sure we need the Parker woman?" The Russian stared at Scott.

"If there is a computer element to this clusterfuck, Everly is very good with hacking a system. It occurs to me that she might be helpful in case there's some security on the diary, and she would likely be more willing to lend a hand if we have her boyfriend here." He looked down at the walkie-talkie and pressed the button again. "Niles? Come in."

"Everly is probably in Brooklyn." Once Gabe got the Russians outside, Dax would have some freedom of movement to get Everly to safety. Connor would likely be waiting for them when they went downstairs. God, he'd joked with the man about being more than an analyst. He prayed he'd been right now. He didn't need Connor's brains. He needed a hunter.

She was either here or she was on her way back to Connor's, where she would be safe. Either way, he had a better chance of getting out of this if they took to the streets. No one knew where Sara was and he wasn't about to tell these men where his sister and her unborn child were. He would die first.

"Niles, come in." Scott cursed at the walkie-talkie. "I thought Everly was staying with you. Isn't she at your place?"

It would take them longer to get to Brooklyn. It would buy him more time. "No. She said she needed some space. We'll find her there, I'm sure. I have a car downstairs. We can go get her right now."

The Russian chuckled. "How quickly they turn on each other. Americans. You're all the same. You look out for yourselves."

Scott's gun was aimed squarely on Gabe again. "That's not his reputation at all."

Shit. "Look, she's just some chick I was banging. I don't want to die."

Scott's eyes narrowed as he studied Gabe. "Really? Just some chick? She was your best friend's sister. Even if I believed for a second you don't have feelings for her, you cared deeply about him. I know she's not in Brooklyn. I've already been there and had a look around so I know you're lying. She's here, isn't she? I thought I heard the elevator earlier, but I wrote it off as paranoia. I was right. She's here and she's hiding."

Panic threatened. He forced himself to stay calm and cool. "I'm alone. I told you. I came up here to get some paperwork."

"Sure you did." Scott strode his way, but Gabe held his ground. He stayed put even when Scott shoved the muzzle of the gun under his chin, pain jarring through his system. "Where is she?"

He shook his head. "I don't know."

It didn't matter if they blew his head off as long as Everly was safe. His brothers would protect her. It would be all right. An odd calm settled over him. Scott and his uncle wouldn't find her.

The Russian looked down the hall. "I don't like the silence. My boys know to answer back. Don't kill him until I return."

As his uncle walked away, Scott tightened his hold. "Everly, sweetheart? Are you here? Because I've got a gun pressed against your pretty boy's head and I'm about to pull the trigger."

Gabe prayed again that she couldn't hear Scott, prayed that she was smart enough to stay hidden.

"I'm here." Her hands came up first. He watched in horror as she slowly rose into sight over the cubicle wall. "Gabe came looking for me. I wasn't supposed to go off on my own."

She placed a heavy emphasis on *own*. Dax was nearby and he intended to make his move.

The gun at Gabe's jaw never faltered. He would give that to the asshole. Scott—if that was even his real name—seemed well trained. "I want that diary, Everly."

Her eyes were wide as she shook her head. "I don't know what you're talking about. I came up here to grab a hard drive. I got a message saying something important was on it. I can get it for you, but you have to let Gabriel go. He doesn't have anything to do with this."

What the hell was she doing? She was obviously bluffing since he knew the diary was on an SD card and not a hard drive. He wasn't going to let her take the heat when the Russians found out they didn't have the right information. "No. She'll tell me where the hard drive is, then you'll let her go."

Of course, he wasn't stupid. Gabe knew how it was going to work. Scott couldn't afford to leave either one of them alive.

Even if he could wait until Connor brought the cops and it turned into a standoff, they could trade Everly for their freedom. Gabe would go with them as a hostage.

"I'm going to get that hard drive one way or another," Scott promised. "Once I'm assured the information is on the drive, I'll need the name of the person who sent it to you. Move. We'll all go to your office."

She nodded and started to move toward the end of the aisle. "Don't hurt him. If you do, I won't help you."

"Everly, baby, the minute you give him what he wants, he's going to kill me. Then he'll kill you. Don't do this." Gabe was going to have to make a move before then and give her a chance to escape. The only problem was, he wasn't sure she would take it.

She stopped as she moved out into the aisle, making herself completely vulnerable. "What you told me earlier? I should have said it back, Gabriel."

She was killing him. "It doesn't matter, baby."

"I love you, too. I'm never going to leave you." Her jaw was tight, and yet her words came out softly, as though she was trying to impart some truth to him.

He had to get them out of this. "Everly, you know what I would want."

Scott jammed the butt of the gun against his jaw again, making pain flare. "You two shut up. Everly, if you want your boyfriend's head on his shoulders for the next few minutes, you'll turn around and walk toward your office. If you try anything at all, I'll pull the trigger. Is that understood?"

She nodded and turned, moving slowly toward the bank of executive offices.

Scott had such a tight hold on him, Gabe found it hard to move. He shuffled forward. If he stumbled, would that give Everly time to flee? Or would she fight back?

If he lived, they were having a serious talk.

A horrible scream stopped them all in their tracks and suddenly Gabe found himself falling forward. He hit the ground with a hard thud, his knees buckling and pain shooting through him. No time for agony. Adrenaline poured through his body, forcing him to turn onto his back. Everly was standing over him. He turned and saw Dax. Damn. The man was good with a gun, but it turned out Dax also excelled at finding weapons in an office setting. He'd stabbed a pair of scissors into Scott's right foot. Gabe winced as he glimpsed how deep Dax had managed to sink them.

"Son of a bitch!" Scott was on the floor, but he hadn't dropped the gun. As Dax got to his feet, Scott aimed at him, the metal glinting in the low light.

"Run!" Dax yelled as he dove for the cubicles. "Get her the fuck out of here."

Gunfire resounded, so close it nearly split his ears. Everly was trying to drag him. She wouldn't leave, and Scott was going to catch them again if they didn't flee. Dax leapt over the wall and disappeared. Scott shot again, this time Dax's way. It was all happening at lightning quick speed. Gabe grabbed Everly's hand.

They had come to a turning point. He loved his brother. They were a family, but the woman he loved came first.

As he ran down the corridor with her, it struck him firmly that the world had changed. He had to put her before all others. They were going to get married and have kids, and he still loved those friends who had been his whole world, but they would forever take second place to her. His childhood, that grand, carefree time when he could be selfish and the world had been his oyster, was over. He served her now. He would be her husband, and that came with other terms—lover, friend, protector.

He ached at leaving Dax, but Gabe would come back for him after he made sure she was safe. Dax was smart and had training. He wouldn't go down easy. Neither would Everly, he knew. But Gabe simply refused to risk her.

They ran toward her office, his feet pounding against the carpet.

He gripped her hand, threading his fingers through hers so he couldn't lose her. God, he couldn't lose her. Just a few more moments and he could lock her in and she would be safe.

A large man rounded the corner, and there was no way to miss the gun in his hand. Gabe stopped, almost falling back. He heard Everly's gasp and felt her stumble against him.

Too little. Too late. He'd been too late. He tried to turn, to run the other way.

Scott was standing at the other end of the hallway.

Gabe shoved Everly behind him, putting her back to the wall, but they were caught.

"Your friend is dead, asshole. You're on your own." Scott walked with a pronounced limp.

Everly gasped, and Gabe's heart sank. Dax couldn't be dead. He couldn't.

Scott kept his aim up but nodded to the new guy. "Where are Niles and my uncle?"

The big guy replied in Russian, but Gabe would bet anything that he was saying he wasn't sure.

Where the hell were Connor and the police? He knew there was no way he could hear the sirens from here, but he kept waiting and praying for those elevator doors to open and the office to be filled with New York's finest, screaming for everyone to get to the floor.

Dax couldn't be dead. He was just shot and pretending. That must be it. They would take him to the hospital and tonight would eventually all become a rousing story they would tell later.

Damn it. None of this was supposed to happen. They were supposed to be friends all their lives. All their *long* lives. They weren't supposed to lose each other in their prime.

Everly squeezed him tight, as though she could feel his pain and tried to take some of it. "It's going to be all right."

"You take Bond. I'll take the girl," Scott said. "If she tries anything, kill him."

"I love you," she whispered as they were pulled apart.

He watched as Scott placed the gun to her head. So precious. She was precious to him and that fucker was treating her like she was an expendable pawn.

"Now we're going to get that hard drive. Then we're all going to take a little trip," Scott said.

"Who is Sergei?" Even as he felt the gun pressed to his temple, he remembered that Mad had mentioned he needed to find a man named Sergei. Was he the Russian boss? Was this Sergei the one pulling the strings?

Scott stopped, fear lighting his features. "How do you know that name? Who the fuck told you that name?"

"I don't know, but I think it's time we found out, don't you?" a familiar voice asked.

Connor was here. Gabe sighed with relief.

The big Russian walked into the hallway, his body stiff. Connor forced Scott's uncle into the room, pointing a gun at the back of his head and using his big body as a shield.

"All right, little boy, I've taken out your muscle and now I'm going to kill this fucker if you don't let my friends go," Connor growled.

"I don't think so," Scott said. "I don't believe you killed them."

"Believe it," the Russian managed between pursed lips. "I saw the bodies. He killed them all with his bare hands. He is animal."

Scott paled, but didn't relinquish his grip. "You have no idea what you're getting into."

"This is Yuri Golchenko," Connor said, moving them farther into the room. "He's a lieutenant with a Moscow syndicate, headed by a man named Ivan Krylov. You're looking for the diary of Natalia Kuilikov, who took care of the president of the United States from the time he was born until he was seven years old. You think there's something in the diary you can use against him. I'm going to give you one chance to save yourselves. Drop your weapons and walk out, and I'll give you a head start. You might have a day or two before I find you again."

Scott shook his head. "I'm going to kill her if you don't let my uncle go."

"Do it," Connor said. "Now that I know where the diary is, she's meaningless. You kill her. I kill your uncle. Hell, kill Bond, too. I can still take the two of you out and leave here with the prize."

"Connor?" Gabe stared at his old friend in perfect horror. He couldn't have meant that.

"Gabe, it's a job, and you know damn well that my job is more important than anything. I told you before, I don't feel much. But I will have that information and I will find Sergei." Connor's stony face stared back at him. "It's like when we played lacrosse, buddy. I got the job done. You were only there to make sure I got to score. Life isn't any different than that game against Whittington."

Shit. Shit. Shit. Gabe had mostly sat on the bench while Connor and Roman had been the stars of the team, but during their senior year, they'd played a game against Whittington Prep. All Gabe had to do was distract the defender long enough for Connor to score.

Connor needed a distraction. When he got out of this, Gabe swore he would never think his cushy job was boring again.

"You're a son of a bitch. You were always a selfish player." He nodded at Connor, then went for it. He dropped straight to the floor. His body hit with a hard thud, pain flaring through his system. He heard Everly's shout, then the ping of a silencer going off.

And he felt the man who had been holding him fall to the floor. Connor wouldn't have missed. He wouldn't have simply injured the man. The dude was dead the moment after Connor's bullet had left the chamber.

"Get his gun, Gabe," Connor ordered.

"Don't you fucking move off that floor or I will kill her." For the first time, Scott sounded a little panicked. Not a good thing. He could freak out and pull that trigger. Then nothing would matter.

"He won't kill her because he still thinks he can win and he's right." Connor's voice was as smooth as any conman's. "You've made a study of Maddox Crawford, Scott. That means you know his friends. You knew I was lying about killing Gabe, but you also know I don't give a shit about some bimbo he's been banging. I want to cut a deal."

Gabe got to his knees, picking up the gun that had fallen. He had to pray Everly didn't believe a word coming out of Connor's mouth. Connor wouldn't hurt her. Gabe trusted him with his life and he had to trust him with hers.

Just for insurance, he gripped the gun and trained it on Scott.

"Take the girl. I'll take your dear uncle here, and when you have the information you need, we'll make a trade. I'll give you your uncle and the diary in exchange for the man who's been feeding the girl information. We both walk away," Connor explained.

"You give him nothing, nephew. You know what is at stake. You know what they will do," Yuri Golchenko said in his thick accent. "I am no fool. This man is CIA. If he discovers—"

A loud bang cracked through the air and a dot of red appeared on the front of Golchenko's white shirt. Blood bloomed as Scott's shot hit him, and Connor couldn't hold the Russian up. He let the man fall.

"Put the fucking gun down," Connor yelled as Scott shoved Everly away.

Gabe caught her before she fell to the floor, and he covered her with his body.

"You want to know who Sergei is?" Scott asked with a fervent light in his eyes. "He's closer than you think."

"Put the gun down now." Connor stepped toward him.

"No, and you can't make me talk." Scott took all the choices out of their hands as he put the gun to his head and pulled the trigger.

Everly shrieked. Connor cursed, and Gabe finally got a really good look at his friend. His previously pristine clothes were covered in blood and he wore the most ferocious look on his face as he pulled out his cell phone. It looked like Connor had taken out more than the Russians. He'd taken out the cell jammer as well.

"This is Sparks. I need a cleaning crew at the Crawford building in Manhattan. Nine bags. Yeah, I've got five who will need cover stories. No. I'm alone." He shoved the phone back into his pocket and raised his gaze. "I just lied to the CIA. I need you to get Everly and Dax and that damn SD card out of here."

"Dax is alive?" Hope sprung inside him.

Connor nodded. "He's got a bullet in his side, but he's alive. Get him to the hospital and tell them it was an attempted carjacking. You were not here. Go. Quickly."

"We need to call an ambulance." Gabe got to his feet and helped Everly up, pulling her into the circle of his arms. She was here and she was alive. He held her for a moment.

"I can't have anyone find you here," Connor insisted.

"Gabe, we have to go." Everly pulled away. "Baby, we have to get Dax to the hospital. Connor, I can erase the cameras for the whole building from my system. It won't take me long. I used my keycard to get in."

"The Russians stole your card," Connor replied. "And I stole Gabe's."

Everly dashed to her office.

"What the hell is going on, man?" Gabe stared at Connor, not certain he recognized his old friend. "Dax needs medical attention and he needs it now. You have to call an ambulance and the cops."

Before Connor had a chance to say anything, Dax stumbled into the hallway, a small towel over his left side. "I swear, if he ever says he's an analyst again, I'm going to beat the shit out of him. After I get some surgery. A little help, buddy? Damn, that's a lot of bodies. I was freaking safer in the Middle East."

Gabe got there just as Dax started to fall. He caught his friend. "I can't thank you enough."

Dax grinned as he leaned heavily on Gabe. "Sure you can. You give me some of that Scotch and get me to a hospital. No cops. We can't, Gabe."

They damn straight could, but it looked like even Everly was against him.

"I've got the SD card," Everly said. She was also holding a laptop. "Oh, poor Dax."

"Hey, have you got a sister, sweetheart?" Dax asked, his voice slightly slurred.

Only Dax could be bleeding out and trying to find a date.

They made it to the elevators and when he looked back, Connor was surrounded by bodies, covered in blood, and utterly alone. A sliver of unease passed through him.

As the doors closed, Everly touched his shoulder and smiled. Gabe smiled back. He'd worry about Connor later. He had to focus on her now.

He looked down at the small SD card in her hand. "It's not over."

When she noticed Dax leaning against the wall, she offered her help as well. Together, they managed to keep him upright. "Nope. But we'll be okay because we're in this together, Gabriel Bond. You and me."

Something settled deep inside him, something he hadn't even known had been out of place. "Yes, baby. You and me."

EPILOGUE

Everly walked into the room, excitement bubbling up. She'd done it. Her father would have been proud. It was time to let her new family know how smart she was. Considering her new family included a CIA agent and the leader of the free world, she had to make a place for herself somehow.

She walked to the door of the guest suite and stopped. A seriously large man in a dark suit and sunglasses stood, standing guard. A couple more lurked outside the front door, along with two more in the kitchen.

She liked Zack, but she was kind of ready to have the place to herself.

And her fiancé.

"Hi, Thomas. Can I sneak past you?"

The big dude stared at her. "No."

He was also very literal. "I need to see my fiancé. May I be allowed into a room in my own house?"

Thomas finally cracked a smile. "Of course."

She started to open the door. "Do you have a name besides Thomas?"

"No."

She would figure it out in the end. Just like she'd figured out the why of Maddox's mysterious death . . . although that seemed to have led to another mystery.

Gabriel smiled as she walked into the guest suite. "Hey, baby." He'd been sitting beside the bed, but he sprang up and crossed the space between them quickly. Whenever she walked into a room, her handsome man made sure she couldn't doubt his affection. He leaned over and brushed his lips against hers. "Has your hard work paid off?"

Dax sat up with only the smallest of groans. "Did you actually manage it?"

"Of course she did." The president of the United States sat across from Dax, a chessboard between them. Despite the fact that Dax still had an IV in his arm, he was sipping on that damn Scotch they all seemed to love so much.

"Maybe we should call Connor," Roman suggested, staring out the window at the street below.

Connor had been to see Dax at the hospital, but he'd slipped in and out without saying much to the rest of them.

"He didn't even bother to call the police when I asked him to." Gabriel was still a little mad.

"No, he managed to get his ass up forty flights of stairs and take out all the bad guys singlehandedly without making a sound." Dax hadn't stopped defending his best friend.

"You could have died," Gabriel shot back. "And so could we. Did he think about what could have happened if he failed?"

"Connor doesn't fail," Zack said quietly. "And if you're going to be angry with someone, Gabe, be mad at me."

Gabriel's eyes narrowed. "Yeah, I didn't say I wasn't."

She was willing to cut Connor and Zack some slack. Connor had a job to do and he'd been forced to choose between doing it and saving his friends. There was more at stake here than any of them really understood. "He chose us, you know."

Suddenly, all four pairs of intelligent eyes focused on her.

"What do you mean?" Gabriel asked.

She'd thought about this a lot in the week since that terrible night. Gabriel had been so angry that Connor had kept the cops out of it. He'd played his part and told the police that Dax had been shot in an attempted carjacking and they'd been so close to the hospital, it had been faster to deliver him there. But he'd silently fumed for days. She had to mend those fences because she intended for everyone to be at her wedding.

"If he'd called the cops, they would have taken the SD card. They would have asked a whole bunch of questions none of us are ready to answer. You do realize what his best play would have been?"

Gabriel shook his head.

Roman frowned. "He would never have done that."

She'd talked this scenario through with Roman the night before as they'd moved Dax into his current room. "If he'd been playing this like a pure agent, he would have. Gabriel, he needs to know why the Russians are so interested in Natalia and he needs to know who Deep Throat is. It's obvious the president is at risk. He gave up answers to both when he chose to save us. His best play would have been to let them take me. He could have easily followed us. Hell, I still had my cell phone on me. He could have tracked us and then planted a couple of bugs and the Russians would never have known someone was spying on them. He would have had his answers, but he chose to save you, me, and Dax."

"And do you understand that the press would have been all over us?" Roman asked. "As it is, there's still a scandal."

Connor had come up with a cover story for the deaths of Tavia and Scott. He used the skimming and Tavia's cocaine problem to pin her death, along with the security guards and the janitor, on a drug deal gone wrong. Scott, in Connor's story, had been unlucky enough to be with her when the dealer came for his cash. Apparently the CIA's cleaning crew also knew how to dummy up a crime scene. Yuri and his henchmen had simply vanished.

"And he promised me that the Agency would do what they can to find the missing girls, and he's already brought one home," Everly added. She'd been talking to Connor via e-mail, but she hadn't gotten him to come to dinner. She'd invited him to drinks this afternoon, and this time, she'd had something to hold over his head, though he still hadn't shown up.

"We'll find the others, too. I promise. We'll work until we find them all. Connor is already looking through the foundation records to locate them." Zack looked at Gabriel. "Come on. He basically committed career suicide. If anyone finds out he lied about what happened . . ."

"And in his line of work, career suicide can become real suicide," Roman admitted. "Well, really well faked suicide to take the place of assassination."

Gabriel seemed to go a little pale. "Fine. Let's not talk about more people dying. When Connor shows up, I'll be civil."

"I'll hold you to that, brother." Connor slipped into the room. He stood there as though utterly unsure of his welcome. It was the only time she'd ever seen him looking vulnerable, but in that moment, she had to wonder what it had been like for him to be the scholarship kid, the only one without money among the incredibly wealthy.

He'd come. She couldn't help but smile. She'd known he couldn't resist finding out what was really on that SD card. She walked right up to him and gave him a hug.

Connor stood there for a moment. "I am unsure how to handle this."

Gabriel finally laughed. "Give in. She wants you in the family, and Everly gets what she wants."

Dax smiled brightly. "My man. It is good to see you."

Slowly, Connor hugged her back.

After a moment, she stepped away, and some of the tension had left the room. She hated the fact that she was about to amp it up again. "I decoded the diary."

She'd discovered that the diary had been written in code and in Russian code at that. When she'd pieced together all the information, she'd found a single item—a handwritten book that had been scanned in. She'd worked for a full week to decode the thing, then given it to a confidential Russian translator.

"I'm sending you all a copy of the translation. The diary begins almost a year into her tenure with the Hayes family. She talks about being happy and how much she loves Zack." The next part was the one she didn't want to get into. She wished she could leave it there.

"And?" Zack had one eyebrow raised as though he knew what was coming.

"She mentions at one point how scared she was when the head of her school had come to her and told her she was being placed. She talks about a mistake she'd made, some sort of shame she brought on the school. Apparently the headmistress told her that by working for the ambassador, she could make everything right again. It's a little cryptic but she writes about work being the only way she could protect something we can't quite decipher. The translator thinks she's talking about protecting her own life. I think someone threatened her."

"Shit," Roman said, his head shaking. "Her school? Tell me it wasn't a foundation school."

"I can't." That was where the real scandal began. It all went back to that day when a poor Russian girl had been told it was time for her to work.

"Damn. Zack, you were raised by a girl who had been trafficked," Dax said, his voice hoarse.

"The question is, did your parents know?" Gabriel asked.

"I wouldn't put it past them. So this was all about embarrassing me?" Zack questioned tightly. "Is this about the next election cycle?"

"I intend to find out," Connor replied with grim resignation. "I think Natalia is alive."

That stopped the room.

"Is she in Russia?" Roman asked.

Connor shook his head. "She came to the States fifteen years ago on a Visa and disappeared. I think she's still here and I think Lara Armstrong knows where to find her. I'm going to figure this out, Zack. I'm not going to let her be used to bring you down."

Connor sat with Zack, Dax, and Roman. They started to plan.

Which was Everly's cue to leave.

She'd made it to the door when Gabriel caught up with her.

"Hey, you don't leave without a kiss," he said, brushing his mouth against hers. "You don't have to leave at all. You have a stake in this, baby."

But some things were meant for the boys. She'd done her part and was happy to put her mind to other things.

She twisted the big engagement ring on her finger. "Nope. Your sister should be here any minute and we're going over arrangements for the engagement party. Hint, I hope you like Asian because Sara's got some crazy cravings going on."

He stared down at her. "I love you."

She didn't hesitate anymore. He was her guy. "I love you, too."

Everly stepped out because sometimes the Perfect Gentlemen needed a little time together.

Deep in the night, Connor Sparks sat in front of his computer, his head buzzing.

He'd almost lost them all. That night haunted his dreams. When he did manage to sleep, he kept seeing Dax dead on the floor, Gabe and Everly riddled with bullet holes.

He hated this. He needed to pull away from them all.

It had been right there, the impulse to let the Russians take Everly so he could follow them and play the game he'd been born to play.

If his superiors ever figured out what he'd done, he would likely find himself in a cell somewhere. He would definitely find himself burned, disavowed, and all the other things that happened to an agent who chose his friends over his country.

They made him feel. Dax, Gabe, Roman, and Zack. They were the only ones left who could.

He kept a grainy old picture of the six of them on his desk. He settled in, poured himself a shot of bourbon, and studied it for a moment. Six kids, five of whom hadn't figured out how shitty the world could be yet. For a long time, it had been Connor's job to keep it that way.

Just like it had been his job to make sure Gabe Bond got to keep the woman he loved.

"Fuck you, Mad." There it was, that wellspring of hated grief that seemed so close to the surface these days. He drank the amber liquid down. "You weren't supposed to die. I was supposed to go first."

He'd always thought he'd die in some stinking hellhole, and the five of them would be left wondering what had happened.

Surviving was worse than dying. But then he'd figured that out a long time ago.

His computer beeped and he turned with a sigh.

Skype. His heart rate ticked up in an oddly pleasant way because only one person instant messaged him at that particular address. Niall Smith had one friend in the world, though if she looked him up online, she would find a diverse selection of leftie friends on his completely fake Facebook, Instagram, and Twitter pages. Of course she would also see a picture of some intern at the Agency they'd used to set up Niall Smith's life so Lara Armstrong wouldn't question him when he wrote to her.

Niall? Niall, are you there?

Her picture popped up beside the words. There she was. Cute, sweet little thing with dark hair and blue pixie eyes. A little rich girl who thought she could change the world through tabloid reporting. Oh, he knew how she justified it. She'd told him she used the scandalous headlines to bring in readers and then hit them with real stories, but he knew the truth. She was a spoiled rich princess with daddy issues. So why did he get hard every time he saw her picture?

Yeah, he needed to get laid.

I'm here. What's up, sweetness?

He wasn't sure why he'd started calling her that, but it was all part of his cover, right? Lara Armstrong had something to do with Deep Throat, and he was going to find out what. She might know where to find Natalia Kuilikov. If she did, he would find out. He would protect his friends and his country. If he got a little blood on his hands, that was all right, too.

Niall, I'm scared. I've gotten involved in something and I think someone is trying to kill me.

A slow smile crossed Connor's lips. Now he had her. *Don't worry. I'll take care of you, sweetness. Tell me everything.*

He sat back and let the game begin.

Connor and all the Perfect Gentlemen will return in

SEDUCTION IN SESSION

Privileged, wealthy, and wild: they are the Perfect Gentlemen of Creighton Academy. But the threat of a scandal has one of them employing his most deceptive—and seductive—talents . . .

Recruited into the CIA at a young age, Connor Sparks knows how dirty the world can be. Only when he's with his friends can he find some peace. So when an anonymous journalist threatens one of the Perfect Gentlemen, Connor vows to take down the person behind the computer, by whatever means necessary—even if it means posing as his target's bodyguard.

Publishing a tabloid revealing Washington's most subversive scandals has earned Lara Armstrong the ire of the political scene—and a slew of death threats. To keep herself from ending up a headline, Lara hires a bodyguard, a man as handsome as he is lethal.

When the bullets start to fly, Lara is surprised to find herself in Connor's arms. But as they begin to unravel a mystery that just might bring down the White House, Lara is devastated when she discovers Connor's true identity—and finds herself at the mercy of forces who will stop at nothing to advance their deadly agenda.

Coming soon from Berkley Books

Don't Miss the Next Wicked Lovers Novel
from *New York Times* Bestselling Author
Shayla Black

WICKED FOR YOU

Ever since he rescued her from a dangerous kidnapper,
Mystery Mullins has wanted Axel Dillon. When he
returned her to her Hollywood father and tabloid life, she
was grateful . . . and a little in love. Mystery wasn't ready to
let Axel go, even after the soldier gently turned her away
because, at nineteen, she was too young.

Now, six years later, Mystery is grown, with a flourish-
ing career and a full life—but she's still stuck on Axel. Dis-
guised, she propositions him in a bar, and the night they
spend together is beyond her wildest dreams. Mystery steels
herself to walk away—except the sheets are barely cold
when her past comes back to haunt her.

Once he realizes Mystery isn't the stranger he thought,
Axel is incensed and intrigued. But when it's clear she's in
danger, he doesn't hesitate to become her protector—and
her lover—again. And as the two uncover a secret someone
is willing to kill for, Axel is determined to claim Mystery's
heart before a murderer silences her for good.

Coming soon from Berkley Books

ABOUT THE AUTHORS

Shayla Black is the *New York Times* and *USA Today* bestselling author of more than forty sizzling contemporary, erotic, paranormal, and historical romances produced via traditional, small press, independent, and audio publishing. She lives in Texas with her husband, munchkin, and one very spoiled cat. In her "free" time, she enjoys watching reality TV, reading, and listening to an eclectic blend of music. Shayla's books have been translated into about a dozen languages. She has also received or been nominated for the Passionate Plume, the Holt Medallion, Colorado Romance Writers Award of Excellence, and the National Readers Choice Award. RT BOOKclub has twice nominated her for Best Erotic Romance of the Year, and also awarded her several Top Picks and a KISS Hero Award. A writing risk-taker, Shayla enjoys tackling writing challenges with every new book. Find Shayla at ShaylaBlack.com or visit her Shayla Black Author Facebook page.

New York Times and *USA Today* bestselling author **Lexi Blake** lives in North Texas with her husband, three kids, and the laziest rescue dog in the world. She began writing at a young age, concentrating on plays and journalism. It wasn't until she started writing romance that she found success. She likes to find humor in the strangest places. Lexi believes in happy endings no matter how odd the couple, threesome, or foursome may seem. Find Lexi at LexiBlake.net.